Praise for Jace Carlton and *The Reunion*

"*The Reunion* is simply exquisite! Masterful storytelling!"

— Terrie Dailey Morgan

"Jace's writing is very riveting, suspenseful, had anticipation, drama, light-heartedness, and tenderness with sadness and tragedy. I found myself trying to put myself into each of these characters and their situations. He brought out all of my emotions – I cried, I laughed, I smiled, I giggled, and I dreamed! I was on the edge of my seat and glued to the words as the hours sailed by way too quickly!"

— Rica Van Katwyk

"*The Reunion* has such detailed emotion, it felt like this was a true story! Jace captured such heartfelt feelings of true love for someone and showed how people can truly care for someone else. It's that once in a lifetime love that escapes most people. *The Reunion* is so well written it would be very easy to turn it into a movie. Hallmark Channel look out!"

— Yvette Rammel

"First, I want to say thanks for making me cry! With everything going on in *The Reunion* I couldn't put it down, which is why I stayed up late most nights.

"My favorite part was how Jace wrote their feelings, they were dead on and I felt like I was in the book. The innocence that Marc and Jenny both have toward each other is heartwarming. I've had the exact feelings in my life. It's easy to understand and forgive someone you truly love."

— McKensie Ocana

THE
REUNION

THE REUNION

JACE CARLTON

1423
PRESS
Eagle Mountain, Utah

Other Books by Jace Carlton

Sounds of Darkness

Reflections

The Reunion
by Jace Carlton

Published by 1423 Press
212 E Crossroads Blvd., #184
Saratoga Springs, UT 84045

Edited by Terrie Dailey Morgan and Tamara Herring
Cover Photo by Frank McKenna on Unsplash
Cover and Book Design by James Woosley, FreeAgentPress.com

First Printing, January 2018

ISBN: 978-0-9996855-0-1 (hardcover)
ISBN: 978-0-9996855-1-8 (paperback)
ISBN: 978-0-9996855-2-5 (e-book)
ISBN: 978-0-9996855-3-2 (Kindle)

Library of Congress Control Number: 2017918368

DEDICATION

The Reunion is dedicated to my Princess Bride, Kathi.

I cannot thank you enough for allowing me the countless
late nights, all-nighters, and distracted spare moments
as the story came together, and for your invaluable insight
during the early re-write stages.

Also, to those who believe that ALL things are possible.

MEMORIAM

In memory of my friend, Rob Dailey,
a giant among men, a loving son, brother, husband,
father, grandfather, uncle, and friend.

He not only stood tall physically,
but also in his character, integrity,
and service to and compassion for others.

God bless you, Rob, for the legacy you left behind.

ACKNOWLEDGMENTS

IT IS WITH DEEP gratitude that I acknowledge the following individuals for their various contributions that made this book so special to share with you.

Kurt Smith, M.D., Trauma/ER Specialist, Vanderbilt University Medical Center for your very thorough medical consultation.

Lieutenant Colonel Tony Barham of the Tennessee Highway Patrol for his detailed operational and tactical advice. Also, to Geoffrey Lack, (Deputy Sheriff, Ret., Alameda County Sheriff's Department) for his additional consultation.

Diane Larsen, one of the very first to review my initial manuscript. Your comments helped me gain a tighter focus and put me on the right path.

Terrie Dailey Morgan and Tamara Herring for your incredible editing! You took my manuscript and enhanced it beyond my wildest dreams, and for that I am deeply grateful! Your insights and suggestions were so helpful, and I hope to have you by my side for my future offerings!

James Woosley, of Free Agent Press, for your amazing design work of my book and the cover. You're the professional designer I was looking for, and I can't thank you enough for all your efforts in bringing *The Reunion* to print. It's been such a pleasure to work with you, and I'm looking forward to a long and successful partnership!

Of course, I can't forget the many friends who offered to read the next-to-last edit. Your encouraging words and spot-on suggestions really helped to make this book the best it can be, particularly Yvette Rammel (Really? A Hallmark movie??), Katie Wright ("Maybe a few more details, please?"), McKensie Ocana ("I felt like I was in the book!"), Rica Van Katwyk, Sara Jensen, Carol Bryant, Lezlie Bibeau, Linda Santillan, and Terri Brinkerhoff.

And finally, to all of the wonderful singers and songwriters who provide the soundtrack to our lives that inspire us in so many ways. Without your knowing it, you kept me company in those late night hours (when I do my best songwriting and storytelling) while I was looking for just the right words to express the joy and heartache in this story, along with my own songs that were inspired along the way.

Author's Note

I'VE BEEN A WRITER all my life – short stories, poetry, songs, motivational / inspirational articles, freelance articles and commentaries, new music, artist, and book reviews, convention keynote addresses, and now novels. Along the way a variety of wonderful events and special people have inspired so much of what I write.

I love movies that uplift and inspire me, and one of my favorites is *The Rookie* with Dennis Quaid. I have the framed movie poster above my desk and the tag line for the movie says it all, "It's Never Too Late To Believe In Your Dreams".

I've been a dreamer all my life. In my late teens my personal "theme song" was *The Impossible Dream* from *Man of La Mancha*. Over the years I've added other songs to my list because of their own message of desire, passion, and belief, including *One Moment In Time* by Dana Winner and *This Is The Moment* by The Moody Blues.

I'm sentimental and I like happy endings, although I do acknowledge that life doesn't always offer them to us. I believe we truly need to experience the inconsolable pain of loss, and of devastating heartbreak, in order to equally experience the exquisite breathlessness of love and joy. I've been there many times in my life, so what I write is, quite simply, the truth from my heart.

I look forward to what each new day holds, because yesterday's memories keep coming back, and the inspiration keeps flowing.

Jace Carlton
October 23, 2017

There's a moment between a glance and a kiss,
where the world stops for the briefest of times.
And the only thing between us
is the anticipation of your lips on mine.
A moment, so intense,
it hangs in the air as it pulls us closer.
A moment, so perfect,
that when it comes to an end we realize …
it's only just beginning.

(Author Unknown)

PROLOGUE

THROUGHOUT OUR LIVES PEOPLE come and go. That's just how life is. Some friends and family members live close by and we see them all the time, especially around the holidays, birthdays, anniversaries, family reunions, and other special events, while others seem as though they live half a world away because we see them so seldom. Classmates that used to be our best friends, and whom we swore we'd never forget, somehow become just a distant memory. Loved ones pass away and we wonder if we'll ever see them again. Some even believe the veil is very thin, so thin that we can feel them watching over us, and there's a hope that one day we'll see them again on the other side.

And then there are the few ... the special few ... the special one or two people that have touched our hearts and our lives so deeply, that we never really let go of those special times we shared, and how they made us feel. Family member, friend or lover ... we pray we might have another chance to see them, to say "I love you" one more time, or say "I'm sorry" and ask their forgiveness for something we said or did that we shouldn't have, or just to say "Thank you" for how much we appreciate all they did for us, and how they changed our lives and helped to make us who we are today.

We pray ... for just one more reunion.

CHAPTER I

Several Years Ago

'WHY?' MARC THOUGHT TO himself as he hit the steering wheel. 'Why today? Why now? Why, after all these years?' He let his thoughts simply hang in the air.

The traffic was unbearably stubborn and it appeared to Marc as if it went on like this for miles. Not the kind of late-morning commute into San Francisco that he was expecting. He'd taken the early morning flight out of Nashville in order to arrive in what he thought would be plenty of time to check into his hotel and grab a quick lunch before he was due downtown for his 1 p.m. presentation.

Normally this would have been just a quick round-tripper, or at the most an overnighter, but since he was arriving on a Friday he had decided to stretch it out for the whole weekend. It seemed like ages since he'd been home, and yet it had only been a few years.

After college things just weren't the same. Everything in his life had changed. He thought that if he could only go back to his senior year, back to before —. Well, anyway, if he could go back he definitely would have done things differently, but it was too late for that now. At this point in his life he knew his chance had passed, for his dream … and for that special love.

After his presentation Marc planned on kicking back, relaxing, and completely enjoying himself. But for now, this horrid traffic was definitely *not* the way he needed to spend his time this morning. At least the traffic was beginning to inch along a little faster, not much perhaps, but some. That eased the tension headache he'd been fighting for the last half hour, but this slow pace also caused his mind to wander, allowing thoughts of things other than the traffic and his memories of the City long ago to creep in … like who he'd seen at the airport earlier.

As Marc was walking through the terminal he had passed by the high glass wall separating the incoming and outgoing passengers and gave only a fleeting glance toward the people working their way through the security lines. As he took a few more steps a strange feeling came over him to take another look. Not seeing anything unusual he continued on until that urge returned, stronger this time. He slowed his pace a bit and started walking off to the side so the people behind him could pass by on their way to baggage claim. Once he was clear of the crowd, he paused and looked back toward the glass wall and slowly walked over to get another look at whatever had caught his attention.

He did a quick scan of everyone in the security checkpoint area, including the security officers and passengers, even carry-ons going through the scanning machines as well as those already having cleared inspection and waiting for their owners to pick them up and carry them away. Nothing, not one thing unusual enough that it might otherwise have caught his attention. He started to walk away and the urge returned, this time with a clear voice inside his head that said with a sense of urgency, "Look again!"

Marc stopped, looked more closely this time at the faces of all the soon-to-be passengers, and was once again just about to walk away when he froze, his eyes locked onto one woman who had just flung her purse over her shoulder and was picking up her carry-on to start the final trek to her gate. She briefly looked in his general direction but he knew she hadn't seen him because their eyes would have met for sure. He stared right at her, not believing his eyes, taking in all of the details. He dropped his carry-on and leaned his hands against the cool glass panels.

It was her! Beyond a shadow of *any* doubt it was her! Tall, slender, with auburn hair that was a little shorter than the last time he'd seen her … if, in fact, it really *was* her. It just *had* to be her, though. Why else would he have felt the urge to stop and look than to be able to see her once again? There was no way to go back and try to follow her because he'd already passed security's "point of no return". All he could do was watch as she gradually disappeared in the crowd. Watch … and wonder. 'Where are you going? That smile on your face … I wish it was for me. After so many years, why here? And why now?'

At the first sight of her standing in that security line a major surge of adrenalin had raced through Marc's body and his heart had been pounding rapidly. The years of memories that came flooding back all at once were nearly overwhelming, but now, as she walked away and out of sight he began to calm down and gain some semblance of composure. He realized that he'd also unconsciously been holding his breath and let it out in a long sigh and felt the normal pattern of his breathing begin again, if ever so slowly.

Looking around he remembered exactly where he was and why. He picked up his bag and proceeded to once again join the crowd that was heading out to parts unknown.

As Marc's full attention returned to the task at hand of driving into the City, he sighed deeply in an attempt to shake the memories of long ago, but somehow he knew they would be with him for the rest of the weekend and, no doubt, beyond. Hopefully his mind would be sharp and focused for the presentation, but how everything else went after that would be anybody's guess.

He heard himself sigh out loud, "Oh, Jenny … why? After all this time, *why* did I have to see you in the airport? And why did it have to end the way it did? I'm *so* sorry!"

CHAPTER 2

Fifteen Years Earlier

MARC JANSSEN WAS THE typical great catch for any girl. Six foot two, a solid 175, light brown hair, with eyes the color of blue topaz, athletic, smart, confident without an ego, and good looking with a chiseled jaw line he'd inherited from his dad.

His parents, Cole and Roni, were originally from Minnesota, but early in their marriage Cole had been offered a promotion and the opportunity to head up his company's San Francisco office and they'd moved to California where both Marc and his younger sister, Alexa, were born. Marc was grateful that his dad had already served his time in the Marines and wasn't a "lifer" so they didn't have to move every couple of years, saving him the anguish of having to make new friends. He'd felt the heartache of young love back in the seventh grade when he found out that Teddy Martin, a girl he'd had a crush on all through sixth grade, moved with her family during the summer because her dad was transferred to an Air Force base in Texas.

He loved music, having taken years of piano lessons, and had also taught himself how to play the guitar. He started writing his own songs and by the end of his freshman year in high school he'd formed his own band, Wild Expectations. They spent the summer practicing so in the fall they'd be ready to play for school dances and anywhere else that would have them. They stayed together a year before breaking up, after which Marc just played solo. His talent as a solo artist became well known and he was asked to play for weddings and company parties, as well as for the local Rotary and Lions Clubs and many Chambers of Commerce events throughout the surrounding cities.

His dreams were big – he wanted to move to Nashville as soon as he graduated from college. Even though he was comfortable performing, he actually enjoyed writing more and wanted to focus his career on writing for the major artists.

Marc was just two when his sister, Alexa, was born, and so they'd shared virtually everything as they'd grown up, especially their interest in music and sports. Alexa tagged along everywhere her older brother went, but he didn't mind because she was more of a tomboy than a princess. She didn't mind getting dirty and wrestling around with her older brothers' friends, and they'd considered her just one of the gang. She could actually run faster than most of the boys her age, and played a great game of baseball, just like her older brother.

Marc loved his little sister and would do anything for her. Alexa adored her big brother and loved being around him and doing the things he enjoyed every chance she had. And, like Marc, she was an excellent student.

Alexa was also very competitive, picking that up from Marc as well at a young age. First there were the games of Monopoly, and then, when they were a bit older, it was basketball or baseball. When they weren't doing homework, they could usually be found shooting hoops in the backyard or throwing a baseball out front. Their parents were amazed at how well they got along.

Because Alexa walked in practically every shadow her older brother cast, it was no surprise to anyone that she was such a good student, athlete, and musician. Even though Alexa appeared to have been Marc's constant companion since she was born, as a teenager she had gradually come into her own. She was not only a popular and attractive young lady, she was also quiet, reserved, and humble about it all. This made her even more appealing, and her big brother watched out for her like a hawk throughout their time together in high school. She didn't mind this at all because it meant only the guys who would treat her right and respect her would dare to approach her about a date. Scumbags need not apply.

CHAPTER 3

The Invitation

AS MARC'S FINAL YEAR of high school began he reflected back on his summer vacation and the great times he'd spent with his friends, as well as the time with his family up at their spacious cabin at Lake Tahoe. He knew all too well that it would no doubt be the last carefree summer he'd ever spend, because from this point on his life would be filled with getting through his senior year while preparing for college, then working as much as possible during college to add to what scholarship money he hoped to earn, and then on to his career after graduation. He was certain that those last few months would definitely remain in his memory for a long time to come.

During the second week of classes Marc was talking with a couple of friends while trying to cram his back pack into his locker before heading to football practice when Lori came up and stood next to him, waiting politely to interrupt. Finally his buddies got the hint and headed off to their classes.

"Hey, Lori! What's up?" Marc asked.

"Hi, Marc!" Lori replied. "I'm throwing a party this Saturday night and I want you to come!"

"Sure, I think I'm free. What time?"

"We're going to barbecue, so come early … 5:30, okay?"

"Sounds cool. Can I bring anything?"

"Yeah, two things. Yourself and a couple of six-packs of whatever kind of soda you like!"

"Okay, I'll be there and I'll bring sodas."

"AND your guitar!"

"My guitar?"

"YES! We want you to sing for us, too!"

"Oh, I get it. I'm the entertainment for the evening, huh?"

"No! Just a few songs, including that new one I heard you wrote! Will you do that? For me?"

Marc hesitated, but noticed the pleading look in Lori's eyes, a look he was all too familiar with.

"Please?"

She'd done it again. For as long as he'd known Lori he just couldn't say no when she looked that way.

"Okay, I'll bring that, too."

"THANKS, Marc!" Lori leaned up and gave him a quick kiss on the cheek, which was noticed by Mr. Harrelson, the Dean of Students, as he was walking by their lockers.

"Sorry, Mr. Harrelson," Lori replied. "I just couldn't resist."

"I understand, Lori," Mr. Harrelson replied with a slight laugh. "Now get to class and don't let me catch you doing that again, okay?"

"Okay!" They laughed off the embarrassment and Lori started to walk down the hall toward her math class when she turned around just as Marc closed his locker.

"By the way, Marc, there's another reason I want you to come Saturday night."

"Oh, yeah?"

"Yeah. There's someone I want you to meet!"

"Who is it?"

"Nope, I'm not telling you … yet," Lori replied teasingly.

"Well, then when?"

"Just come to my party and you'll see."

"Ah, so that's the *real* reason why you want me there, huh?"

"Well, one of many."

"Many?"

"Yes, I want you there because we're good friends, and because we want to hear you sing, and … well, just because."

"What's her name? Maybe I already know her."

"I'm not telling you. And besides, I know you don't know her."

"And just how do you know that?"

"Oh, come on, Marc. After all these years that we've been friends, you should know me well enough to know that I have my ways."

"Yeah, you sure do. But … not even a hint?"

"Not a single one, buster. Now, head off to practice before you're late and have to run extra laps of the field or whatever Coach makes you do when you're in trouble."

Marc just shook his head knowing he wasn't going to get anywhere trying to get anything out of Lori. One of her trademarks was how coy she loved to be, but it was one of the many reasons he'd always liked her.

In the locker room Marc's best friend, Dave, was already changing for practice when he walked up to his own locker.

"Hey, Dave, have you heard anything about a party at Lori's house Saturday night?"

"Yeah, she invited me today at lunch. You going?"

"Yeah, she just invited me, and then she told me she has someone she wants me to meet."

"Oh, yeah? Who?"

"No clue. She wouldn't say a thing."

"Yeah, that's Lori for ya. Always flirting, always teasing, *always* trying to keep ya guessing."

"Yep. That's her."

They laughed as they headed out to the field for practice.

§

"It's all set, Jenny," Lori confided with a wink to her best friend as they sat on Jenny's bed, failing miserably in trying to concentrate on their homework.

"What is?" Jenny asked, quizzically. Lori was always cooking up something, so she wasn't sure what Lori was referring to this time.

"My Saturday night party, and the great guy I'm going to introduce you to."

"Aw, Lori, I wish you wouldn't. I told you this feels just like a blind date and I hate blind dates."

"Aw, come on, Jenny. How many have you been on?"

"Two, and that's two too many."

"Well, just believe this … the third time's the charm!"

"I have to admit, I love your enthusiasm, but that doesn't mean I have to like this whole thing. And I swear, if he turns out to be some jerk, I won't be speaking to you again for a long time, got it?"

"Relax, Jenny, you don't have a thing to worry about. And neither do I, for that matter."

"What do you mean?"

"Believe me, Jenny, you'll be thanking me before Saturday night is over!"

"Can't you at least tell me something about him? Anything?"

"Not without giving my secret away. I know you know him, well, at least I know you know *of* him, and I'm pretty sure that if I were to tell you anything more then you'd guess who he is and that would spoil my surprise."

Jenny let out a long sigh and shook her head, frustrated that she couldn't get at least *something* out of Lori.

"Believe me, Jenny, I've known this guy for a long time and you two are going to hit it off perfectly."

"Well, if you've known him for so long, and me as well, for that matter, why haven't you ever introduced us before now?"

"Stop and think about it for a moment, Jen. If you'll remember, you were kinda spoken for last year, right?"

"Don't remind me."

"Well-l-l-l?"

"Okay, I'll admit last year was … well, let's just say I never want to go through anything like that again, especially the way it all ended."

"How many times do I have to tell you? Please just trust me, Jenny. You're really gonna love this guy!"

"I'm not ready to start falling in love again anytime soon."

"Hey, *when* you fall in love is completely up to you, but *who* you fall in love with … well, that just might be up to … *me*, at least I might have a little hand in it."

"Oh, Lori, what are you doing? I'm not ready to even *think* of falling in love again. Troy hurt me so bad, I just—"

"Stop worrying, Jenny. Nothing's going to happen right away. I'll introduce the two of you at the party where there'll be lots of our friends around so it'll be a very casual and comfortable place. No pressure at all. You guys will have a chance to talk and laugh and have a good time, no strings attached. And then, whatever happens after that is completely up to the two of you, okay? If anything special comes from it, great! If not, well … at least you'll have made a new friend, right?"

"Yeah, I guess. Now, can we get back to prepping for the history test?"

CHAPTER 4

Jenny

TO SAY THE LEAST, Jennifer Kincaid was very attractive, with long, auburn hair that curled four inches below her shoulders, emerald green eyes, olive complexion, and a very sweet smile. She was tall and slender, standing 5' 10". She was trusting to a fault, and this had led to many hurt feelings and heartaches over the years. As far as she was concerned everyone started at the top of the scale with her, and only their comments or actions could lower themselves in her eyes. She was also forgiving, as she could never really hold a grudge for long, particularly with her girlfriends, and especially if there had been a genuine apology. But when it came to affairs of the heart she was more cautious.

As a naïve 16-year-old junior, Jenny had been swept off her feet by a senior who she initially thought was her "perfect guy". Troy was a little taller than her and his chocolate brown eyes made her melt every time he looked at her. He was a three-sport letterman, but struggled a bit in the classroom. It had taken a lot for Troy to win her over because Jenny's shyness toward jocks had prevented her from seeing herself with such an accomplished athlete. Occasional notes in her locker, and a friendly smile at lunch or while passing in the hall between classes had finally broken the ice. She had told her best friend, Lori, that he'd seemed like a nice enough guy.

They'd dated for a few months, and throughout that time Troy had treated Jenny fairly well. After getting to know him better, though, she began to see a few rough edges. It was probably just a macho thing brought on by some of his friends' challenges, but it wasn't anything she couldn't handle.

A couple of times Troy teasingly flirted with other girls in Jenny's presence just to see how she'd react. The first time Jenny just let it go, not wanting to make a big fuss, but since she hadn't said anything he apparently thought that she didn't mind, or wasn't the jealous kind, and so he did it a few more times and that's when she sat him down one night to have a heart to heart talk with him. Troy had been remorseful and apologized, promising it wouldn't happen again.

A month later Troy had broken his promise and Jenny stopped answering his calls, ignored him at school, and refused to see him when he came by her house. He was not the kind of guy who found it easy to put his thoughts down on paper, nevertheless he wrote Jenny a long letter of apology and mailed it to her. If she refused to see him or answer his calls, then he was hoping that perhaps she'd at least read his letter and respond the same way. A couple of days later he received his answer in the form of a thick envelope. Anxiously opening it to see what she'd written he found his original letter, still in the envelope, torn to pieces, and the pieces partially burned. 'Whoa', he thought, 'what's it going to take to get her to see I'm sorry?!'

The next day a dozen long stemmed red roses were delivered while Jenny wasn't home. Her mother, Adele, had answered the door and accepted the box of flowers from the florist's deliveryman. An hour later Jenny walked in the door and noticed the shiny gold box on the dining room table.

"Oh, no. Are these from Troy?" Jenny asked disgustedly.

"I didn't read the card, honey, but I suppose they are," her mom replied calmly.

Jenny sighed heavily, "Oh, great," she mumbled. "Mom, what am I going to do? I'm *really* upset with him, and he knows exactly why. I don't want anything more to do with him but he won't get the message!"

"Sweetheart, I know. This has been hard on your dad and me, too. We've never seen you feeling so down. Perhaps," her mom sighed, "as hard it may be, perhaps you should just talk to him the next time he calls. Tell him how you feel, and then see how it goes. If it's over, it's over, and you can move on."

Jenny looked at her mom, wondering if talking to Troy was the wisest thing to do. She looked at the box of flowers. "Maybe you're right, mom."

That evening, a nervous and humbled Troy called.

He tried sweet-talking her, hoping her heart had been softened by his gesture but, in fact, it hadn't. She made it clear to him how much he'd hurt her. He begged her for another chance, promising he'd do anything to make things right.

"Forget your promises," Jenny replied. "You promised me once before and you broke that promise. How am I supposed to ever trust you again?"

He said he'd learned his lesson, acknowledging that this was his "second strike" and promised her there wouldn't be a third.

Tension hung in the air as Jenny remained silent for a long time before finally telling Troy in no uncertain terms that she'd give him that chance, but it would absolutely be his last. After that he had been on his best behavior and she thought he'd finally learned his lesson. That's when the memory of the final blow-up came flooding back.

About a dozen of their friends had decided to have a big beach party blow-out before Troy and some of his friends headed off to college. Jenny's best friend, Lori, was there, too.

Many trips were made back and forth from their cars to the beach to haul all of the coolers, beach umbrellas, towels, and other supplies they'd brought for the day. The weather had started out overcast, but it didn't take long for the sun to burn through the fog and begin to bake everyone.

Shortly after everyone was settled on the beach Jenny thought of something she'd forgotten back in Troy's car and asked him for his keys. When she returned Troy was already involved in a volleyball game with a few of their friends along with some others they'd met shortly after they'd arrived. She dropped his keys into her backpack as she walked out to join Lori under one of the big umbrellas.

As they were sitting there talking Jenny noticed Troy paying a bit too much attention to a bikini clad blonde on the other team. She kept a close eye on him, but nothing further happened.

That night, while they all sat around a blazing bonfire under the moonlight, Troy excused himself from Jenny and told her he'd be right back. When he didn't return in a reasonable time she went looking for him, and that's when she saw Troy kissing the bikini clad blonde. He had no idea he'd been caught. Strike three!

Jenny didn't make a scene, she just walked off and sat quietly by herself in the shadows, crying. Lori saw her and walked over and asked if she was okay.

"No, I'm not okay. I just saw Troy with that, that ... blonde he'd met this morning during those volleyball games."

"What?! Where were they? What were they doing?"

"They were over there, on the other side of the dunes, and they were locked in a pretty heated kiss!"

"Oh, no, Jenny! I'm so sorry."

"I just can't believe it, Lori! He's done some hurtful things in the past and we've had some long talks about them and he *promised* me he'd never do anything that would ever hurt me again. He was doing so well, too, and now ..." Jenny couldn't continue through all the tears that were flowing.

Lori put her arm around Jenny for emotional support and asked in between her own tears, "Oh, Jenny, what are you going to do? You still have to ride home with him, and ..."

"Wait! That's it!" Jenny exclaimed. "I've got it!"

"Huh? Got what?"

"When we first arrived here this morning I'd forgotten something back in his car so I asked him for his keys. By the time I got back he was already off playing volleyball with the guys so I just put his keys away safely in my backpack. I still have them!"

"Um, Jenny, what are you thinking?"

"It's not what I'm thinking, Lori ... it's what I'm going to *do*." And with that Jenny explained to Lori what her plan was and asked her to wait at least 15 minutes and then give Troy a message. She then gathered up all of her things and quietly slipped away from the party and headed out to the parking lot. Once she made it over the hill separating the party from the cars she knew it would be no problem to jump into Troy's car and drive off with no one hearing a thing.

A little while later, Troy came sauntering in from over the dunes. He first headed toward one of the coolers to grab a soda, then after chugging down half the can, he started glancing around. Not seeing Jenny right away he walked over to the bonfire and asked some of his friends if they'd seen her. With one "No" after another he kept going until he saw Lori sitting off by herself.

"Hey, Lori, have you seen Jenny anywhere?"

"Yeah, a little while ago."

"Oh, yeah? Cool, where can I find her?"

"Well, actually she asked me to tell you something and give you something."

"Huh? What?"

"She said to tell you she saw you earlier."

"Saw me? What are you talking about? Come on, Lori, where is she?"

"As I said, she asked me to tell you something and give you something. What I'm trying to tell you, if you'll stop interrupting me, is that she saw you with that blonde a little while ago, and she told me to tell you, and I quote, 'It's OVER! Strike three and you're OUT!'"

That, of course, caught the attention of everyone around the bonfire.

"What are you talking about, Lori?" Troy replied indignantly, his anger now rising.

"And," Lori continued as she stood up from the picnic bench, "what she wanted me to give you is this," and with that Lori slapped Troy so hard she knocked him off his balance and onto the sand.

"WHAT THE –"

"And as for me, you and that blonde can both go to hell for breaking Jenny's heart! Oh, yeah, and one more thing," Lori continued as she looked down into Troy's bleeding face, "Looks like you'll be hitchhiking home, because Jenny's already on her way home … in your car."

"WHAT?!" Troy screamed as he tried to stand up.

Shoving Troy back down into the sand with her foot Lori warned, "If you know what's good for you, you'll stay right where you are. Don't even think of calling the police on her, because what's she's done isn't illegal. And, I'm not sure how you'll get your car back, because her daddy will be waiting to get his hands on you."

As Lori walked away Troy's head bounced back down onto the sand with a thud as he painfully tried to comprehend everything that had just happened. By now everyone at the party was fully aware of what happened and no one was making any effort to come to his aid. It looked like he was going to have to figure out what to do next all by himself.

§

The bitter end had taken a deep toll on Jenny's heart. And now Lori was talking about introducing her to someone new? 'Oh, why, Lori?' she pondered. 'Why now? I'm just not ready for anything like that for a long time.'

CHAPTER 5

The Party

MARC ARRIVED EARLY AT Lori's house so he could help her out with any last minute preparations. He retrieved the soda from the trunk of his car but left his guitar behind because he didn't want it to be in anyone's way.

A sign on the front door read, "Don't bother knocking! Just come right in!", so Marc opened the door and called out for Lori.

"I'm in the kitchen, Marc!"

He made his way through the living room and found Lori scurrying around wildly.

"Hey, calm down! What's the rush?"

"Well, if you're here then that means everyone else will also be here soon and I'm not ready!"

"What can I do to help?"

"Fire up the grill?"

"Got it!" and Marc headed for the backyard.

Lori's parents had spent a small fortune landscaping their whole backyard. Marc made his way across the patio, passing a beautiful four-level stone water fountain along the way. Around the far edge of the curved patio were a half dozen Tiki torches which he lit as soon as he had the barbecue going.

The temperature was perfect for an Indian summer evening. There would soon be the aromas from the barbecue mixed with the perfumes from the young ladies, and who was this new girl that Lori was going to introduce him to? He tried picturing in his mind as many of Lori's friends as he could, but no one stood out as being new.

More friends began arriving, and the chatter coming from the kitchen was mixed with laughter. Lori had finally caught her breath moments before her guests arrived and was now being the perfect party hostess. The guys found their way to the backyard and joined Marc near the barbecue, while the girls stayed in the kitchen to gossip about the guys.

Jenny arrived a few minutes later along with her friend, Monica. As they joined Lori and the other girls in the kitchen Jenny felt it was getting rather congested and asked Lori if there was anything she could take out to the patio tables.

"Yes, if you could give a shout out to the guys and ask if they'd move the ice chests out near the serving table, that would give us a little more room in here."

Jenny opened the patio door and caught the attention of the guys. "Would a couple of you please move the ice chests out of the kitchen?"

"Sure," Marc replied, asking Dave to join him.

Jenny held the door open for them as they did their casual "guy thing", quickly jogging across the patio and smoothly strutting into the kitchen among all of the fine looking young ladies who'd just cleared a path for them to get to the ice chests. Marc and Dave each lifted one of the large chests full of ice and chilling sodas and headed back toward the door, with Jenny outside still holding it open for them.

As Marc stepped out he glanced toward Jenny, nodded, and thanked her. The scent of her perfume definitely caught his attention. She smiled sweetly and nodded her head gently, realizing she had just come face to face with one of the stars of their football team, ace receiver Marc Janssen!

After setting the ice chests down Marc turned toward Jenny, but she'd just stepped back into the kitchen. 'Hmmm,' he thought to himself. 'Who was that?'

At first Jenny hadn't noticed Marc's glance, but just as she closed the screen door behind her she glanced out toward Marc and their eyes met ever so briefly before they both quickly turned away. There was just something about him and she couldn't resist the chance to get a closer look at him. She glanced around the kitchen for something to take out to the serving table, saw the chips and dip and, before anyone noticed, was back out the door and heading straight for the table. Without hesitating she turned back toward the kitchen and headed back in, all the while thinking about what to do next.

Marc was already back at the barbecue and tending the fire and hadn't noticed Jenny's return. His thoughts were wandering and he didn't hear the punch line of the joke Dave was telling, but when the rest of the guys all started laughing he snapped out of it.

"Hey, what did I miss?"

"A great joke, buddy. Where were you?" Dave asked.

"Right here, but—"

"But your brain was elsewhere, right?"

Marc laughed, "Yeah, something like that."

Just then Jenny came back out to the patio and headed toward the serving table again, this time carrying a stack of paper plates, napkins and plastic utensils. Marc didn't hesitate to break ranks and made a beeline to help her out.

"Need any help with that?" Marc asked as he noticed the mysteriously attractive young lady startle just a little.

"Huh?! Oh, yeah, sure," Jenny replied, trying her best to calm her rapidly beating heart.

"I'm Marc," he said calmly and confidently.

"Hi. I'm J-Jenny," she replied, trying to hide her nervousness.

"Glad to meet you."

"Same here. Great game last night. You really played well." Jenny was trying to think of something, *anything*, to keep the conversation going.

"Thanks. I appreciate it. It was nice to get another win under our belts this early in the season. We've got some tough competition in the league this year, but we're determined to make it to the championships. Coach has us totally focused on winning, but will smack us down the moment our heads start getting too big for our own, or the team's, good."

"He sounds like a great coach," Jenny replied, grateful that she'd hit on such an easy topic to get their conversation off to a comfortable start.

"He really is. All the guys respect him. He's tough as nails on us, but fair, and that makes us respect him even more because we know he really cares."

"That must be a good feeling," Jenny said with a smile.

"Sure is. Um … is there anything I can do to help you get things ready?"

"Actually, I was about to ask you the same. Lori seems to have everything under control in the kitchen. How's the barbecue going?"

"Huh? OH! The barbecue! Yeah, I almost forgot. I better check on it."

Jenny smiled with the knowledge that she'd just been responsible for derailing Marc's attention.

"Yeah, why don't you do that and I'll go get the burgers and hot dogs. I'm sure people are getting pretty hungry."

"I know I sure am," Marc replied over his shoulder as he headed back to the barbecue.

"Hey, Lori, are the burgers ready?" Jenny called out as she opened the kitchen door.

"Yeah, almost. Why?"

"Because Marc's just about ready to put them on the fire, and I, for one, am starving," to which several of the other girls near her agreed wholeheartedly.

Lori and Monica had been working diligently to make the hamburger patties just right and then stacking them on the platters to take outside. When they finished Lori scooped up both platters and headed in Jenny's direction. She was just about to hand them to Jenny when she froze with a startled look on her face.

"Wait a minute!!" Lori exclaimed. "What did you say about the barbecue just now?!"

"I said that Marc's getting ready to—"

"Oh my GOSH, Jenny!" Lori said, almost in a whisper. "You've already spoken to Marc Janssen?"

"Sure, why? He's a nice guy and—" Just then Jenny noticed a very excited look on Lori's face.

"What?"

"That's him!"

"Him who?"

"Marc! It's him! He's the guy I was going to introduce you to this evening!"

"What?! Really?! Oh, my gosh! Well, it looks like you're a little late. He already introduced himself."

Lori squealed, followed by equally excited responses from the other girls who had been listening intently. "Well, it looks to me like the 'third time's the charm' is going to work after all," Lori said excitedly.

Jenny smiled, looked out through the screen door toward the barbecue, and then back at Lori and smiled.

"Yeah. I think this one's going to be just fine," and Jenny reached out and took the platters before Lori dropped them. "I'll be right back."

Jenny headed out to the barbecue while all the other girls watched in great anticipation through the kitchen windows and door.

"Here ya go, Marc," Jenny said with an inviting smile.

"Hey, thanks, Jenny. I'll get these going and we'll all be eating in no time. Tell Lori thanks for getting them ready."

"Oh, I will," and with that Jenny turned around and headed back to the kitchen. As she walked through the door there was a collective squeal from all the girls which definitely caught the attention of all the guys.

"I wonder what *that* was all about?" Dave asked.

"Yeah, me too," Marc added.

"Hey, I don't suppose …" Dave left his comment hanging.

"You don't suppose what?" Marc replied.

"I don't suppose *that's* the girl Lori was going to introduce you to tonight, is it?"

"Who, Jenny?"

"Yeah, Jenny Kincaid!"

"You know her?"

"Don't *you?*!"

"I do now, but I've never seen her before this evening."

"Are you serious?"

"Yeah, why?"

"Because she's so ... so ..."

"Watch what you say, buddy."

"Okay, okay. Let's just say that she's just ... so right for you, okay?"

"I hope that's what you were thinking in the first place."

"Yeah, it was," Dave replied, but the look on Marc's face made it evident he didn't believe him.

"So, are you going to ask her out?"

"What?! Easy, man. I just met her a few minutes ago!"

"So, what are you waiting for, an embossed invitation?"

"No, I'm just waiting for the opportunity to be able to talk to her some more and get to know her a little better."

"Well, if I were you—"

"Which you're not!"

"Right, right, I get it. But just listen to me for a second, will ya?"

Marc didn't respond, he just folded his arms and stared at his best friend.

"If I were you I wouldn't wait too long."

"And why is that?"

"Because ... she's a very popular girl, and you wouldn't want her to get swept off her feet by any other guy, now would you?"

Again Marc didn't reply, but he unfolded his arms and just smiled.

"Do me a favor, Dave, will ya?"

"Sure, what's that?"

"Just let me do this my way, okay?"

"Yeah, okay, but just remember what I said."

"Yeah, yeah," Marc replied, and just before he turned back toward the barbecue to begin putting the burgers on the grill he glanced toward the kitchen and noticed all of the girls looking in his direction, with Jenny front and center right inside the kitchen door. And she was smiling. A very warm and beautiful smile. The most beautiful smile he'd ever seen.

§

The rest of the evening seemed like a blur to Marc. He hardly remembered fixing the burgers, even though everyone thanked him and said they were perfect; it was the same for Jenny. Lori tried several times to engage her in conversation, but all Jenny did was answer in short replies. Lori had seen this look before and just knew that something, or *someone*, was distracting Jenny that night.

After dinner Jenny walked to the far end of the backyard and sat on a bench in the deepening shadows. Marc had kept an eye on her all evening and soon quietly broke away from the party to join her. A couple of Tiki torches flickered about a dozen feet away, casting dancing shadows on the ground and surrounding foliage.

As Marc approached, Jenny looked up and smiled.

"Is this a private party, or may I join you?"

"It's a private party … for two," Jenny replied with a flirtatious wink.

"Oh, yeah? Well, I only see two of us out here, so I guess if I'm the next one to sit down then the party will be closed to others?"

"Yeah, something like that."

"Okay … works for me," Marc replied with a wink and a smile of his own and before long they were lost in conversation, oblivious to whatever else was going on at the other party.

As they were talking Marc noticed Lori begin to walk out toward them. She stopped, moved her arms in front of her as if she was playing air guitar to see if Marc would get his guitar and sing a few songs, but he shook his head imperceptibly and she nodded. A knowing smile lit up her face and she turned back toward the party. She knew not to bother them again.

Time had passed swiftly, and Marc and Jenny had been so lost in their conversation that they hadn't noticed the party was starting to break up. Lori teasingly flipped the patio light on catching their attention.

"Oh, wow, is it that late already?" Jenny asked.

"Let's just ignore it," Marc pleaded teasingly.

"I'm sorry, Marc, I can't. I wish I could though. Monica is probably waiting for me because she came to the party with me."

"Okay," Marc replied, with a hint of disappointment. "May I walk you to your car?"

Jenny looked up into Marc's eyes and felt a tingle ripple through her. She smiled. "I'd like that."

They made their way through the garden and past the Tiki torches and helped Lori and Monica carry in the last set of dishes from the patio. Neither of them wanted the evening to end. Without saying a word they looked at each other as if to say, "Let's do this again!" Their smiles were the only answers they needed.

Monica was heading out to the car as Jenny and Marc were saying good night and thank you to Lori.

"I'll see you both on Monday!"

"Sounds good," Marc replied with a wave. Jenny gave Lori a special look that simply said, 'Thank you SO much!' and winked. Lori nodded and winked back.

As they reached Jenny's car, Marc was finding it hard to talk. 'Why am I so nervous?' he thought. 'Shake it off. You're going to see her again.'

Jenny unlocked the doors and Monica climbed in. As she opened her own door Jenny hesitated and turned toward Marc. 'Will he kiss me?'

"I had a great time tonight, Jenny."

"I did too, Marc," Jenny replied, nervously biting her lip.

"I'll see you, Monday?"

"Yes, you will."

With his hand resting on the top of the door Marc cleared his throat. "Well, I guess I'd better let you go." He leaned down to look at Monica.

"Take care, Monica."

"You too, Marc," she replied with a smile and a wave.

As he leaned up Jenny hesitated just in case Marc might want to say something else, but when he didn't she lowered herself onto her seat and Marc closed the door after her.

"Drive carefully."

"I promise. See ya, Marc."

"Bye, Jenny." She started the car and a moment later drove off. She hadn't realized it, but she'd driven off with Marc's heart.

"Wow! He's nice!" Monica beamed.

Lost in her own warm glow Jenny said, "Huh?"

"I said, Marc's nice!"

"Oh, yeah. He is," Jenny replied, dreamily.

"Uh-oh. Are you falling for him?"

"Well, I *could* be. I *might* be." Jenny paused. "Yeah, I think so." They both giggled.

"Oh, girl, you've got it bad!"

"Do I?"

"Yes! It's written all over your face!"

Jenny blushed. "Yeah, maybe I do."

As Jenny drove Monica home their conversation was light, with Monica just letting Jenny bask in the feelings of this special night.

"Do you think he's going to ask you out?"

"I sure hope so."

"You've gotta let me know the minute he does, alright?"

"Huh? Oh, sure. I promise."

They pulled up in front of Monica's house, said their goodbyes, and Jenny was off.

Later, as Jenny was lying in her bed unable to sleep, she replayed the whole evening over and over in her head. Every word of their conversation. Every look. 'Could he be the one?'

She wondered why he hadn't tried to kiss her. 'He didn't even give me a hug before I got in the car! What's up with that?' She laughed at herself, realizing how silly she must look right now.

Finally she softly drifted off to sleep, hoping she'd see Marc again … in her dreams.

§

Jenny's phone rang early Sunday morning, waking her up from her best dream ever.

"Hello?" she answered sleepily.

"Okay, spill it!" Lori playfully demanded.

"Wha—? Lori? Do you know what time it is?"

"Yes! It's time for you to tell me all about how everything went with Marc! The two of you were off by yourselves for a long time and I'm dying to know all of the details!"

"Well, you can just keep dying a little longer because I'm going back to sleep."

"No, Jenny, don't hang—"

"Bye, Lori. I'll call you later," and with that she hung up the phone and moments later she was fast asleep.

Jenny called Lori back a few hours later. She told her what a nice guy Marc was, how easily they seemed to get along, and how comfortable she felt around him. Then she proceeded to tell Lori all about the dream she'd been so rudely awakened from earlier. Over two hours later they were still going strong when Jenny finally explained that she needed to get to her homework since she hadn't been able to get any of it done the day before because she'd been so nervous about the party.

"Lori?"

"Yeah, Jen?"

"Thanks … for everything. I don't want to rush into anything, but Marc sure seems like a great guy, a real gentleman. So much better than Troy ever was, that's for sure."

"Oh, I'm so glad you feel that way. I hope things work out for the two of you."

"Yeah, it would be nice if it did, but I just want to take things slow and easy. There's still a lot of lingering hurt from Troy, and I need to be completely free of all of that before I can even think of caring about another guy, and Marc seems like just the guy I need right now who'll let me have that time to work things out."

"Believe me, Jenny, he is."

"Good. I'll see you tomorrow in class."

"Yep! See you then!"

CHAPTER 6

Monday

MARC ARRIVED AT SCHOOL thirty minutes early to see if he could catch Lori before her first class and find out where Jenny's locker was.

"Hey, Marc!"

"Mornin', Lori! That was a great party Saturday night. I had a good time!"

"And it looked like you and Jenny were having fun," Lori replied with a sly grin.

"Aww, I've seen that look before. I'm guessing Jenny was the girl you wanted to introduce me to?"

"As a matter of fact, yes! And even though I didn't get to make the actual introduction it seemed like the two of you hit it off okay."

"Yeah, you could say that," Marc replied nonchalantly.

"Well, I think she was pretty happy, too."

"Really? Did you talk to her?"

"Don't girls *always* talk about things like this?"

"I don't know, do they?"

"Of course, we do! We chatted for *hours* about you yesterday."

"Really?"

"You act surprised."

"Yeah, I guess. I mean *hours?*"

"Well, okay, I guess I did most of the talking, asking her lots of questions, you know me."

"Yes, I sure do," Marc replied with a laugh.

"Anyway, she said she had a fun time."

"That's good to know."

"So, are you going to ask her out?"

"Yeah, I was hoping to catch her before class. Where's her locker?"

"It's down the hall on the right, #423."

"Thanks."

"Hey, before you go, I think you need to know something."

"What's that?"

"She was hurt badly by her last boyfriend, so just go easy."

"What happened?"

"Well, it's not for me to tell you the details, but if Jenny wants to she will, in her own time, okay?"

"Yeah, sure. Listen, I'm going to try to catch Jenny at her locker before she heads to class so I'll see you later, okay?"

"Sounds good! Bye, Marc! And," making sure she had his attention, "you treat her right, or else!"

Marc smiled, "You have nothing to worry about, Lori. And neither does Jenny."

Lori smiled back and headed for her class.

Just as Marc was nearing her locker Jenny turned into the hallway. Their eyes met, and they both paused for just a moment, before meeting at her locker.

"Hi, Jenny," Marc said calmly, but with a hint of excitement.

"Hi, Marc!" Jenny replied, her heart beat jumping upon seeing him.

"Hey, I know we only have a few minutes before class but I wanted to ask you, would you like to go out with me Saturday night?"

"Yes, I'd like that."

"Great! I was thinking we could go out for pizza and then go for a drive."

"Yeah, that sounds like fun."

"Can I call you tonight?"

"Sure!" and Jenny gave him her number.

"Thanks, Jenny. I'll call you around 8, if that's okay?"

"Yes, that'll be fine."

"Cool, so I'll see ya later."

"Okay! Thanks, Marc!" Jenny couldn't think of a better way to start off her week than by being asked out on a date by Marc Janssen!

At lunch Jenny saw Lori and ran up to her grinning from ear to ear!

"Guess what, Lori?!" Jenny couldn't wait for Lori to even open her mouth. "Marc asked me out!"

"YES!! That's great, Jenny! I'm so excited for you!" Lori replied.

"He's taking me out for pizza and then we're going for a drive."

"Did he say where?"

"For pizza or the drive?"

"Both!"

"No, but it doesn't matter. I'm sure it's going to be fun!"

"Oh, Jenny. I'm so happy for you. And to see you this excited just makes me feel so good."

"Thanks, Lori. It *does* feel good! I'm curious where he's going to take me on the drive."

"Where would you like him to take you?"

"Oh, I don't know. Hopefully the weather will be nice and we could go someplace and maybe go for a walk? I know there are some nice parks around."

"Mmmm, that sounds lovely!"

"Yeah," Jenny replied with a sigh. "He's calling me tonight so maybe we'll talk some more about it then."

"And you'll tell me all about it tomorrow, right?"

"Of course!" They laughed as they went into the cafeteria for lunch.

§

That night Marc called right at 8. His promptness impressed her. They talked about Lori's party and the good time they both had, and then Marc jokingly quizzed her about her call with Lori the day before, but Jenny remained coy about what was said between the two of them and changed the subject.

"So, where are we going for our drive?"

"Oh, I have a few ideas in mind. I think I'll wait and see how the weather is Saturday evening and then surprise you."

"Can't I have any hints?"

"No, I said it'll be a surprise."

Even though Marc couldn't see Jenny he could somehow tell she was playfully pouting.

"Tell ya what. I promise it'll be worth it."

"Oh, I don't know. Can I trust you?"

"I guess you'll have to."

Jenny thought to herself for a moment, 'I do, too.'

CHAPTER 7

And so it begins!

AS JENNY WAITED FOR Marc to pick her up she realized that she had no idea what kind of car he drove. She kept peeking out her bedroom window whenever cars drove by until one pulled up in front of her house. The butterflies she'd been feeling up until that moment were nothing compared to what she was feeling now!

Jenny's dad answered the door right after Marc knocked.

"Hi, Mr. Kincaid?"

"Hi, you must be Marc," Jenny's dad replied.

"Yes, sir."

"Well, come on in. Jenny will be right down."

"Thank you, sir." They exchanged a firm handshake.

Just then Jenny's mom joined them in the foyer. "Sweetheart, this is Jenny's date, Marc."

"Hi, Marc! We're pleased to meet you. Jenny's been telling us all about you."

"Thank you, Mrs. Kincaid. I'm glad to meet you, too."

Before their conversation could go any further Jenny came down the stairs.

"Hi, Marc!"

"Hey, Jenny! You look great!"

"So do you!"

Jenny turned toward her parents and gave them each a hug and kiss. "I love you, mom and dad. See you later."

"Love you too, sweetheart," her mom replied. "You two have fun and be careful."

"We will," Marc and Jenny replied in unison, then looked at each other and laughed.

Marc held the door open for her and she slipped in, admiring his car.

"Nice ride, Marc! What year is this?"

"It's a '66 Chevy Malibu. Both my dad and I are into classic cars and he helped me buy it and restore it."

"Well, I love it!"

Marc smiled as they headed to the Pizza Joynt.

As expected, the place was packed and they saw some of their friends from school but decided to be on their own and found a small booth near the back where it wasn't quite as noisy.

They talked a little about Marc's football game the previous night, and the tough loss they'd suffered at the hands of this year's best team in the league. Jenny had found him after the game before the team boarded the visitor's buses but he was in a bad mood. They had been undefeated the previous year and had won the North Coast Section championship. In fact, Marc couldn't remember when the last time was that they'd lost a game, but none of that mattered now; all he could think about was *this* game.

The emotional pain of the loss had subsided by Saturday evening, but he was still feeling the effects from some ruthless tackles. He tried his best to mask the stiffness as he moved. He was just about to change the subject when their pizzas arrived – hot and loaded with cheese! The extra cheese was a trademark of this place.

They saw a few more friends who briefly stopped by their booth to say hi. Marc noticed Jenny's mood change.

"Hey, what's up? You don't look too happy about something."

"Oh, it's nothing really. Lori and Monica and a few other friends just came in, probably to spy on us. Maybe they won't see –"

"Hi, Jenny! Hi, Marc!" Lori exclaimed. Monica and the others were close behind.

"Hey, how are you?" Marc replied.

"Your pizzas look delicious!"

"Yes, they are!" Jenny added.

"Well, we won't bother you. You have more important things to do tonight than chat with us!" The girls all laughed and Marc smiled and shook his head as they left.

"You know, Jenny, I'm surprised we never saw each other before last Saturday night. I mean, I've known Lori for a long time, and you said she's your best friend, so how come we never made this connection before?"

"I don't know. I've known about you since junior high, and then I've seen you playing football, but I didn't know you knew Lori."

"Well, regardless of what we may have missed out on in the past, I'm glad we've met."

"Me too, Marc."

"So, how's your pizza?"

"It's hot, but I love it!"

"Yeah, this is one of my favorite places."

"Mine too. I was here once before, but it's been a while."

"Well, we'll just have to come here again."

"Sure, I'd like that," Jenny replied as she saw the look in Marc's eyes; a look that said he was probably thinking the same thing as she was … more good times are coming!

They continued to chat about school, sports, and friends while they finished their pizzas.

After Marc left a nice tip for their waitress he took Jenny's hand and she felt the exquisite thrill of that moment. His hand was strong but he held her gently and she instantly felt safe. She looked up at him, their eyes met, he smiled, her heart melted, and she sighed in complete contentment.

They walked over to say goodbye to Lori and the other girls. Lori gave Jenny one of those looks and then whispered, "You are such a lucky girl!" Jenny just smiled and winked.

Marc paid the cashier and they were off to enjoy the rest of their evening!

§

Marc was captivated by Jenny and it was hard for him to not show it. He remembered what Lori had shared with him about Jenny getting over a horrible relationship. So far the evening had been light and fun and he intended to keep it that way so Jenny wouldn't feel any pressure from him in any way.

"So, do I get a clue where you're taking me on our drive?" Jenny asked.

"No, just sit back and relax and we'll just let the rest of the evening unfold in the moment." Marc replied with a sly grin.

"Ooh! Would you turn the radio up?" Jenny exclaimed. "This is one of my favorite songs!"

"Sure!" As Marc turned the dial up Jenny began singing along and a moment later he joined her.

"I love your voice, Marc! I didn't know you could sing."

"Yeah, I've done a little here and there. And I love your voice, too. Have you ever thought of recording a song or singing with a band?"

"Me? No, but thanks."

"Why not?"

"Just consider yourself lucky that you heard me singing this one time. I normally only sing to myself in my bedroom. Or once in a while when I'm driving."

"Ah-h-h, I can see it now," Marc said with a far off look. "Standing there in your room, the music rocking, and you're holding a hairbrush for a microphone, right?"

Jenny laughed. "Yeah, something like that." 'This was fun!' she thought. Every minute with Marc was another minute away from her memories of Troy.

"We're heading to San Francisco?!" Jenny exclaimed as they headed for the approach to the Bay Bridge.

"In a way, yes."

"What's that supposed to mean?"

"Just that we're heading *toward* San Francisco, but we may not be *staying* in the city."

Jenny sat back. "You're enjoying this, aren't you?"

"What?"

"Torturing me like this. Keeping me guessing."

"Yeah, as a matter of fact I am." Marc replied smugly.

Jenny elbowed him in the ribs.

"Hey! What was that for?"

"Just because."

"You are *so* going to get it!"

"Promise?" Jenny asked teasingly.

"Absolutely!"

'Hmm-m, I wonder what he has in mind,' Jenny thought.

Marc turned the radio back up to listen to one of his favorite songs and it wasn't long before they were both singing along. Time didn't seem to matter to them as they crossed the bridge and drove through the City, took the Fell Street off ramp and made their way through Golden Gate Park and finally out to the coast.

The sun was setting, casting a beautiful hue of colors across the horizon, as they drove down the Great Highway. Marc found a place to park along Ocean Beach and helped Jenny out of the car. She felt a momentary sting of apprehension as she remembered the last time she had been at the beach, but she tried her best to shake off the feelings and focus on who she was with this evening.

"This is beautiful, Marc," Jenny said wistfully.

"Yes, you are," Marc replied as their eyes met. Jenny blushed.

"I've – ." Jenny caught herself before she could say what she was thinking.

"Pardon me?"

"Oh, nothing. Thanks for bringing me here, Marc."

As Marc took Jenny's hand that same feeling of safety came back to her that she'd felt earlier. They walked across the soft sand and made their way to the wet, hard packed sand being kissed by the waves.

They walked down the beach, occasionally chasing seagulls, tossing stranded starfish back into the ocean, and being careful not to get drenched by an onrushing wave. The twilight was romantic, and they let the sounds of the crashing waves drown out the sounds of the cars passing on the nearby highway.

They turned and headed back up the beach. Jenny stopped for a moment as she felt something. Marc turned and saw the look in her eyes.

"Is everything okay, Jenny?"

"Yes," she replied softly. Then she stepped closer and gave Marc a hug. His strong arms enveloped her and she lost herself in the moment.

"Thank you, Marc."

"For what?"

"For being you. For bringing me here. For this whole night. I mean, you hit a home run on our first date. Great pizza, a fun drive over here – "

"Listening to you sing!" Marc interrupted.

"Oh, stop. I'm not that good."

"Yes, you are."

Jenny just smiled as she lowered her eyes. "Thank you. You're sweet." She let out a gentle sigh. "And bringing me here, at just the right time to see that beautiful sunset, and then walking along the beach with you ... it's ... lovely."

"You're welcome, Jenny," Marc whispered softly. He reached down, placing his fingers under her chin and gently raised her head until their eyes met. As he looked deeply into her eyes he couldn't hold back anymore.

"I'm falling in love with you, Jenny."

Just then Jenny looked away and it seemed that romantic spell was cast away by the breeze. "What is it?" he asked.

"I'm sorry, Marc. I've spoiled this special moment for us. I need to tell you something."

"What is it?"

Jenny held her breath as she gathered her thoughts. "Let's walk while I explain a few things."

"Okay."

As they continued to walk back up the beach Jenny told Marc all about Troy, how she'd fallen for him, how he'd been nice to her to begin with but then how things went downhill. She told him about Troy's broken promises, including how everything crashed for good, at the beach party.

"Oh, Jenny, I'm so sorry. And here I brought you to the beach on our first date. I really screwed up."

"No, Marc, you didn't! You didn't know anything about my past before just now."

"Well, Lori had mentioned to me that you'd been really hurt by another guy, and I'd asked her about it but she didn't go into any details saying that it was up to you to share that with me if you ever wanted to."

"Well, I was hoping that I wouldn't have to – "

"And I blew it."

"No, you didn't, Marc. It's actually better that I'm able to tell you this now instead of holding onto it any longer."

"Still, I'm sorry, Jenny."

Jenny looked up at Marc, gently touched his cheek with her hand, and said, "It's okay, Marc. Really, it's okay."

They just held each other for a while as the waves rushed to the shore a few feet away.

Finally they leaned back and looked at each other.

"Marc, can we just take it slowly."

"Absolutely. We'll take things as slowly as you'd like."

"Thank you," she replied softly, and gave Marc another hug.

§

The drive home was quiet as Jenny rested her head on Marc's shoulder. She felt herself drifting into a peaceful reverie ... dreaming of what might yet be.

CHAPTER 8

In The Moonlight

AFTER THAT SPECIAL NIGHT Marc and Jenny spent as much time together as they could which, because of their mutually busy schedules, meant only a couple of nights a week to study together, and then Jenny attending Marc's football games on Friday nights, and a dance or movie or party on Saturday nights.

Marc hadn't felt badly about telling Jenny he was falling in love with her on their first date, only that he hadn't waited longer. Lori had told him to go easy but everything about that night seemed so perfect and it just happened. Jenny's hesitation wasn't what he'd been hoping for but after Jenny told him about Troy he'd understood and promised to give her all the time she needed.

On Jenny's birthday in late October he dropped by her house just after eight. She'd heard his car as he approached and was anxiously waiting at the door when he knocked.

"Happy birthday, Jenny," Marc said as he held out a large, beautifully wrapped present.

"Thanks!" Jenny replied as she opened the screen door and let him in, taking the present from him.

"I guess this is for me?"

"It's your birthday, isn't it?"

Jenny smiled, but didn't need to answer. The look they shared seemed to say it all.

"Hmm. It's large, but not that heavy. Any hints?"

"Nope. Not a single one."

Jenny proceeded to quickly unwrap her present.

"Oh, Marc, it's so cute!" she replied as she lifted the soft, fluffy teddy bear out of the box. "Thank you so much, sweetheart!"

"You're welcome. Happy birthday."

"Thanks!" she replied and then leaned into Marc and gave him a big hug and kiss. She was just about to give the teddy bear a hug when something caught her eye. She noticed a slight reflection of light near the ribbon that was tied in a bow around the teddy bear's neck. She held it closer to get a better look, then burst into tears as she fell into Marc's arms.

When she was finally able to control her breathing she leaned up and looked into Marc's eyes. Nothing was said, at least not out loud, but the unspoken feelings were strong and genuine.

She looked back down at the teddy bear and untied the ribbon around its neck, removing the shiny item that had caught her eye. She began to cry again as she handed it to Marc and asked him to put it on her. She threw her arms around his neck and pulled him close for a loving kiss, then with her arms still wrapped tightly around his neck she raised her left hand and cried once again as she admired Marc's class ring on her finger.

§

Three weeks later Marc and Jenny were heading to a ranch in the hills several miles away from their homes and getting ready to join about two dozen other friends for a hayride and dance.

It was an unusually balmy evening for the middle of November. The windows were rolled down and Marc and Jenny, along with Marc's friend, Dave, and his girl, MariAnne, were all singing along to the radio. They were having a great time when Marc thought that he'd just passed the entrance to the ranch, easy to do since there wasn't a sign posted, only an opening in the brush that marked the way.

Marc stopped in the middle of the road and proceeded to make a Y turn using the left shoulder when it felt like he'd hit something with his car. He stopped abruptly, paused to try to remember if he'd seen anything in his turning path, but couldn't remember anything nearby. He put the car in reverse and gently stepped on the gas. Nothing. He stepped on the gas harder, and was only spinning his rear wheels. He put his car in park and got out to see what the problem was. Walking around the front of the car Marc was stunned to see the right front tire was deep in a hole.

The four of them talked over what to do next and Marc suggested everyone else should get out and sit on the back of the car so they could get more traction on the rear wheels and he'd pop it into reverse and get out of the hole that way, but the only results they got from that was a cloud of dust and the smell of burning rubber from the spinning tires.

"Tell ya what, buddy," Dave began, "I'm pretty sure I saw where that side road is to the ranch, so MariAnne and I will walk back there and see if we can get someone out here to pull you out."

"I don't know that we have any other alternative," Marc replied. "Thanks. Jenny and I will be right here."

The full moon shone brilliantly in the cloudless sky as Dave and MariAnne walked off down the road with enough light for them to see their way safely.

Marc let out a sigh of frustration.

"What's wrong?" Jenny asked.

"I just feel so *stupid* for driving into a *stupid* hole in the ground."

"Hey, did you actually *see* the hole before you drove into it?"

"No."

"Well, then, don't feel stupid. It just happened, okay?"

Marc was reluctant to agree, but he saw her point.

"Besides," Jenny continued, her voice softening to almost a whisper, "We're all alone … in the middle of nowhere … with a *beautiful* full moon up above."

"Yeah? So?" Marc replied, teasingly.

Jenny proceeded to lean Marc up against the driver's door and then pressed tightly into him, putting her arms around his neck and pulling him close for a kiss. As their lips parted what seemed like an eternity later Jenny looked into Marc's eyes.

"I love you, Marc," she whispered softly, and the pace of Marc's heart exploded.

"Oh, I love you too, Jenny!" and they were once again lost in another kiss.

The next look they shared also brought big smiles as they both realized an important moment had just occurred – Jenny had finally let go of the hurt from Troy and had committed herself completely to loving Marc.

"I can't believe it, Jenny! I've waited so long to hear you say that!" he said breathlessly.

"Well, to be honest with you, you didn't have to wait quite this long," Jenny replied with a teasing smile.

"What?"

"Well, think back to my birthday, when you gave me your ring."

"Yeah, I remember."

"I was hoping you were going to say you loved me that night."

"But … you'd asked me to hold off just a few weeks earlier and I—"

"I know, but the moment I saw your class ring I felt all of the hurt and pain from my past just wash away and I knew I was ready to really give my heart away again completely."

"Then why didn't you tell me you loved me that night."

"Because … I wanted to hear it from you first."

"Okay … then … now, don't get me wrong, I love that you told me tonight, but why didn't you wait for me to say it first before telling me you loved me?"

"Because! I couldn't wait any longer!"

CHAPTER 9

Carmel-by-the-Sea

MARC AND JENNY ENJOYED one exciting and loving moment after another throughout their senior year. Dances, movies, parties with friends, bike riding, walks along the beach, horseback riding in the hills – it was a wonder they were both able to keep up their grades!

As their senior year was drawing to a close they were looking forward to one very special night – their Senior Ball. It was being held at the Claremont Hotel in the Berkeley hills. Jenny and Lori had put in long hours on the planning committee while Marc and Dave were leading their baseball team to another league championship, their third in four years.

The theme for the ball was "The Promise" and the whole evening seemed like a slice of heaven for both of them. Lori had invited them to a party at her house afterwards but they had other plans. After the last dance, Marc and Jenny jumped in his car and headed across the bay to the City and ended up at the beach where they kicked off their shoes and walked along the shore and thought about what the rest of their friends were missing out on.

Once again the setting was perfect for this romantic evening – another full moon lingered high above. The sky was perfectly clear and the air was surprisingly comfortable with no chill or fog in the air. It had been a truly magical evening for them but they still had more plans for the weekend. After spending an hour walking along the edge of the crashing surf they knew they needed to get home and get some sleep. On the ride home Jenny rested her head on Marc's shoulder and fell asleep, not waking again until Marc pulled off the freeway.

It was nearly 2:30 a.m. when they pulled up in front of Jenny's home and there was a light on in the living room. Jenny's dad was old fashioned and very protective, and she just knew he must be waiting up for her. They exchanged one more special kiss in the car and then Marc walked Jenny up to the door. They kissed goodnight, and as Jenny opened up the front door they heard her dad, Tony, say, "Is that my special princess?"

"Yes, daddy, I'm home," Jenny replied cheerfully, rolling her eyes as she smiled at Marc. All of a sudden Jenny's dad appeared in the doorway.

"Marc?" Tony said in a firm voice.

"Yes, sir?"

Tony smiled. "I just want to thank you for bringing my little princess home safely."

"You're welcome, sir. We had a great time, and thanks for letting me have her out longer than normal."

"No problem, young man. Adele and I trust you with our daughter, and we're glad everything went well."

"Yes, sir. And thank you again, sir."

"Well," Jenny interrupted, "if we're heading out early in the morning to *wherever* you're taking me, I better get my beauty sleep. Good night, Marc. I had a *wonderful* evening! I love you!"

"I love you too, Jenny. Good night. I'll see you at 8!"

"I'll be ready!"

Jenny watched as Marc walked back to his car and then slowly closed the door as he drove away.

As she lay her head on her pillow a while later and began to drift quickly off to sleep she couldn't help but think about the theme for the dance … "The Promise" … and thought about the promises they'd made … as well as those yet to come.

§

Eight a.m. rolled around early, but Jenny was up, dressed, and ready for Marc as he pulled up.

"I'll be right out, sweetheart," she called, as she rushed to give her mom and dad a hug and kiss goodbye.

"Don't wait up for me!"

"Wait, honey," her mom said. "Are you guys going to be really late again tonight?"

"I don't know what Marc has planned for us, so to be perfectly honest with you I have no idea when I'll be home, but I'm sure it won't be as late as last night."

"Or … this morning?" chided her mom. Jenny just smiled.

"Okay, honey. Well, you two have a wonderful time, and be careful wherever you go."

"I will, mom. Love you. And I love you too, dad!"

"Bye, Princess. Love you, too."

Jenny bounded out the front door and soaked up the beautiful spring morning.

Marc was waiting next to her side of the car with the door open.

"So, good looking," she said as she paused to kiss him before jumping into the car, "where are you taking me on this righteously beautiful day?"

"I told you, it's a surprise."

"Have we ever been there before?"

"I have, and you may have, but we've never been there together."

Jenny curled up next to Marc in the front seat, secured herself into his seatbelt, and teasingly ran her fingers through his hair knowing how much this drove him crazy.

"And you won't even give me a clue?"

"Nope."

"Not even a little hint?" she playfully pouted.

"Not even a hint, so just sit back and relax because it's going to take us a while to get there."

"Oh, yeah?" she asked innocently. "How long?"

"No way! You're not getting anything out of me about this surprise. My lips are sealed."

"Oh, really? Well ... sealed lips are not kissable lips," and with that she unbuckled their seat belt and started to move away from him.

"Hey! Hang on! I haven't sealed them yet."

Jenny just couldn't resist the look in Marc's eyes and caved into him with a nudge.

"I love you, big guy."

"Love you too, babe."

The first forty-five minutes or so of the drive wasn't so interesting as they made their way south on I-880 to San Jose and then shifted over to Highway 101 heading further south. They talked and laughed, sang along with songs on the radio, and recalled memories of the previous night. Morgan Hill ... Gilroy ... the towns went flying by. Then, as they headed into the coastal range Marc noticed Jenny's silence.

"Hey, darlin', are you okay?"

"Yeah, just admiring how beautiful it is through this area. I'm hoping some day to live where there are lots of trees and not so much congestion."

"Oh, yeah? That's good to know. I'd like that, too."

Jenny gave Marc a look that didn't need any words. They just ... knew.

Another twenty minutes or so later they descended out of the hills, heading west.

"Are we going to the beach?!" Jenny asked excitedly.

"Better."

"What's better than the beach?"

"This coming from a girl who just a little while ago said she hoped to someday live where there are lots of trees?"

"You know what I mean!"

"I know. I just had to tease you," and Jenny proceeded to jab Marc in the ribs.

"Hey! What was that for?"

"For teasing me."

"Oh, I get it. It's okay for you to tease me, but I get jabbed when I tease you?"

"Yep! Something like that," Jenny replied with a flirtatious wink and a smile.

"Oh, you are *so* going to get it!"

"Promise?!"

"Wha—?" and they both laughed.

There was another quiet pause in the conversation as they reached the coast of Monterey Bay and Jenny waited for Marc to take one of the off ramps that would lead them closer to the beaches, but instead he kept driving.

"Have you figured out where we're heading yet?"

"Well, I thought we were heading to the beach, but you just keep on driving and so, no, I haven't figured it out yet."

"Good!" Marc replied triumphantly.

"Good? Why good?"

"Because … that makes my surprise even that much more special!"

Jenny just looked at Marc for several moments, trying to figure out what this big surprise could possibly be. She then resigned herself to just going along for the ride and let it all happen as he wanted it.

"Does any of this look familiar to you?"

"Well, kind of. I vaguely remember that my parents brought me down here when I was a little girl, and then we went to some place near the water where there were lots of little shops."

"Yeah, that's probably Fisherman's Wharf."

"Yeah, that was probably it, but I don't remember too much after that other than being tired and wanting to go home."

"Well, today is going to be a lot better than that."

They drove past a sign for Seaside, and a few minutes later they spotted signs for different off ramps in Monterey, while all along Marc remained in the fast lane, giving no indication that he might be pulling off anytime soon.

Before she knew it the freeway was ending and turning into Highway 1 and the last turns for Monterey had already gone by.

"Wherever we're going, can we at least get something to eat soon? I'm starving!"

"Sure. We're actually almost there."

"Really?! Ooooo, I can't wait!"

Marc looked at Jenny. She was beaming! "Just like a little kid at Christmas."

They finally came to a stop at the corner of Highway 1 and Ocean Avenue and Marc flipped on his signal and turned right.

"Okay, we're here."

"We are?!" Jenny asked with unbridled excitement. "What town is this?"

"Carmel-by-the-Sea."

"Long name for a town."

"Well, most people just call it Carmel."

"I love it already!"

They drove to the end of Ocean Avenue which dead-ended at the beach and then turned around and drove halfway back up toward Highway 1. Marc turned onto a side street and drove a few blocks and found a place to park with no parking meter, which suited him just fine since he had no idea how long they'd be there and he didn't feel like running back every couple of hours to feed the meter.

They started their day with a visit to a small café and each had a large croissant and juice. Then it was off to explore the beautiful world of Carmel with all of its various gift and clothing shops, art galleries, and souvenir stores blended in with a variety of aromas emanating from numerous cafés and restaurants.

§

There was an exhausted but comfortable silence as they began the drive home later that night. The day had been filled with one new and exciting discovery after another. Jenny's eyes lit up with excitement with every new store they ventured into as if she were still a little girl and Carmel were her own personal Christmas gift shop. They even spent some time out on the beach. Marc had simply watched with amazement as the joy in her smile and in her eyes just got brighter and brighter all day.

"What a beautiful surprise, Marc. Thank you so much!"

"I had a feeling you were enjoying yourself today. That smile of yours never left your lips."

"Well, except when that little girl out on the beach lost her balloon. That just broke my heart to see her crying like that."

"Yeah, I know what you mean."

"But other than that the day was perfect! I love you so much, Marc!"

"I love you too, Jenny! So, what was your favorite part of the day?"

"Being with you!"

"Thanks, but you know what I mean."

"I know, but there were just too many special moments to just pick one or two. I know one thing, though."

"What's that?"

"I know I'll never forget this day. Carmel is *our* place. Ours, and ours alone!"

"Sounds good to me, but what are we going to do with all the other people who live there and the other people, like us, who come to visit?"

"Oh, I guess we can share it with them."

Marc just smiled and shook his head.

"I love you, babe," Marc said as Carmel disappeared in the rear-view mirror.

"I love you too, sweetheart. Thanks for a truly beautiful day," Jenny replied softly as she leaned up and kissed Marc on the cheek and then rested her head on his shoulder and closed her eyes.

CHAPTER 10

Jenny

GRADUATION CAME AND WENT so fast, along with a quick trip to Lake Tahoe for Marc and Jenny and his parents, and before they knew it three weeks of their summer vacation had already flown by. Marc's dad had helped him secure a summer job working at the Lake Chabot Golf Course in the Oakland hills where his dad frequently played.

As often as Cole went golfing he had never taken his son with him because Marc had always been so busy with his studies, sports, and music. Even during previous summer vacations Marc had earned money by tutoring other students as well as performing at various events, but now that high school was behind him, and college yet to come, he wanted to spend his summer doing something completely different. When his dad suggested working at the golf course Marc jumped at the chance!

Of course he had initially assumed that he'd be out on the course as a caddy, but his dad gently burst that bubble the day before he was supposed to go in for his job interview.

"Sorry, son," Cole confided, "Your duties will probably include many other things, but being a caddy will not be one of them."

"But, dad—"

"Son, how much do you know about golf?"

"Nothing, really. Just what I've seen once in a while on TV."

"Okay, a caddy doesn't just carry a golfer's clubs. A caddy needs to not only know and understand the game, but he needs to know and understand the course, and every minute idiosyncrasy of every green and hole. It takes time to develop that skill. I'll take you golfing with me sometime and I'll show you what I mean. Fair enough?"

Marc paused before responding, then looked at his dad. "Yeah, dad. Fair enough. Thanks."

"Besides, because of the terrain of the course we use carts to get around and our bags are strapped into the carts."

§

Jenny was busy spending her summer splitting her time with her friends and an evening part-time job at an upscale steak house where the tips were known to be exceptional. She hustled to offer her customers first class service, sharing her irresistible smile with everyone equally and she was rewarded for her efforts with generous tips from her satisfied customers. Many even returned on a regular basis and specifically asked for her.

With Marc working full time, Jenny spent most of her days hanging out with her girlfriends and lounging around someone's pool or playing tennis to keep her radiant tan, or shopping for nothing in particular at the mall. When she wasn't working or hanging out with her friends, she'd spend as much time as possible with Marc, and when she was working, Marc could usually be found restoring his classic '66 Malibu.

Having his dad help him pay for and restore the Malibu had been a great experience. While the car was turning out great, Marc especially enjoyed the time he was able to spend just talking with his dad. They'd always been close, but working together on a father/son project like this had brought them even closer. Now that he was soon heading off to college Marc wanted to take advantage of every chance he could to pick his father's brains about what to expect over the next few years as he entered manhood, and the advice Cole offered him was invaluable.

§

As the end of summer approached and the time for Marc to leave for college crept closer day by day, Jenny began to feel apprehensive, not so much about starting college, but more about Marc being so far away. It was taking an emotional toll on her and she had to find a way to talk to him about it.

Marc was home working on his car in the driveway with his buddy, Dave. They'd been best friends since elementary school and had done nearly everything together over the years. Dave was even a member of Marc's band back when they were sophomores. Now that summer was ending and college was about to begin they were about to go their separate ways.

Dave had earned a boat load of scholarships and had chosen to attend UC Berkeley. Marc had also earned many scholarships and had finally decided on attending the University of Utah. He'd chosen Utah because of its proximity to so many great skiing venues, having developed his love for skiing from spending so much time with his family at their cabin at Lake Tahoe. Leaving for college, however, was going to have to wait for at least another week because he and Dave had one final getaway planned. Marc had gotten permission for the two of them to use his parent's cabin for a long weekend, and they were looking forward to getting away for some fun in the sun before college and dorm life set in.

Marc was under the dash checking the wiring on a new stereo and speakers he'd just installed in his car while Dave was checking the oil and other fluid levels.

"Hey, Marc?"

"What?"

"Is anyone home besides you?"

"No, why?"

"The phone's ringing in the kitchen."

"Would you mind running in and getting it?"

"Sure." Dave ran through the garage thoroughly wiping the grease off his hands before opening the kitchen door, hoping to reach the phone in time.

"Hello?"

"Hi, Marc?" Jenny said in a voice that she hoped masked her faltering emotions.

"No, it's Dave. Marc's out in his car. Can I get him for you?"

"Sure, would you mind?"

"Not at all. He'll be right with you," Dave replied and placed the phone down on the counter.

"Hey, Marc!" Dave called as he reentered the garage, "it's Jenny!"

"Great! Coming!" Marc slid out from under the dash and sat on the edge of the seat for a moment before standing up so he could let the blood that had gone to his head begin to recirculate.

"She's wai-ting."

"Yeah, yeah, I know. I just didn't want to pass out."

"Wiring all set?"

"Yep, all set. It's going to sound great!"

Marc jogged through the garage and into the kitchen and swept up the phone, anxious to talk with his sweetheart.

"Hey, beautiful! How's it going?"

"Good. I just got off the phone with Lori and we're going to get together tomorrow for some girl time at the mall."

"Sounds like fun for you."

"Yeah, we're looking forward to it. We both need more clothes for school and—" Marc's laughter interrupted her.

"Uh, you *need* more clothes, or you just *want* more clothes?"

"Well, Marc Janssen, how dare you question what a girl needs or wants when it comes to clothes," Jenny replied mockingly.

"Yeah, I know that's a touchy subject, but you have to admit I just couldn't pass up the chance to tease you about it, right?"

"True, you never seem to miss a beat." Jenny took a deep breath and bit her lip before continuing.

"Hey, are you busy?"

"No, Dave and I are just finishing up a few things on the car before we leave tomorrow. Why, what's up?"

"Just wondering if I could come by for a few minutes."

"Sure! Come on by!"

"Okay, see ya in a bit."

Dave was just lowering the hood as Marc rejoined him. "You've done a great job restoring this beauty," Dave commented with a slight hint of envy. "I can't believe you're driving it to Utah for school. I know it's no problem now, but what about when winter hits? Aren't you worried about driving it in snow, or about someone else sliding and crashing into you? I mean this baby is a classic and I don't know if I could do it. Why not just leave it home? You'll be living on campus, you could probably bum a ride from your room-mate if you need to, your girlfriend is here so you won't be dating,—"

"I know, I know, but I'll be fine, and so will my car."

"Well, just think about it, okay?"

"I have, Dave, and I'm truly not worried. Now, what time can you be ready to leave tomorrow?"

"As early as you want."

"Okay, I'll pick you up at 5."

"A.M.?"

"Yep!"

"What?! Why so early?"

"Why not? It gets us out of the Bay Area and through Sacramento before the morning commute, and once we get up there we've got the whole day ahead of us to do whatever we want!"

"Okay, I'll be ready," Dave sighed, adjusting to the idea of get-ting up while it was still dark, something he'd rarely done in his life, much less during this last summer before college.

Just as they were wrapping things up Jenny drove up and got out of her car. Normally she would have bounced right out and quickly jogged right up to Marc and given him a big hug and kiss, but not this evening. And it wasn't because Dave was there that she hesitated. It was just that her emotions were running all over the place, even to the point of feeling very scared.

"Hey, beautiful!" Marc called out.

"Hi, Marc," Jenny replied with as much enthusiasm as she could show under the circumstances, still trying to mask her emotions. "Hi, Dave."

"Hey, Jenny. How's it going?"

"Good. So, you guys are getting ready for the big trip, huh?"

"Actually, we're all ready and we were just talking about what time we're leaving tomorrow."

"And your crazy boyfriend wants to leave at 5!" Dave exclaimed with mock disgust.

"That early?" Jenny asked timidly.

"Yeah, we figured—"

"Correction," Dave interrupted. "*You* figured."

"Okay, *I* figured it would be good to be on the road early enough to be way ahead of the commute traffic here and up around Sacramento."

"Yeah, I guess that makes sense," Jenny agreed.

"Hey, it's still light out, how about if we wash the car and give it a coat of wax."

"You guys go ahead," Dave replied. "I'm going home to pack and get to bed early."

"Okay, see you tomorrow … EARLY!" Marc replied with a wicked smile.

"Don't remind me," Dave shot back as he walked down the driveway to his car.

"So, beautiful," Marc said as he took Jenny's hand and walked into the garage, "Wanna help me wash and wax my car?"

"Okay," Jenny replied, trying to show a little more enthusiasm.

Marc let go of Jenny's hand and began to reach for the box labeled Car Cleaning Supplies when he sensed something wasn't quite right. He stopped and looked back at his sweetheart. The look on Jenny's face said it all.

"Hey, what's up? You're not your usual bubbly self."

Jenny paused for a moment, lowering her head as she tried to find the words to say while her heart was so desperately trying not to break. Suddenly she threw her arms around Marc and buried her face in his neck and burst into tears.

"Whoa! What's wrong, sweetheart? What happened?" Marc asked as he held her close. Jenny just continued to cry, so he held her tight until she was able to calm down a bit.

"Marc, I'm scared," she replied through her tears with her face still buried in his neck.

"You're scared? Of what?" But Jenny couldn't answer, as her sobbing became more intense. They just stood there in each other's arms for several minutes. Finally, Jenny's sobbing eased up a bit and her breathing began to calm down. Marc reached for his handkerchief and handed it to Jenny.

"Always the gentleman," she replied, then took a deep breath and let it out in a rush of air.

"So, can you tell me what's going on? Why are you scared, or what are you afraid of?"

"Us," Jenny replied softly.

"Us? What do mean?" Marc asked, totally bewildered by Jenny's reply.

"Oh, Marc, I don't know. I can't really put it into words."

"Try, please? I need to know what's made you so upset."

Jenny looked up into Marc's eyes, reached up and touched his cheeks with her hands, and then once again held him close, resting her head on his shoulder and sighed deeply. After several more moments of silence Jenny leaned back a bit in Marc's firm but gentle embrace, lifted her arms up and put them around his neck and looked into his eyes once again.

"I love you, Marc. I need you to know that with all of my heart. I love you more than anything else in my life."

"And I love you too, Jenny. I always have and I always will."

"Promise?"

"Of course, sweetheart. Why? What's made you so upset? And why did you say you were afraid of us?"

Jenny sighed again, gathering her thoughts.

"I guess afraid or scared might be the wrong words. I've been … thinking. And I've been worried about … Oh, Marc, it's just that as I was driving over here to see you my emotions just got more intense as I was thinking about …"

"Thinking about what?"

"Thinking and worrying about us."

"But why? Nothing's happened between us, has it?"

"No."

"And nothing is going to happen between us, right?"

Jenny didn't answer right away and that made Marc worry even more than he had been.

"Jenny? Nothing is going to happen between us, right?" he repeated more slowly.

She looked deeply into Marc's eyes, searching for the reassurance she so desperately needed to see and feel at that moment.

"I hope not."

"Sweetheart, what are you talking about? What could possibly happen? Are you afraid we're going to break up or something?"

Finally the words that had been eluding Jenny came to her all at once, and without hesitating she let them flow.

"Marc," Jenny bit her lower lip to keep it from quivering, "next week you're leaving for college—"

"Yeah?"

"Shhhh," Jenny said softly as she gently placed her finger on his lips. "Just listen, okay?"

Marc nodded.

"Next week you're leaving for college, and I'm staying here. We won't see each other until Christmas, and then for only a brief time. After that I won't see you again until late next spring. That's a long time to be apart, and … I'm … I'm just afraid you're going to meet some cute co-ed who'll steal your heart and you'll forget about me and fall in love with her. And—"

"And this is where I need you to listen to me, okay?" Marc softly replied, placing his finger gently on her lips.

He looked deeply into Jenny's eyes, cupping her cheeks in the palms of his hands.

"You have absolutely nothing to worry about, Jenny. I love you. I love *only* you, and while I'm away, my heart is going to be right here with you, so there's not a chance for anyone else to take it, okay?"

Jenny nodded as a smile came to her lips and tears once again filled her eyes. She had seen exactly what she needed to see in Marc's eyes.

"I'll be writing to you all the time, and calling as often as I can. We'll spend as much time together as possible over Christmas break, and I'll be home next spring before you know it!"

"I love you so much, Marc. I'm sorry I went so crazy on you."

"Nothing to be sorry about, Jenny. I'm just glad you talked to me about it so that you aren't scared the whole time I'm gone."

"Yeah, me too."

"And, Jenny … I love you, too. And that's never going to change, okay?"

"No, that's not okay. I want it to change all the time and just get better and better!" Jenny said laughingly.

"Okay, okay. That kind of change I'm fine with," he conceded with a smile, and they lost themselves in a tender kiss as they held each other tightly for several minutes without saying another word.

"Forget about washing and waxing the car. Let's go for a ride," Marc suggested.

"Sure!" Jenny replied, her loving, joyful smile having returned. "Where to?"

"Somewhere special."

Marc ignored the fact that he had to get up early in the morning. Spending this time with Jenny was more important, and they'd be lucky to have even one more time like this before he left in just seven days.

Marc opened Jenny's door for her and as he walked around the front of the car to his side she started to smile in a sly way.

"What's that look for?"

"Oh, I just love to watch you as you walk – those tight jeans and all."

Marc just smiled as he slipped a CD into his new stereo system. With the windows down, the music playing, and their hair blowing in the breeze they headed for the coast and their favorite secluded beach.

CHAPTER II

One Year Later

JENNY WAS SITTING ALONE in the campus library. Once again, she was finding it hard to study as her mind wandered back, as it had so many times before, to the first couple of months of their freshman year. She'd been so lonely with Marc being so far away. She thought about all of the letters, cards, and phone calls that she and Marc had exchanged back and forth at a steady pace from the time he got settled on campus.

By the end of October, though, she'd noticed that Marc's calls and letters had begun to come less frequently, and, in spite of his deeply sincere promise, she had begun to feel that he'd found another girl. But why? He'd never given her any cause to doubt him before, why now? All of this worrying had caused her to lose sleep, and losing sleep had made it harder to pay attention in class, and the snowball effect had affected her grades. Not hearing from Marc, her grades dropping, and her spiraling emotions caused her to not even be able to think straight anymore.

She became convinced that Marc *had* found someone new when his letters and calls stopped altogether a couple of weeks later. She thought about calling him just to see if he was okay, but hesitated. What if he really *was* okay, but busy ... with someone else? Just the thought of that possibility broke her heart. She was gripped with fear and the uncertainty was crippling. She'd never liked confrontation of any kind with anyone over anything, so in order to protect her heart from being broken she had decided to do something before she lost her mind altogether.

She'd cried as she penned the "Dear John" letter and was grateful she hadn't tried to break up with him over the phone. Knowing he'd probably try to call her after receiving the letter she had changed her number and made it unlisted so she wouldn't have to worry about giving in and then continuing to wonder and worry with Marc so far away. It literally tore her to pieces to walk away, especially like that, but she thought it was for the best … for both of them.

She flashed back on the call she had made to her mother.

"Mom, I have to ask you a special favor."

"Sure, honey, what is it?"

"Mom, please don't ask me to explain, but … if Marc or his parents or Alexa should try to call or write to you about anything, anything at all, PLEASE don't give them my new phone number."

"Jenny! Oh, my word! What happened?"

"Mom, you promised."

"But sweetheart, I—"

"Mom?"

"Yes, honey, okay. I … I just don't understand, but … we'll do as you've asked."

"Thanks, mom."

"Honey?" Adele asked cautiously.

"Yeah?"

"We love you."

Jenny paused as she fought back tears. "I love you too, mom."

Now, nearly a year later, she was still struggling. She had barely hung on through her freshman year, and her sophomore year had started off just as bleak. She had loved Marc so much, and she had truly believed that he had loved her. How did it all go so wrong? How?

§

Since trying to study proved to be useless Jenny decided to head over to the student union where she hoped to get something to eat and chat with some friends; anything to help her get her mind off of her loneliness and her struggling grades.

She walked into the student union and found her best friends, Lori and Monica, chatting about their upcoming mid-terms. Lori and Monica were both fairly confident they'd pull off decent grades, if not better, but Jenny wasn't so sure. Her mind had been distracted for too long over too many other things. Even though it had been nearly a year since she broke up with Marc, time still hadn't healed her heart.

Somehow Jenny knew she had to do something to pull off better grades. Monica saw the distant look in her eyes as they'd been talking.

"Jenny, what's up? You look like you're lost or something. You're just not yourself. In fact, you haven't looked this upset in a long time."

Jenny had tried to keep her troubles to herself, but the burden was becoming unbearable and she felt she had to say something to someone or she'd probably burst into tears at the wrong moment … like in the middle of a class.

"There's actually two things. First are my grades, because I'm struggling with a couple of my classes."

"No! Not you, Jenny!" Lori replied. "You've always gotten good grades! What's going on?"

"Well, that's the second thing. It's Marc."

"What? What about him? Have you heard from him recently?"

"No. I just … I just miss him so much, and I'm so distracted that it's making it hard to study."

"Have you tried to call him, or at least write to him?"

"NO! How could I do that? *I* broke up with *him*, remember?"

"Oh, Jenny," Lori replied. "I'm so sorry. What can I, well, what can *we* do?" she added as she looked over at Monica.

"Well, there's nothing you can do about Marc, but do you know anyone who might be able to help me boost my grades?"

"You mean like a tutor or something?" Monica asked.

"A tutor?" Jenny asked, kind of bewildered by the suggestion.

"Sure," Lori replied. "There's always lots of tutors around to help out."

Jenny sat there motionless for a moment while she considered the idea. 'A tutor? Hmmm, maybe that would work.'

"Well, if I were to get a tutor, how would I go about it? I mean, this just seems so weird. I've always worked hard and never needed any help."

"There's nothing to be ashamed of," Monica replied.

"No way, Jenny," Lori added. "Look, I've seen postings about tutors on bulletin boards around campus from time to time, and …"

"And the counseling office can probably help you find one too," Monica interjected.

"Really? Okay, I guess I could look into it."

"Sure!" Monica replied. "What have you got to lose, except for good grades if you don't do anything?"

"You're right," Jenny conceded with a sigh. "Maybe I better go check into it now, while I still have the nerve."

"Want some company?" Lori asked. "I'll walk over there with you if you'd like?"

"No. I know I haven't been very good company for a while because of this thing with Marc, so I'll just let you guys go and head over there by myself." Jenny stood up from the table, swung her backpack over her shoulder and right into someone walking behind her.

"Oh! Excuse me! I'm so sorry I—"Jenny exclaimed as she turned around to apologize to whomever she'd bumped into.

"It's not a problem at all. I was just—" Their eyes met, and for a moment they both just froze mid-sentence. Monica and Lori looked on with wide eyes!

"Jenny?!"

"Marc?!"

"It's … good to see you."

"You too … Marc. What … uh, what are you doing here?"

"Well, I transferred here during the summer hoping to run into you, but someone said they thought you'd transferred to State.

I went by your apartment but I was told you'd moved. I've kept calling information for your number and the operator keeps saying there's no listing, so I just figured it was true, and didn't know what to do after that."

"Yeah, my parents moved and I was planning on moving with them and, you're right, I was planning on transferring to State, but at the last minute I decided to stay because I really do love it here, and my friends are here, and ... well, you know."

All this time Monica and Lori sat watching this interchange between these two, not believing what they were seeing.

And now, here they were, face to face, and Monica and Lori looked at each other and silently agreed, these two *needed* to be back together!

"Listen, Jenny, I really hate to rush off, but I need to get to my next class. Umm ... do you mind if I get your new number before I go?"

"Wha ...?" Jenny asked dreamily, then snapped out of it as Monica nudged her. "What? Oh, my number? Sure," she replied, reaching for her pen and some paper.

"Cool, thanks, Jenny. Sorry again that I have to run, but are you going to be, well ... home, wherever that is, tonight?"

"Yes. After 8. I work at the mall till 7 and then I have to pick up a few things at the store on my way home, but I'll be there by 8."

"Great! I'll call you tonight."

"OK. Thanks, Marc. It's ... good to see you," Jenny said hesitantly, fighting her warring emotions.

"Same here," Marc replied over his shoulder as he jogged toward the door of the student union on his way to another History class.

"Oh, wow!" Jenny exclaimed, as she sat down on her chair just in time because her legs had suddenly given out on her. She just sat there with a bewildered look on her face.

"Jenny!" Lori shrieked. "He's actually HERE!!!"

Monica couldn't wait to add her two cents worth. "Do you think ... I mean, do you have any idea why he transferred here? I mean he *did* say he'd been looking for you and tried calling you. Do you think he wants to try to get back together?"

Jenny didn't know what to say. Just moments ago she was feeling so low because of all of the struggles she was having with her grades, and missing Marc, and now he shows up unexpectedly?! Not only shows up, but they bump into each other and stood there talking face to face!

"I ... I ...," Jenny was trying to find the words, but they simply eluded her.

"Well, I think the answer is YES!" Monica said.

"I do, too," Lori agreed enthusiastically!

Jenny let out a very long sigh. "It's just ... so sudden. I really don't know what to think."

"Well, regardless of what you think," Lori said, "he's calling you tonight!"

And with that a smile came to Jenny's lips, the kind of warm, gentle, and carefree smile that her friends hadn't seen in a long, long time.

"I'm so happy for you, Jenny!" Monica gushed. "It'll be so good to see the two of you back together again, right where you belong!"

"Whoa, what a minute! Hold on!" Jenny said, trying to calm her friends down. "I'm not going to rush into anything. There's a lot of time and too many miles that's passed between us, and I just need to take this slowly. I don't want to get my heart broken again."

"Again, Jenny?" Lori asked.

"Yes, again," Jenny replied.

"Umm, as you mentioned earlier, Jenny," Monica said, "it was *you* who broke it off between the two of you. So what are you talking about a broken heart?"

"Yeah, you're right, I did break it off between us. But don't you think it tore me up to do that?"

"Well, sure," added Lori, "but you never told us why you did it in the first place?"

"Because ... I was sure he'd ... he'd found ... another girl."

"You never told me that," Lori replied.

"Me, neither," Monica added. "Why would you think that?"

"I know. I just kept it to myself. It just hurt so much that I didn't want to talk to anyone about it, not even you two."

"Jenny, may I remind you," Lori said, "*that's* what best friends are for! We're here for each other, no matter what."

"I know, but I … oh, I don't know. Right now I'm just so confused."

"What's there to be confused about?" Lori asked.

Jenny let out another long sigh. "Everything just seems to be happening to me all at once. My grades, Marc, …"

"Yeah, your hunk of a guy who's come back for you," Lori interjected.

"Oh, stop it, will you please?" Jenny pleaded in exasperation. "I don't know that, and neither do you. I'm just going to need some time to … to think, and figure things out, and right now my head is spinning. I have to go over to the counselor's office and see what I can do about arranging for a tutor before I really lose it, OK?"

"Sure, Jenny," Lori replied. "My offer still stands, though, if you'd like me to walk over there with you."

"No, I'm sure I can find my way just fine, thank you," Jenny replied with a tired grin. The sparkle was mostly gone from her eyes once again as she remembered what she really needed to be concentrating on at this time … her grades. Marc would just have to wait.

"I'll see you guys later," Jenny said. "Well, I guess tomorrow since I need to head over to work later."

"And don't forget to rush home quickly so you won't miss Marc's call at 8," Monica added for good measure.

"Oh, for crying out loud, guys! Leave it alone, okay?"

"Well, at least call me after you get off the phone with him," Lori pleaded. "I need to hear all about it!"

Jenny gave Lori a very rare steely look that could only mean one thing … back off!

"Uhh," Lori began hesitantly, "tomorrow will be fine."

"Thanks for understanding," Jenny wearily replied as she swung her backpack over her shoulder, more cautiously this time, and waved goodbye to her friends.

"See ya, Jenny," Monica added.

"See ya. And thanks for the tip about the tutors and the counseling center. I sure hope this works, otherwise I don't know what I'll do."

§

Jenny arrived at the counseling center, took a number, and then found a seat to wait her turn. After about ten minutes she became bored and stood up and walked over to the bulletin boards to read the random notices posted there.

"Dance after the game this Saturday night. Fraternity Row."

"Roommate wanted! FAST! Just kicked out my roommate for getting drunk and throwing up all over my term paper! Call me! No, never mind! Just come by! You can move in today! 47 Lester Street. Ask for Mike!"

"Looking for a few good men! U.S. Marine Corps Recruiting Center 1191 Manor Blvd."

"Struggling with your grades? Notify the Student Counseling Office and let us know you'd like to speak with a tutor. Don't wait! Save your grades now!"

'Hey, this sounds good,' Jenny thought. She sat back down to wait her turn and didn't have to wait long.

"Number 23?"

Jenny stood up and walked to the next open space at the counter to speak with the lady waiting for her.

"Hi there, young lady, my name is Adele. How may I help you?"

"Hi, Adele, I'm Jenny, and your name will be easy to remember because that's my mom's name."

Smiles were exchanged between them as Adele replied, "Wonderful! Now, how may I help you today?"

"Well, I need some help with a couple of my classes so I'm here to sign up for a tutor."

"Certainly," Adele replied, reaching for a folder in a drawer below her. "Just fill out this form, listing the subjects you'd like help with, and we'll do our best to match you up with the best tutor for your needs."

"Thank you," Jenny replied as she accepted the form.

Before she walked back to her seat Adele continued, "When you're finished filling out the form just bring it directly to me. You don't have to wait in line again, okay?"

"Thanks, Adele, that's very nice of you." Jenny replied. They exchanged smiles again and Jenny returned to her seat. A few minutes later she was finished filling out her request, returned to the counter to turn it in, and waited until Adele was finished answering a question for another student.

Adele noticed Jenny, smiled, and said to the other student, "Would you please excuse me for just one moment?"

Turning her attention to Jenny she reached her hand out for Jenny's form, "Here, I'll take that for you." She briefly looked over the form to make sure all of the necessary information was there, then thanked Jenny and reassured her that she'd take care of it right away.

"Do you have any idea how long it will take to process my request?"

"Sure, you should hear from someone within a day or two at the most. In fact, if you'd like, why don't you check in with me tomorrow, perhaps around lunchtime, and I may have an update for you at that time."

"Oh, that's wonderful. Thanks, Adele!"

"My pleasure, Jenny."

'What a sweet young lady,' Adele thought, as Jenny walked away.

Adele took a closer look at Jenny's request form, particularly the classes she had requested help with, then zeroed in on the box labeled "Referred by", added her name, and next to that, in the box labeled "Referred to" she paused for a moment and then thought, "Yes! I think this is just the right tutor for her." Adele smiled as she wrote down the name, and then placed the form in the "EXPEDITE" file.

CHAPTER 12

The Call

AFTER WORK THAT EVENING Jenny stopped by the grocery store before heading home to be ready for Marc's call. She couldn't believe that he was actually right there, on campus, face to face with her that afternoon! She was still feeling so overwhelmed by the whole idea. Why did he come home? Why did he transfer to her college? Why now? What did he want to talk about? How did he take her Dear John letter? And what about his girlfriend? Oh-h-h, so many questions!

Jenny put away her groceries and looked at the clock. Only 7:50. 'What am I going to do for 10 more minutes,' she thought. A quick glance around her apartment to make sure everything was neat and in its place, and then ... "Wait a minute!" she exclaimed out loud. "He's not coming here, he's only calling me!"

'Only calling me?' she thought. This was no time to be taking his call lightly. Butterflies in her stomach were replaced by a knot, twisting ever so slowly. 'He was nice to me today, but was that because we were in public, and in front of my friends? What will I say if he wants to grill me over that letter?'

'"Well, why'd you stop writing to me? You had a new girlfriend, I just knew it, right?" 'Yeah, that's what I can say.' Jenny had it all worked out in her mind, or so she thought. As the minutes continued to tick away her doubts and more questions returned. 7:54.

'I know! I'll just start working on my term paper. That will keep my mind busy, and after all, he didn't say he'd call right at 8:00 sharp, did he? No, I'm sure he didn't. I just told him I'd be home by 8.'

Jenny pulled her history and biology books, along with a notebook, out of her backpack and set them on the desk, then walked into the bathroom to brush her hair. 'What am I doing?! How many times do I have to remind myself he's not coming here?!' She placed her brush down on the counter and sighed as she took one more glance at herself in the mirror. She turned off the light and returned to her desk. 7:59. Almost time!

She was just about to open up her notebook when she noticed out of the corner of her eye that, according to the clock on her desk, it was now 8:00. 'Anytime now,' she thought. The knot in her stomach was getting tighter.

'8:07 … he's late,' she joked to herself. 'Okay, that's cool. Perhaps this is his way of punishing me for my Dear John letter. That's okay, I can take it. I probably deserve it. After all, I never knew for sure that he had a new girlfriend, but every ounce of me just screamed he did so I had to do something, didn't I? I mean, how else could he explain his letters and calls just dropping off like that? Besides, why didn't he ever attempt to reach me after that? Oh, yeah, I'd changed my number and made it unlisted. But he didn't even write!!! No, he had a new girlfriend, alright. I'm sure of it. A girl just knows these things. So, explain yourself, buddy!'

Jenny looked at the clock again – 8:08! AAHH!!! 'Time is just dragging! Why doesn't he call?' She sighed. 'Why can't you make up your mind, Jenny?! First you're excited about his call, then you're scared, then you're nervous, and now you're upset that he's late! Good golly, what's it gonna be, huh?' Jenny had to laugh at this conversation going on inside her head. If she didn't know better she'd think she wa—

The ringing phone startled her! 'OH, MY GOSH! IT'S HIM! Okay, calm down, Jenny. You can do this. Breathe. Calm down. Don't be too anxious, it'll give him the wrong impression.' She picked up the phone after the fourth ring.

"Hello?" Jenny answered casually.

"Hi, Jenny?"

OH! It was *so* good to hear Marc's voice on the phone again!

"Yeah. Hi, Marc. How's it goin'?" The knot in her stomach kicked her. Hard! She was *so* nervous!

"I'm good. How are you?"

"Fine." 'Fine? FINE?! That's all you can think of to say to him? FINE?! Sheesh, Jenny! Snap out of it!'

"That's great. I'll tell ya, it was really good to run into you in the student union today."

"Um, was that pun intended?"

"Wha— OH! Ha, no. But, I guess it fits, huh?"

Their mutual laughter eased the tension Jenny had been feeling for too long.

"Yeah, it sure does. So … how is it that you've come to be at my college now?" 'Oh, no!' Jenny thought, 'I can't believe I just asked him that so soon!' She heard Marc clear his throat. 'Okay, hold on … here it comes.'

"I … I just felt like coming back home. I missed it and thought it would be cool to go to college closer to home, ya know?" Marc replied, not knowing whether Jenny would believe him or not.

"Oh, that's cool. It was just such a surprise to all of a sudden see you right there in front of me today after we hadn't talked in so long."

"Yeah … I know." Marc realized his answer came out awkwardly, but he didn't know how else to respond. He was still feeling the pain from her breaking up with him so suddenly, and for no reason.

Jenny had to change the subject quickly to avoid their conversation from spinning out of control.

"So, how's your family?"

"Huh? Oh, they're good." Jenny had caught him off guard with the switch, but he was relieved that they could talk about something else for a while. Sometime, hopefully soon, they'd be able to talk about … the letter.

"Oh, that's great, Marc."

"And how're your folks?" Marc asked, still stumbling for the right words, and realizing this was getting more awkward with each minute, something he truly hoped wouldn't happen.

"Oh, they're doing well. They really like their new home. Well, it's not new, just newer than our other home was."

"That's cool. I'm happy for them." At this point Marc couldn't think of anything to say and he was afraid of the silence that was building between them. He decided to bite the bullet.

"So, um, Jenny … um," 'Oh, this is so hard!' he thought. "Are you doing anything this Saturday?"

'Oh, my gosh! Is Marc asking me out?!' Jenny panicked!

"Well, midterms are approaching and I have a lot of studying to do, so yeah, I guess I'll be kinda busy with that."

"Oh, okay."

"Why? What did you have in mind?" 'WHAT?! Did that just come out of my mouth?! What am I doing?' Jenny was really panicking now!

"Well, I was wondering if we could get together for just a short time, like maybe for lunch or something?" Marc managed to stammer out.

"Lunch? Oh, uh, yeah I guess that would be okay." 'Jenny! Do you have any idea what you've just done?!'

"Okay. Um, what's a good time for you?"

Jenny paused, trying to get her wits about her before saying anything more. She felt like she was slipping into an abyss that she might not want to be getting into, especially right now with her need to keep her mind on her studies. She let out a deep sigh which she hoped Marc couldn't hear on the other end of the line.

"How about 12:30?"

"12:30 it is. May I come by and pick you up, or would you prefer to meet somewhere?"

"How about if I just meet you? You pick a place and let me know and I'll be there, okay?" 'Smart move, Jenny! Now you're thinking!'

"Okay, um, I'll check out a couple of places and give you a call tomorrow, okay?"

"Sure, that sounds fine, Marc. Listen I hate to cut this short, but I've already lost a few hours of valuable studying time because of work today, so I better let you go, okay?"

"Yeah, sure Jenny. And ... thanks for the .chat. It'll be good to see you on Saturday."

"Yeah, it will, Marc," she replied nervously.

"Catch ya tomorrow."

"Hmm? Oh, yeah, to let me know where we're meeting. Yeah, that's cool. Bye, Marc."

"See ya, Jenny."

CHAPTER 13

Jenny

O N ANY GIVEN DAY Jenny would normally head right over to the student union after her last class of the morning to meet up with Lori and Monica and grab something to eat, but today she took a detour and headed over to the Counseling Center in hopes that her tutoring appointment had already been set up.

As Jenny walked through the doors she looked for Adele and saw her helping another student. Adele waved to her to let her know she'd seen her and would be right with her. She sat down and opened one of her textbooks to try and take advantage of the few moments she might have to squeeze in a little more studying. Moments later she heard Adele calling her name.

"Hi, Adele," Jenny replied as she approached the counter.

"Hi, Jenny! How are you today?"

"Well, honest?"

"Sure, lay it on me," Adele replied with a wink, trying to sound like she was just one of the students.

"Hey, you're pretty good! Ever think about being a comedian?"

"Oh, sure, all the time! But I think it's smarter for me to just keep my day job."

"Yeah, it's probably best." They both laughed.

"So Adele, I was just wondering if you had any news on my tutoring request."

"As a matter of fact, I do. Based on the information you listed on your request you're available on Saturdays, is that correct?"

"Yes."

"Good. Well, I have something set up for you this Saturday."

"Hey, that's great! Oh, wait a minute. I'm actually busy in the morning and into the early afternoon this Saturday. What time is the appointment?"

"I set it for 3:00 p.m., is that okay?"

"Oh, yes, that'll be perfect. So, I just come here to meet with my tutor, is that right?"

"Yes. We have rooms available right down that hall. When you arrive just check the list that will be posted on that bulletin board for your assigned room, and then head on down the hall and your tutor will be waiting for you. We have a reduced office staff here on the weekends, but someone is here in case anyone needs any additional help. I'm not normally scheduled to work on Saturdays, but my boss just asked me a few minutes ago if I might be able to cover for one of my co-workers who's out sick for a few days and I agreed, so I'll probably see you."

"That'll be nice. Thanks so much for all your help, Adele. I really appreciate it."

"Oh, it's not a problem. I love my job!"

"Well, it certainly shows."

Jenny gave Adele one more of her charming smiles and then headed for the student union. She'd skipped breakfast that morning and now she was starving! Two of those dark chocolate power bars just weren't enough to get her through the morning.

Entering the student union she headed for the table where she usually sat with her friends and saw Marc a few tables away. Her heart skipped a beat when she saw him and then shook off the feeling as quickly as she could. 'I can't afford to get involved with him again. At least not right now. Maybe … maybe not at all. Oh, Marc, why did you have to come back into my life right now? It's just not a good time.' The thoughts twisting in Jenny's mind were so unsettling that it caught Monica's attention.

"Hey, Jenny, are you okay?" Monica's question startled Jenny back into the moment.

"What?" Jenny asked, still in a daze.

"I asked if you're okay. You came in with a big smile on your face and then all of a sudden you looked like you were lost in another world. What's up?"

"Oh, nothing."

"Are you sure?"

"Yeah, it's nothing. Where's Lori?"

"Oh, she'll be right here. She had to pick up a book in the library."

"Okay, cool. I have something to tell you both so I'll wait until she's here. In the meantime, I'm starving so I'm going to get something to eat."

Jenny made sure she took a wider route to the food court that was further away from Marc's table and hoped he wouldn't notice her. But she wasn't so lucky. Just as she was paying for her lunch Marc appeared and seeing him approaching as she looked up from the cashier startled her a bit.

"Hey, did I scare you?"

"Oh, no, I was just kinda lost in my thoughts for a moment."

"Oh, good. Hey, I just wanted to see if you wanted to meet up at the Pizza Palace?"

"Huh?"

"You know, this Saturday for lunch?"

"Oh yeah. Yeah, the Pizza Palace? Sure, that's fine. 12:30, right?"

"Yep! I'll see ya there."

"Okay, Marc. Bye."

As Marc passed by her to get his own lunch Jenny let out a sigh of relief as she walked back to her table. Just then the faint and familiar scent of his cologne wafted past her and she was once again lost in her thoughts.

"So," Lori started, "I just saw you talking with Marc."

"Yeah? So?"

"Hey, I was just saying ..."

"It's no big deal. I was just getting my lunch and he passed by me while he was heading in to get his."

"You seem a little edgy today," observed Monica. "Are you sure you're okay?"

"Yes, I'm fine. I just have a lot on my mind."

"About Marc?" Lori asked.

"NO!" Jenny replied in exasperation. "My studies! What is this obsession you guys have with Marc?"

"Nothing," Lori replied defensively. "We've both seen you feeling a bit out of sorts over your studies, but ever since you saw Marc yesterday it just seems like there's something else going on."

"There's nothing else going on, okay?"

"Okay, sorry," Monica replied calmly. "May I ask just one more question?"

Jenny heaved a huge sigh. "Sure. What is it?"

"Did everything go okay with the call last night?"

"What call?"

"What call?!" Lori asked. "Marc's call!"

"Oh, that one," Jenny answered nonchalantly. "Fine."

"That's it?" Monica enquired. "Just fine?"

"Yeah, just fine, okay?"

"Sure. Sorry to bug you about it."

Jenny looked at her friends. "I'm sorry. I know you mean well, but I'm just so … I'm just feeling overwhelmed with everything going on in my life right now. I didn't need to have another complication come up."

"Marc?" Lori asked softly.

"Yes. When he called me last night it was kinda awkward. We didn't really say very much; mostly just the general 'hi's and "how are you's" kinda stuff. And then he asked me out."

"What?!" Monica and Lori exclaimed in unison. They tended to do that a lot.

"Well, not really on a date. He just asked if he could see me for a few minutes over lunch."

"Are you going to go?" Lori asked, trying to hide the excitement in her voice and on her face, but Jenny saw it before it faded.

"It's not like that. It's not like a regular date. I'm just meeting him for lunch."

"Well, that's cool, Jenny!"

"It's no big deal, really."

"If you say so," Monica replied skeptically.

"Yeah, I say so," Jenny replied with finality in her voice.

Monica and Lori looked at each other debating which one would dare ask. Lori jumped first. "You *will* tell us about it afterwards, though, right?"

"Aw, come on! Give it a rest, will ya?!"

CHAPTER 14

Truth

JENNY'S ALARM WAS SET for 6 a.m. even on Saturday mornings (she gave herself a break on Sundays) so she could get in a good run to start her day. This not only kept her in shape, it also helped her stay disciplined and this, in turn, helped her in other areas of her life, especially her studies. Well, until this semester. She hadn't been quite as enthusiastic about her running of late, but she also hadn't missed a regular workout in so long that she couldn't even conceive of missing one now, no matter what.

Jenny dressed quickly, brushed her hair and pulled it back into a ponytail, and then did some basic stretching while she walked through her apartment. She took her vitamins with a couple of swallows of juice and then headed for the door. Stepping outside into the cool autumn morning she breathed deeply and began her real stretching exercises in earnest. A few minutes later she was on her way.

As she ran Jenny thought about the day ahead of her; studying in the morning, lunch with Marc, and then her three o'clock appointment with her tutor. That would probably go for at least an hour, maybe a little more, so now what to do with her evening? She really wasn't looking forward to doing any more studying, but she figured that she might have to do some, depending on what her tutor recommended. But what she was mostly concerned about right now was her lunch with Marc.

'Ahhh, Marc. What's on your mind? Will you allow us to just keep the conversation light and friendly, or will you want to start digging into the past, our past. I remember every word of that Dear John letter as if I'd written it yesterday, but it's been nearly eleven months. And now you're back in my life. Well, let's just say you're back and leave it at that for now, shall we?' As she ran through the park on the other side of the hill from her apartment she listened to the sound of birds in the trees and watched an occasional squirrel scamper across her path, no doubt in search of a morning meal. Even though the morning was cool, the slight warmth of the rising sun felt good.

The pace of her jogging picked up as she approached the last hill leading up to her apartment. She always loved this hill. Sure, it was hard to attack it at the end of her run, but she loved the challenge of giving it everything she had at the very end just to show the hill it couldn't beat her after all the miles she'd already put in. She finally slowed down as she approached the stairs leading up to her apartment and walked around a bit, doing some more stretching to keep her muscles limber as they cooled down. She'd be in the shower in a few minutes and then on with her day, but for now she wanted to enjoy these last few moments of this beautiful autumn morning. Perhaps she'd eat her breakfast out on the patio before starting her studies. 'Then again,' she thought, 'I could study out there, too!'

Jenny enjoyed spending time on her patio, whether she was studying, reading, or just relaxing. There was only a short time at midday when the sun was on the deck, otherwise the tall trees on the hill behind her apartment shaded her from the morning sun, and the afternoon sun was blocked by her townhouse apartment.

After her shower Jenny slipped on some casual sweats since the sun was still a few hours away from warming up the deck. She fixed herself a big cup of tea, toasted some English Muffins, added a light layer of jelly just for taste and headed out to her deck with a notebook.

She curled up in a deep cushioned chair, sipped her tea, reviewed her notes from the previous day's history lecture, and started thinking about what to wear for her "non-date" with Marc. She also needed to prioritize a list of which classes she needed to focus on first with her tutor that afternoon. 'It's going to be a busy day. I wonder if I'm going to have much of an evening before heading to bed and starting all over again tomorrow. It's been so long since I've been out and just had some fun with friends.' She let out a long sigh before taking another sip of tea.

"I've got it!" Jenny exclaimed out loud as she sat up straight in her chair, almost spilling her tea. A squirrel that had been gradually making its way toward some crumbs from her English Muffin suddenly scampered away.

"Instead of worrying about whether Marc will bring up my Dear John letter or not I'll just go ahead and bring it up myself so we can get it over with." Jenny felt a sense of calm and empowerment with this sudden decision, a welcome relief to the angst she'd felt ever since she and Marc met in the student union the other day after such a long time.

"If I take the upper hand I can direct the conversation the way I want it instead of worrying about what he's going to bring up next. After we're past the pleasantries and are searching for the next topic I'll just bring it up and watch his reaction. Then we can discuss it, *and* his girlfriend, and move on. This could very well make our lunch shorter than expected and then I can just move on with my life and Marc can move on with his."

With that settled, and her plan firmly worked out in her mind, it was time to get down to some serious studying. She only had a few hours before getting ready for her "date". She didn't plan on getting too fancy; this was, after all, just a casual get together at best. She was also curious what his plans were for his future and why he'd *really* returned. Perhaps they wouldn't even get to that, though, once the truth was on the table about his suddenly dropping her without any warning the previous fall.

'And perhaps … just perhaps … the Dear John letter wasn't enough,' she thought. 'Perhaps I need to just make it perfectly clear that his letters and calls just dropping off like that had really hurt me, and if he was, in fact, hoping to start anything again, I'll just make him understand I don't want my heart to be hurt like that again. I just can't take it. Not now. Especially not now. He would just be a distraction; an unnecessary one, at that.'

She nodded in acknowledgment of her coming to such a clear assessment of her situation with Marc. He would just have to take it or leave it. Either way didn't matter to her because she didn't figure to be a part of the equation. She had school and work to think about and that was enough.

§

Marc arrived at the Pizza Palace a half hour early. He wanted to get just the right booth where he would be able to see Jenny when she arrived, and yet back and out of the way so they could have some privacy. The restaurant opened at eleven, but on Saturdays the usual crowd of students didn't start flowing in until closer to twelve thirty. Most would be sleeping off their dates from the previous night.

The crowd would no doubt be larger than some Saturdays because the football team was away and they needed *some* place to hang out.

As much as Marc tried to deny it, he was nervous. This wasn't going to be like meeting Jenny in the student union, this was ... well, it was just different. Jenny had seemed hesitant to commit to anything this weekend except her studies, but something must have made her change her mind. Whatever it was he was glad. Now he just hoped everything would go okay. And maybe, just maybe ... well, if it did, then she might be willing to go out with him on an actual date sometime.

In the last few days, Marc hadn't seen any evidence of a boyfriend, and obviously if there was someone else in her life, even if he was away at another college or in the military, Jenny would have said something the other night and not agreed to see him today. So, maybe he might still have a chance to get something going with her again after all. Then again, maybe she'd just started dating someone and it would still be too soon in that relationship to know where it might be going. Whatever the case may be, she'd said she'd meet up with him, so he'd make the best of it.

That letter she'd sent him last November had literally destroyed him. Obviously she didn't know what had happened to him because he knew she wasn't the kind of girl to not care. But why hadn't she called first, or even written, before just sending that letter?! He thought better of bringing it up today, he just wanted to keep everything light and fun on this "almost-a-date". Another time and another place would no doubt be better.

Marc glanced at his watch, noting that Jenny would be there in a few minutes. Their waitress had already come by to give him a tall glass of water, offered him a menu and asked if there was anything else he'd like to drink. He accepted the water and asked for a second menu, mentioning that a friend would be joining him shortly. The attractive co-ed smiled, said "Sure!" in a pleasant voice, and returned a moment later with the second menu and a second place setting and napkin.

Jenny walked in a few minutes early. Marc took one look and froze in place for a moment. Even though he could tell that she was trying to only look casual, she was still beautiful; the most beautiful girl he'd ever seen. That's one thing he'd noticed about her when they first met over two years ago. She could make a pair of Wranglers, Sketchers, and a simple blouse look like a million bucks, especially the moment she smiled. Today was no different, even with the jacket and knit cap she'd added due to the cool autumn air.

Marc stood up, smiled, and began to wave his hand to catch her attention but just his standing had caught her eye. Jenny nervously smiled back at him and he remained standing until she'd gotten to the booth.

"Hey, Marc," Jenny said breezily as she approached.

"Hi, Jenny." Marc did his best to hide his excitement at seeing her.

Jenny took off her cap, stuffed it into her purse, and then began to unbutton her jacket. As she started to slip it off her shoulders

Marc was right there to help her.

"Oh, thanks Marc. I see you haven't lost your gentlemanly ways."

"Actually, I've turned into kind of a slob … except when I'm around you." Marc was trying to keep things light, but wondered after he'd said that if it was a bit too forward at this point. He reminded himself that he needed to tread lightly for now.

Jenny smiled again. "Oh, I know you better than that. Once a gentleman, always a gentleman. I'm sure I'm not the only pretty girl you've ever been nice to, right?" 'Whoa, am I going to get right into the Dear John letter deal so soon?' she wondered.

"OK, guilty. But you can blame my parents, especially my dad, for teaching me to be one. My dad had me practicing regularly with my mom. Even at home!"

Jenny giggled, "What?!"

"Yep. He wanted to make sure it was just second nature to me so that no matter where I was or who I was with I wouldn't even think twice about opening a door for a lady or helping her with her chair."

"Or helping her take her jacket off," Jenny said with a wink and a smile.

"Yeah, that, too." There was that wink. His heart began to melt.

"So, how hungry are you? Want to share a pizza, or …"

"Oh, I'm not too hungry. I might just get a salad and some water or tea."

"Oh, come on," Marc said teasingly. "This is the Pizza Palace! Let's order a pizza and if you need to watch your weight you can eat just a couple of slices."

"Oh, and I suppose you'll be glad to eat all the rest, is that it?"

"Yeah. Something like that."

"Well, I've got news for ya, buddy. I'm actually hungry and I'm going to order one for myself."

"Really?"

"Yeah, why?"

"Oh, I don't know. I just …" Marc felt flustered. He hadn't expected Jenny to take charge like that. It was kind of fun to see this feisty side of her.

"You just what?" Jenny sensed she had the upper hand and was going to milk the situation for everything it was worth and take advantage of the moment while she could.

"Oh, nothing. That's fine, we'll just order a couple of pizzas and sodas. How about some garlic bread, too?"

"Garlic bread? Oh, no! I mean, don't get me wrong, I love garlic bread, but I'm meeting up with someone later this afternoon and I can't smell like garlic."

'Ah-HA!' Marc thought. 'She *does* have someone else she's seeing.'

"Okay, no problem. Just pizzas and drinks."

"Sure. That works for me."

Their waitress arrived and asked Jenny what she'd like to drink.

"May I have root beer, please?"

"I'll have one, too," Marc added.

"Absolutely! I'll be right back!"

She returned a few minutes later with two tall glasses of root beer and asked if they were ready to place their order. Marc looked at Jenny who was glancing quickly over her menu and then closed it, nodding at Marc. "You know what you want?"

"Yeah, I've been here a couple of times so I'm good to go." They proceeded to place their order, and their waitress collected their menus and was off.

The next several minutes passed in idle conversation, just chatting back and forth about their families and school.

"So, Marc, are you still the smart guy you've always been, or have you slacked off?"

"Oh, I've started slacking off since I transferred," Marc replied, willing to go along with Jenny's good-natured ribbing.

Jenny was fully aware of how good a student he was and always had been. She'd been politely envious of his study skills when they were in high school. She always had to 'burn the midnight oil', as her parents had called it, while Marc hardly seemed to study at all and aced everything. It was just so wrong!

"How are you doing?"

"Oh, not bad."

"Why do I get the feeling that's not quite right?"

"Huh? No. I'm doing fine, really," Jenny replied in such a way to hopefully convince him so he'd drop the subject.

"Okay. I was just asking. Just so you know, I can help with just about any subject, if you're interested."

"No, I'm fine, Marc. But thanks."

'After all,' Jenny thought, 'in a couple of hours I'll be meeting with my very own tutor, and then I WILL be fine.'

"Just saying."

"And I appreciate it, Marc. I really do, but I'm fine, okay?"

"Sure."

The conversation lagged a bit once again as they both tried to figure out where it should go next.

Their waitress arrived with their pizzas and sodas, asked if they'd like anything else, but Marc and Jenny said they were fine, so she was quickly on her way to another table. A smile along with efficiency … yeah, she was hoping for some pretty decent tips this afternoon, especially from this large of a crowd.

Jenny took a big drink of her soda. She'd been building up her courage for a while and was fairly confident she was ready for what was about to transpire. Little did she know she wasn't.

"Marc?" Jenny began.

"Yeah?" Marc replied, noticing Jenny's voice seemed different somehow.

"We need to talk."

"Okay, what about?" Marc had noticed the seriousness in Jenny's voice, but he was doing his best to try to keep everything light and relaxed. He certainly wasn't ready for Jenny's bombshell.

"The letter." Jenny watched Marc's reaction carefully.

Marc stopped mid-bite and just stared at Jenny in confusion. 'Why does she want to bring up that letter now?' He set his partially eaten piece of pizza down on the platter and slowly chewed what was in his mouth as he tried his best to gather his thoughts. He let out a deep sigh and cleared his throat.

"So … what do you want to say about it?" Marc asked cautiously. Sure, he wanted to know what her reason was for writing it in the first place, but he didn't expect to be discussing it today, right now, in the middle of lunch.

"Well …" Jenny paused to collect her thoughts, "I guess … I'm curious about your reaction. What did you think, or do, when you read it?"

Marc felt himself begin to experience the emotional pain he'd originally felt when he'd first received that letter almost eleven months ago. At this point, though, he didn't know whether to feel hurt or angry. His response showed a little of both.

"First off … I was crushed because I couldn't figure out why you'd written it. You didn't mention anything about having a new boyfriend, so I was deeply confused. I tried calling, but I got the message that your number was no longer in service. I sent a letter that was returned with it stamped, 'No longer at this address'. I mean, what was I to think, Jenny? What was I to do?" Marc did everything he could to fight back his emotions.

"Well, I'll tell you, Marc. When your letters and phone calls slowed down I began to worry, and when they stopped coming altogether, I knew there could be only one reason. I didn't have the courage to call you out of fear of what you would say, especially about having a new girlfriend."

"A new girlfriend?!" Marc was stunned.

"Yes."

"Why would you even think that?"

"I just knew, okay?"

"No, Jenny, it's not okay. I made a promise to you —"

Students at a nearby table looked over to see what the commotion was about, even though Marc and Jenny were trying to keep their voices down.

Jenny was beginning to feel her anger well up inside, and she fought hard to maintain a sense of calm.

"Listen, I just knew you had to have a new girlfriend and that had to be the reason you stopped talking to me. It hurt me so bad just thinking about it, but I also knew that I just couldn't stand to hear you tell me that you loved someone else, so I … I … I wrote the letter to end it with you first."

"What?!" Marc was clearly overwhelmed by this revelation. 'So, the truth was finally out on the table,' he thought. 'Great! What's next?!' He took a deep breath and let it out slowly, collecting his thoughts and trying his best to calm down.

"Listen, Jenny," Marc softly replied, while looking deep into her eyes. "There's not another girlfriend —"

"Oh, sure, not now maybe. You're probably just reaching out to me now because you're on the re-bound, but last November—"

"But nothing, Jenny. There isn't another girlfriend now, and there wasn't then. Remember, when we started college I made you a promise. I left my heart right here with you. Even when my room-mate and some of our friends wanted to go out on a few big "group" dates I didn't go."

"You … you didn't?" Jenny asked, not sure whether she could believe him.

"Not once."

Jenny paused. Her head was spinning with new questions. This just didn't make sense.

"But then … why … why did …," she paused again and took a deep breath, "then why did you stop writing to me and calling? Why, all of a sudden, did you cut me off like that? Marc, try to understand, I couldn't figure out what I'd done or said wrong. I cried myself to sleep for over two weeks worrying about what I'd done and nothing made any sense."

By now Jenny was in tears as she, too, was reliving the anguish she felt from her rejection by Marc. She looked away, not able to look into Marc's eyes anymore. The pain was becoming unbearable. 'Why did I have to bring this up now? Why?!' she thought as she buried her face in her hands.

Noticing that Marc wasn't responding she somehow found the courage to raise her eyes up to meet his, only to find him looking down at the table, wiping away his own tears.

In a hushed voice, Jenny reached out her hand to touch Marc's. "Marc … I'm sorry. I'm so sorry, but … do you … can you under-stand what I was going through? It was just so hard on me and I just couldn't take the heartache any longer."

Marc gently pulled his hand away from Jenny's, wiped away more tears, then pushed his now cold pizza away as he'd definitely lost his appetite. He tried to gain some composure by taking a drink of water. Great. Cold pizza and warm water. The small amount of ice that had been there at the start had melted long ago. Their waitress, apparently noticing that they were in a very private conversation, had left them alone. He breathed deeply, trying to calm down.

"Jenny ... "

"Yes, Marc?" Jenny asked hesitantly through her sniffling.

"May I ask you a question?"

"Yeah. I guess so."

"When my letters and calls stopped ... why didn't you try to write to me or call me right then?"

"Because ... they had come so regularly during the first couple of months you were gone. When they slowed up a bit I figured it was only because of mid-terms, so I didn't worry about it. But when they stopped altogether I just put two and two together and realized you must have met someone else around the time that they were coming more slowly, and when they stopped, I just knew you had fallen in love with someone else and didn't have time for me anymore. And that's when I fell apart. I'm sorry for the letter, but it was the only thing I could think of to do."

Marc sighed deeply and then spoke softly, almost in a whisper. "I wished you'd called."

"Why, Marc?" Jenny asked abruptly. "What good would that have done? All I would have heard was your 'Gee, I'm sorry I haven't written or called lately, Jenny, but I have a new girlfriend now.' My heart just couldn't take that."

"I've already told you, Jenny, there wasn't anyone else. Still," Marc continued, his voice breaking up, "I ... I wish you had tried. I ... I needed you."

Marc had spoken those last few words so softly Jenny hadn't understood them. Her countenance changed suddenly as she softly asked, "Excuse me?"

Marc looked deeply into Jenny's tearful eyes, searching for

something, some hint, perhaps, that she would understand what he was about to tell her.

With his voice still barely audible he said, "I needed you."

"You needed me?" Jenny's eyes were searching Marc's, trying to understand what he'd said and what it meant. "You needed me, Marc?" she repeated.

"Yes, Jenny, I needed you ... badly."

The look in Jenny's eyes changed from confusion to concern and worry.

"You needed me? But ... why?"

"Because ..." Marc choked up as painful memories were flashing back faster than he could control them.

"Marc ... why? Please tell me." Jenny reached out both of her hands to hold Marc's. She felt the need to touch him, to encourage him to tell her what he was fighting to say. She let go of one hand to wipe tears away from one cheek and then the other. Marc responded to her touch with a slight smile which disappeared a moment later. Jenny looked at him, and with her eyes she pleaded with him to continue.

"Near the end of October I got really sick, and it was all I could do to try to stay up with my classes. I didn't tell anyone, not even you or my family, because I didn't want anyone to worry about me. My roommate had to take me to the hospital one night, but it turned out it was all stress related. I was falling behind so fast that I feared I'd have to take incompletes in all of my classes, but I started to get better and I worked hard and managed to catch up by the Thanksgiving break. At that point I was going to call you and apologize, but instead I decided to apologize face-to-face. I wanted to surprise you by coming home for Thanksgiving."

"But ..." Jenny stopped mid-thought.

"But something happened and I couldn't."

"Why not?"

"Because ... of the ... accident."

Jenny froze, stunned by what Marc had just said. She noticed that her gentle hold on Marc's hands was growing much tighter.

"What?! Marc! What accident? Oh, my ..." Jenny's hands

covered her mouth as she gasped. Looking into Marc's eyes she began to cry again, but this time for a much different reason.

"Sweetheart, what accident? When? What happened? Are you okay? Oh, Marc ... I ... I ..." Jenny lost the words she was looking for.

"It was a car accident. Thanksgiving week. Like I said, it was supposed to be a surprise for my family, but especially for you."

"What?! Oh, Marc, I ... I'm so sorry! Oh, baby ... how? Where? ..." Jenny was frantic with anxiety over Marc's revelation.

"I had packed everything I needed for the trip, jumped into my car and hadn't gone very far. It was raining hard on the interstate and the other driver lost control, crossed over the median, and crashed into me and another car."

Jenny's tears were now unstoppable.

"Sweetheart, I'm okay. It took a while, but I'm okay now."

"It took a while? What's 'a while'?"

"Seven months."

"What?! Seven months?! Oh, baby, what happened? Oh, my gosh, Marc! I didn't know! I didn't know!" Jenny wept as she felt so much anguish from the realization that she had misunderstood Marc's silence. 'Why didn't I try to reach him?'

"Yeah, it took a while for everything to heal up along with physical therapy and counseling."

Jenny couldn't take her eyes off Marc. What had she done? How could she have been so thoughtless, so selfish, to only think of herself, when all along Marc had needed her so desperately?

"Why ... Marc, why didn't your parents or Alexa call me to let me know?"

"They told me they'd tried just before rushing off to the airport to fly to Salt Lake City. They got the recording that said your number had changed and there was no forwarding number. They tried your parents and the phone just rang and rang. Then, out of time, they had to leave for the airport."

"Oh, Marc ..."

"They told me that they were so panicked about the accident that the next few days were just a blur for them. My roommate came to the hospital every day, and one day he brought my mail. My mom opened it all to read to me, saving your letter for last thinking it would really lift my spirits. As she began to read it to me she stopped and began to cry. She couldn't continue so she handed it to my dad to finish reading it to me, but as he started he choked up, too, and stopped. I begged him to keep reading. When he was finished it was clear that, for whatever reason, it was over between us. My mom said she wanted to at least let your parents know about the accident, but I asked her not to, that you'd apparently been planning this long before the accident so it wouldn't make any difference."

Jenny couldn't look at Marc. She just cried.

Marc had nothing further to say so he just sat there staring out the window in the distance.

"Marc, I want you to tell me all about this, okay? But first I need to ask you a question."

"Okay."

"Marc ... do you think," Jenny breathed deeply, "do you think you'll ever be able to find it in your heart ... to forgive me? Oh, Marc ... I'm just so very sorry. I wasn't there for you when you needed me because I was so selfish and concerned about myself, and that wasn't fair to you. It wasn't right. Oh, Marc ... can you ever forgive me?"

Marc reached out and touched Jenny's tear-stained cheek, her mascara mostly gone with the rest streaking her face. She reached up and held his hand to her cheek tightly. She'd missed that touch, that look he was giving her right now, his love, his tenderness, his caring. And to think, she'd almost lost it forever, but somehow, by some miracle, here he was, back in her life.

"Jenny, I ... yes, I forgive you. How could I not?"

Jenny looked at him with a look of curiosity. "How could you *not*? Easy. I wasn't there when you needed me. Simple as that."

Marc smiled and Jenny's sobbing began to subside as she began to breathe a little easier.

Marc rose from his side of the booth and Jenny's eyes followed him as he moved closer and knelt next to her.

"Sweetheart, I can forgive you … because I love you." Jenny burst into tears again as she reached out and hugged Marc. She released him long enough to be able to look into his eyes.

"Oh, Marc … I love you, too." Marc held her tear stained face in his hands just the way he'd held her so many times before. Happier times? Perhaps. But then again, what could make them happier than finding love … again. Their eyes closed as they shared a tender kiss.

As they separated, they simply smiled at each other.

"I've missed you, Jenny."

"Oh, Marc … I've missed you, too. And I'm so-o-o sorry."

Marc gently placed his finger over Jenny's lips. "Sh-h-h-h-h … it's okay, sweetheart. It's okay."

"Oh, baby, I love you!"

"I love you too, Jenny."

§

After that revelation hit Jenny, and after they'd had a chance to catch their collective breaths, she excused herself from the table and headed for the ladies room to freshen up and try to fix her makeup. It helped a little, but she knew she'd still have to swing past her apartment to get it done right before heading over to see her tutor.

Her tutor!! Oh, why did she have to see him, or her, today?! All she wanted to do now was stay with Marc! She felt so bad for not being there for him after his accident. 'Why didn't I at least try to get in touch with him before I wrote that STUPID letter?!' she asked herself as she looked in the mirror. Just then another girl came in so Jenny tossed her makeup kit back into her purse, took one more glance at herself in the mirror, quickly ran her fingers through her hair and left.

Marc and Jenny spent the next hour just talking. In fact, they were so absorbed in conversation that they were totally oblivious to anyone else around them.

"Marc, I don't want to, but I'm going to have to leave soon. I have some place I have to be in a little while and I look like a mess so I'm going to have to go back home and freshen up."

"Anything special?" Marc asked, wishing they wouldn't have to separate, even for a moment; though he just remembered that he, too, had to be somewhere.

"Yes, and no. It's kinda complicated. I can explain it to you later. I'd just prefer to not get into it right now, if that's okay?"

"Oh, sure. Any idea how long it might take? I guess I'm asking because ... well, because I'd like to see you again afterward."

"Yes, I'd like that. I'll make it as fast as I can, but it's possible it'll take at least an hour, maybe longer? I just don't know."

Marc reached for his wallet and pulled out cash to cover their bill and a sizable tip.

"Okay. Well, maybe we can get together after that? You could call me when you're done and I could meet you at your place?"

"I'd like that, Marc," Jenny replied wistfully.

"Great. Let me walk you to your car." Marc got up and stepped closer to Jenny and offered his hand to help her up.

"There you go again, Mr. Gentleman," Jenny replied with a wink and a smile.

"Babe, did I ever tell you what that wink of yours does to me?"

"Oh, you may have mentioned it ... about a hundred times." Jenny giggled.

"Ha! Is that all? I apologize. I must be slipping."

Jenny leaned forward and kissed Marc on the cheek as they started to leave. "Then you better get busy, buddy. You've got a lot of catching up to do," she said with another wink.

"Hmmm ... I think I know what I'll do."

"What?" Jenny asked because she wasn't sure what he'd just said. She was so pleasantly distracted.

"I said, I think I know what I'll do."

"About what?"

"Whenever you wink at me." Marc held the door open for Jenny as they exited.

"What's that?"

"Oh, you'll find out."

"I will?"

"Yes."

"Promise?"

"Absolutely!"

Jenny stopped Marc dead in his tracks just as they stepped into the parking lot, turned to face him, and looked him right in the eyes. She smiled sweetly ... and winked. Faster than she could even think of teasing Marc by winking at him again he planted a kiss on her lips. As they pulled apart ever so slightly, they looked deeply into each other's eyes.

"I love you, Marc."

"I love you too, Jenny."

They held each other close for a very long moment.

"GET A ROOM!" someone shouted from across the parking lot.

Marc and Jenny turned to see Monica and Lori approaching, both smiling from ear to ear.

"Hey, there!" Monica and Lori just couldn't stop smiling.

"Hey, girls! What are you doing here?"

"Hi, Marc!" they said teasingly. "Oh, we heard you guys might be here."

"What?" Jenny was stunned. She hadn't told anyone where she was going. "That's not possible."

"True, but we have our ways, or should we say our ... sources."

"Well, I'm just going to have to find out another time because I have to be somewhere in a little while.

"Oh, you're going to—?"

"Yes," Jenny responded abruptly, stopping Monica's question before she said too much.

Marc looked puzzled. 'Apparently Jenny's friends know about what she's doing this afternoon?' He wondered.

"Oh, okay. Got it. Well, we'll let you two lovebirds go." Looking at Jenny, Lori continued, "and I'll talk to *you* later."

"MUCH later, okay, girls?"

"O-kay," Monica responded in a playful pout.

"Come on, Marc. Walk me to my car. Bye, girls!"

"Bye, Jenny!" Monica and Lori headed into the Pizza Palace, giggling.

"I wish you didn't have to go, Jenny."

"I know, me too, but the sooner I go, the sooner I can be with you again."

"Ah-h-h, okay. Deal!"

They arrived at Jenny's car, she unlocked and opened the door, then turned to give Marc a big kiss. "I love you, sweetheart."

"Love you too, Jenny."

"You be good, and I'll call you as soon as I can, okay? Oh, wait! I need your phone number!" She reached for a piece of paper and a pen from her purse, handed it to Marc, who feigned a loss of memory for a second, causing Jenny to gently smack his arm.

"Hey, I'm thinking. I don't ever call myself so sometimes it takes a while to remember my number."

"How could that be? Your memory is perfect."

"Well, I'm getting a little older, and some things just don't work like they used to." Marc had to say something funny in order to keep from divulging the real reason for his pause in remembering his number. Hopefully he'd be able to keep it from Jenny a while longer. "Here ya go. Don't lose it."

"Are you kidding me? I'll protect this with my life!" Jenny smiled. No wink this time, just a sweet and loving smile. She climbed into her car, slipped the key into the ignition and rolled her window down as Marc stepped back a bit. He gave her the "all clear" sign and she started her car, slipped it into reverse, and backed out.

Swinging her car around, she paused before driving off.

"Did you forget something, babe?"

"Yeah. This!" Jenny winked and sped away.

"I owe you one!" Marc called after her.

"Yeah! A BIG one!" Jenny yelled back. One turn, a pause at the street to check traffic, and she was on her way.

'I wonder where she has to go?' Marc pondered.

CHAPTER 15

Lucky

JENNY DROVE HOME AS quickly as she could without drawing the attention of any police. She raced up the steps and through the door of her apartment, headed for her bathroom to re-do her make-up, then changed her clothes.

She thought briefly about the too casual outfit she'd worn to see Marc and wished that she'd made a better choice. Since she was going to see him as soon as possible after her session she decided to add those special touches now. Hopefully her tutor, if it's a guy, wouldn't get the wrong idea about her. After all, how many students bothered to get dressed up nicely on a Saturday afternoon, especially for a tutoring session?

Jenny glanced quickly at her watch ... she was still on time. She had originally planned on being there early, but spending those extra few minutes with Marc had been more important to her. She grabbed a jacket that matched her new outfit, and she was out the door, down the steps, and into her car.

She drove through traffic as cautiously as possible while still thinking solely about Marc. Thinking about what he'd told her brought new feelings of regret and sadness, but she took a deep breath when she felt tears begin to well up in her eyes because she didn't want to mess up her makeup again.

Thirty minutes later she pulled into the college parking lot and headed toward the counseling center. She was grateful her appointment was on a Saturday afternoon because the lot was mostly deserted, allowing her to park in the first row. Less than two dozen other cars were scattered nearby. She retrieved her backpack from the trunk where she'd put it earlier before heading over to meet up with Marc. Marc! Just the thought of him made her smile and feel all warm, despite the cooling temperatures of a mid-autumn afternoon.

Not far from the doors to the counseling center was a ladies room and Jenny dashed in to take a final look. She unzipped her jacket and brushed her long auburn hair, grateful for the fact that she rarely had bad hair days, even when she wore a cap. A quick glance at her makeup and she was ready. She took a deep breath and headed out the door toward the counseling center.

As Jenny walked through the doors she looked toward the counter and saw Adele working at her desk. Adele looked up as she heard someone coming through the doors and when she saw it was Jenny she immediately rose and came toward her to say hello.

"Hi, Jenny! Right on time, I see."

"Hi, Adele! It's good to see you. Oh, you wouldn't believe what it took to get here on time. I'm so glad I was able to skate through traffic as easily as I did and was able to park nice and close."

"That's great, honey. Well, your tutor is already here and waiting for you down the hall. He's in room 7."

"He?"

"Yes. He's a very nice young man. Polite, intelligent, and pretty charming if you ask me," Adele added with a wink.

"Oh, great!" Jenny replied with a slight giggle. "I'm just here for tutoring, NOT a date."

"Oh, I know. I just had to tease you. But I'm sure you'll enjoy your session with him. He's been very helpful for other students this semester, and many have actually left comments with our staff raving about how easy it was to work with him. But I shouldn't keep talking about him or I'll make you late. Have a good session, Jenny, and I'll chat with you later."

"Okay, thanks, Adele. Oh, what's his name?"

Adele smiled. "Lucky."

"What?! Lucky? Are you serious?"

"Well, it's not his real name, but when he came in this afternoon he asked me to just say his name was 'Lucky' if anyone should happen to ask. Don't ask me why. He just seemed to be in a particularly good mood when he came in, so perhaps he's just having a really good day and thought he was such a lucky man."

"Aw, that's nice. Okay, then Lucky it is. Maybe he'll be lucky for me and I'll catch on quickly to what he's going to try to teach me."

"Oh, I'm sure you will, honey. He really is that good."

"O-o-o-o, sounds wonderful. Thanks again, Adele. Catch ya later."

Jenny waved over her shoulder to Adele as she walked down the hall. Adele smiled and waved back.

"Let's see … room 7, huh? Okay, here it is." Jenny paused for a moment before knocking to collect her thoughts and try to calm down. She took a couple of deep breaths and let them out slowly. That trick always worked whenever she was nervous. It gave her a quick shot of extra oxygen to her brain and helped to calm her nerves. She thought it appropriate to knock before entering.

"Come on in!" came the voice from inside.

For just a split second she thought the voice sounded familiar, but shook it off and reached for the door knob. She opened the door with fresh confidence and a smile. "Thank yo—" Jenny stood there frozen in the doorway, still holding the door knob.

"MARC?!"

"Hi, Jenny," Marc replied softly with a loving smile.

"Wha … how … wait a minute! Marc, what are you doing here?" Jenny's emotions were all over the place at the moment; thrilled, surprised, speechless.

"What do you think I'm doing here?" Marc's smile broadened.

"But how … Marc, what's going on?"

"Sweetheart, I'm your tutor."

"My tutor? But how did you do that?"

"Adele."

"What? How ... Oh, Marc!" Jenny finally let go of the door and ran to Marc's arms. She hugged him tightly. "Oh, Marc."

"Surprised?"

"Surprised?! YES! But ... wait a minute. How did you know where I was going this afternoon?"

"I didn't. This is where I'M supposed to be right now, too."

"What?! So ... ," Jenny continued, still trying to grasp what'd just happened, "you really *are* my tutor?"

"That's right."

"Oh, wow! Oh ... wow! Oh, my gosh! I can't get over this!"

"Well, sweetheart, it's really me, and I really am your tutor."

"Okay. Okay." Jenny stood there looking at Marc, her arms around his waist. "Wow, you've managed to take my breath away. I mean, this is a total shock to me. I was not expecting to see you in here."

Marc chuckled. "Yeah, that was pretty obvious by the look on your face as you came through the door."

"But did you know I would be here?"

"Not until I arrived today. When I got here about 15 minutes ago I chatted with Adele for a couple of minutes, asked her what room I was assigned to, and then asked her what the name of the student was that I'd be working with today. When she said 'Jenny Kincaid' I couldn't believe it. I quickly tried to hide my excitement, but I'm sure Adele could tell I was at least happy, but she had no idea why, and still doesn't."

"Okay, but what's with this 'Lucky' bit?"

"Oh, that." Marc laughed. "I just said that because that's how I felt right at that moment, plus I didn't want her to give anything away about who you were seeing just in case you asked what your tutor's name was. I wanted to surprise you and see the look on your face as you walked through the door."

"Well, you certainly did. I suppose I must have put on quite a show for you standing there like that in the doorway with my jaw dropping to the floor."

Marc chuckled politely. "Yeah, you were pretty stunned. The operative word here being 'pretty'."

"Oh, Marc." Jenny leaned into him again and gave him a big kiss. "Well, sir, I've come here for a tutoring lesson. Am I still going to get one, or —"

"Absolutely! I want to see if I can score another great rating from another satisfied student so the college will continue to use me."

Jenny smacked him playfully on the arm. "Oh, I'll give you a rating, alright, mister." They laughed and then let go of each other and sat down.

§

The hour they spent in the room could just as well have been spent anywhere else, even at Jenny's apartment where they'd planned to meet later anyway. Some tutoring actually did take place, but they were both so distracted with each other that they weren't able to get much accomplished. They finally decided to just pack up and leave.

As they headed down the hallway they laughed as they thought about what Adele would say or do when she saw them together. They weren't disappointed. As they came into view, holding hands and laughing, Adele stood up from her desk and came to the counter with her eyes popping and her mouth dropping open.

"Wow!" Adele exclaimed, as Marc and Jenny burst out laughing. "What went on back there? You two look absolutely ... oh, gosh, what's the word I'm searching for?"

"It's actually two words," Marc replied.

Adele looked at him with curiosity. "Pardon me?"

"It's actually two words you're looking for. In ... love."

"WHAT?! But, how? I mean, wow! That was fast! I guess my little matchmaking effort really paid off big time!"

"What do you mean?" Jenny asked with a puzzled look on her face.

"Well, Marc's been one of our star tutors this semester, and after you turned in your request a few days ago and I had a chance to look it over and see what your needs were, I just felt inspired to select Marc as your tutor. And now look!"

Jenny looked up at Marc who was already looking at her and asked, "Shall we tell her?"

"Tell me what?" Adele demanded playfully.

"Sure, babe, go ahead," Marc said with a nod.

"Well-l-l … you see …"

"Come on! Tell me! The suspense is killing me!"

Jenny continued, "Well, you see, Marc and I actually already knew each other."

"What? Really? How long have you known each other."

"Over two years."

"Really?"

"Yeah, but after our senior year I came here and Marc went off to the University of Utah, but he transferred here at the beginning of this school year."

"And so you're back together."

"Well, yeah, we are, but in a different way than you're thinking."

"I'm sorry, I don't think I understand."

"Well, it's a long complicated story, but the short version is while Marc was away at school a year ago I misunderstood something that happened and overreacted and broke up with him. He had tried to reach me but I had changed my phone number and my parents had moved about that time so his mail was being returned to him. Yeah, like I said it's a long complicated story, but as of today, this afternoon at lunch, actually, we're officially back together."

"Well, however it worked out, I'm sure it was meant to be. And I'm SO glad that it did."

Marc and Jenny looked at each other and then back at Adele. "We are too," Marc replied with a smile.

"Yeah, we are," Jenny added, looking into Marc's eyes.

CHAPTER 16

The Promise

JENNY MADE IT THROUGH the rest of the semester with flying colors. In spite of Marc becoming a very pleasant distraction for her she was able to improve her grades for the classes she'd been struggling in, thanks in large part to his loving and patient assistance.

However, they would be spending some of the holidays apart. Marc would be staying in town to be with his family, while Jenny was going to join her parents to visit her Grandma in Twain Harte.

Marc had asked Jenny if he could see her before she left on her trip, and that was more than fine with her since she had a surprise for him. She'd been thinking about something special like this ever since they'd gotten back together, and when they were at the mall a couple of weeks ago she'd finally found the perfect one.

Marc's sister, Alexa, happened to notice as Jenny pulled up in front of their house.

"Marc! Jenny's here!" she called, not sure if he'd be able to hear her upstairs in his room. As she'd passed by it a few minutes earlier she noticed he was playing his guitar and listening to music with his headphones on. Not hearing any movement from upstairs she quickly made the climb before Jenny had even gotten out of her car.

"Marc!" Alexa called from his doorway, finally getting his attention.

""Yeah?" he replied, lifting his headphones away from one ear.

"Jenny's here," Alexa announced joyfully before heading back downstairs to the family room.

"Great! Thanks, Alexa!" He quickly tossed his headphones onto his desk, set his guitar on the nearby stand, stopped the CD player and ran down the stairs. After taking a quick glance in the foyer mirror and running his fingers quickly through his hair he opened the door just as Jenny was about to knock.

"Hey, Jenny!"

"Hi, Marc!"

"Come on in!"

"Thanks," Jenny replied, leaning up to give him a kiss as she stepped in.

"I hope your parents weren't too disappointed about leaving a little later."

"No, they were cool about it. They understand we have a hard time being apart." Jenny added with a flirtatious smile.

"Well, I hope to make it worthwhile, at least to you," Marc replied with a special smile of his own.

"Oh, yeah? What do you have in mind?"

"Well, why don't you come into the family room and find out?"

Marc and Jenny walked past the living and dining rooms and back toward the rear of the house. They noticed Alexa relaxing on the couch and watching a DVD.

"Alexa?"

"Yeah, Marc? Hi, Jenny! It's good to see you!"

"You too, Alexa," Jenny replied with a sweet smile.

"Um, I hate to interrupt but would you mind giving us a few minutes?" Marc asked.

"Sure! Anything for my big brother and his sweetie," Alexa replied with a wink aimed at Jenny.

"Thanks, sis. I appre—, excuse me, *we* appreciate it."

"Yeah, thanks, Alexa," Jenny added, still smiling.

"Hey, no problem. Just behave, you two. You don't want mom and dad coming home and catching you doing anything you shouldn't," Alexa added as she jogged toward the stairs.

Marc and Jenny looked at each other and shook their heads and laughed.

"Oh, Marc! I know I've said it before, but I just have to say it again, I really love the way your family decorates your home for the Christmas season. There's always such a sense of warmth and love!"

"Yeah, I love it, too. My mom and Alexa do all the work on the inside, while my dad and I handle all the lights outside. The lights are actually the easy part compared to what mom and Alexa do. And they always add something every year without telling my dad or me what it is and make us try to guess what it is. The first one to guess always gets a little something extra under the tree on Christmas morning."

"How fun! I sure love your family, Marc!" Jenny said with a special glow in her eyes.

"And they love you too, Jenny," Marc replied, almost in a whisper.

Jenny looked into Marc's eyes, saw the love he felt for her and melted into his arms before sharing another tender kiss.

"Why don't you sit on the sofa while I get something," Marc said as he turned and walked toward the Christmas tree.

"Would that be something for me?" Jenny teased.

"As a matter of fact … it could be," Marc replied as he removed a small package from deep within the branches. As he turned around and returned to sit next to Jenny her eyes lit up with excitement.

"Merry Christmas, sweetheart."

Jenny looked deeply and lovingly into Marc's eyes. With great anticipation she carefully unwrapped her present. With the ribbon and paper set gently on the sofa next to her she held a small, slightly rectangular jewelry box. Before opening it she had to give Marc one more look that she hoped would convey what she was feeling but unable to say at the moment. Then she looked down, tears beginning to pool in her eyes, and slowly opened the box to expose a silver necklace with two entwined silver hearts. The tears let go, and raising one hand to her mouth, Jenny began to cry. Still unable to speak, she simply leaned into Marc as he placed his warm, strong arms around her and held her close.

It took several moments before Jenny was able to regain her composure. Marc had offered her his handkerchief which she quickly grabbed to dab her eyes. It was soaked in no time.

"Oh, Marc, it's ... so beautiful."

"I'm glad you like it, Jenny."

"Like it? I *love* it! Thank you *so* much!!! Would you put it on me, please?"

"Sure!"

Jenny took the necklace out of the box and handed it to Marc, then lifted her hair up off her shoulders and away from her neck. Marc slipped the necklace around her neck and attached it, then leaned down and gently kissed her on the back of her neck. His kiss sent shivers down her back and she dropped her hair and melted right back into Marc's chest with a sigh of sheer ecstasy. Marc held her in his arms and they sat quietly for several minutes.

"I was looking for something really special that would express my love for you and show you how grateful I am that we're together again, and that our love for each other is forever."

"It sure is, sweetheart. Oh, I love you so much, Marc," Jenny whispered.

"Merry Christmas, darling!"

"Merry Christmas," Jenny replied, wiping away more tears, and leaning back into Marc's arms. They sat there in a silent reverie for several more minutes, simply enjoying each other's warmth and comfort.

Once Jenny was able to breathe almost normally again, she sat up and shifted on the sofa so she could look more easily into Marc's eyes. She reached out and took his hands in hers, took a deep breath, and was about to start when she paused again to collect her thoughts.

"Are you okay, Jenny?" Marc asked with a worried look.

"Yes! Yes, of course. I'm ... I'm sorry. I'm just not used to doing anything like this. I mean ... I've never done anything like this before."

"Like what?"

"Made this kind of promise." There it was. It was out.

"A promise? What are you talking about?"

"Oh, sweetheart, I blew it. This isn't the way this was supposed to go. I've gone over and over this in mind for days and I had it all worked out! I really did!"

"What, babe?" Marc's eyes were searching, and he was feeling a bit confused.

Jenny sighed deeply. "If it's okay with you … I'd like to start over."

Marc smiled the smile that, when combined with that special look in his eyes, always made Jenny melt. "Sure. Would you like to start from when you drove up?" he asked teasingly.

Jenny smacked him on the arm as she giggled. "No, that's okay. Just from where I shifted on the sofa a moment ago."

"Okay, works for me."

Jenny cleared her throat and shook her arms in an animated fashion in front of her in order to ease some of her tension and further lighten the mood. She rested her hands in her lap for a moment, then reached for Marc's hands as she did a few moments earlier, and finally looked deeply into his eyes. Ahhhh … there it was. The look of love. Jenny smiled, and this time she felt more relaxed and focused.

"Marc—," Jenny began.

"Yeah?" Marc interrupted.

"Shhhh," Jenny replied, as she softly put her finger on Marc's lips. He kissed it and made her giggle again. "Stop it, Marc! I'm trying to be serious here."

"Sorry, I just couldn't resist."

"Okay, now behave. And be quiet so I can get through this." Marc pinched his lips and whipped his fingers across them as if to zip them shut causing Jenny to shake her head and smile.

"Marc … I know you love me. And I know you know that I love you."

The look in Marc's eyes began to reflect his thoughts, 'Where is she going with this? I wish she'd just get to the point, because this is killing me!'

"As much as I've tried to put it behind me I've been haunted by what happened between us just over a year ago. I know you said you forgave me, but at a time you needed me the most I wasn't there for you and I've cried myself to sleep several times since I learned the truth. I'm so grateful for your forgiving heart."

Marc started to say something, but Jenny's look stopped him in his tracks.

"As Christmas was approaching I had been trying to think about what I could get you that would show you how much I love you and how committed I am to you and our relationship."

"I don't need anything but you, Jenny," Marc interjected as he touched her cheek with his fingers.

"I know that," Jenny replied as she held his fingers to her cheek, and closed her eyes slowly for a moment as she reveled in his tenderness. "I know." She paused, looked into his eyes again, and then leaned forward and kissed him.

"I've spent every spare moment since we got back together going from store to store until I found the exact thing I was looking for, and the one I got couldn't be more perfect. Now, I need you to close your eyes and promise you won't peek."

"For how long?"

"Only a moment. I just need to reach into my purse for a second."

"I know what you got me!" Marc exclaimed, almost opening his eyes in the excitement of it all.

"Oh, I doubt it."

"Yep, I do! I hear what sounds like keys ... car keys ... YEP! THAT'S IT! You've bought me a new car!" Marc opened his eyes and threw his hands up in excitement.

"Not a chance, buddy. I'm still a struggling college co-ed, getting by on a part-time job and student loans, remember? Now, close your eyes so I can get through this."

"Sorry. Just had to tease you."

"I know, now ..." Jenny paused as she reached for and finally found what she was looking for in her purse. She lifted out a slim rectangular box, wrapped in sparkling red paper with matching ribbon and bow.

"OK, sweetheart, you can open your eyes now." Her heart leapt with anticipation! "MERRY CHRISTMAS!"

"Aw, you bought me a pen and pencil set," Marc joked.

"Aw, shoot! How'd you guess?" Jenny replied in mock frustration. "Actually, it's a bread box."

"Yeah, right. For just the crumbs, right?"

"Yep! OK, enough fooling around. Open it! The suspense is killing me!" Jenny held her hands in her lap as she watched in anticipation while Marc unwrapped his present … slowly, ever so slowly, just to drive Jenny crazy.

The bow and ribbon off, the paper now tossed aside, Marc was looking at a long and slim black box with a classy gold design on top. "It's got to be a pen and pencil set. Or, perhaps just a pen, right?" Marc thought out loud as he slowly lifted the top. He was stunned to see its real contents. Jenny was pleased by the surprised look on his face. She'd done it! She'd completely surprised him!

"A ring?" Marc asked in wonderment.

"Not just *any* ring, darling."

"Well, it's a beautiful ring, that's for sure. But …" Jenny saw Marc was speechless. It was exactly the effect she was hoping for.

"Merry Christmas, darling! It's a very special ring, from me to you, from my heart to your heart."

"But sweetheart, I … I don't know what to say."

"Just tell me you love me and I'll be fine."

"Well, of course I love you, Jenny, but I didn't expect anything like this in this kind of box."

Jenny laughed, "I know. I worked with the jeweler to make this special box just for the ring."

"That must have cost you extra, right?"

"A little, but it was worth it to see the look on your face. It was priceless! Do you like it?"

"Of course! It's incredible."

"Sweetheart … the most special part of this ring is that it's a promise ring. And I know that it may seem strange for a girl to give a guy a promise ring, but I'm promising you that you will never go through what you went through last year. I'll always be here for you, right by your side, no matter what and no matter where you go, okay? I promise."

"Oh, Jenny ... I love you so much!"

"I know, darling. I know. I love you, too."

Jenny slid closer to Marc and melted in his arms as they fell into a tender kiss that was interrupted a few moments later by the sound of Marc's parents coming in the front door.

"Hi, everyone! We're home," Roni called out as she and Cole, walked into the foyer.

Marc and Jenny reluctantly broke their kiss and sat up. From where they were sitting his parents couldn't see them, but they still didn't need to be caught by his parents even though they weren't doing anything 'wrong'.

"Hi, mom! Hi, dad!" Alexa called from upstairs.

"Hi, sweetheart," Roni called in return. "Is Marc here, too?"

"Yeah, he's in the family room with Jenny."

"And Jenny's here too! Wonderful! I thought I recognized her car in front."

While Cole headed for the kitchen with some groceries, Roni made her way toward the family room and saw Marc and Jenny cuddled up on the sofa.

"Hey, you two, how are you?" Roni called.

"Great, mom," Marc replied as he leaned up.

"Hi, Mrs. Janssen! Merry Christmas!" Jenny added.

"Hi, Jenny! Merry Christmas to you, too! It's so good to see you again! We thought you'd already be on your way to your grandmother's by now."

"I know. Marc asked my parents if they could wait just a bit so we could get together this morning and my parents agreed!"

"Well, that's wonderful. How's your grandmother?"

"She's doing well. Thanks for asking."

"Well, we hope you have a safe trip up there and a wonderful visit with her."

"Thank you so much, Mrs. Janssen. I really appreciate that."

"Well, I don't want to be in your way, so you two have fun, and we'll see you after the holidays, Jenny?"

"Yes, you will, Mrs. Janssen," Jenny replied enthusiastically, looking up at Marc with a big smile. "Yes, you will."

"Okay! Merry Christmas, Jenny!"

"Merry Christmas to you and Mr. Janssen, too! Oh, wait! Look what Marc just gave me!"

Jenny stood up and raised her necklace to make it easier for Roni to see.

"Oh, Jenny! It's lovely!" Then looking at her son she said, "You sure do have good taste."

"I sure do, mom," Marc replied, looking into Jenny's eyes.

"I meant the necklace, son."

"I know, mom, but my good taste started with Jenny."

"Yes, you're so right." Jenny and Roni shared a smile, and Roni winked at her along with a look that once again made her feel so welcome in their family. Yes, she certainly felt lucky to be a part of their lives.

"Well, you two have a good time and I'm going to go find my husband."

"Thanks, mom."

"Yes, thanks, Mrs. Janssen."

Roni smiled and waved over her shoulder as she walked toward the hallway.

Marc and Jenny looked at each other for a moment, and then shared a brief kiss before Jenny spoke. "Marc, I hate to break the mood, but I better be going."

"Yeah, I know. I wish you didn't have to go, but I understand. Be careful and I hope you have a good visit with your grandmother."

"Thanks, sweetheart. That means a lot to me."

"Jenny?" Marc asked softly.

"Yes, Marc?"

"Thanks for my ring. It really *is* incredible. But, how'd you know I'd like this one?"

"Remember when we were at the mall a couple of weeks ago?"

"Yeah."

"As we walked passed that jewelry store and slowed up just a bit, I noticed your eyes light up when you saw it."

"Really? But we only slowed for a second."

"That's all it took. I'm a very observant young lady. I see

everything, so you better be good while I'm away because I also have my spies posted to keep an eye on you. I don't want some other co-ed to come along and snatch you up while I'm not around," Jenny added with a laugh.

"Oh, yeah, as if that'll happen."

"Well, you never know, and I can never be too careful. You're quite the catch, Marc Janssen, and I'm not letting you go again."

"Promise?"

"I gave you that ring, didn't I?"

"Yes," Marc replied as he looked down at his hand. "You sure did. I sure love you, Jenny."

"And I love you too, Marc."

"And … I need you, too … now, more than ever."

"Oh, baby, I need you too, but are you alright? I mean, you sounded … oh, I don't know, kind of … well, not quite yourself there for a moment."

"Yeah, I'm fine, sweetheart. Don't worry about me. You just go and have a good time with your parents and grandmother and I'll be here waiting when you get home."

Jenny still wasn't completely convinced that everything was okay with Marc, but he'd just reassured her that it was, so she'd have to take his word for it … for now.

As they walked hand in hand toward the front door Alexa heard their footsteps and bounded enthusiastically from her bedroom.

"Heading out, Jenny?"

"Sure am, Alexa. It was good seeing you again!" Jenny replied.

"Same here. Have a good trip and Merry Christmas!"

"Merry Christmas, Alexa! Bye!"

Marc reached for Jenny's coat from the rack near the front door and helped her put it on.

"Thank you, Sir Marc!" Jenny said with a smile.

"Sir? Where'd this 'sir' come from?"

"Well, you're my knight in shining armor and that was a chivalrous thing to do for me, so thank you, Sir Marc," she repeated, this time with a wink. And with that Marc planted a big kiss on her lips.

"There, hopefully that'll hold you until you return. If not, then you'll just have to come back sooner," Marc added with a smile. "Come on, I'll walk you out to your car."

"Aren't you going to grab a coat? It's in the 30's out there this morning."

"I'll be alright. I won't be out there that long."

"Perhaps. Then again … Oh, never mind."

"What?"

"I said never mind."

"That's not fair!"

"Ha! Whoever said love is fair?"

Marc held Jenny tight as they walked to her car. A cold gust of wind blew Jenny's hair into her face and she tucked it behind her ears and then reached into her coat pocket for her keys. Before she unlocked the car she looked up at Marc.

"I love you, Marc. Merry Christmas, darling. And thank you for my necklace. I love it!"

"I love you too, Jenny. Merry Christmas, and thanks again for my ring. It's perfect."

"You're welcome. I'm *so* glad you like it!" They shared one more lingering kiss and then Jenny turned, unlocked her door, and climbed in. Marc walked around the car and backed up toward the lawn as Jenny rolled down the passenger window.

"Hey, buster, you keep that ring in plain view when you're out and about, you hear? I don't want to come home to find some other girl has stolen you."

"Not a chance, babe! And please be careful while you're gone, okay? I really need you."

"Need you too, Marc!" Jenny called out as she started to drive away. "I love you!"

"Love you too, Jenny!"

As Jenny drove away Marc shivered as another bitterly cold gust of wind hit him from the side. He continued to watch until Jenny's car eventually disappeared down the hill and around the corner.

"Come home to me, Jenny," Marc said softly. "I really need you … more than ever."

CHAPTER 17

The Drive

JENNY WAS FILLED WITH mixed emotions on the drive. Part of her wished she could be by Marc's side every moment of every day; she just couldn't get enough of him! Another part, though, knew her place was by her grandmother's side for Christmas. But still, she was worried about Marc.

'… and I need you, too … now, more than ever.' Jenny thought back to those words Marc had said just before she left. There was something in the way he said it that was a little unsettling to her. But what was it? 'Marc, are you okay?'

"Dad?"

"Yes, honey"

"I know it's still a while, but how much longer before we get there?"

"We still have less than two hours," Jenny's dad, Tony, replied.

"Okay. Thanks, dad." Jenny leaned back, feeling suddenly tired. She just wanted to rest.

"Everything okay, sweetheart?" Tony, asked, looking in the rear-view mirror.

"Yeah, dad," Jenny responded, unconvincingly. "I'm fine."

Jenny closed her eyes for several moments as she listened to the rhythm of the road. The radio was on low, playing a song that seemed to fit the same rhythm.

§

"Jenny? Sweetheart?"

"Yeah, mom?"

"Are you okay?"

"Yeah, I'm fine. Just resting my eyes."

"Uh-huh. Well, you're going to have to give me the recipe for that."

"For what?" Jenny replied as she opened her eyes and lifted her head away from the head rest, feeling just a bit light headed.

"Resting your eyes."

"Huh? Why?"

"Because. You've been asleep for over an hour."

"What?!"

"We're almost there, sweetheart," added her dad.

"What?! How … ? I can't believe it! I just leaned back, closed my eyes. I was listening to the radio and —"

"And the next thing you knew I was waking you up."

"Yeah." Jenny sat there, a bit dazed and confused. "How did I do that? I wasn't even that sleepy."

"Honey, you must have needed it. When was the last time you got a really good night's sleep?"

"Too long ago to remember."

"That's what I thought."

"Well, between my classes, studying, papers, tests, work, and spending as much time as I can with Marc I don't really have much time to treat myself to a good night's rest."

"So how are things going with Marc?"

"Oh, mom, they're wonderful! Look what he gave me for Christmas!" Jenny leaned forward and held out her necklace.

"That's beautiful, darling! He sure has good taste."

"Yeah, that's what his mom said, too!"

"You know, your dad and I were so surprised when you called us back in October to say you two were back together again. After last year we—"

"Mom, please don't bring that up, okay?"

"I was just trying to say that we were surprised about the turn of events, and we're happy for you now. If you'd prefer to not talk about it we can respect your privacy."

"Thanks, mom."

"But if you ever change your mind—"

"MOM!"

"Sorry, dear. I'll drop the subject."

"Thanks."

Except for the music on the radio they rode in silence for several more miles.

"Mom?"

"Yes, honey?"

"I'm sorry," Jenny replied softly.

"For what, dear?"

"I didn't mean to cut you off like that. It wasn't right. You know I love you guys, right?"

"Sweetheart, you don't need to apologize. Whatever happened between you and Marc, good or bad, is your business, not ours. And yes, we know you love us. And we love you, too."

"I know, mom, but you care. You care about me and you care about how I'm doing."

"Yes, we do, very much, sweetheart."

"Then I want to explain what happened."

"Are you sure, honey?"

"Yes. I'm sure."

For the balance of the journey to her grandmother's, Jenny explained to her parents what Marc had shared with her, including the details she'd just learned from him a week ago.

She told them about Marc's letters and phone calls dropping off, and how she feared the worst ... that he had a new girlfriend. She started to tear up as she told them about how she'd overreacted and written the Dear John letter, and now they finally understood why she'd changed her phone number. She had just moved to her own apartment at the first of November and hadn't sent Marc the new address yet, and as a part of her "Dear John" reaction, she chose not to. She took a deep breath and wiped away her tears. Letting out a long sigh she continued.

Next came all the details that she could remember from what Marc had told her about the accident. He had explained everything to her without going into any of the horrible details, wishing instead to spare Jenny the agony of it all, but she had still cried the whole time he was talking.

Jenny told her parents about the other driver who'd lost control of his car during a heavy rain storm and crossed over the median and into oncoming traffic, slamming into two cars, including Marc's. Miraculously there were no fatalities, but everyone had sustained serious or critical injuries.

She explained how Marc had seen the other car coming but wasn't able to get out of the way in time. The next thing he knew, he woke up in the hospital with two broken legs, a broken arm, three broken ribs and a serious concussion. The broken legs had taken him months to recover from, and the physical therapy had continued until mid-summer. After realizing everything that had happened to him she told her parents how she was so amazed at how fast he'd recovered, because when she had first seen him in October, he looked perfectly fine, as if he'd never even been hurt at all.

"There's something else, though, that …" Jenny paused a few moments to try to figure out how to share her concerns. "I'm really starting to worry about something Marc has said to me a couple of times."

"What is it, sweetheart?" her mom asked softly.

"Well, maybe I'm just reading too much into it, but he said to me 'I really need you' then he pauses before continuing with, 'now, more than ever.'"

"Actually, Jenny, that's very romantic. Don't you think?"

"Yes, the words are, but mom … it's the *way* he says them. And the look on his face when he says it that also makes me think something's wrong, but I just can't seem to put my finger on it."

"Have you asked him about it, honey?"

"No, because he's only said it a couple of times and it was just as I was leaving for something, like joining you this morning to go see Grandma."

"Well, honey, I think if it was anything serious he'd tell you, so in the meantime try not to think about it, or at least try not to worry about it, okay?"

"Okay, mom." Jenny replied halfheartedly, not convinced she could, or would, even try.

With only a few minutes left before arriving at her Grandma's house, Jenny sat back and just watched the pine trees whiz past her window. Even with troubled thoughts of Marc, as well as thinking about how much she was going to miss him over these next few days, she was still looking forward to seeing her Grandma again.

There was always something so special about the times they spent together. Her Grandma and Grandpa had made quite a difference in her life as she was growing up.

One of her favorite memories from spending many of her summers with them was hearing the stories they loved to share with her, especially about how they grew up in a little town in Iowa, how they met and courted. 'Oh, my! Courting!' Jenny thought, as a smile crossed her face. 'They sure don't do things today like they used to.'

CHAPTER 18

Six Months Later

THE JANSSEN'S WERE SO excited as Alexa's senior year in high school came to a close. They all remembered another big celebration two years earlier when Marc had graduated, and afterwards they had started their summer off with a small get together at their lake house on the northwest shore of Lake Tahoe. With some gentle encouragement from Marc, Cole and Roni had extended an invitation to Jenny and her parents to join them that year, which they'd gladly accepted.

The week at the lake that summer was especially exciting for Marc and Jenny as they had looked forward to sharing as much time together as possible knowing that Marc would be going away to college near the end of summer which was coming all too soon.

That first year apart had been a difficult one, but they'd been able to get back together. And now, to celebrate Alexa's graduation, both families were once again heading back to the lake house for another small celebration.

Alexa had graduated valedictorian of her high school and had earned several excellent scholarships, but the one she was most excited about was her full ride scholarship to Belmont University in

Nashville, Tennessee. Her plan was to major in musical composition and performance.

Choosing to attend Belmont had been an easy decision for her to make, even though she had many very substantial offers from other excellent colleges and universities. But, in one respect, it was a difficult one for her parents to deal with, mostly because she would be the last one to leave home and the empty nest syndrome was already beginning to edge its way into Cole and Roni's thoughts. However, they genuinely felt very excited and happy for their lovely daughter and knew this was an important step for her. They wanted to do all they could with this time they would have together at their lake house, and for the rest of the summer, to make it as special as possible for Alexa. They wanted to provide a treasure trove of memories to last everyone a lifetime.

It took less than four hours to make the drive from the Bay Area to the north shore of Lake Tahoe by way of Truckee. The day was sunny and it felt more like spring as summer was officially still a couple of weeks away. The temperatures at the lake that week were expected to be mild during the day and cooler in the evenings, with no rain in the forecast. Meals and activities had been planned for the week, with everyone taking his or her fair share of the responsibilities. The schedule itself would be light, allowing for plenty of quiet, restful times throughout the week, as well as spontaneous activities like walks along the lake or hikes on nearby mountain trails. Marc and Jenny were anxious to take off on their own a few times, while still spending plenty of time with their families. There were a couple of gift shops they'd discovered their last time up at the lake and they were anxious to see what new things they might find.

The lake was perfectly calm. A few boaters were out that morning, but it was still fairly early in the season for the summer vacationers to be crowding into the area.

After lunch everyone gathered outside on the upper deck to enjoy the cool pine-scented breeze, with the parents on one end of the deck, and Marc and Jenny sharing a love seat, with Alexa nearby, toward the other end.

Jenny drew Marc close to her and whispered an 'I love you' in his ear and gently kissed him. He returned her affection and held her close for a few moments.

"I just love it here, Marc. Promise me we'll continue to come up here often."

"I love it too, babe, so yes, I can certainly promise that."

Jenny snuggled in under Marc's firm embrace and closed her eyes. "This sure feels good," she whispered softly.

"Hey, it's getting too mushy over here!" chided Alexa from a few feet away. Marc and Jenny looked at her and noticed her big, cheesy grin. "Yeah, I thought that would get your attention. You two better behave yourselves. This is a *family* vacation, understand?"

Marc and Jenny looked around and noticed their parents all enjoying a good laugh over the bantering going on.

"Yeah, you're just jealous, sis."

"Actually … you're right, Marc," Alexa sighed. "I've tried not to think about it too much, but it sure would be nice to have someone special like the two of you have."

"I know it may be easier said than done, Alexa," Jenny added, "but there *is* someone out there just for you, and you'll find him when the time is right. In the meantime, is there anyone you're kind of interested in?"

"No, not really." Alexa leaned back against her chair.

"What about the guy who took you to the Senior Ball?" Marc asked.

"You mean Dusty? No, that was more of a friend kind of date than anything else. We've known each other for so long, since fourth grade, I think, and we've never had any romantic feelings toward each other."

"Are you sure?" Marc kept the questions going.

"Yeah, we just have a really good friendship. He's always been there when I needed someone to listen to my problems and he's never gotten upset when any of those problems happened to have been about another guy."

"Sounds like just the right kind of guy to hold on to, Alexa," said Jenny. "In more ways than one."

Alexa leaned up and glanced over at Jenny just as Jenny gave her a little wink as she added, "If you know what I mean."

Alexa laughed as she leaned back against her chair. "Yeah, Jenny, I know what you mean."

The three of them sat in silence for several minutes listening to the breeze blow through the pine trees and the lighthearted chatter among their parents. By now in their relationship, both Marc and Jenny had looked at each other's parents and thought about them as future in-laws, and couldn't be happier to see how well they all got along. Their love was bringing together two wonderful families, and at some point in the future they knew they'd seal that bond for good, but not yet. They weren't in any rush in spite of how much they loved each other.

"Hey," called Roni, "you guys are sure quiet over there."

"Just thinking, mom," Alexa replied.

"Yeah, mom, she's thinking about the guy she's going to marry," Marc shouted teasingly.

"I am not!" Alexa replied and playfully smacked his leg with her fist.

"Hey! What was that for?" Marc asked, rubbing his thigh and trying not to laugh.

"You know darn well what it was for."

"Well, it's true, isn't it?"

"No!"

"Yes, it is." Marc just loved teasing his sister. He'd always been such a gentleman and protector toward her, but it was at times like this that he just couldn't resist letting her see his other side.

"No, it's not, and that's final!"

"Hey, you two, be nice to each other," Cole interjected. Marc noticed that there was an edge to his dad's voice and it caught him off guard. Roni looked at her husband with a 'where-did-that-come-from?' look, and he gave her a quick glance before turning forward to look out over the lake again. Marc looked at his sister and whispered "Sorry" and Alexa quietly replied, "Me too, bro." The parents resumed their chatting, but silence reigned supreme on the other side of the deck.

Alexa leaned closer to Marc. "What's up with dad?"

"I have no idea, sis," Marc whispered back. "That just came out of the blue. Has he been like this around the house lately?"

"No, he's been fine, at least when I've been around."

"I think I'll talk with mom later and see if she knows what's going on."

"But didn't you see the look she gave him, and the look he gave her back? I have a feeling this was the first time."

"Could be, but I still want to find out what mom might know."

"Okay. Let me know what you find out, okay?"

"No problem. As soon as I know, you'll know."

The look Alexa gave her brother was a simple way of saying 'I love you, bro' and Marc nodded back in reply. The three of them spoke in hushed tones for quite a while.

Cole seemed temporarily subdued, leaving Roni to maintain the conversation with Jenny's parents. It certainly helped that the four of them had become close friends.

"Tony and I have been up here to the lake so many times over the years," Adele said, "but it's more fun when we can share it with friends! And your view is breathtaking!"

"I know, isn't it? Cole and I have really enjoyed this place as a special retreat whenever we can. It's the perfect vacation getaway!"

"I'll say!" Cole added.

Marc and Alexa looked at each other quizzically as they listened to their dad once again in a more upbeat mood, but each chose not to make a comment.

§

The rest of the day had gone smoothly. The edginess that had been apparent in Cole's voice and attitude earlier had since seemed to dissipate, which made everyone else feel a bit more relaxed.

As Roni began preparations for dinner Marc took the chance to ask her about what was going on.

"About what, son?"

"About dad. He just didn't seem like his normal self this morning."

"Well, honestly Marc, that caught me by surprise too."

"I asked Alexa if she'd noticed anything different about dad recently, but she said he's been fine."

"Yeah, he has been. That's why what happened this morning was such a shock."

"You could say that again! Alexa and I just looked at each other and —"

"Hey, Roni," Adele said as she walked into the kitchen. "Anything I can do to help with—Oh! Am I interrupting something? I'm so sorry!"

"No, Mrs. Kincaid, it's fine. Mom and I were just chatting."

"Oh, how fun! It's so nice to be up here with your family!"

"And now, ladies, if you'll excuse me, I have a pretty young lady to find," and with that Marc left the kitchen in search of Jenny.

CHAPTER 19

Father and Son

A S THEIR WEEK TOGETHER was drawing to a close, Marc noticed his dad becoming gradually quieter with each day. This just wasn't like him and Marc was wondering if his dad was ill but not saying anything about it so as not to disrupt any family activities. He talked to Jenny about it one afternoon as they went for a drive around the lake and she suggested that Marc just ask his dad about it. The opportunity came up early Friday morning as they were both early to rise.

"Mornin', dad," Marc said with a yawn as he came down the stairs.

"Good morning, son. How're you this morning?"

"Still kinda tired. I didn't sleep very well last night."

"You and me both, it looks like," Cole replied with a sigh.

"Really? Anything wrong, dad?"

"No, just restless I guess. What about you?"

"Actually … actually, dad, I'm worried about you."

"Me? Why?"

"I don't know, it's … it's just that you haven't seemed like yourself this week. I mean, you seem to be having fun right along with everyone else, but there just seems to be something else, maybe something on your mind, or not feeling well?"

"Very observant, son, but it's nothing for you to be concerned or worried about."

"Are you sure, dad? I just can't remember you ever being this quiet and reserved, especially when family and friends are around."

"Maybe I'm just in a quiet mood?" Cole replied, trying to deflect Marc's questions.

"Dad, the only mood I ever recall you being in is a positive one. Not overly so, but just genuinely optimistic. That's why this mood, if you want to call it that, stuck out, and I noticed it early on. Usually you're talkative, not needing to be the life of the party, but still pretty much a part of the party. But when we first got here you didn't say very much for most of the day. You seemed to be back to your normal self by Wednesday, but then slipped back into your mood yesterday."

"Well, I appreciate your concern, son, but really, I'm fine."

"Nevertheless, just to remind you of something you've always told me, if there's ever anything you need or want to talk about, I'm here for you, okay dad?"

"Fair enough, son. And thanks."

"You're welcome. I love you, dad."

"I love you too, son."

Marc decided to take advantage of the cool mountain air to get in his morning run. Stepping out onto the porch and looking across the lake he took in the beautiful view his family had enjoyed for many years. His only regret was that they hadn't spent more time at the lake, but his family had always been busy with normal life situations. Coming up here two to three times each summer and the same each winter just wasn't enough. Still, he wanted to make it a point that he wouldn't let life get too busy to be able to enjoy it and unwind regularly.

Cole watched Marc go through his stretching exercises and pondered at the man his son had become. He'd always been proud of his son. The decisions he'd made and the actions he'd taken during his teen and young adult years had been very mature for his age. The concerns that he'd had on his mind throughout the week had been taking their toll on him, but he thought he'd done a fairly good job of masking them. Leave it to his son to notice.

A few minutes into his jog Marc picked up his pace, perhaps to ward off the concern he was still feeling about his dad. Somehow he needed to find a way to get his dad to talk to him before the week came to an end.

Cole wandered into the living room, picked up a magazine, and glanced outside again in time to see his son jogging further and further down the beach. As he turned toward the sofa he let out a long sigh. 'I'll tell him later today.'

§

Friday turned out to be a day for everyone to just relax and do whatever they wanted. It had been a full and busy week and everyone had certainly enjoyed themselves. They'd be packing up early the next morning and leaving for home, but this last day at the lake together they could just kick back.

After breakfast Marc and Jenny decided to go for a ride. They started out heading to the north shore. There was one shop there that featured gifts and souvenirs from all over Europe, but they specialized in gifts from Scandinavia. Marc had always loved going there from the time his family first started coming to the lake when he and Alexa were children. That morning he introduced Jenny to his Norwegian heritage and afterwards they headed down the east shore of the lake and stopped for lunch at a deli near Stateline.

As they sat down at a table on the patio overlooking the lake Marc adjusted the umbrella to keep them in the shade while they ate.

"I talked with my dad this morning," Marc said. "Well, at least I tried."

"About what's been bothering him this week?"

"Yeah, but he wouldn't say very much. He said he was fine, but I could tell something is on his mind."

"Have you said anything to your mom?"

"Not since the other day when we were both surprised by his outburst. Hopefully I can pull him aside after dinner this evening and try again."

The rest of their lunch time was spent talking about their plans for the rest of the summer, including the possibility of throwing a going away party for Alexa.

They finished their lunch and headed out in search of a few more gift shops before finally heading back up the west side of the lake.

§

Marc finally managed to get his dad away from everyone else after dinner and went for a walk along the lake. "Marc, I can't help feeling like there's something that's going to happen," Cole was trying his best to explain. "I don't know why I've been feeling this way, or what it might be, but it keeps coming and going."

"How long have you been feeling it, dad?"

"Oh, I guess off and on for a couple of months, but it's been getting more intense lately."

"Are you feeling okay, dad? Any problems with your health, like your heart?"

"No, I'm fine. Just had my annual check-up and everything's in great shape, especially my heart."

"Good."

"Anyway, because of these feelings, I feel a need to ask you a favor."

"Sure, dad, anything."

"If, and that's a *big* if, anything happens to me, or me and your mom ... I'm sure you'd do this anyway, but just the same, I need you to promise me that you'll look after Alexa."

"Of course, dad, but nothing's going to happen to you or mom, okay?"

"Well, I hope not, but ..." Cole didn't finish his thought.

"Dad ... no matter what, I'll be there for Alexa. I promise."

'Thank you, son. I love you."

"I love you too, dad."

They shared a strong father-son hug and then headed back to the house.

CHAPTER 20

Alexa

THE FIRST OF JULY rolled around and over dinner Cole and Roni announced they were heading up to the lake house in the morning to enjoy the 4th of July festivities and would be staying for the week.

"This is probably the first time in a long time that just the two of you have managed to get away and head up to the lake, isn't it?" Marc asked.

"Just about, son," Cole replied.

"Wish I could go," Alexa said wistfully. "I just love it up there!"

"Well, I'm sure we'll all be able to go again before you head off to college," Roni replied.

"Good! I'm sure I'm going to need it before college life hits me square between the eyes."

"It's not as bad as you might think, Alexa," Marc added. "Sure, there's a lot more work than what you were accustomed to in high school, but I know you're up for it. You'll do great!"

Alexa had always been so grateful for Marc's enthusiastic optimism.

The rest of their dinnertime was spent chatting about Alexa's plans for after she arrived in Nashville. In just seven weeks she would be settled into her dorm room, getting to know her new roommate, and ready to start on the next journey in her life. But for now, this evening, she was happy to be with her family.

After dinner Marc and Alexa left to pick up Jenny, and the three of them headed to the County Fair. They knew that for a Saturday night it would be packed, especially because of the nice weather. However, it would still be better than showing up on the 4th when the crowds were always unbearable and the temperature traditionally scorching.

They spent the evening walking along the midway, playing games, munching on snacks, sitting in on a free twilight concert in the amphitheater and then walking along the midway again before heading home. Marc and Jenny were going to go out for ice cream afterwards and Marc asked Alexa if she'd like to join them but she declined, saying that she was really tired, and asked her brother to just drop her off at home. Marc and Jenny then headed to Fentons in Oakland for ice cream sundaes and then went for a drive and ended up in a spot in the Oakland hills that looked out over the lights of the Bay Area. In spite of all of the bright lights below them, they were still able to see plenty of stars in the moonless night.

A night like this, in a place like this, was made for spending together, and for Marc and Jenny the night was still young.

§

The next morning Cole had just finished packing the car when Marc pulled in next to him on the driveway. Even though he'd been out quite late the night before Marc had come over early to have breakfast with his family before his parents left.

"Mornin', dad!" Marc called out as he got out of his car.

"Good morning, son! You're up early for a Sunday morning."

"Didn't want to miss seeing you and mom before you guys left."

"Well, thanks, son. We appreciate that."

"Looks like the weather is going to be perfect for the drive up there."

"And for the whole week," Cole added. "Hey, son, do you remember what we talked about up at the lake last month?"

"Yeah, dad. Do you still have that unsettled feeling?"

"It comes and goes. I try to ignore it because it just doesn't make any sense."

"Have you said anything to mom about it yet?"

"No, I don't want to worry her. I'm sure it's nothing and I'll get past it soon."

"Yeah, I'm sure it is too."

"Hey, you two good looking men," Roni called from the front porch, "breakfast is just about ready!"

"Thanks, mom, we'll be right in!" Marc replied with a wave and a smile.

"Just relax and have a great time up there, dad."

"Thanks, we will."

"I mean you specifically."

"Okay, son, I promise I will," Cole replied, putting his arm around Marc's shoulders as they walked to the house.

"Mornin', mom!" Marc said as he walked into the kitchen.

"Good morning, son! I'm glad you could join us."

"Sure! It's so nice out this morning, is there any chance we can eat out on the patio or in the gazebo?"

"I don't see why not. Would you let Alexa know we're almost ready?"

"Okay, be right back."

"Alexa's not up yet?" Cole asked.

"Not yet," Roni replied.

"Hmmm, she's always up and about by now. I wonder what's up."

Marc tapped on Alexa's bedroom door but heard no response. He waited another few moments before trying again.

"Alexa?"

"Yeah," she replied groggily.

"Mom asked me to let you know that breakfast is about ready."

"Thanks. I'll be out soon," she responded with little emotion.

"You okay, sis?"

"Yeah."

"Are you sure?"

"Yes, Marc. I'm fine. I'll be out in a minute, okay?"

"Sure. I'll let mom know." Marc walked off without any further response from his sister.

"Not sure what's up with Alexa, mom, but she sure seems grumpy this morning."

"Hmm, that's unusual. She's always so upbeat, and usually up before the sun. Maybe she ate too many hotdogs at the fair last night," Roni commented with a smile, knowing full well how conscientious Alexa was about her diet.

"All I know is we asked Alexa if she wanted to join Jenny and me for some ice cream afterward and she said she was getting kinda tired. She asked if we could just take her home, so we dropped her off. Then Jenny and I drove to Fentons to meet up with some friends we'd met at the fair."

"Oh, honey!" Roni exclaimed to Cole, "We haven't been to Fentons in *too* long!"

"Okay, we'll go next week after we get home from the lake."

"I'll hold you to that, big guy," Roni said teasingly.

"I'd rather you'd just hold me, babe," Cole replied with a certain look in his eyes and Roni turned and leaned into Cole's arms and planted a kiss on his lips.

"AHEM! Hey, you two!" and they all had a good laugh.

"What's so funny?" Alexa asked as she slowly walked into the kitchen, still looking sleepy.

"Good morning, sunshine!" Roni exclaimed as she walked over and gave Alexa a hug which was barely returned.

"Hey, are you okay, sweetie?"

"Yeah, just tired, I guess."

"Okay, well your timing is great because breakfast is ready. We're eating outside because the weather is so gorgeous this morning!"

Everyone pitched in to carry the food and dishes out to the patio, and Cole went back in and turned on the stereo for some relaxing Sunday morning background music.

Cole offered a blessing on the food and the serving trays were passed around. The conversation was upbeat, although Alexa remained subdued. They mostly talked about the trip to the lake, along with how Marc's job at the golf course was going and Alexa's preparation for college.

"Hey, son, can I ask you to do something for me while we're gone?"

"Sure, dad. What's that?"

"Would you do me a favor and just check in on Alexa once or twice—"

"DADDY! I'm NOT a little girl!" Alexa exclaimed.

"I know you're not, honey, but just the same I'd like Marc to call you or drop by a couple of times just to make sure you're safe and all's well, okay?"

Alexa didn't immediately respond, but just sat there at the table looking perturbed.

"You're still my little girl, Alexa, and—"

"Daddy, I'm 18 years old. In a few weeks I'll be going off to college, not close by, but 2,000 miles away. Nobody can just drop by to see how I'm doing there."

"But, we can call you. In fact, I want to make sure we chat at least once a week, just to see how you're doing."

"Daddy ..." All Alexa could do was sigh.

"Honey, perhaps we could compromise?" her mom added.

"How so?" Alexa wondered.

"Well, maybe to begin with, just to make sure you're making a smooth adjustment we can chat with you once a week, or more if you'd like, and then we can ease it off to just a couple of times a month?"

Alexa thought about her mom's suggestion for a long moment. "I guess that's okay," she replied with a reserved sigh.

Not understanding where this particular attitude from his daughter was coming from Cole proceeded cautiously.

"So, honey, are you okay with Marc checking in with you while we're gone this week?"

Alexa sighed again. "I guess so. Yeah, that's fine, daddy," she replied, still with less than her usual enthusiasm.

Roni was just about to say something more when Marc caught her eye and shook his head imperceptibly. She nodded in return to acknowledge she understood.

"Mom? Dad? May I please be excused?" Alexa softly asked.

"Sure, sweetie, but you haven't eaten very much. Are you okay?" her mom asked.

"Yeah, I guess I'm just tired. I didn't sleep very well last night. I had a strange dream that upset me."

"Do you want to talk about it?" her dad asked.

"No, I think I just want to go lie down on my bed for a few minutes. Promise me you'll let me know before you leave?"

"Sure, sweetheart," her dad replied. "You bet we will."

"Thanks," and with that she pushed her chair back, excused herself from the table, and headed to her room.

"Did everything go okay last night, Marc?" Roni asked after Alexa was out of ear shot.

"Yeah, we all had a fun time. I doubt that whatever's bothering her, if there is anything other than that dream, has anything to do with last night."

"Okay, just checking."

"Don't worry, dad, I've always watched out for her when you weren't around."

"I know, son, and I appreciate it."

"Honey," Roni gently interrupted, "what time did you say you'd like to leave for the lake?"

"I guess around 9:30 or so," Cole replied, looking at his watch. "Wow! It's almost 9 already? Well, there's no rush. Sometime between 9:30 and 10 is fine with me."

As they finished breakfast Marc helped his mom clear the table while Cole went inside to see if he could talk with Alexa. He was about to tap on her door when he was stunned to hear Alexa crying. He choked up and paused another moment. Finally, he tapped softly and waited.

Alexa thought she heard something in between her sobbing and held her breath for a moment. She heard someone tapping on her door.

"Who is it?" she asked weakly.

"Princess, it's dad. May I come in?"

"Just a minute."

"Sure, sweetheart."

Alexa sat up on her bed, reached for some tissues on her night stand and wiped away the tears. She couldn't wipe away the redness or the sadness in her eyes so she just resigned herself to letting her dad see her that way.

"Okay, daddy."

Cole eased open the door, unsure of what he'd see. "Princess? Honey, what's wrong?"

"I guess I'm just tired daddy, and I haven't had a good cry in a long time."

"But was there something that triggered it this time?"

"Oh, daddy!" With that Alexa burst into tears and ran to her dad's strong arms, burying herself deeply into his embrace.

Roni heard Alexa crying and ran up the stairs and down the hallway to her room, but Cole caught her attention and nodded that everything was okay. She stood in the doorway for another moment before backing away and walking downstairs to the kitchen.

Cole held Alexa firmly in his arms for several minutes letting her just cry it all out. As her sobbing began to subside she leaned back and noticed her dad's tear stained shirt.

"Oh, daddy, I'm so sorry."

"For what, Princess?"

"I messed up your shirt, and—"

"Sh-h-h-h, it's okay, sweetheart. It's easy enough to change," her dad softly reassured her.

It took Alexa a few more minutes to get her sobbing under control enough to be able to breathe almost normally again.

"Let's go sit down on your bed, okay?" Alexa nodded without replying.

"So, whatever it is, something seems to have upset you a lot, huh?"

Alexa half chuckled, "Yeah, you could say that." She inhaled quickly, then took a few more shallow breaths until she felt like her emotions were finally calmed down enough to talk about it.

She looked up from the tear soaked tissues in her hands and directly into her dad's eyes. "Daddy … I'm scared."

"Of what, sweetheart?"

"That's just it, I don't know."

"When did you start getting these feelings?"

"I don't know … maybe a week ago, I think?"

"Any idea what started it then?"

"Not really."

"Can you tell me anything about it?"

Alexa looked deeply into her dad's eyes and began to tear up again but courageously fought them back. Taking another deep breath she continued.

"Daddy, can I ask you something?"

"Anything, sweetheart, anything at all."

"Are you okay?"

"Pardon me?"

"Are you okay?" Alexa's eyes searched her father's for reassurance.

"I'm not sure I understand. If you're asking if my health is okay, yes, I'm fine. Why?"

All Alexa could do for a long moment was to keep looking deeply into her father's eyes, then she leaned into his arms and let out a gentle sigh. Cole just held her close in silence and wondered if his precious daughter was beginning to feel the same uneasiness he'd been feeling for a few months, a feeling that seemed to be increasing with each passing day. But why? Why had he been getting these feelings? And now, why Alexa?

"I really am fine, sweetheart."

"I know, daddy. I know. It's just—" and what she was trying to say just couldn't be said. The thought of it was just too horrible.

"May I ask you something?"

"Sure, daddy."

"Do you think that your going away to college might have anything to do with this? Perhaps the fear or anxiety of the unknown?"

"I don't know. Maybe."

"I know it's going to be a big adjustment for you, but I also know you're capable of handling it. Just try not to make too big of a deal out of it. Everything you're going to be facing can be handled just fine if you remember to just take it one step at a time. You don't have to tackle everything all at once. All of your preparation can be handled one day at a time, and once you get there the same rule applies … one day at a time. You'll have a roommate who will be just as scared and unsure of herself as you, so you can both tackle everything together. Okay?"

"Okay, daddy. Thanks."

"Does that help, at least a little?"

"Yeah, I think so."

"Good. Now, is there anything else you'd like to talk about?"

"No, that's fine, daddy. I know you and mom want to take off soon."

"That's not going to get in the way of my being here for you, princess. I'll stay here with you as long as you need or want me to."

"I know, and I appreciate it, but I think I'm fine now."

"You think?" Cole asked with a smile on his face.

"Okay, daddy, I *know* I'm fine."

"Are you sure?"

"YES, daddy, now go! Mom's waiting. Have a good time," she added jokingly, gently shoving her dad off the bed.

"Okay, okay, I'm going," Cole laughingly replied with raised hands, fending off her loving eviction from her bedroom.

Cole had taken a few steps toward the bedroom door when Alexa called to him. He stopped and turned, and Alexa ran into his arms, giving him a very loving hug.

"Thanks for caring, and thanks for loving me, daddy."

"Of course, Alexa. Remember, your mom loves you too, just as much if not more than I do. I'm not sure that's possible …" Cole said with a wink and a smile. They laughed and Alexa gave her dad a kiss on the cheek.

"I love you, daddy."

"I love you too, Alexa," he replied as he kissed her forehead.

This time as Alexa left her room she seemed back to her normal exuberant self. Almost.

§

Thirty minutes later Cole and Roni were ready to leave, and Marc and Alexa walked outside with them to say goodbye.

As Cole and Roni began to pull out of the driveway, everyone waved and exchanged their "I love you's".

"Just relax and have fun!" Marc called out.

"And be careful!" added Alexa.

"We will!" Roni replied as she blew them another kiss. "You guys be good and have fun, too!"

"We will!" Marc and Alexa replied in unison.

As the car headed up the street Alexa added under her breath, "Please ... be careful."

"What did you say, sis?" Marc asked.

"Nothing."

CHAPTER 21

Premonition

WITH THEIR PARENTS UP at their lake house for the week Marc kept busy with his job at the golf course, and Alexa kept making progress with her preparations for college. Jenny had helped her get a part-time job at the same restaurant where she'd worked for the last few summers, and they often worked the same shift.

Marc had called Alexa each day to briefly see how she was doing, and all was fine. Until Friday morning. He was just about to call her when his phone rang.

"Hello?"

"Marc?"

"Hey, sis! How's it going?" Marc asked in a cheerful voice.

"Oh, Marc …" Alexa replied in the midst of sobbing.

"Alexa! What's wrong?! What happened?!" All he could hear was his sister continuing to sob heavily.

"I'll be right there, sis!" His own fear rising.

"No, Marc," she interrupted. "No, don't."

"Alexa, what's the matter?"

"It's mom and dad …"

"What about them?"

"Something's wrong."

"What? Did they call you?"

"No. I ... I ... I had that horrible dream again."

"Again? What dream?"

"The same one I had on Sunday."

"What?"

"Remember Sunday morning when I wasn't doing so well?"

"Yeah."

"Well, I had that stupid dream again."

"What dream, Alexa?"

"Oh, yeah, that's right, I was too upset to tell anyone about it that morning." Alexa sighed heavily and shuddered just thinking about having to talk about it.

"Please don't think I'm crazy, okay?"

"Sis, I love you. Whatever it is, you can tell me."

"Something's happened to them."

"Who, mom and dad?"

"Yeah."

"What happened?"

"Marc ... I don't know how ... but they're ..... "

"Alexa, calm down. Calm ... down. First off, it was just a bad dream. Second, we can solve this by just calling them. Do you want to do that or should I."

"Would you? I'm too afraid they won't answer ... because they can't."

"Alexa, *please* calm down. It was only a bad dream, nothing more."

"Then why do I keep having this stupid dream?!"

"I don't know, but you'll feel a whole lot better after you talk to them."

"Me? I thought you were going to call them."

"I changed my mind. You need to hear for yourself that they're just fine."

"But—"

"Alexa?"

"Yeah ... I know."

"Call them now, okay? And then call me back."

Alexa sighed. "Okay, bro. Thanks. I love you."

"Love you too, sis. Are you calling them now?"

"Yes, yes! As soon as you hang up."

"Hanging up!"

Alexa set the phone back down on the night stand and looked for her address book for the phone number of the lake house, her hands still trembling. She found the number, dialed and waited for what seemed like hours for the phone to ring the first time. Second ring. Third ring. Fourth! Panic was definitely setting in.

"Come on! Pick up!"

Fifth ring.

"COME ON!!!!!" she yelled!

"Hello?"

"DADDY?!"

"Alexa?

"YES! DADDY!"

"Honey, are you okay? Why are you yelling?" His questions were answered with the sound of sobbing.

"Sweetheart, who is it?" Roni asked as she came in from the deck.

"It's Alexa. She's upset about something."

"Let me talk to her, okay?" she asked as she reached for the phone. Cole handed her the phone and sat down on the nearby love seat.

"Sweetie, it's mom, are you okay?"

"MOM!"

"Honey, what's wrong? Did something happen?"

"No … are you guys … okay?"

"We're fine, honey. Why? What's wrong?"

"I had a horrible dream that something had happened to you and dad, and I've had it more than once recently. Why, mom? Why am I having this dream?"

"I don't know, sweetheart. Listen, dad and I were going to come home tomorrow, but would you rather we come home today instead?"

Alexa thought about it for a long time as she tried to calm down. "No, I don't think so. I'll be fine."

"We love you, Alexa. We'll be home tomorrow evening around dinner time and we'll take you out to dinner, okay?"

"Okay, that sounds good. Love you, mom, and tell dad I love him, too."

"I'll let you tell him yourself, he's right here," Roni replied as she handed the phone back to Cole.

"Princess?"

"Hi, daddy."

"Are you okay, sweetheart?"

"Yeah, I am now. I just needed to hear your voices to know that you're okay."

"Yeah, we're fine. And we'll see you tomorrow, okay?"

"Okay. Miss you. I can't wait to see you guys."

"We miss you too, Alexa. Love you!"

"Love you, too, daddy."

As Alexa hung up the phone she fell back onto her bed and just lay there staring at the ceiling. Her heart, which at one point had been pounding so hard she thought it would burst, was calming down. Her breathing was returning to normal, and she thought about how grateful she was to have been able to talk with them. She didn't want to even think about what she would do if she lost them.

As she sat back up she remembered she'd promised to call Marc.

"Hello?"

"They're safe, Marc," Alexa replied with a sigh of relief in her voice.

"See, I knew it. I'm glad you called them."

"Yeah, me too. Thanks for listening, Marc."

"Hey, what are big brothers for, right?"

"To be there for their little sisters."

"Always have been, always will be. Hey, how about if Jenny and I come over after I get off work this evening and we'll hang out, just the three of us?"

"Yeah, I'd like that."

"Okay, sis. See you around 6:30?"

"That'll be fine. See you then. And Marc?"

"Yeah?"

"Thanks. And I love you."

"I love you too, sis. See ya tonight."

"Bye."

CHAPTER 22

The Visitor

MARC HEADED RIGHT HOME after work to get cleaned up, and then left to pick up Jenny. He'd called Alexa that afternoon and offered to pick up pizzas and sodas for dinner, and despite the heavy commute traffic, he'd managed to time everything so that they arrived at 6:30 sharp.

"Wow, right on time, bro! I'm impressed!"

"Why, I'm usually on time, aren't I?"

"Yes, but I heard about the accident on the freeway and figured you'd probably been caught behind it."

"I know some short cuts so I took an off ramp, worked my way through the city, and got home about the time I normally do. After that it was just a breeze to pick up Jenny and the pizzas."

"Good! Well, let's eat, cuz I'm *starving!*"

"Me too," Jenny added.

They were sitting comfortably in the living room and about half way through dinner when the doorbell rang. Marc looked out the window as he crossed the living room and noticed an Alameda County Sheriff's car parked in front of the house.

"Hey, any of you have any unpaid parking tickets?" Marc asked jokingly.

"No, why?" Jenny asked.

"Because the Sheriff's here to haul someone away," he added with a sly smirk.

"Good evening, I'm sorry to disturb you this evening. I'm Deputy Higgins with the Alameda County Sheriff's office."

"Hi, what can I do for you, Deputy Higgins?"

"Is this the Janssen residence?"

"Sure is."

"May I come in for a moment?"

"Sure." Marc stepped back and held the door open for the deputy as he stepped into the living room. Alexa gasped, which caught Marc's attention. He gave a slight wave to her to signal not to worry.

"Thank you."

"How can I help you, Deputy?" Marc asked as he closed the door behind him. Jenny and Alexa looked on anxiously.

"Mr. Janssen—"

"Oh, you can call me Marc. Mr. Janssen is my dad." He responded nervously, trying to keep the atmosphere light. He sensed by the tone of the deputy's voice, though, that this might be a serious visit, especially since he asked to step inside.

"Okay. Well then, Marc, our office received a phone call a little while ago and I was asked to come by and see you."

"A phone call? From whom? What was it about?" Marc's curiosity was now certainly getting the better of him. He knew he didn't have any outstanding tickets.

"The call was from the California Highway Patrol—"

"No! No, no, no!" Alexa exclaimed and burst into tears. Jenny immediately was by her side and holding her.

"I'm sorry to have to tell you this, Mr. Janssen, but … your parents—"

"NO!!!!" Alexa screamed again and continued crying uncontrollably.

Marc looked into the deputy's eyes, searching for anything other than what he was almost certain he was about to hear.

"Your parents were killed in a single car auto accident late this afternoon."

"Oh, NO! Oh, ... no-o-o-o-o, no, no, no!" he repeated over and over, as he felt his legs start to give out. The deputy noticed and helped him into a nearby chair, and glanced over toward Jenny and Alexa. In his nearly 27 years on the force he'd only had to make a call like this a few times. It was always so hard on him to share tragic news like this. It never got any easier because there are just no words he could think of to comfort the families at a moment like this.

"I just talked with them this morning," Alexa said amidst her crying into Jenny's shoulder.

Marc just looked at the deputy with a blank stare, disbelieving what he'd just heard.

"There must be some mistake. Please, there *has* to be some mistake," Marc pleaded.

"I'm sorry, Marc, there's no mistake."

"But ... how? Does anyone know what happened?"

"Well, witnesses described the car braking suddenly and swerving to the right, flipping over a couple of times when it hit a roadside ditch, and then crashing into a tree all to avoid a deer that had suddenly jumped into the road. They ran to the car to see if they could help, but it appeared like your parents were killed on impact. This was later confirmed by the paramedics."

No one knew what to say, they just sat there in disbelief, crying.

The deputy reached into his shirt pocket for his card and handed it to Marc. "If you need or want to you can reach me at this number. I've also written down the number for the Highway Patrol on the back, since you'll probably want to contact them as well."

"Thank you," Marc replied awkwardly, his hand shaking as he accepted the card. He willed enough strength into his legs to stand up and open the door for the deputy.

"Once again, Marc, I'm really so very sorry."

"I know. I appreciate it. This is ... probably one of the toughest parts of your job, right?"

"One of the worst, if not *the* worst."

Marc couldn't find any more words to say so he just half-heartedly waved as the deputy walked toward the driveway.

After closing the door he turned toward Alexa and Jenny who were both already rushing to him. He opened his arms wide and held them both as they all cried together.

"I *knew* it!" Alexa exclaimed amid her tears.

"So did dad," Marc replied softly.

"What?" Alexa asked, not sure if she heard her brother correctly.

"Dad knew," Marc replied in almost a whisper.

"What are you talking about, Marc?" Alexa questioned as she pulled back from his arm. "Dad knew what?"

"Remember when we were up at the lake after your graduation, and that time on the deck early in the week when he was pretty uptight?"

"Yeah, what about it?"

"I was finally able to talk to him about it at the end of the week and—"

"You never told me about it! What did he say?" Alexa demanded.

"He said he felt something was going to happen. He didn't know what, and he didn't know when, but he just felt very unsettled about everything."

"How long had he felt that way?" Alexa demanded, still stunned by Marc's revelation.

"Off and on for a couple of months."

"WHAT?!" Alexa was finding it nearly impossible to comprehend these revelations.

"He said he tried to ignore it hoping it would just pass, but it just wouldn't go away. He tried to downplay it with me, but I'd never seen him so concerned about anything like this before in my life, so I think he was really tormented by it."

"Did he at least tell mom about it?"

"I doubt it. At least, not that I'm aware of. He told me he didn't want to say anything to anyone, mostly because he didn't understand it himself, but also because he didn't want to worry anyone unnecessarily."

"Then ... how did you get him to tell you?"

"He knew I was aware that something was up. Plus, he asked me to do him a favor."

"What kind of favor?"

Marc paused for a moment before continuing. "He told me that he had this feeling that something might happen to either him or both he and mom, and if it did he asked me to take care of you."

Alexa fell back into Marc's shoulder and just cried as he held her and Jenny close. "What are we going to do, Marc?"

"I don't know, sis, but we'll figure it out."

"I want to help in any way I can, sweetheart. Anything at all," Jenny added.

Marc looked into Jenny's eyes but couldn't say anything. He just held her tighter. Suddenly, his head began to throb with a headache the likes of which he'd rarely felt since just after his accident.

'No!' he thought to himself. 'Not now!'

CHAPTER 23

A Quiet Day

THE SERVICE HAD BEEN simple, but beautiful. The chapel was packed, as well as most of the available overflow. The eulogy and other comments shared during the service, along with the poignant music selected by Alexa and Marc, made it a special celebration of Cole's and Roni's lives, individually and together.

The day was sunny and clear, but unusually comfortable and cool for mid-July. The setting was peaceful in the shade of the sprawling oak tree as they were laid to rest next to each other on a hillside, with a serene view of San Francisco Bay.

Jenny's parents, Tony & Adele, had coordinated a get together at the Janssen's home, and family and friends comfortably, but solemnly, mulled around for a few hours sharing fond memories. Eventually they began to leave and Marc and Alexa graciously thanked each person individually for coming. They had actively mingled with their guests throughout the get together, making everyone feel as much a part of their family as they could. Their appreciation, love, and gratitude seemed boundless, but it was clear to those who knew them best that they were still incredibly overwhelmed with grief.

After the last guest had gone Marc and Alexa were joined by Jenny and her parents as they sat around the living room, exhausted.

"Alexa and I would like to thank you for all of the love and incredible support you've given us over these last several days."

"Oh, Marc," Adele began, "you and Alexa are just like family to us. How could we not help you two out through everything?"

Marc just nodded as Alexa dabbed her eyes with a tissue.

"Just the same, we couldn't have done any of this without you."

"If you need any help with anything, Marc," Tony added, "please don't hesitate to let us know, okay?"

"Fair enough. I may have my work cut out for me in going through my parents important papers, but they were both pretty organized so I'm hoping it won't take me too long. I've already spoken with our attorney and we have an appointment to meet with her on Friday."

"Her?" Tony asked. "I thought Dean King was your attorney. Your dad always spoke so highly of him, though I'd have to admit we haven't talked about any legal matters in a couple of years."

"Yes, Dean was our attorney for as long as I can remember, but he retired last year and his daughter, Samantha, is head of the firm now."

"That's good, very good," Tony replied with an agreeable nod. "Well, if she's anything like her father I'm sure you're in good hands."

"Thanks, we are."

"Well, listen, Tony and I should be going," Adele said with a gentle sigh, "but please call us with anything you need, okay?"

"Thanks, Mrs. Kincaid," Alexa replied, giving her a loving hug just before they left.

As Jenny's parents drove away she turned to look at Marc and Alexa and ran into their waiting arms. They'd been through so much together over the last few years, and now this. The special bond between the three of them seemed absolutely unbreakable.

"Okay … what now?" Alexa asked through her tears.

With a distant and somber look in his eyes Marc held the two young ladies in his arms. "We find a way to keep going."

§

By the end of the following week most of the legal and financial matters regarding the estate had at least been initially dealt with. The home and the lake house were left to both Marc and Alexa to share equally. As executor of the estate Marc had asked Alexa to join him when they met with their attorney and accountant, even though she quite comfortably deferred to his counsel and wisdom regarding how to handle all of these matters both now and in the future.

A copy of the report from the Highway Patrol, which Marc had requested, had also arrived and confirmed the witness's reports that their parents had swerved to miss a deer; their deaths had been instantaneous. As horrific as those few seconds must have been for them, he was grateful that they hadn't suffered.

With Alexa going off to college in a month Marc considered giving up his apartment and moving back home, though he wasn't sure how he would handle the emotional vacuum. It was one thing to have to deal with his parents being gone, but how would he deal with the expectations of seeing his parents at various places throughout the only home he'd ever known?

Cole and Roni had handled their investments wisely and conservatively and over the years these investments had made them quite wealthy, although they were never ones to show off that wealth through material possessions. They enjoyed living in a nice home in a safe middle-class neighborhood, though certainly not living a spartan life. They could have easily afforded to move to one of the many upscale areas anywhere in the Bay Area, but they were comfortable where they were, they liked their neighbors, and enjoyed living a more comfortable, relaxed lifestyle that keeping things simple allowed.

Living in the home he grew up in would offer some level of comfort, but without his parents? Well, he'd deal with that when the time came. Sure, it was certainly much larger than what he needed to live in alone, but Alexa needed a home, their home, to come home to on her breaks from college. There was just no way he would even consider the possibility of selling their home, at least not for the next few years.

CHAPTER 24

Moving On

As ALEXA WAS PUTTING the final touches on her packing for college, making those hard decisions of what to take and what to leave behind, she thought about how upsettingly surreal her summer had been; from the elation of graduating from high school and enjoying the family trip to Lake Tahoe, through the devastation of her and Marc losing their parents and dealing with the aftermath.

Now, just a few days away from leaving for Nashville, she sat on her bed and cried because she was about to move on with another part of her life and wouldn't have her parents to help her along. Sure, as always, Marc would be there to help, but it just wasn't the same. Now more than ever, though, she was committed to make her parents proud. They might not be around to cheer her on and smile at each new accomplishment, or even to call when she needed their advice, but she knew they were smiling down on her from Heaven.

Alexa had always been close to God. She'd read her scriptures and said her prayers twice a day like her parents taught her, so her faith had brought her through the tragedy. She decided that she also needed to pack a few more things that hadn't been on her original list … some special things that had belonged to her parents that she could put in her dorm room to help her remember them by.

§

Marc had completed the difficult transition from his apartment to the house. It was so hard to think of it as a home because his parents would no longer be there to talk to, but Alexa was there, at least for a few more days, so there was still love at home. How he would deal with it after she headed off to college was anyone's guess.

Even though he was well-liked and had plenty of friends, he'd never been known as a party guy, so filling up the emptiness with non-stop noise was out of the question. Jenny, college, and his music had been his only real priorities beyond his family, but Alexa was now equally a priority that he was very willing to accept. He considered himself lucky that the two of them had always been close as brother and sister, and now that it was just the two of them they were already beginning to draw even closer. A promise had been made and a promise would be kept ... he would always be there for her, no matter what.

CHAPTER 25

Nineteen Months Later

IT WAS ONLY MARCH, but the unusually warm spring-like weather made it seem more like April or May as Marc jumped in his car and drove off with his windows down and music playing. It felt more like a day to head to the beach than to sit inside and listen to professors talk about history, literature, or econ, so instead of heading in the direction of the college he headed off in the other direction, toward Jenny's apartment. She didn't have an 8 a.m. class like Marc, but she was always up early for her morning jog.

Marc knew the route she usually ran, and just by a nice coincidence he noticed her up ahead as he slowed down for a stop sign. It was a quiet neighborhood so as he pulled up from behind, he shifted his car into neutral and revved his engine a bit to get her attention but not loud enough to scare her or bother the neighbors. Jenny slowed down and ran in place to keep her pace going as he stopped, put the car in park, and got out. Even with perspiration on her face and running down her back she was incredibly attractive. He knew he was *so* lucky!

"Hey, good lookin'! What are you doing here? Don't you have Dr. Harris' class at 8?"

"Not today!"

"How come?"

"Haven't you noticed? It's too beautiful this morning to be cooped up in his class! Besides, I'm already acing the course anyway, so it won't matter if I skip his class and all my others today," he replied with his famous Cheshire cat smile.

"And just what do you have in mind, Mr. Dean's List?"

"It's a surprise! How soon can you be ready?"

"What?! Ready? For what? Have you forgotten I still have classes today?"

"Oh, I guess you didn't get the memo."

"And what memo is that?" Jenny asked coyly.

"The one that said your hunk of a boyfriend was coming by this morning to sweep you off your feet and take you for a special ride."

"No, I guess I missed that one. But if, as you say, my 'hunk of a boyfriend is coming by to sweep me off my feet', then you better get out of here before he shows up, because he's likely to get jealous and want to start something with you, and knowing him like I do it won't be pretty, because he's also very good at finishing things he starts," Jenny replied as she shot him a teasing smile.

"O-o-o-o-o, you are SO going to get it!" Marc slyly snapped back.

"O-o-o-o-o," Jenny teased back, "is that a promise?" And with that Jenny took off running for her apartment again with Marc hot on her trail.

"Oh, sweetie," Jenny said over her shoulder, "aren't you forgetting something?"

"Like what?" Marc asked as he caught up to her.

"You left your engine running, and if you leave it there like that and my boyfriend shows up he's likely to grab the keys and throw them down into the river."

"I swear, Jenny, sometimes you can be so, so ..." Marc replied, breaking off his pace as Jenny continued on toward her apartment.

"So, what? Huh? Beautiful? Charming? Breathtaking? Irresistible?"

"All of the above ... plus maddening! Be ready in an hour, OK? I'll be back."

As Marc ran back toward his car Jenny called out, "What do I tell my boyfriend when he comes by?"

Turning and taking another long look at this beautiful young lady he'd been in love with for so long he shouted back, "I guess you're just going to have to tell him it's over, cuz I want you all to myself!"

Jenny flashed him an alluring smile just before she turned to run up the stairs toward her apartment. 'Yeah,' she thought to herself, 'I have him right where I want him!' She smiled gleefully at herself as she entered her apartment, locked the door, and headed for the shower. Whatever Marc had in mind she just knew it was going to be a *great* day!

§

The early morning drive through the hills near Jenny's apartment was incredible! Clear skies, the sun shining through the leaves of the tall, broad trees arching over the lanes, a light breeze, all four windows rolled down on Marc's classic '67 GTO, his replacement for his '66 Malibu which had been totaled in his accident, and Jenny's long, auburn hair was flowing in the breeze. Oh, yeah-h-h … the perfect start to a perfect day.

As Jenny rested her hand on his leg, she leaned teasingly toward him and with her sweet 'Please may I have a cookie?' little girl voice she asked, "So, Mr. Dean's List, where are you taking me on this breathtakingly *beautiful* morning?"

"Why do you keep calling me 'Mr. Dean's List'?"

Playfully pouting Jenny said, "Well, you *are*, aren't you? For as long as I've known you you've always done so well in your studies, so I just thought it would be kinda fun to call you Mr. Dean's List. Is that OK?"

"Yeah, I guess so," Marc replied, resigning himself to accept whatever nicknames Jenny wanted to give him, just as long as they weren't shared with anyone else.

"Now, back to my original question … where are you taking me on this breathtakingly *beautiful* morning?"

"Ah-h-h, wouldn't *you* like to know?"

"As a matter of fact, yes!"

"Sorry, but as I told you earlier, it's a surprise."

Not to allow Marc the chance to just put this line of questioning to rest she kept it up. "How about, while you drive, we play twenty questions, and we'll see if I can guess the correct answer?"

"And how about if we don't?"

"Aww, come on, sweetie. Why won't you play along? Afraid I might guess and spoil the whole surprise?"

"All I'll say is we're going somewhere you've wanted to go for a while, but we've both been kinda busy."

Jenny chuckled, "Now *there's* a clue! But … that could be a *lot* of places."

"Yeah, I know, so just sit back, enjoy the music and the ride, and we'll be there soon."

"Ah- HA! Another clue! Hmmm … soon, huh?"

"Guess all you want, I'm not saying anything else."

"Kill joy," Jenny replied, giving Marc a gentle jab in the ribs.

"Hey, I can always turn around and take you back home."

"You *could* … but I know you won't."

"Oh, yeah? And just how do you know that?"

"Because I'm so beautiful and irresistible. And besides, if you took me home right now I'd be sad, and I'd cry, and—"

"All right! All right! You win."

"So you'll tell me?"

"No."

"WHAT?!" Jenny exclaimed and leaned back in her seat, crossed her arms and stuck out her lower lip in a playful little girl pout.

"I promise it will be worth it."

"It *better* be!"

Marc kept her guessing for a few more minutes while they made their way through Oakland on the MacArthur Freeway, approaching the interchange that could take them in one of two directions, north through Berkeley, or west to San Francisco. Jenny closed her eyes in anticipation, waiting for the movement of the car to give her a clue.

"YES!" she exclaimed, as she felt the car drift into the turn for San Francisco. She opened her eyes, looked at Marc with a big smile, and leaned over and gave him a big kiss on his cheek.

"Thank you, sweetheart! Yeah, this is going to be a *great* day!"

Over the next few hours Marc and Jenny enjoyed the beautiful weather while exploring shops along Pier 39 and Fisherman's Wharf, then headed west to more of Jenny's favorites, The Cannery and Ghirardelli Square.

They were having so much fun they hadn't noticed how hungry they were getting until it hit them both as they were walking past the Ghirardelli Chocolate Manufactory. They fought off the temptation of having dessert before lunch and opted for deli sandwiches and sodas from a nearby deli, then headed across the street to San Francisco Maritime Park where they relaxed and enjoyed their lunch in the cool shade of a tree.

"I want to ride on a cable car!" Jenny said with a smile of joyful anticipation.

"Sure! This day is all yours, babe!"

Marc's easy willingness made Jenny pause in her thoughts as she looked deeply into his eyes. She set her sandwich down on the wrapper, leaned toward Marc and tenderly placed the palms of her hands on his cheeks.

"Marc Channing Janssen, I love *so* much!"

"I love you too, Jenny." They shared a brief, but tender kiss. As their lips parted they looked deeply into each other's eyes and felt their unspoken love and desires. They sighed together, and then laughed. So much love ... so much to live for! They were just perfect together!

They finished their lunches and hopped on the next cable car which took them directly into downtown. They'd done enough little shop hopping during the morning so they decided to just take the cable car back, jump in their car and drive down the coast on Highway 1. By late afternoon they were pulling into Santa Cruz and headed to the Boardwalk. Since it was still March the rides weren't running, but the arcades were open so they spent some time there before walking out onto the pier.

After such a beautiful morning in the City a more typical weather front for March was moving quickly into shore – clouds and a chilly breeze. Because the weather had been *so* beautiful that morning they hadn't bothered to bring sweaters or windbreakers, so they didn't stay out on the pier for long. By the time they made their way back to their car Jenny's teeth were chattering in spite of Marc holding her close to try to get her warm. They quickly jumped into the car and Marc started it up and cranked on the heat.

"Who would've thought we'd need this when we left this morning!" Marc exclaimed.

"I know," Jenny replied, shivering.

The car was soon warm enough that they could relax a bit, and they began their trek home through the Santa Cruz Mountains. When they finally made it to Silicon Valley they were grateful to be behind the evening commute because hunger was urging them to stop.

"I know just the place," Marc said, with a wistful look in his eyes. "It's been a while since we've been there. Too long, as a matter of fact, but it's the perfect way to end this perfect day."

"Wherever you want, sweetheart," Jenny replied. "I'm with you, anywhere you want to take me."

"You know that could mean a few different things," Marc answered teasingly.

"I know, but just behave yourself, mister."

"Just sayin'." Marc smiled and then put his eyes back on the road. Next stop, their favorite pizza place.

§

Before dropping Jenny off at her apartment that night they took one final drive up into the Oakland hills to enjoy the lights of the city below. In spite of the fog that had rolled in, the view was still beautiful. Or, did it just seem that way because they were so much in love?

CHAPTER 26

Storm Front

ALEXA WAS HAVING THE time of her life. Her first year at Belmont University had been amazing, she'd made many friends, her grades, as usual, were great, and she was also enjoying the night life around Nashville, particularly with her roommate, Lacy.

The scholarships she'd earned allowed her to focus her time on her studies and her music, so as soon as her classes were over each day she'd head straight to the library or her apartment to get her studies done allowing her as much time as possible each evening for her music. The time was either spent at home writing and practicing, or participating in one of the many songwriter open mics going on around town.

She'd spent the better part of her freshman year just getting to know her way around town, developing a sense of which places she enjoyed playing at the most and which ones she preferred to shy away from, usually because of the type of crowds that would be there.

The Bluebird Café was, by far, her favorite place to hang out with her friends. There were always such great shows with the "songwriters behind the hits", and she dreamed of someday playing there regularly, right along with some of her favorites.

She knew it would take time and a lot of effort to pay her dues in Music City. An overnight success was typically defined as someone who'd spent about ten years in the business, always improving their craft along with constantly strengthening and increasing their circle of contacts. Networking was a vital key for anyone who dreamed of making it in the business.

But having talent and the "right" contacts wasn't enough for Alexa. She was determined to live her life in a way that would make her parents and her brother proud of her, no matter how much or how little success she attained.

Oh, if only her parents could see her now, though in a way she just knew they could. She felt their presence around her often. She remembered something Jenny had told her, about when she'd visited her grandmother just before she passed away early the previous spring. She said her grandmother had spoken often about the "thin heavenly veil" that separated her from her late husband, Peter. At the end she acknowledged that she'd had a wonderful life, but that she was now ready to pass through that veil so she could once again be reunited with her "Sweet Pete", as she loved to call him. Jenny was sure it had been a wonderful and joyous reunion!

Alexa felt the same way about her parents. She missed them dearly, and wished they were still alive so they could come visit her from time to time and see how much fun she was having with her music! She played regularly around town and was becoming fairly well known and it showed in the number of engagements filling up her calendar.

She'd even had a few 'producers' approach her about 'helping her' with her career. Each had claimed that they could do 'x' for her, gave her their card, and said 'call me tomorrow.' 'What do they do here in Music City?' she wondered, 'clone these guys?' Alexa knew to be wary of people like this thanks to Marc. She took her brother's advice and did her research on these guys just to make sure they were legit. The ones who'd already approached her weren't. She wasn't disappointed, simply relieved. She knew, and had faith, that when it was her time the right person would come along and make her an honest offer.

Alexa felt that her dream shot as a singer/songwriter was coming closer every day and she could hardly wait! She'd auditioned at the famous Bluebird Café one Sunday and was so well received that she was invited back several times, and was finally placed on a mid-week schedule to perform 'in the round' at an upcoming 6 p.m. show. She realized that being invited to play 'in the round' at the Bluebird was a huge step for her and her budding career.

In the meantime, she was looking forward to a co-writing session with her friend and roommate, Lacy, another singer/songwriter she'd met in one of her classes at Belmont during their freshman year. They'd become such good friends that they decided to share an apartment when summer arrived. All summer long it was a popular hangout for their music friends, with regular Saturday afternoon barbecues and guitar pulls.

Lacy and Alexa made the perfect roommates. Their personalities and interests matched, they were the same size, a slender 6, and height, 5' 9", so they could share all of their clothes, and they also shared many of the same classes as they both had their sights on careers in music. Whether they sang alone or as a duo at open mics, their voices were like those of angels. And wherever they went they nearly always went together.

On that particular day, though, Lacy had taken off for her parent's home about 30 miles south of Nashville in Spring Hill right after her last class of the day. She wanted to help her mom with the plans for her dad's surprise birthday party coming up in a few days. She'd invited Alexa to join them for dinner, and then spend the evening writing. It was a good thing that neither of them had early morning classes the next day because with the storm that was due that evening they had decided earlier in the day that they'd spend the night at Lacy's and then head back into Nashville in the morning in time for their first classes.

Alexa finished her homework, slipped her songwriting notebook and wallet into her backpack, grabbed her windbreaker and car keys and headed out. No sooner had she stepped out of her apartment than she was hit by a chill wind. Looking at the sky she noticed dark and ominous clouds approaching from the west and decided she better bring along her umbrella, because this fast moving storm system appeared unlike any other she'd ever seen. As she approached her car she remembered hearing something on the radio as she was eating breakfast that morning about a big thunderstorm coming to the area later that night, but she thought it would be much later. Now it looked as if it might even start before she reached Lacy's parents' home. Intuition told her she needed to go back into the apartment and call Lacy and let her know she might be a little late for dinner because of the storm and potential traffic tie-ups. Lacy thanked her and reminded her to drive carefully.

As Alexa made her way down Wedgewood Avenue toward I-65, the sky went black and began to unload. 'Fortunately,' Alexa thought, 'I'm heading out before most of the commute starts so hopefully traffic won't be too heavy,' but before she'd even gotten to the freeway her windshield wipers were at full speed. She knew then that commute traffic or not, she would be in for a tough drive.

Entering the freeway cautiously, along with a long line of cars ahead and behind her, it took her a while to find her place in the flow of traffic and get to a decent speed, which, at this point, was completely dictated by the weather. Forget the speed limit – no one would even come close to it in a downpour like this. All she hoped for now was for her fellow travelers to drive sanely. If they did, she thought she might just make it to Lacy's on time for dinner.

The rain was relentless and Alexa's wipers strained mightily to keep up, but at times they were unable. She soon realized that other drivers must be having the same problem because their speed was diminishing ... 45 ... 40 ... 35. 'At this rate I'll definitely be late,' she thought. A few minutes later the rain let up a bit and the speed gradually increased ... 40 ... 45 ... 'Okay, that's a little better.' Perhaps she'd make it on time after all.

The drive down I-65 from Nashville through Brentwood and Franklin continued pretty much the same way. The rain, along with some occasional sleet blown by a powerful wind, pelted them from every direction, then let up, back and forth. So far Alexa had seen a couple of accidents on the other side of the freeway, but none on her side. However, she still had another ten to fifteen miles to go before her turnoff. Anything was possible.

Finally, Alexa could tell that the rain must be letting up a bit because her wipers weren't straining to keep up with the downpour. She was grateful that Lacy's boyfriend, Terry, had been kind enough to replace both Lacy's and her wipers two weeks earlier.

So far the new blades had held up in spite of the incredible downpour she'd been in for the last … oh, my gosh! An hour? Yep, she'd be late. She glanced out the windshield, and in spite of how dark it was getting with this storm, she was relieved to see that in the event that she might need to stop quickly she knew she had clearance on her left to bail out altogether, if necessary. There was a shoulder on the left side of the freeway and then a very wide grassy median area in between the south and northbound lanes which, due to this deluge, would now be more like mud but still an alternative to getting stuck behind, or worse, being involved in an accident.

A tall pickup truck came up too close for comfort behind her, and even though he didn't have his bright lights on, his normal lights were so high above the road that they lit up the inside of her car and shone directly into her mirrors blinding her for a few moments. She attempted to adjust her mirrors, but to no avail. She wondered why they had to ride her bumper so close, especially in this storm. It wasn't like she could move over to let them pass.

If this had been any other kind of afternoon when it was sunny, or even mostly cloudy, it wouldn't have been a problem, but this storm was like no other she'd ever experienced and hoped she never would again. The wind and rain had been so intense, and the clouds so dark and ominous, that she'd just be glad as soon as she could pull up in front of Lacy's house and run inside to safety.

The idiot in the pick-up truck behind her was relentless! 'What are they thinking?! That they can pass me?!' They flashed their high beams twice, and even though she had already adjusted the inside mirror to nighttime mode, the flash was so bright that it momentarily blinded her again. She couldn't help it, she had to slow down. She didn't care if it upset the other driver. They were all in this together, and there was nowhere else for any of them to go. The truck slowed down momentarily, but the driver must have gotten really upset because he flashed his high beams one more time and left them on. Alexa felt so helpless.

Just as she looked forward again she couldn't see through her windshield – it looked like she was under water! The deluge had suddenly returned, more fiercely than she'd ever experienced before.

The next thing Alexa saw was the simultaneous flash of brake lights from the cars in front of her, and as the windshield briefly cleared, the last thing she saw was a semi-truck ahead in the right lane as it jackknifed and began to swerve into her lane.

CHAPTER 27

Marc

THE BEAUTIFUL WEATHER IN the Bay Area the day before was replaced by the typical foggy winter day, leaving a chill in the house while Marc had been in classes. As he walked in the door at a half past two he headed for the thermostat to crank up the heat. Jenny was out with her mom for some "girl time", shopping in the City, and they'd be eating dinner there too, so he didn't expect to hear from her until later that night.

Marc grabbed his phone and called Alexa to see how she was doing but his call went right to voicemail. He figured she was probably studying in the library or with some friends. He fixed himself a late lunch to tide himself over until dinner, but even that would be leftovers of the previous night's lasagna. It always seemed to taste just as good the next day, but the same couldn't be said for the garlic bread. It was always best when it was fresh out of the oven, not the microwave.

Marc walked into his bedroom, sat down at his desk and began looking over his notes, getting ready to prep for his tests the next day. His mind wandered to thoughts of Jenny and the weekend ski trip they were planning. He'd only been to his parent's lake house a couple of times since the accident. Each time the memories flashed back to the last time they were all together for the family reunion after Alexa's high school graduation. They'd all had so much fun that week, but the accident just three weeks later had turned his and Alexa's world upside down.

Now, nearly two years later, he and Jenny were going to do their best to have a good time. They'd invited two other couples to join them, so the group atmosphere would help considerably to keep the mood light and the festivities fun. The snow pack in the Sierras was especially deep, so they all looked forward to skiing. He stopped his mind from wandering and got back to the task at hand; preparing for his tests.

Marc looked at his watch, almost three o'clock, wrote out his study plan and was buried in textbooks and notes when he heard a knock on the door. He walked out of the bedroom, down the stairs and glanced out the front window, noticing an Alameda County Sheriff's car parked in the street. Concern bordering on fear gripped his chest from memories of the last time a County Sheriff was parked in front of the house, but he did his best to hold his emotions in check. Looking through the peep hole in the door he saw a deputy on the other side, and he took a deep breath as mounting fear gripped his chest again.

"Hi, Marc." The deputy's greeting was somber, but still one meant for someone more like a friend than for official business because saying "good" afternoon just felt wrong. The look on his face was a cross between 'official' and 'sorrow' as he recognized Marc.

"Deputy Higgins? What ... ?" Marc stammered as he recognized the same deputy who had told him about his parent's accident.

"Um, Marc, may I step inside for a moment?"

The request seized Marc's heart.

"Please don't tell me this has anything to do with my sister." Marc's heart was pounding furiously.

"I'm afraid so."

"Oh, no! What happened to Alexa?!"

"Marc, perhaps you should sit down," Deputy Higgins calmly suggested.

"I don't want to sit down! Just tell me what happened, please!" Marc implored impatiently.

Deputy Higgins began as calmly as he could. "There's been an accident—"

"Oh, NO! Not Alexa!" Deputy Higgins noticed the look of terror on Marc's face and eased him into a chair near where they were standing.

"Marc, I'm sorry to have to tell you this but Alexa was involved in a very serious accident, and—"

"NO! Is she alright?!" Marc was in sheer panic!

"I'm sorry, I don't have many details. From the information passed on to me your sister survived the accident."

"What happened?!"

"There was a severe thunderstorm that hit the Nashville area this afternoon and caused numerous accidents, and your sister was involved in one of them. I can give you the name and phone number of the trooper who'll be writing up the report with all the details. I can tell you, though, that she was flown by LifeFlight helicopter to Vanderbilt University Medical Center in Nashville. Do you have any other family or relatives in the Nashville area?"

Marc just listened in stunned disbelief, his thoughts racing wildly. 'Not Alexa! Oh God, please don't take Alexa!'

"Marc?" Deputy Higgins asked when he didn't get a response. "Marc?!" he asked again, a bit louder this time, trying to get Marc's attention.

"What? Oh, sorry."

"Did you hear what I said, Marc?"

"Y-y-yes, I did. I just … I just can't believe it."

"Do you have any family or relatives in the Nashville area?"

"No. It's just me and Alexa now since our parents died."

"I wish I had more information to pass on to you now, but I should probably let you go in case you want to make any phone calls or make plane reservations to go see her."

"Yes, calls. I need to make some calls," Marc replied in a daze. "Thanks, Deputy."

"You're welcome, and goodbye, Marc. And on behalf of our department, our prayers are with you and Alexa and I hope she'll be okay."

"Thank you. I appreciate that."

"Oh, I almost forgot," Deputy Higgins said as he reached into his shirt pocket to retrieve his card. "If you'd like to talk with the trooper who was on the scene of the accident and gathered all of the information for the report, I've written down his name and phone number on the back of my card."

"Thanks. And yes, I'll need to talk with him. Bye."

"Goodbye, Marc."

Marc closed the door behind the deputy and leaned against it in utter shock. His legs became shaky and began to give out on him and he slid to the floor. "Oh, Alexa!" he cried out loud. "Oh, please be okay. PLEASE!"

It took a few minutes but Marc finally gained his composure and stood up. He took a moment to look around the house, trying to clear his head and figure out what to do next. He reached for his phone and started to call Jenny, and then remembered she was in the City with her mom. He called anyway and left a message, then he called and left a message on her mom's phone. He did his best to remain as calm as possible, but after hanging up he had the feeling he still sounded very upset. He had simply left enough of a message to let them know that Alexa had been in an accident, was hospitalized in critical condition at Vanderbilt, and that he was heading to the airport shortly to catch a flight. He promised to call Jenny as soon as he could. He finished his message with "I love you, Jenny. Please pray for Alexa. I don't want to lose her, too."

Marc had flown Southwest Airlines from Oakland into Nashville many times and knew they'd have a flight soon so he called them and got a seat on an afternoon flight that would arrive around 11 p.m. Central. The late arrival meant he'd need to secure a rental car now so it would be waiting for him when he arrived and could take right off for Vanderbilt. Catching this flight so quickly also meant he wouldn't get a chance to talk with Jenny before he left. Oh, how he needed her now!

Next came his call to Vanderbilt. He didn't have time to look up the number himself so he called the operator and was connected in less than 30 seconds, though it seemed to him to be an eternity.

He was finally directed to a nurse in ER. He gave her his name and explained that he was calling about his sister, Alexa. When she started to hesitate in giving out any information Marc began to lose his temper and interrupted her, telling her he was calling from California, that he'd just been told by a Deputy Sheriff of the Alameda County Sherriff's Office that they'd received a call from the Tennessee Highway Patrol about his sister, Alexa, being in critical condition at Vanderbilt after an accident on the freeway and had been flown by helicopter to Vanderbilt.

"I apologize, Mr. Janssen. Due to hospital regulations there's only so much information I can give out over the phone without some sort of positive identification."

Marc took a deep breath to calm down and exhaled loudly before continuing. "Okay, I know you're only doing your job, but what *can* you tell me about my sister? I'm catching a flight out of Oakland soon and I'll be there at Vanderbilt sometime after 11:00 this evening. I just need to know how serious her injuries are. Please, can you just tell me if Alexa is going to live?!"

"Mr. Janssen, what I can tell you is that your sister was flown from the site of the accident by the LifeFlight helicopter and she was taken into the ER about forty-five minutes ago. I'm sorry, but beyond that I just don't have any further updates."

Marc took another couple of deep breaths. All he could feel right now was fear that he'd lose his beautiful sister before he could even get to her side. He thanked the nurse for the information and for her patience with him, and said he'd be there in a few hours. He hung up and called his buddy, Mike, who lived just fifteen minutes away.

"Hello?"

"Mike! It's Marc! I need a favor!"

"Anything, buddy. What's up?"

"I need a ride to the airport and I'll explain on the way. How soon can you be here?"

"On my way right now, Marc! See ya!"

"Perfect. Bye."

He ran to his bedroom, pulled out his suitcase and a carry-on from his closet, and started grabbing clothes and shoes. He jammed as much as he could into the suitcase, not knowing how long he'd be there. Hopefully, when he arrived at Vanderbilt, he'd find that Alexa was already out of surgery and in recovery. He didn't give another thought to his classes; all that mattered was Alexa. He'd be there in just a few hours and would stay by her side for as long as it took to see her through this. He'd keep that promise he'd made to his dad … no matter what.

When his suitcase was ready Marc grabbed his shaving kit and a book and tossed them into his carry-on. He knew he probably wouldn't be able to concentrate, so taking his textbooks would be futile. He even gave a second thought to taking *any* books, but he also knew he would need *something* to help him try to take his mind off of the stress and panic he was feeling right now. All part of the orders his doctors had given him after the concussion he'd suffered in his own accident over three years earlier.

The doctors had warned Marc to avoid any and all stress related circumstances in order to combat the headaches he'd had during the first seven months of his own recovery. It concerned him deeply that he was headed into a critically stressful time over these next 24-48 hours, and knew he would have to remind himself to breathe deeply and stay as calm as possible. He decided to keep repeating to himself. 'Alexa's going to be fine. Alexa's going to be fine.'

His heart ached that he wasn't going to be able to talk to Jenny before he left, but the voice messages he'd left would have to do for now. What he wouldn't do to be able to talk to her, to just hear her voice. She always had a way to calm him down, to soothe his nerves. And he needed her *now*, more than *ever*!

CHAPTER 28

ICU

MARC ARRIVED AT VANDERBILT'S Medical Center just before 11:30 p.m., having run into delays picking up his rental car, along with traffic delays due to flooding from the storm in a few areas on the freeway as well as in Nashville itself. He stopped at the Guest Services desk in the lobby, identified himself, and asked about his sister. Deanna, one of the two twenty-something's behind the desk, turned to her computer, noticed that Alexa was in Medical ICU, and checked to see who her attending physician was.

"Dr. Macilyn Carr is the head of Alexa's critical care team," Deanna said. "I'll call and let her know that you're here."

"Thanks, Deanna. I appreciate that."

"Your sister is in the intensive care unit and that's located in the Critical Care Tower. You can get there by going down the short hallway to your left, then you'll come to a long hallway on your left. Follow that down until you come to another set of elevators on your left. Those are for the Critical Care Tower. As you enter the elevator alcove you'll take one of the elevators on your right to the eighth floor where Medical ICU is located. As you get off the elevator turn to your right and Dr. Carr will meet you in the waiting room down the hall."

"Thanks again for your help, Deanna."

"And, Mr. Janssen, for what it's worth, I hope your sister will be okay." As Marc started to walk away he gave her a slight smile and a nod.

Marc found his way to the long hallway and hurried to find the next set of elevators. In spite of there being so many people in the lobby, no doubt waiting to hear word about a loved one, traffic in the hallway was sparse so he was able to pick up his pace to a jog without fear of bumping into anyone. Moments later he saw the CCT elevators. Someone from the Vanderbilt staff had just stepped into one so he slipped in behind her.

"What floor, sir?"

"Eighth, ICU, please … Lynette," Marc replied anxiously as he noticed the name on her name tag.

"Okay, here we go," she said with a cheery voice that caught him off guard. Marc realized at that moment that he'd been in such a fearful state since the deputy sheriff had told him about Alexa that the cheerfulness of this young lady allowed him a moment of calm and reassurance, even though his destination was ICU. A moment passed before she spoke again.

"I get the feeling you're here to see someone?"

"Yes, my sister," Marc answered sadly, as he lowered his head.

"Hey," Lynette replied softly as she stepped closer to Marc and looked up into his eyes. "She's going to be okay."

"I hope so," Marc whispered.

"Trust me," she answered quietly, but confidently. "The doctors and nurses here are the best. Your sister is going to be fine."

Marc raised his head a bit and looked into Lynette's eyes. "I wish I had your confidence."

"Just try," she replied with a gentle smile.

"I don't even know what happened to her. I was told she was in a really bad accident on the interstate this afternoon and was rushed here by helicopter. I just flew in from California and so I haven't even had a chance to see her or talk to her doctors to find out how bad it is."

Just then the elevator arrived at their floor and they exited together.

"Let me introduce you to Sahara, our Guest Services rep on our floor."

"Oh, you don't need to bother."

"It's no bother at all!"

As they approached the Guest Services desk, Sahara looked up with a warm smile. "Hi, Lynette!"

"Hi, Sahara! This is, um, I guess I didn't get your name," Lynette said with a blush.

"Mr. Janssen?" Sahara asked.

"Yes," Marc replied, a bit stunned that she would know his name.

"I just got off the phone with Deanna downstairs and she told me you were on your way up."

"Yes, I'm here to see my sister, Alexa, but first I'm supposed to see Dr. Carr?"

"Yes, Mr. Janssen, Dr. Carr's been alerted that you're here and she said that she'll be out in a few minutes."

"Thanks. And thanks, Lynette."

Lynette looked back at Marc with a puzzled look on her face. "Thanks? For what?"

"For your encouraging words."

"Oh, sure! Anytime!" She left him with a friendly smile that did its trick to ease Marc's troubled heart just a little. He raised his hand and half waved as she turned and headed down the hall.

"And thanks again, Sahara. I'll be right over here." Marc turned toward the waiting area to his right. He passed by four people who appeared to all be there together, and another couple with what he thought might be their daughter who all looked as distraught as he felt. Their conversations were low, some of them even whispering, but Marc turned his attention to his own troubled thoughts and, in the stillness of the moment, said a silent prayer.

A moment later the young lady sitting closest to him looked his way, momentarily catching his attention. She looked to be about the same age as Alexa, and the look in her puffy eyes led him to believe that she'd been crying for quite some time. He assumed the older couple next to her were her parents and he made brief eye contact with them as well. They appeared to be almost as distraught as their daughter, and looking back at the young lady made him think of his sister and he fought back the tears. He took a breath, looked away, and closed his eyes as tears rolled down his cheeks.

"Excuse me, sir."

Marc opened his eyes and quickly wiped away his tears with the palms of his hands.

"Excuse me. I'm sorry to disturb you," the young lady said, "but I heard the girl at the desk say your name was Janssen? Are you Alexa's brother?"

"Yes, I'm Marc."

"I'm Lacy Kensington, Alexa's roommate, and this is my mom, Catherine, and my dad, Robert."

Marc glanced toward Lacy's parents and nodded with half a smile. They smiled back through looks of deep concern.

"It's good to meet you," Marc replied softly, almost as if he were losing his voice. He cleared his throat and realized how thirsty he was. "Would you excuse me for a moment? I need to find some water."

"Sure," Lacy replied.

Marc spotted a drinking fountain near the elevators and took his time re-hydrating. Sahara looked up from the book she was reading and smiled as he walked back toward the waiting area. Sitting back in his chair he looked over at Lacy.

"How did you know about Alexa's accident?"

All of a sudden Lacy's eyes filled with tears. "I feel so bad, Marc. If it hadn't have been for me none of this would have happened," she replied as she began to sob uncontrollably.

Marc moved over to sit next to her and rested his hand on her shoulder. "None of this is your fault, Lacy."

"Yes … it is. Normally we would have been in our apartment a few blocks away from here on a stormy night like this, but she was coming down to our home in Spring Hill to have dinner with us. I had driven down earlier today to help my mom get things ready, and Alexa called before leaving our apartment to let me know she might be late because of the storm that was moving in. I told her not to rush, that we'd wait until she got there to eat, whenever that was.

"We started getting nervous when she was about half an hour late. We had the TV on and were watching the weather reports about the storm. Then the news came on and they were talking about all of the accidents on the freeways and we just figured that Alexa had gotten stuck behind one and hoped she hadn't ended up with a fender bender. When they talked about the jackknifed truck on I-65 and how a young lady had been flown from the accident scene on one of the LifeFlight helicopters to Vanderbilt we prayed it wasn't her.

"When she hadn't arrived about 45 minutes after we knew the accident had cleared I called her cellphone and when she didn't answer we were hit with the reality that it might have been Alexa, so we called Vanderbilt and asked about her. We finally found someone who confirmed it was Alexa since they'd received word that her family had been notified. They weren't able to share any details about her condition, so we jumped in the car and drove here."

"And you've been waiting ever since?"

"Yes, and even though we're not family we were hoping somebody might be able to at least give us a clue if Alexa is going to be all right."

"Well, I was told her doctor would be out in a little bit so we'll hear together."

"Oh, thank you so much, Marc."

"Sure, it's no problem, and thank you for caring so much about her."

"It's not hard. She's my best friend."

"She's a lovely girl, Marc," Lacy's mother, Catherine, added. "She's been in our home so many times we've lost count, and she's just like part of the family now. She's become the sister Lacy never had, and we love her as if she were our own daughter."

These kind and wonderful sentiments touched Marc deeply as he nodded while fighting back more tears. "Thank you," he whispered.

Dr. Carr arrived a few minutes later. As she approached the Guest Services desk Sahara noticed her and pointed toward the far corner of the waiting room. "Hi, Dr. Carr. The brother is the gentleman in the dark blue sport coat sitting over in the corner."

"Thanks, Sahara."

As Dr. Carr walked into the waiting area the heads of the other people waiting there turned and followed her. Perhaps they had been hoping she'd have an answer about their loved one. A couple of the men, though, watched her because of her stunning beauty.

Dr. Carr was quite petite, just five feet tall, with blond hair down past her shoulders and a perfect complexion accented by a warm smile and beguiling green eyes. In spite of her being a trauma/ER doctor, and having to deal with all that implied on a daily basis, she somehow managed to maintain a gentle air of calm, poise and compassion that was perhaps more befitting a pediatrician, not someone who faced such trauma and tragedies as she saw each day in her work.

As she approached Marc stood up to greet her.

"Mr. Janssen?" Dr. Carr asked gently.

"Yes." Marc replied with barely more than a whisper, trying to clear his throat.

"I'm Dr. Carr, and I'm the head of Alexa's critical care trauma team," she said while extending her hand.

"Hi," Marc replied, this time with a little more strength in his voice, shaking Dr. Carr's hand.

"Please, have a seat."

"Sure. Thank you."

Knowing how family members are usually so distraught and bewildered after a loved one has been in a critical accident, Dr. Carr wanted to find out about Marc's state of mind.

"Are you doing okay, Mr. Janssen?"

"Yeah, it's just been a long day, and please call me Marc. How's Alexa?"

"Well, how much do you know so far?" Dr. Carr looked over at Lacy and her parents. Marc realized that perhaps the doctor was concerned about his privacy in these matters.

"Oh, Dr. Carr, this is Lacy, Alexa's roommate, and her parents, Catherine and Robert."

"Hello. It's nice to meet you too," Dr. Carr replied, extending her warm smile to them as well.

"So please, Dr. Carr, whatever you can tell me is fine for them to hear as well."

"Okay, thank you. So, what have you heard about the accident or your sister so far."

"Nothing about Alexa, except that she was in a severe accident on the freeway and brought here by helicopter. Do you know what happened?"

"I don't have any of the details from the accident other than I know there was one of the most severe thunderstorms ever recorded here in middle Tennessee this afternoon that caused scores of accidents on the interstates as well as on city streets. Based on other accident victims that have been rushed here during the storm, and judging from what I gathered from the LifeFlight crew that airlifted Alexa here from the accident scene, your sister's accident was apparently the worst of them all, involving at least two dozen vehicles, including a jackknifed semi."

The look on Marc's face was one of sheer disbelief.

"Oh, Alexa," Marc replied under his breath, with tears welling up in his eyes once again.

"When she arrived here she was immediately brought down to ER and I, along with a team of specialists, examined her injuries and confirmed she needed to be taken directly into surgery. We just finished operating on her about two hours ago, then she was in recovery for about an hour. She was moved into the ICU about 15 minutes ago, and that's where I was when you arrived.

"Now, Alexa is in critical, but stable, condition. As a result of massive blunt force trauma she has suffered a severe concussion—", Lacy gasped and Marc rested his hand on her leg to reassure her.

"— including some bleeding in the brain, along with a broken neck and collarbone, and back. Her left leg is broken, the right leg is fractured, and she has a broken arm, several broken ribs, and a punctured lung, and multiple internal injuries.

"As I said she's stable and in ICU right now, but we still won't know about the chances for her full recovery for a few days at the earliest."

Marc sat there with tears flowing down his face. Remembering everything he had gone through with his own accident, including his concussion and the lingering after effects, he looked at Dr. Carr and couldn't seem to form the words for the questions he wanted so badly to ask. She recognized his reaction and proceeded.

"Marc, you're probably wondering about Alexa's prognosis." All Marc could do was nod his head.

"Well, it's far too early to tell right now. Because of the injuries she sustained to her head we've put her in a medically induced coma to reduce brain activity which should give her brain a chance to rest. In that state it should also keep her brain from swelling thus allowing proper blood supply to her brain. We're monitoring her brain activity very carefully and sometime within the next twelve to twenty-four hours we should know more about how her recovery is going and when we may be able to bring her out of the coma. One thing I noticed as we were operating is that she appears to be in excellent physical condition."

"Yes," Marc replied, attempting to wipe away his seemingly unstoppable flow of tears, "she's always been in great shape, playing several sports and jogging."

Dr. Carr nodded in approval, "That's a big plus in her favor. Now, I'll be straight with you—"

"Dr. Carr, would you ... would you mind giving me the best case scenario, and then we can go from there?"

Dr. Carr looked at Marc, as well as at Lacy and her parents with deep compassion, understanding the emotional trauma they were all dealing with. "Sure, Marc." She paused a moment to gather her thoughts.

"Best case scenario based on her injuries, and taking into account her being in such excellent physical condition prior to the accident, I'd say she's looking at being in ICU for perhaps two to three weeks before we can move her to a private room where she'll then be for an additional three to four weeks. If speech therapy is necessary we'll want to start that as soon as possible. Otherwise, we'll begin physical and occupational therapy once she's moved to her private room, and then, once she's made enough progress with all of that, we'll transfer her across the street to Vanderbilt's Stallworth Rehabilitation Hospital. They'll continue with her full rehab, monitoring her progress and determining when she'll be capable of taking care of her own basic needs, even if it's from a wheelchair."

"Do you have any idea how long she may need to be confined to a wheelchair?"

"Well, it depends on how well she does in rehab. May I be candid with you, Marc?"

"Yes."

"Okay, I just gave you the best case scenario, now I'm going to give you the worst case scenario. Fair enough?"

Marc hesitated, taking a deep breath, and then said, "Go ahead."

"Alright, worst case scenario … it's possible that Alexa may never walk again, and depending on what we're able to find after she's awake it's possible she may have difficulty speaking. A lot depends on any nerve damage she suffered in the accident. There are two nerves that come down from the brain, pass along each side of the throat toward the heart, then back up again and run right along the vocal chords. If both nerves have been damaged or severed she'll never talk again. If only one has been damaged or severed, she may regain the ability to speak, though her voice may sound raspy."

Marc looked away as his heart stopped. He thought he could take it, but it just kept getting worse and worse. Alexa may never walk or talk again? He prayed another silent and fervent prayer that this would not be her fate.

Dr. Carr continued. "We really have to wait until the swelling goes down in order to begin to get a better idea about her prognosis. Best case scenario, she recovers quickly and rehab goes well, we're looking at three to four months until she's up walking and talking and on her own again. Worst case, easily six months or more, with all of the damage I spoke of a moment ago being permanent. More than likely we hope it will at least be somewhere in the middle, if not better, of course."

Marc was very distraught. "On the good side you mentioned

three to four months and she'll be walking and talking again. When she regains her ability to talk does that mean she'll also be able to sing again?"

"Oh, she's a singer?"

"Yes, she's attending Belmont on a full ride scholarship in musical performance. She's an excellent singer/songwriter with a ton of talent and a lot of promise for a career in music."

Dr. Carr took a deep breath and then made sure she had Marc's undivided attention. "I think it's important for you, and Alexa, to think of the possibility of her never being able to sing again. Just based on the damage she suffered to her throat in the crash, the indications are that there will more than likely be problems, but like I said we'll know more, one way or the other, sometime in the next few days."

Marc nodded to acknowledge he understood. "One more thing, Dr. Carr. Our parents passed away almost two years ago and they left a sizeable estate to us, so whatever it takes, anything at all that you can do for Alexa to help her make a full recovery, just do it. We can cover it."

"You're talking to the wrong person about that. I'm Alexa's doctor here in ICU, not the billing department. However, you can count on me and our staff to do everything humanly possible for your sister, Marc. I promise."

"Thank you, Dr. Carr. How soon can I see her?"

"I can take you to see her right now, but I need to give you fair warning. She's connected to several monitors, with several IV's going as well. She's bandaged from head to toe with only her face, toes and a few fingers exposed."

Marc nodded, acknowledging that he understood and was ready. They rose from their chairs and Marc gave Lacy and her mom a hug and shook her dad's hand and thanked them for coming.

"Give me a few minutes with Alexa, and then I'll come out and see you again, okay?"

"Yes, that's fine, Marc," Lacy replied as she took a deep breath to help her try to hold back more tears.

Dr. Carr led Marc into ICU and to Alexa's room. Even though

she had attempted to prepare him he still wasn't ready for what he saw as he entered her room. He gasped, and tears welled up in his eyes again.

"Oh, Alexa. I'm so, so sorry!"

"Don't let all of these machines and tubes scare you, Marc. I know this is very difficult for you to take in all at once, but believe me, these are all necessary to help Alexa during this early stage of recovery after the trauma she suffered today."

"I know, Dr. Carr, I just … it's so …" Marc sighed heavily as he looked away from Alexa.

"You might want to sit down, Marc. You're looking a bit pale."

"Yeah, I … I think I better."

"Do you need me to explain any of this equipment to you, Marc?"

"No, that won't be necessary, at least not now. I'll be here with Alexa for however long it takes for her to recover so if I have any questions about any of them I'm sure I'll ask at that time."

"Very well. I'm presuming you'll want to spend the night here with your sister?"

"Yes. I hope that's okay."

"Certainly, Marc. We're prepared for that and I'll make the necessary arrangements."

"Thanks, Doctor."

As Dr. Carr left, Marc leaned forward in his chair while staring at all of the equipment hooked up to Alexa and let out a shaky sigh while wiping away more tears. With a ventilator gently filling her lungs, a cardiac monitor tracking how her heart was doing, and IV's delivering medicine and fluids to his sweet sister, Marc could only watch and pray.

A few moments later Dr. Carr returned, opening the door slowly and found Marc on his knees next to Alexa's bed holding her hand and heard him whispering a prayer. She backed out quietly and waited for a few minutes before peeking through the slit in the door once more and this time found Marc once again sitting on his chair. As she entered Marc looked her way.

"I've notified the staff that you'll be staying here tonight with Alexa, and Sahara will be bringing in a blanket and pillow for you.

Your chair reclines so you should be fairly comfortable. I'll be coming by to check on your sister off and on through the night along with the nurses. We'll be as quiet as possible so as not to disturb you, but I promise you, Marc, that if anything occurs during the night we will wake you."

"Are you anticipating any problems, Dr. Carr?" Marc asked with concern in his tired eyes.

"No, not really. But these are critical, life threatening injuries she sustained. The surgery went fine, but we still have to keep a very close eye on her for the next 24 to 36 hours just to make sure she's progressing as we expect her to."

"Okay, thanks," Marc replied with a noticeable sigh of relief.

"I hope you can get some rest."

"Yeah, me too."

As Dr. Carr began to walk toward the door Marc stood up, catching her attention.

"Dr. Carr, I just want to say thank you for everything you and your team have done for my sister. She's all I have left and I just can't bear the thought of losing her, too."

"Don't worry, Marc. Personally, I believe the worst is over and Alexa will be fine. It'll just take time and also a lot of love," Dr. Carr replied with a warm, reassuring smile.

"Well, I've got plenty of both for her."

"And that's going to make all the difference in the world to her, too, Marc. She's lucky to have you for a brother."

"Thanks, Dr. Carr. Good night."

"Good night, Marc." Dr. Carr opened the door as Marc turned back to his sister, gently holding one hand while ever so softly touching Alexa's bandaged cheek with the back of his fingers.

"You're going to pull through this, sis. I just know you are. I love you, Alexa." And the tears once again flowed freely down his already moist cheeks.

Dr. Carr smiled to herself as she gently closed the door behind her, having witnessed a truly loving moment.

§

After spending several quiet minutes with his sister, Marc walked back out to the waiting room to talk with Lacy and her parents once again. He sat down next to Lacy, and she reached out and rested her hand on Marc's knee. He looked down toward the floor, took a deep breath and let it out slowly, gathering his thoughts, then looked up at each of them.

"I can't begin to tell you what it means to me to have you here tonight. I am so grateful for your love and support for my sister. Alexa probably told you that we lost our parents almost two years ago in a car accident, and now, today, I almost lost Alexa, too."

"We're praying for Alexa and you, Marc," Lacy's dad, Robert, said. "Like Catherine said, Alexa's been like a daughter to us, and we love her very much."

"Thanks. Listen, I have to get back to Alexa, but can I get your phone number or something? I'd like to stay in touch with you and keep you posted on Alexa's recovery."

"Oh, thank you, Marc," Catherine replied. "That would mean the world to us." Robert reached into his inside coat pocket for one of his business cards, wrote down their home number and cellphone numbers on the back, and handed it to Marc.

"Thanks. I'll keep you posted with any change, and as soon as I can get it worked out with Dr. Carr I'll give you a call so you can come up and see her. I know Alexa will need to see some other friendly faces after a day or two of putting up with me." Marc half smiled as he surprised himself with that slight hint of a sense of humor, lifting the ominous black cloud that had hovered over them in the waiting room.

Lacy looked at Marc and then leaned forward and gave him a big hug. She started to cry again and didn't want to let go.

"Marc, I'm so terribly sorry," she sobbed.

"Hey, hey, hey, Lacy," Marc replied, easing her back. Lacy's shaking arms remained outstretched as her hands rested on Marc's hips.

"This isn't your fault, okay?" Marc replied with deep compassion. "It's just that—"

"It's just nothing, Lacy. We don't know why this happened, but that doesn't matter. What matters most right now is that we're all here for Alexa, and she's going to pull through this just fine."

"Do you really think so?"

"Yes, Lacy. I do."

"Oh, Marc ..." and she leaned into him and gave him another tight hug. With tears in her eyes also, Catherine stepped forward and hugged them both, and Robert stepped forward and rested his hand on Marc's shoulder.

"Everything's going to be okay, son. We're just a phone call away if you need *anything*, okay?"

"Yes, sir. Thank you."

"No, thank you, Marc." When Robert saw the bewildered look on Marc's face he continued. "Thank you for being the kind of brother that Alexa can count on to help her through this. You're the kind of son I wished we'd had."

Marc managed a half smile and nodded his appreciation for Robert's comments, then closed his eyes and rested his head against Lacy's.

"God bless you all," Marc said, and a moment later they separated and Lacy and her parents began to gather their things.

"Thanks for the phone numbers, too. I'll give you a call as soon as I find out anything."

"We'll be waiting for your call, Marc," Catherine replied with genuine gratitude in her heart. "Thank you for allowing us to be a part of this with you. You don't have to face all of this alone, you know. Call on us anytime, okay?"

"I promise. Well, I better get back to Alexa. Thank you all so much for coming."

"Sure, Marc," Robert replied, offering his hand to Marc and shaking it firmly. "Listen, you probably haven't had the time to figure out where you might be staying, but we have a couple of extra rooms in our home, and we'd be honored if you'd like to stay with us while you're here in town."

Marc looked warmly at Robert and Catherine. "Thank you. I appreciate that. I need to stay by Alexa's side for now, then in a couple of days I'll probably find a place close by so I'm not far away … just in case."

"Sure, son," Robert replied. "We understand. But in case you change your mind just remember that the offer is open ended."

"I will. Thanks."

They walked out of the waiting area together and Marc paused near Sahara's desk while Lacy and her parents walked down the short hallway in front of him toward the elevators. When the elevator doors opened Robert and Catherine were the first to step in, while Lacy paused a moment longer and looked back toward Marc. With tears in her eyes but a slight smile on her lips, she waved to Marc and he waved back as he whispered "Thank you, Lacy."

"Thank you, Marc."

This time his walk to Alexa's room wasn't quite so hard to make.

CHAPTER 29

Jenny

JENNY ARRIVED HOME JUST after nine after a full day with her mom in the City. She was looking forward to calling Marc and was surprised to see that he had called her a few hours earlier. She checked for messages and yes, he'd left one for her. Even though she was anxious to hear his message and then call him so she could hear his voice for real, she decided to fix some tea and get ready for bed so she could curl up on her bed while talking to him. Eight minutes later she was in her night gown with tea cup in hand as she checked her voicemail. She was stunned to hear fear in Marc's voice.

"Jenny, I can't talk long. Alexa's been in a terrible accident and hospitalized at Vanderbilt in critical condition. I'm catching a flight to Nashville in a short while, but I promise to call you as soon as I can. I just have to find out more details first. I love you, Jenny. Please pray for Alexa. I don't want to lose her, too."

At first Jenny sat on the edge of her bed in stunned silence, then her hands began to shake so bad that it was all she could do to set the mug down on her night stand before dropping it on the carpet.

She realized there was no way she could reach Marc since he'd either be at Alexa's side or still on his way to reach her. Her next thought was to call her mom, but the phone was already ringing.

"Jenny, are you sitting down?" her mom asked with deep concern in her voice.

"No, but if—"

"Honey, Alexa's been in a horrible accident and—"

"And Marc's on his way to her now. Yes, mom, I know," Jenny finished her mom's sentence, trying to hold back tears.

"He called you?"

"No, he left a message and I just heard it. Oh, mom, I feel so terrible, and Marc is so scared. I could hear it in his voice."

"Did he say what happened?"

"No, just that she was in critical condition. Mom, I need your help. I have to get a flight to Nashville as early as I can in the morning and I'm going to need a ride to the airport, but I don't know how early that will be."

"Don't worry about it, honey. After you have your flight just call me back and let me know. I don't care how early it is, I'll be there."

"Thanks, mom. I love you."

"I love you, too. Talk to you soon."

"Bye, mom." Jenny set the phone down and sat back down on her bed, her head spinning, trying to organize her thoughts. She decided to make the reservations first and then pack.

She checked with Southwest Airlines and found an early morning flight, then called her mom back and arrangements were made for Adele to pick Jenny up at 5 a.m. and get her to Oakland International Airport in plenty of time to make her 6:40 a.m. flight to Nashville. With any luck she'd be in Nashville with a rental car by mid-afternoon, and then find her way to the medical center at Vanderbilt University and in Marc's arms within minutes thereafter.

Not knowing how long she'd be in Nashville, Jenny went through her closet and drawers, trying to pick out a variety of clothes to cover her for at least several days.

By eleven Jenny had finished packing, and now she needed to try to get some sleep. She'd be up by 4 a.m. to shower and dress and possibly fix something quick for breakfast, something that she could also just wrap up and take with her in the car if she ran late. Besides, she could also catch a few more hours of sleep on the flight if need be. Yeah, right. She wouldn't be able to sleep. Not on the flight. At this point she just hoped she'd be able to get to sleep now.

She looked at the clock as she climbed into bed … 11:23. Alarm set for 4? Check. Lights out.

§

Jenny was startled awake by her phone ringing.

"Hello?" she answered sleepily.

"Hi, Jenny," came a somber voice on the other end.

"Marc?!" Jenny bolted upright in bed.

"Yeah, it's me," Marc replied quietly. "Sorry to wake you."

"No! No, it's fine. Really it's fine. What time is it?" Jenny asked, adjusting her pillows behind her back as she leaned against the headboard. "Are you okay? How's Alexa? What happened?"

"Whoa, baby, one question at a time."

"Sorry. I'm just grateful to hear from you. I've been so worried."

"That's okay. I understand. It's just after 5 a.m. here, so 3. your time. I hope to get the details of the accident from the highway patrol sometime later today or tomorrow, but I've had a chance to talk with the doctor who's heading up Alexa's trauma team and she's in critical condition but at this point she's stable."

"Oh, Marc! No!" Jenny gasped, holding her hand over her mouth, as tears filled her eyes.

"She has all of these monitors and tubes hooked up to her, and she's bandaged from head to toe. I'm doing okay, but … oh, Jenny, I'm just so scared. I need to hear her voice. I need her to hear my voice so I can tell her everything's going to be okay.

"I don't have any details about what happened yet, just that there was a massive accident on the freeway during a heavy thunderstorm. She hit a jack-knifed truck and was airlifted here to Vanderbilt and was in surgery for several hours, and then in recovery. She's been in ICU since shortly before I arrived and I've taken a break to call you."

"Marc, I'm so sorry. She's going to make it, isn't she?" The tears continued to flow.

"Yes, the doctors are confident that she'll live, but they won't know for a few days about her chances for a full recovery."

"Oh, my gosh! What happened to her?"

"It's pretty extensive. She's in critical condition with a broken neck and broken back, with several broken bones, a punctured lung, multiple internal injuries, and a concussion. Oh, and blunt force trauma to her chest and throat. She got out of surgery about seven hours ago, but due to some initial swelling of her brain they put her in a medically induced coma to calm her brain activity. They're monitoring her closely and if all goes well they hope to bring her out of the coma within the next 24 hours or so." Marc could hear Jenny's sobbing.

"There was one good thing her doctor mentioned and that was they'd noticed while she was in surgery that she appeared to be in excellent physical condition."

"Yeah, she's always been so active."

"Yeah, and that didn't appear to have changed since moving away. They said that will be a big benefit in her chances for a faster recovery."

"Oh, thank goodness. Marc, is there anything I can do?"

"You've already done it. I just needed to talk to you and I'm glad you were there."

"I always will be, sweetheart."

"I know, Jenny. You have no idea how much that means to me."

"Marc?"

"Yeah?"

"Are you doing okay?"

"Yeah, I'm just really exhausted." He didn't mention anything about the fierce headache he was dealing with. "I haven't been able to get any sleep all night and I'm—"

"I mean emotionally, too. I'm worried about you."

"I'll be fine after I can get some rest."

"I'm flying to Nashville in a few hours, and—"

"No, Jenny, that's not necessary."

"Yes, it is, Marc. I need to be there with you and for Alexa."

"No, really, Jenny, stay home and I'll call you whenever I have updates. You shouldn't miss your classes, especially when you're so close to graduating."

"You mean especially when *we're* so close to graduating."

There was no reply on the other end of the line.

"Marc? Marc, are you still there?" Jenny asked, her voice beginning to show panic.

"Yeah, I'm still here."

"Did you hear what I just said?"

"Yeah."

"And?"

"And nothing."

"What do you mean?" Jenny sat up on the edge of the bed, wiped away her tears and suddenly became very concerned about Marc.

"I mean exactly that."

"Sweetheart, I don't understand."

"Jenny ... I'm not coming back—"

"WHAT?!" Jenny was now in full panic mode.

"Let me finish, Jen. I was going to add at least not anytime soon."

"But—"

"Jenny, I know what you're going to say. I've worked so hard for my degree and I'm so close to finishing everything, but you need to understand ... Alexa needs me. I'm all she has left, and I need to be here with her and for her until she's completely back on her feet ... however long that takes."

"I understand, Marc," Jenny replied solemnly. "Really, I do. I'm just so sorry. You've come so close ..."

"I know, Jenny, I feel the same way, but Alexa is all that matters to me right now."

A lump began to form in Jenny's throat.

"All?"

"You know what I mean. I love you, Jenny, and of course you matter to me too, but please don't make this difficult for me right now. I'll come back home, and to you, as soon as I can. In the meantime I'm going to stay right by Alexa's side until she's better."

The lump in Jenny's throat began to ease, but now her heart began to feel heavy.

"Okay, sweetheart," Jenny replied, suddenly feeling so alone. "I … I do understand. Listen, I better let you go so you can get some rest."

"Thanks, Jenny. I appreciate that. Listen, I'll call you again later today as soon as I get a chance to find out anything new from the doctors."

"Okay. Marc?"

"Yeah?"

"I miss you so much." Jenny stifled the overwhelming urge to cry and was careful not to sound desperate.

"I miss you, too. I love you, Jenny. Take care, okay?"

"Yeah, you too."

"Bye, Jenny."

"See ya, Marc."

The click she heard next rang unexpectedly loud in her ear and set off a wave of emotions. She dropped her phone, slumped over sideways on the bed, reached for her pillow, held it tight and buried her head into it, crying uncontrollably for Marc, for Alexa, and yes, even for herself. She longed for Marc, to see him and talk to him, to hold him and have him take her in his arms and hold her tight. She needed that more than anything right now. And even though he'd told her not to come to Nashville, she needed to, if for no other reason than to just be there for Marc. She knew Alexa wasn't the only one in pain right now. Marc must be going through his own private hell. And she knew, she just knew beyond a shadow of any doubt, that he needed her desperately.

CHAPTER 30

Stable

WHEN MARC RETURNED TO Alexa's room a nurse was checking her vitals.

"Good morning, Mr. Janssen. I'm Rae Marie," the nurse whispered.

"Good morning," Marc replied, whispering in return.

Listening to all of the monitors and equipment make their rhythmic hisses and beeps he watched the nurse as she replaced one of Alexa's IV bags.

"How's she doing?"

"She's stable and everything looks good," Rae Marie replied, trying to sound encouraging.

"Good. Thank you," Marc replied as his eyes wandered back to the equipment.

"Were you able to get any sleep last night?"

"None. I'm just too worried about ..."

"I understand."

"I'm really hungry. I suppose there's a cafeteria somewhere?"

"Yes, Mr. Janssen,—"

"Please, call me Marc."

"Yes, Marc, it's downstairs. Just take the elevator down to the first floor, turn to your left when you get into the main hallway, and the cafeteria will be on your right."

"Thanks. I'll be back in a while."

"Take your time, Marc. We'll take good care of your sister. The doctor will be making his rounds in about an hour in case you'd like to chat with him."

"Him? I thought Alexa's doctor was Dr. Carr."

"Yes, Dr. Carr is Alexa's main attending physician, but Dr. Kendall is taking over for her during the day. Dr. Carr will be back on again this evening so you'll see her then."

"Oh, okay. Thanks," he replied wearily.

As Marc headed for the elevator he remembered he needed to call the local Highway Patrol office and decided he'd grab something to eat first and then make the call.

He entered the elevator alone, pushed the button for the first floor, and the doors closed. Within a few floors, others, mostly hospital staff, had joined him. By the time they'd reached the second floor it was so full that the last person in couldn't even turn around to face forward. The pretty brunette blushed for a moment as she realized her predicament and then smiled. Everyone else seemed to be lost in their own worlds. A moment later the doors opened and the exodus of bodies flowed outward and Marc could breathe comfortably once again.

He found the cafeteria without a problem, paid for a bagel and cream cheese with some juice and found a small empty table. Within just a few minutes he was finished, but really couldn't even remember eating anything.

As far as he could tell from what Dr. Carr and the nurse he saw this morning said, Alexa was critical but stable, but what did that mean? Hopefully he'd be able to get some more specifics soon. The lack of sleep hadn't helped his state of mind, or his blistering headache, but he knew he needed to know more before he could feel any sense of assurance that Alexa really would be fine.

Marc searched in his wallet for the card the sheriff gave him the day before with the name and number of the Tennessee Trooper he needed to talk to. Finally finding the card he bussed his plate, juice glass, and tray and began his search for a quiet area from which to place his call. As he rounded the corner into the lobby he noticed a fairly large area where no one was sitting.

"Tennessee Highway Patrol, how may I direct your call?" The young female voice was warm and friendly.

"Good morning, my name is Marc Janssen and I'm calling for Trooper Dailey."

"I'm sorry, Trooper Dailey is out on patrol right now. May I leave him a message?"

"Yes. I was given this number to speak with him regarding an accident he responded to yesterday afternoon that involved my sister, Alexa Janssen. It happened during the storm and she was airlifted by helicopter to Vanderbilt. I flew in from California last night to be with her, and I was wondering if you could just give him my name and my cellphone number where he can reach me when he has a minute?"

"Certainly, Mr. Janssen, I'll be glad to pass along your message." Marc gave her the phone number and they ended the call. He debated about calling Jenny again before heading back upstairs to be with Alexa. It was still early back home so he decided to hold off for a couple of hours. Chances are he'd only get her voicemail since she'd no doubt be off to her morning classes, but by then he might have an update after talking with Dr. Kendall.

'Aw, what the heck,' he thought. 'I need to hear her voice again.'

Jenny's phone rang several times. 'Come on, Jenny,' he anxiously thought, 'I know it's early but I really want to talk to you again.' Finally, her voicemail kicked in and he cleared his throat before leaving a message.

"Hey, Jenny. Sorry I missed you. I know we just talked a little while ago but I was wishing I could hear your voice again. I guess this will have to do for now. I'm heading back upstairs to Alexa's room. One of her doctors will be coming by in a little while so I'm hoping to find out some kind of an update from him.

"I have to go, but I'll call you again later, hopefully this afternoon.

I love you, Jenny. And I'm missing you like crazy. Take care." He turned to head upstairs and suddenly felt dizzy from his headache. It took a long moment, but he was finally able to regain his balance and head back upstairs.

Shortly after Marc returned to Alexa's room Dr. Kendall arrived. Introductions were shared, followed by Marc stepping back and allowing the doctor to check on Alexa's condition while he anxiously awaited the doctor's update. A few minutes later, after adding some comments of his own to Alexa's chart, Dr. Kendall turned to face Marc with a calm and reassuring smile.

"Marc, initially it appears that Alexa is going to be okay."

"Thanks so much," he replied with a deep sigh of relief.

"According to Dr. Carr's notes it appears that your sister was involved in a pretty horrendous accident yesterday afternoon."

"That's correct."

"Do you know any of the details yet?"

"No. I flew in from California last night and a little while ago I placed a call to the Highway Patrol office and they're supposed to have the Trooper who was first on the scene and filing the accident report get back in touch with me some time today and I'll find out then."

"Good." Dr. Kendall glanced at Alexa's chart again.

"From what I saw on her chart, Dr. Carr was very descriptive of the injuries your sister sustained and that included a pretty serious head injury. She probably mentioned that many times with a severe concussion there can be swelling and/or bleeding in the brain. They noticed some bleeding and induced her coma and it appears that stopped it fairly quickly. Other than that, all of her vitals are good and she's doing as well as can be expected so we'll just keep a close eye on her."

"Okay, thanks, Dr. Kendall."

"Sure, anytime."

As Dr. Kendall left Marc sat down on the recliner that he'd unsuccessfully tried to sleep in, and thought about the doctor's remarks. Between her two doctors he felt confident that Alexa was truly in good hands, and he said another silent prayer of thanks.

With Dr. Kendall's visit complete, and the reassurance he felt that Alexa was doing okay, Marc thought about trying to get some sleep. He made sure the recliner was far enough away from Alexa's bed that he wouldn't be in the way in case any nurses came in, and then leaned back and tried to get comfortable.

After suffering from exhaustion for so long Marc thought he'd be asleep in no time. Fat chance. After what was only about ten minutes of trying to get comfortable, and it feeling more like an hour, he was frustrated to still be wide awake. Part of him thought it was simply a false illusion, and that he should just close his eyes and try again, but his brain just kept going a mile a minute, thinking about Alexa, about her accident, about everything that could possibly be involved in her full recovery, and wondering how long it would take, and then thinking about the future. He reached for his bag on the floor next to him and took out his notebook.

He started writing notes about things he needed to do, the things that mattered most. From this point forward he knew his life would never be the same, but he wasn't feeling sorry for himself, just taking stock of his circumstances. Finishing college was out of the question, at least for now. Taking care of Alexa was what mattered most. Staying in touch with Jenny was equally as important, but helping Alexa get through this immediate ordeal was paramount above all other concerns.

There was a soft tapping on the door and as Marc looked up to see who it was Rae Marie slowly opened it.

"Hi, Marc. I wasn't sure if you were trying to get some sleep again or not," she said softly.

"Yeah, I wish," Marc replied in a light, sarcastic manner.

"Well, I just wanted to let you know that I just received a message from a Trooper Dailey—"

"What? Why didn't he call me?"

"He said he tried but his call just went to voicemail, so he called us next."

Marc checked his phone and there was a message waiting. Then he remembered that he'd turned the ringer down when he entered the room so he wouldn't disturb Alexa.

"Is he on the phone right now?!" Marc asked excitedly, but still trying to keep his voice down.

"No, he needed to make a few more calls, but he told me that if you were able to call back within the next ten minutes he'd be able to talk with you briefly."

"Great. I'll be right back."

§

Marc anxiously returned the call to Trooper Dailey. The receptionist he spoke with earlier put him right through.

"Trooper Dailey."

"Hi, this is Marc Janssen returning your call."

"Yes, Marc. You wanted to talk to me about your sister's accident?"

"Yes, I wanted to find out if I could come by and pick up a copy of the accident report so I could understand what happened."

"Well, I'm still in the midst of putting that report together, and it won't be ready until early next week, but if you'd like to come by some time I can meet with you and give you what information I have."

"How soon can I do that?"

"Well, are you available this afternoon?"

"Yes!" Marc replied anxiously.

"Then how about if you come by around one o'clock?"

"That's fine. I'll be there. Thanks!"

"Sure," and Trooper Dailey gave him the address and directions to the office from Vanderbilt. They said their goodbyes and Marc headed back to Alexa's room.

In spite of not having slept in over twenty-six hours, Marc knew there was no way he'd be able to get any rest until he was able to meet with the trooper. He returned to making notes in his notebook including specific questions to ask at their meeting.

As he wrote Marc occasionally looked up at Alexa, scanned all of the equipment and their various readings, and said yet another prayer for her. While the staff had been encouraging, he was very aware that anything could still happen that would cause her condition to worsen, but he stopped short of thinking about not only the worst case scenario he and Dr. Carr had discussed the night before, but also the very worst case ... Alexa not making it. Somehow he just knew she would. She *had* to!

CHAPTER 31

Trooper Dailey

TROOPER DAILEY ARRIVED AT the Highway Patrol office just a few minutes before Marc and was talking with the receptionist when Marc walked in. When he identified himself to the receptionist Trooper Dailey introduced himself and invited Marc to join him in a small conference room. Before they sat down the Trooper asked Marc if he wanted anything to drink, but Marc passed. He just wanted to get the details of the accident and get back to Alexa.

"You mentioned on the phone this morning that the accident report won't be available until next week?"

"Right. We write up our reports during the week, turning them in by the weekend. Then the Lieutenant gathers them all up on Sunday and takes them to headquarters to review them. Once they're given the okay they're prepared and filed at the beginning of that next week. So if you'd still like to get a copy you can drop by next week and pick one up."

"Okay. So what can you tell me at this point?"

"To begin with, we had one of the worst thunderstorms on record hit us hard yesterday. Torrential rains, strong winds, and then it all let up for a short time which gave drivers a false sense that it was over, only to have it slam them again even stronger. Wiper blades couldn't keep up most of the time, and streets and highways couldn't drain fast enough. At least the drivers on the freeways tended to keep their speed down early on, mainly because at times they couldn't see through their windshields, but there's always those reckless drivers that cause most of the problems, especially in the accident that involved your sister."

"What exactly happened?"

"Well, it was a chain reaction of sorts. From the witnesses I was able to get statements from, most of them referred to a car that moved into the slow lane without a signal, cutting off a semi who nearly ran over him. It turns out he just wanted to get into that lane so he could take the next off ramp a couple of miles down the road, but he misjudged the amount of room he had and the speed of the car he pulled in behind, and when the car ahead of him hit his brakes, he also slammed on his brakes, and the semi behind them had nowhere to go. The truck driver turned his wheels to avoid rear-ending the guy and ended up jackknifing his truck. Then all hell broke loose."

Marc took a deep breath, preparing for what was to come, as Trooper Dailey cleared his throat.

"The best witness I have is one who had been next to or very near Alexa in another lane from just south of Nashville. He saw the whole accident unfold before his eyes, his own car getting pretty bashed up from other cars hitting him moments later.

"He said he was in the middle lane and a bit behind your sister's car, and he noticed a big pickup with a lift kit come up behind her and relentlessly rode her tail for miles.

"He said the guy would pull up behind her and hit his high beams. He was worried for your sister, while at the same time getting really mad at the guy, just knowing that if there was an accident, that guy would surely be involved, if not the cause of it. He added that traffic in his own lane, as well as the lane to his right was just as heavy, but everyone else seemed to be driving with some sense of sanity.

"Once the semi began jackknifing, cars started swerving to avoid the truck, but the freeway was too slick and they were simply getting mangled into each other. He noticed your sister's brake lights come on and that she started to turn toward the center median area but the big pickup behind her was too close at the time she hit her brakes and he rammed right into her. The last thing he saw before impact was that pickup truck behind her pushing her right toward the mid-section of the trailer of the semi. He thought for sure she was dead. Fortunately, there were several parts of the trailer's undercarriage that prevented her car from going under very far, but from what I was able to see it was still far enough that she's very lucky to have survived.

"I was actually fairly close when the accident occurred. I was on Highway 96 in Franklin and approaching the freeway when I got the call about the accident. I was also advised that ambulances and fire trucks had already been dispatched. I hit my lights and siren and took the on-ramp. By then all of the southbound traffic was obviously at a complete standstill, but I managed to work my way down along the right shoulder until I was on the scene a few minutes later.

"The rain had begun to let up a bit, so there were some drivers and passengers out of their cars and trying to help out others, especially your sister. When I finally reached her car I shone my flashlight in the windows but I couldn't see any movement. I also knew by the initial appearance of her injuries that she might already be dead. Taking no chances I made the call for one of the LifeFlight helicopters from Vanderbilt. They must have already been alerted because it seemed like only a few minutes before they were landing on the south side of the accident.

"Multiple fire department crews were also there quickly, and they had to use the Jaws of Life to free your sister from her car. That was the hardest part of the whole scene for me because with as much damage as her car sustained in the crash I knew she might not have long to live, but she was rescued in time and the LifeFlight crew airlifted her to Vanderbilt."

"What about the driver of the pick-up behind her?" Marc asked angrily.

"What about him, Marc?" Trooper Dailey calmly replied.

"Well, did you at least arrest him and throw him in jail for ramming my sister's car and causing her to go under the trailer?"

"He was initially held in custody while we investigated the accident further, comparing the statements from other witnesses, and finally determined we had enough evidence to place him under arrest and he's in jail as we speak."

"I want to see him, and I want to see him alone."

"Marc, you know I can't do that. I know you're thinking that he's already guilty so why don't we just flip a switch and be done with him, right?"

"That's where you're wrong. I want him to suffer the same way my sister is! I want him to feel that same fear she felt, and sustain the same injuries she did! I want to make his life a living hell like he's made mine and my sister's!"

"Marc, I know what you're going through and how you feel."

"Do you? DO YOU?!" Marc yelled while slamming his fists down on the conference table. "Because unless you've gone through what I'm going through right now, and felt the way I feel right now, you have no right to say you *know*. NO right at all!"

There was silence for nearly a minute while Marc sat there at the table seething, while Trooper Dailey remained calm. Finally the trooper broke the silence.

"Marc ... I *do* know. I lost my own sister two years ago in a senseless accident on another Tennessee freeway. Bad weather, idiot drivers, horrendous accident ... only my sister didn't make it. She died at the scene. She left behind a loving husband and three precious children. None of us could even say goodbye. And believe me, Marc, we're all still hurting big time over it. So ... yes, I do know what you're going through, and I'm really sorry. I just hope your sister is able to recover. I really do."

Silence hung over the small conference room for several minutes as Marc cried and Trooper Dailey respectfully gave him all the time he needed to pull himself together. Finally, Marc raised his head and used his already soaked handkerchief to try to wipe his face.

"I'm sorry," Marc said in a whisper.

"It's okay, son. I know how it feels, and I know you have to get this out. This is a good and safe place, and I'm just the right guy for you to let it all out with."

"Yeah ... I guess so," Marc replied with a slightly stronger voice. He took a deep breath and then let it all out in one big sigh. "Thanks for understanding."

"I do, Marc. I do."

They wrapped up their meeting by making arrangements for Marc to come back the next week to pick up the official report.

"If there's anything else, Marc, just give me a call, okay? And if you want to talk again when you come in for the report next week just let me know and I'll be here."

"Thanks, I appreciate that."

CHAPTER 32

Jenny

JENNY'S FLIGHT FROM OAKLAND landed in Nashville right on time at 1:15 p.m. She wished there was a way to instantly transport herself into her awaiting rental car with her bags already in the trunk, then she shook her head realizing that if she could do that, then why not have just transported herself directly from home to Nashville and have her bags already waiting for her at her hotel. Her hotel! She knew she'd forgotten to do something the night before. No matter, she'd find out which ones were close to Vanderbilt and deal with it later. In the meantime she couldn't wait for the plane to get to the gate and unloaded so she could grab her luggage, get her car, and be on her way. Oh, how she longed to be in Marc's arms! Soon! But not soon enough!

Thankfully, Nashville International wasn't too busy that afternoon and Jenny was able to pick up her luggage and secure a rental car fairly quickly. She asked for the address of the Vanderbilt University Medical Center, and was on her way. She set the GPS in her car and as she began to pull out of the rental car area the bright mid-day sun nearly blinded her. She fished around in her purse for her sunglasses, put them on, and resumed her departure from the airport.

The sky was crystal blue with no hint of a cloud anywhere, and the interstate and streets showed little trace of the storm that had raged through the area the previous day.

As Jenny drove west toward Vanderbilt she passed a few hotels located near the airport and gave another brief thought to where she was going to stay, but quickly waved the thought away, knowing that she'd decide that after seeing Marc. Knowing him like she did he was no doubt still at the hospital and hadn't bothered with finding a place for himself yet.

Arriving at Vanderbilt Jenny was able to quickly find a space in the parking garage right in front of the entrance to the medical center. A short walk through the garage and across the street and entrance drive in front of the medical center and she was inside the lobby. She identified herself to a young lady, Mary Ann, at Guest Services, and asked her where she could find Alexa Janssen's room. Mary Ann checked her computer and informed her that Alexa was in Medical ICU.

"Do you know if her brother, Marc, is with her?"

"I don't, but I can call up there and find out."

"Well, is there a waiting area near the ICU that I could go to? Maybe I could meet Marc there?"

Mary Ann confirmed that there was, indeed, a waiting area outside the ICU and directed her how to get there.

"Thanks," Jenny replied as she broke into a half jog, excusing herself after nearly knocking over a few people rounding the corner into the long hallway that led to the Critical Care Tower.

Mary Ann called upstairs.

"Medical ICU Guest Services, this is Danielle."

"Hi, Danielle, this is Mary Ann."

"Hey! How are you?"

"I'm doing great, thanks! I'm calling about one of the patients in ICU, Alexa Janssen."

"Yes, the young lady that was brought in here yesterday from that bad accident?"

"Yeah, that's the one. Do you know if her brother, Marc, is in her room with her?"

"No, he left here a couple of hours ago, saying he'd probably be back around three." Looking at her watch she continued, "and that would be soon."

"Okay, thanks. There's a young lady named Jenny on her way up who apparently knows Marc and his sister and I told her about the waiting area right next to you. I mentioned that she could wait there, so when you see Marc again let him know she's there, okay?"

"Will do, Mary Ann."

"Thanks."

A few moments later Danielle noticed Jenny anxiously exiting the elevator and greeted her with a warm smile.

"Hi, are you Jenny?"

Surprised, but pleased, Jenny replied, "Yes."

"Hi, I'm Danielle. Mary Ann called from downstairs so I knew you were coming."

"Oh, good. I'm here to see Alexa Janssen, or at least her brother, Marc. Is he here?"

"Not right now, but he should be back fairly soon. If you'd like to have a seat in our waiting area I'll let him know when I see him."

"Thank you. I appreciate that."

"Sure. No problem."

Even though Jenny was *so* excited to see Marc, under the circumstances she knew she needed to control herself so she could be strong for him. The run through the hallway downstairs, and the general tenseness she'd felt ever since getting off the plane and driving to Vanderbilt had left her a bit winded. If Danielle was right she'd hopefully have a few minutes to calm down and compose herself before the love of her life arrived. Hopefully, he'd have some good news about Alexa.

Jenny found a seat, thumbed quickly through the stack of magazines on a nearby table and finally selected one, though she wasn't really interested in reading anything. She nervously flipped through the pages before putting it down and choosing another, continuing this pattern over and over while she waited for Marc.

She worried about how he'd react. Would he remember that he'd told her not to come and be angry, or would he be happy to see her and sweep her up into his arms? She prayed it would be the latter.

Knowing exactly what direction he'd come from once he reached the floor she kept glancing up from her magazine, hoping she'd see him before he saw her and be able to discern his mood.

Several minutes passed and Jenny got restless so she set aside another magazine and stood up and walked over to the windows behind Danielle's desk and looked out onto the indoor courtyard several floors below. She took a few slow, deep breaths to rush some much needed oxygen to her brain in a futile attempt to calm down. That's when she recognized the unmistakable sound of Marc's boots approaching from behind.

"Jenny?" The sound of his voice thrilled her, but she still paused for just a moment before turning around to see Marc just a few feet away.

"Jenny? What are you doing here?" Marc asked, half surprised, half bewildered.

"Well, that's a fine greeting for the girl you love who's just flown 2000 miles to see you," Jenny replied, trying to lighten the mood.

"I'm sorry, sweetheart, I'm just so surprised," Marc replied with a tired half smile. "I said it wasn't necessary to come."

"I know, but I needed to see you. I needed to be here for you, and Alexa."

"Thanks, Jenny." His voice seemed flat.

"You'd better sit down, sweetheart, before you fall down," Jenny said, noticing how exhausted Marc looked. "Have you been able to get any sleep at all?"

"None. I started to drift off a bit late last night, but then I woke up, looked over at Alexa, and was too worried about her to sleep."

"Has she been awake at all?"

"No, she's still in the coma. They check on her regularly but apparently they're not ready to bring her out of it."

"Then you probably haven't had the chance to find out any of the details of the accident?"

"Actually, yes. That's where I've been."

"Where?"

"The Highway Patrol office."

"Really?"

"Yeah," Marc replied softly, starting to choke up. "I called their office earlier this morning and was told that the trooper I needed to talk to would be in the office around one o'clock, and that he'd be available to meet with me for a while and try to answer my questions."

Just then Marc's mood changed, recalling the details that Trooper Dailey had relayed to him, and the look on his face was a mixture of sheer terror and pure hatred.

"Oh, Jenny ... it was horrible." His eyes just couldn't hold back the tears any longer.

Jenny leaned toward Marc and rested her head on his shoulder while she hugged him.

"It's going to be okay, Marc," she whispered.

"I sure hope so, for Alexa's sake."

Jenny suddenly felt Marc tense up and she leaned back to look at him. The look in his eyes frightened her.

"Because if she doesn't make it I'm going to personally kill him," Marc said in a hushed but intense voice.

"What ... what are you talking about? Who are you going to kill?" Jenny asked with fear rising in her voice.

"The idiot responsible for nearly killing Alexa!" he hissed through gritted teeth.

"Wait a minute, sweetheart. I don't understand."

"Alexa's in critical condition and they say it's too early to tell exactly what her recovery chances are."

"Oh, Marc,—"

"And I swear if she dies, I'll go after—"

"Marc. Marc! Hold on. You can't think like that. Not about that guy, and certainly, not about Alexa."

They found a couple of empty seats at the far end of the waiting area and Marc began to relate to Jenny everything Trooper Dailey told him. She sat with rapt attention, trying her best to keep Marc as calm as possible.

§

Twenty minutes later Marc finished giving Jenny all of the details, as well as filling her in on more details of Alexa's injuries. As he did so, he leaned his head forward into his hands and cried uncontrollably. Jenny did her best to comfort him, knowing that the emotional release was no doubt long overdue, but at the same time realizing that just her being there for him wasn't enough.

As Marc's sobbing began to ease a few minutes later he could finally speak.

"Jenny … oh, Jenny, I'm so scared. I know the doctors have told me Alexa's going to be okay, but now … now I just don't know. I … I just don't know."

Jenny leaned forward and rested her head on Marc's.

"Sweetheart, is there anything I can do, or can I get you anything?" she asked softly.

"Just about ten hours of sleep would be nice."

"Well, I might have an idea on that," Jenny replied hopefully.

"What do you mean?" Marc asked as he raised his head from the palms of his hands.

"Well, how about asking her doctors if it's okay for me to join you in her room, and if they say it is, then perhaps you could get some sleep while I stay awake and watch over Alexa, and I'll wake you up if anything changes."

Marc paused a moment before responding, the idea floating through a very groggy brain.

"Yeah," he replied. He was so exhausted there was little to no emotion in his voice. "Come on, let's see. It should be okay since you'll be with me."

The walk down the hallway was quiet and somber. Jenny walked near, but not too close to Marc. She could clearly see how exhausted he was and wanted to avoid upsetting him more than he already was.

As they approached Alexa's room Marc reached over and took Jenny's hand and her heart gently leapt in her chest. She sighed softly, reassured by his touch that he wasn't too upset that she'd come even after he'd told her not to, and that he still cared. Or was it just that he wanted it to appear like they were 'together' as they walked passed the nurse's station?

"Jenny, before we go in, I need to warn you that what you're going to see could really upset you. I know it hit me harder than I expected when I got here last night. I told her doctor I was ready, when I actually wasn't because I really had no clue."

"It's okay, Marc. I'm a big girl. Besides … I have you holding my hand, and that's all this girl needs right now. Let's go."

Marc eased the door open and the sounds of all of the equipment hit them first before Jenny saw Alexa. When Alexa finally came into view, Marc could feel the tenseness as Jenny squeezed his hand tight and she caught her breath.

"Oh, Marc," she softly gasped as she held her other hand up over her mouth. Marc was right. There was just no way to prepare her for seeing Alexa like this. Not the fun loving, high spirited, vivacious young lady she knew. This just couldn't be Alexa. She looked for a chair as her knees became weak.

§

Marc was able to sleep, although fitfully, for a couple of hours. Once he closed his eyes, knowing that Jenny was there, it was only a matter of minutes before he'd nodded off.

He'd been awake for nearly thirty-five hours, and even though there'd been many times in his life when he'd skipped sleep for one night, it was either because he'd been studying for exams or so excited about some project, usually his music, that he just couldn't sleep. But this was different. The last twenty-four hours had been pure hell for Marc, and Jenny had seen the incredible toll it was taking on him. She only hoped that by her being there she could relieve some of the stress he must be feeling from the trauma of Alexa's accident.

As Jenny sat next to Alexa's bed, watching the lights and listening to the sounds of the monitors that were hooked up to her, she reached out and gently laid her hand on Alexa's.

"Alexa?" Jenny whispered. "It's Jenny. We're here for you. Marc and I are right here for you." Tears welled up in Jenny's eyes and began flowing ever so slowly down her cheeks. "We're so sorry this happened to you, but we're going to help you through this."

Jenny kept her hand in place and lowered her head, lying it on the edge of Alexa's bed, a silent prayer forming on her lips. She not only prayed for Alexa, but knowing how all of this must be affecting Marc, she prayed for him, too.

When Jenny opened her eyes she glanced up. Nothing had changed - Alexa's stillness, the beeps of the monitor, the IV bags still dripping their fluids, the distant noises from the hallway. She looked up at the clock and was stunned that over an hour had passed since she'd laid her head down on the bed! 'What?!' she wondered. 'That can't be right! Did I fall asleep?'

She turned her head in Marc's direction as she heard him stir. Oh, how she loved this wonderful man. He'd been through so much in the last few years, and now this! She prayed he could handle the stress, and she recommitted herself to be there with him every step along the way.

CHAPTER 33

The Courtyard

WHEN MARC WOKE UP he felt worse than before he'd fallen asleep. His head was throbbing. Somehow Jenny became immediately aware of his sour mood and hesitated to say anything.

He sat up, rested his elbows on his knees, his head in his hands, and sighed deeply.

"Honey?" Jenny asked softly.

"What?" Marc replied with a sharp edge to his voice.

"Are you okay?"

"No." Marc's voice was now flat, but still held a dark cloud within it.

"What can I do?"

"Nothing. Just give me a minute, will ya?"

Jenny sat back to give Marc some time to collect his thoughts and clear his mind. Finally as he sat up she was able to see the dreadful look in his eyes and it scared her.

"Honey, what's wrong?" Jenny asked, trying to minimize the shaking in her voice. When he didn't answer she eased forward in her chair ever so slowly.

"Sweetheart, let's step outside for a minute. Maybe that'll make you feel better." Without replying Marc labored to stand up, almost losing his balance, but catching himself in time to avoid falling. Jenny led the way to the door.

They walked down the hallway in silence, and as they passed the nurse's station Jenny told the nurse on duty that they'd be back in a while. As they went through the security doors they headed for the waiting area but there were only a couple of scattered seats available.

"Come on," Jenny urged, "let's go downstairs. There are lots of chairs open in the courtyard."

"I don't want to go downstairs. I need to stay close to Alexa. I need to be there for her."

"You will be. We're just going down for a few minutes. We've both been sitting or lying down for too long and we need to get moving around a bit."

"Jenny, I said I need to stay close to Alexa."

"Marc, she's still in her coma."

"I know, but I still need to be with her."

"Just before you woke up one of the nurses came in to check on her and I asked her if she knew if the doctors would be taking her out of her coma anytime soon, and she said it might be this evening. Please, sweetheart, let's go down."

Marc just looked at Jenny without saying anything for a few moments. Then he gave her a slight nod to indicate he'd go and they continued walking toward the elevators.

They waited only a moment for an elevator heading down to stop at their floor, then stepped in and joined three Vanderbilt staff members. Silence hung like a dense fog between them as they exited.

Marc still appeared to be in a fog so Jenny gently reached for his hand, and although Marc didn't accept it eagerly, at least he didn't pull away.

The indoor courtyard was nearby and Jenny led Marc to a couple of chairs that were furthest from anyone else. As Marc settled into his chair Jenny asked him if he wanted anything from the cafeteria, but he declined. Then he leaned back and rubbed his head, especially around his temples.

"Do you have a headache, sweetheart?"

"Yeah," Marc replied as he sat up and leaned forward, trying to find a comfortable position.

"You still look exhausted, Marc," Jenny said, reaching out to brush back the hair that had fallen in front of his eyes.

"So what else is new?" Marc replied coldly, brushing her hand away.

"I just meant—"

"Look. I'm tired, and I'm tired of feeling tired."

"I know, darling, but—"

"But nothing, Jenny. I'm at the point where I don't really know what I'm doing. I can't do anything to help Alexa so I feel helpless, and I hate feeling this way."

"You're wrong, Marc," Jenny replied softly, attempting to calm him down. "You're doing more than you realize for Alexa."

"Oh, yeah? What? What am I doing for her? I sit next to her bed for hours, I walk around to loosen up sore muscles and I go back and sit down again. I should be up there beside her right now. I can't really leave her side to do anything else until I know she's going to be okay. I should be up there right now —"

"She's going to be perfectly fine, Marc —"

"She is? She *is*?! How do you *know* that, Jenny? The doctors haven't said so. The nurses haven't said so. Do you have some medical knowledge they don't have and that I don't know about?

"No, Marc, I'm just saying—"

"Stop! Just stop!" Marc took a deep breath and let out a long sigh as Jenny looked on with deep concern mixed with a growing fear. She'd never seen Marc like this. She collected her thoughts and responded softly.

"Marc. Please listen to me."

"Why," he responded gruffly, but at least not as belligerently.

"Because … I have something I'd like to say to you … from my heart." Marc took a long moment before looking up and out across the courtyard at nothing in particular. 'At least he didn't yell at me again,' Jenny thought.

"What is it, Jenny?" Marc's response was still edgy, but at least a sense of calmness appeared to be returning.

"I'm worried about you, sweetheart."

"Why?"

"You're just not yourself right now."

"Oh, I'm not? And just who am I right now? Who am I suppose to be?" The sharpness in Marc's tone had returned, but Jenny was determined to stay calm.

"Please, Marc, just listen, okay?" Marc just looked at her without responding. "All I'm saying is that you've been under a tremendous amount of stress and anger and fear, and I understand all of that. I know how much you love Alexa, how much she means to you, and I understand about the promise you made to your dad. And while you're afraid for Alexa ... Marc, I'm afraid for you."

"Me? Why are you afraid for *me*?"

"Because, even though you weren't in the accident, and even though you haven't been physically hurt in any way, you've been terribly hurt emotionally."

"What are you talking about, Jenny?"

"I'm talking about the fear you have that Alexa won't make it, and that I know you're blaming yourself, right now, for Alexa getting in this accident and being here in the hospital—"

"Jenny—"

"No, Marc, you need to wait this time because I have something to say that you need to hear." Once again Marc remained still and just looked at Jenny, but with more of a cold stare this time. He crossed his arms in defiance and slouched back in his chair.

"After your parents died you didn't want Alexa to go away to college. You wanted her near us so you could keep an eye on her to make sure she'd be safe, but you knew in your heart that wasn't right. It wasn't what she wanted, and you know it wasn't what your parents would have wanted. She'd worked so hard for those scholarships to be able to come here to Nashville. It was her dream—"

"And now her dream is over," Marc replied bitterly.

"No, it's not, Marc. And I know you know, deep down inside your heart, that it's not over. Alexa is going to come out of this, she's going to recover, I just *know* it, sweetheart. I truly believe this, and Alexa needs you to believe this, too. Yes, she's hurt terribly right now, but she's going to get better and she needs you to be strong for her right now. Listen, there's something I learned from my grandmother that I want to share with you.

"A long time after my grandfather died my grandmother got really sick. We didn't know what it was at the time and I remember my mom being really worried about her. I was worried too, but there was also a sense of calm I felt when I visited her in the hospital.

"You see, she had always maintained a positive attitude through-out her life, and even though she was in the hospital she still managed to maintain that same upbeat attitude and expected everyone around her to do the same.

"During one of our visits my grandmother noticed how distressed my mom was about her illness and my grandmother just told her straight out that if she couldn't change her attitude she could leave and not come back until her attitude was better. And she also went so far as to put her doctors and nurses on notice to do the same. She refused to have any negative words expressed in her presence, whether inside her room or out, even if she was sleeping. And she added that if, God forbid, she should ever slip into a coma, whether on that visit to the hospital or any in the future, they were to do the same thing. She absolutely believed that, while her conscious mind might not be able to hear their conversations, her subconscious or unconscious mind could, and she would only allow positive comments to be made around her. She was convinced that by keeping a positive attitude she'd recover faster.

"Marc, deep down I know you know this, and I don't want it to seem like I'm preaching to you about this. You've always maintained an attitude of positive expectations, expecting nothing but the best in any given situation, and now is the time to really show that. You alone can make more of a difference for Alexa than anyone else in this world. She needs you, she needs your love, and she needs your encouragement, not your worry and not your fear. And she needs your strength to help her regain hers. You need to stop feeling sorry for yourself—"

"I'm not feeling sorry for myself, Jenny," Marc replied sharply.

"Yes, you are, Marc. You're feeling sorry for Alexa, and I believe all of this exhaustion you're suffering from is causing you to also feel sorry for yourself."

Marc sat silently for a few moments trying his best to calm his emotions. The last thing he wanted to do now was say something he'd regret, but it was getting harder and harder.

"Marc, I know I've said a lot, but now I need to know what you're thinking."

"No, Jenny, I don't think you do," Marc replied quietly, but firmly.

"Yes, Marc. I need to know. We've always been able to talk to each other about anything and everything, openly and honestly, and this is no different."

Marc uncrossed his arms, sat up, rested his elbows on his legs, buried his face in his hands and sighed loudly. Jenny reached over and placed her hand gently on his back, only to have Marc jerk away, not wanting to be touched.

"Sorry," Jenny replied softly.

Still resting his head in the palms of his hands Marc took a deep breath, and Jenny braced for what might be coming next. He lifted his head, looked out in front of him without focusing on anything in particular, and then slowly closed his eyes. As he opened them a moment later he looked at Jenny without any sense of emotion on his face, especially in his eyes.

"You need to leave, Jenny," Marc answered quietly.

"What?" Jenny asked, not quite sure what Marc had said.

"I said, you need to leave."

"But, Marc—"

"No, Jenny … just leave."

The look in Marc's eyes scared Jenny. The love and warmth that had always been there for her, especially after they'd gotten back together again over two years ago, and that had seemingly gotten stronger, deeper, and more loving ever since, seemed like it was gone. In its place was sheer emptiness.

She tried to tell herself that it was all because of his incredible exhaustion, but her fears seemed to be telling her it was something more. She hung on tightly to the belief that he still loved her, and that things would improve between them, perhaps ever so gradually, over the next few days. All Marc needed was to hear from Alexa's doctors that she would be fine. Yes, that would do it!

So, she'd leave the hospital for now and find a place to stay. Hopefully tomorrow things would be better for all three of them. She'd stay by Marc's side because he'd asked, even begged her to always be there for him. She'd promised then, and she'd sealed her promise by giving him that special promise ring for Christmas over two years ago. Her friends had thought it strange, a girl giving a guy a promise ring, but she didn't care if they understood or not. This was simply between her and Marc. A commitment she would never break.

Jenny looked for her purse and found it on the chair next to her. She slipped the straps over her shoulder, looked at Marc who was still sitting lifeless with a hollow look in his eyes, and stood up. She leaned forward to give Marc a kiss on the forehead and this time he didn't pull away from her. A good sign? She couldn't tell. Not yet, anyway.

"I'll see ya, Marc. Take care, sweetheart." She took a deep breath and said a silent prayer … for Marc, for Alexa, and yes, even for herself. She could only imagine what the two of them were going through right now, their own private hells, but she'd be here to help both of them heal. Somehow. No matter what.

CHAPTER 34

Jenny

STUNNED AND HURT BY Marc's comments, and confused by his seeming indifference, Jenny walked hesitantly out of the courtyard, praying that Marc would call her back. As the door closed behind her she took a few more steps before turning to look at Marc through the glass-paneled wall. He had leaned forward once again, with his elbows on his knees and his face buried in his hands. She could see his body shaking and knew he was crying. All she wanted to do was rush back in and hold him. She knew he was lost and afraid, and she also knew he needed her in spite of the fact he had just sent her away.

She rounded the corner into the main hallway and out of Marc's line of sight, unable to walk any further, she leaned against the wall. She tried desperately to hold her emotions in check but her knees weakened and she slid down to the floor with her legs doubled up in front of her. She leaned her head forward into her folded arms and cried as passersby simply walked around her, perhaps understanding but not wanting to get involved.

Several minutes later her sobbing subsided enough for her to begin to breathe a bit more easily. Jenny reached into her purse in search of some tissues to wipe away the tears. She rested her head on her arms again and thought to herself, 'Oh, Marc, please let me help. Please don't shut me out.'

Jenny lifted her head once again, realized where she was, and felt embarrassed for blocking part of the hallway. She stood up, took a deep breath, and made her way down the hallway.

She found a remote corner in the lobby to sit and try to gather her thoughts. The day had begun filled with prayers for Alexa's survival from her accident, concern and worry for Marc, and an overwhelming desire to be by their side to help. Everything had now turned completely upside down and she felt so lost about what she would, or even could do, next.

Marc had made it painfully clear that he didn't want her around, at least not now. 'Maybe later,' Jenny thought, 'sometime after Alexa wakes up and Marc's able to talk to her and get the reassurance he needs that she's going to recover, maybe then he'll accept my love and support.' In the meantime all she could do was wait.

Attempting to refocus on her own circumstances Jenny decided to leave the medical center for now and drive around to find a place to stay. As she made the long walk to her car she felt a sense of overwhelming sadness ... and heartbreak. And dread for what the future held.

She figured that there would be a number of hotels fairly close to the campus, and checking out her GPS to get her bearings she discovered that West End Avenue and Broadway were close and decided she'd start there. Within fifteen minutes she'd seen several options and decided on the Holiday Inn on West End Avenue, not far from the medical center.

Jenny parked in the lot in front of the hotel, grabbed her suitcase from the trunk and headed in. She quickly found the registration desk and asked for a room, saying she'd be staying for a few nights. She said another silent prayer, this time praying that Marc would ask her to stay longer, saying that he really did need her, and giving her a new sense of hope. She had no idea, though, when, or even if, he'd come around.

She made her way to her room, laid her suitcase on the bed and opened the patio door for some fresh air. Yesterday at this time she was in San Francisco with her mom, enjoying a fun girl's day out. Now she was nearly 2000 miles away in Nashville, with Alexa in a hospital in critical condition, and Marc not speaking to her. She decided to try to ease her shredded emotions by taking a long, hot shower. When she finished she called her mom and talked to her for over an hour, mostly through tears falling like rain.

When Jenny finally hung up the phone she dried the remaining dampness out of her hair and then lay down on her bed. She was neither interested in eating or watching TV. What she wanted, what she needed more than anything, she couldn't have. With an indescribable aching in her heart, and a longing to be held safely and lovingly in Marc's arms, she said a silent and desperate prayer and drifted off to sleep.

CHAPTER 35

Marc

AFTER JENNY LEFT, MARC eventually made his way to the cafeteria for something to drink before heading back up to Alexa's room. Exiting the elevator once again on the eighth floor he didn't pay any attention to the young lady at the Guest Services desk, even though she was waiting to give him a reassuring smile. He entered the ICU through the security doors, and then passed the nurse's station without acknowledging the two nurses there before continuing down the hall toward Alexa's room. He paused before entering and took a deep breath.

As he opened the door he was greeted once again by the sounds of all the equipment in the room monitoring Alexa's condition. As long as he didn't hear any kind of warning signal from them he was able to relax a bit and try to reassure himself that Alexa truly was going to be all right.

He sat down hard in the recliner, still feeling so exhausted even though he'd slept for a couple of hours. Well, his conscious mind might have been asleep, but his subconscious mind had kept flashing images of Alexa's accident based on the description Trooper Dailey had given him earlier that afternoon.

He kept seeing himself in the car with Alexa, trying to imagine the sheer terror she must have experienced as the accident unfolded in a matter of seconds with no chance to escape. Then, after the accident, he kept seeing himself in the median area looking at the scene and wanting desperately to reach Alexa and get her out of her car. He also tried to get to the driver of the truck that had forced Alexa into the semi, but he was being held back by some unseen force. He had struggled mightily to break free, but without any luck at all.

Next, he saw the LifeFlight helicopter landing and the medical staff recovering Alexa from her car after the fire department had freed her with the Jaws of Life. He wanted desperately to join her in the helicopter, but once again was restrained by that same unseen force. Finally, he saw Alexa being taken into the emergency room and being surrounded by doctors and nurses checking out Alexa's injuries with extreme urgency, followed by the decision to rush her into surgery in a desperate effort to save her life.

The whole scenario played over and over in Marc's subconscious while he was trying to sleep, leaving him even more exhausted when he awoke. Now, as he sat in the recliner, his head throbbing, he thought of all of the emergency personnel from Trooper Dailey who'd been first on the scene, to the firemen who were there in time to cut her car open so she could be rescued by the LifeFlight crew and flown to Vanderbilt, to Dr. Carr and her staff who had operated on Alexa and saved her life, and finally to those attending to her now.

While his emotions were being torn to shreds, there was a remote place in his heart where a small seed of gratitude had been planted and that was helping to ease his splitting headache at the moment.

"Alexa," Marc pleaded silently, "I love you, sis, and I need you to live."

Tears once again began to pool up in his eyes as he said another silent prayer.

"Oh, God, please let my sister live. I need her so much." And he buried his head in his hands and the tears flowed steadily once again.

§

Marc was resting with his eyes closed when he heard someone entering the room.

"Marc?" a familiar voice asked.

His eyes began to flicker open but it took a moment for them to focus.

"Yeah?" he replied, still trying to shake the cobwebs from his mind.

"Hi, Marc. It's Dr. Carr."

"Hey, Dr. Carr," he replied, this time with more strength as he rose to greet her properly.

"How's our girl doing?" Dr. Carr enquired.

"Okay, I guess. Do you think you'll be able to bring her out of her coma soon?"

"Well, let me check on a few things and I may be able to give you a better idea.

"Sure."

Dr. Carr proceeded to check out the monitors and make notations on Alexa's chart. She paused for a few moments and then turned to Marc.

"I have good news for you, Marc. All of the monitors are showing consistent readings for her, so that's a good sign. She's been stable for about 18 hours now and we'll be able to bring her out of her coma very soon. That doesn't mean she's going to wake up right away. My best guess would be within about 12 hours or so."

"And she'll be able to make a full recovery?"

"Well, we still won't know that for a while, but based on a variety of factors that I see right now I believe so, though there may be some lingering affects regarding her speech."

Marc sighed loudly.

"I know, you were hoping for a better prognosis and a lot sooner results, but she's been severely traumatized. With time she should recover just fine from her physical injuries like her broken bones but, what we find after the swelling goes down will determine her recovery time here and in rehab, and if she'll be able to walk and run again like she did before the accident. Once she's awake we'll also be able to see if she has any trouble talking. If she does then I'll examine her vocal chords more carefully to see what corrective measures may need to be done."

"Well, earlier this afternoon I was able to meet with the trooper from the Highway Patrol who was first on the scene of her accident and from what he described it's lucky Alexa's alive."

"Yes, that's pretty much what the LifeFlight crew shared with me yesterday afternoon when they brought her in."

They both looked back at Alexa and Marc reached out and gently held her hand.

"Come on, Alexa. You can do this! I'm here with you, sis."

CHAPTER 36

Jenny

WHEN JENNY AWOKE HER room was dark and she was cold and hungry. The clock on the nightstand read 12:14. She had a pounding headache that had set in after the emotional upheaval with Marc and she rubbed her head to try to ease the pain.

She continued to lie in the dark for several minutes, confused and scared. The day before the accident had been so romantic and magical for them. Now she felt so lost by Marc's reaction to her being in Nashville, and afraid for Alexa, not to mention also being afraid for Marc.

Nothing made any sense. Sure, he'd said it wasn't necessary for her to come, but why wasn't he glad that she had come anyway? They loved each other so much and did everything they could to always support and uplift each other, regardless of whatever situation or challenge they faced. So why wasn't he grateful for her coming to be with him and Alexa, even for a short time? And where did his anger come from?

The only explanation that made any sense was his exhaustion, but she'd seen Marc exhausted for any number of reasons before and he'd never responded like that. She was simply at a loss for what she could do. He refused to leave Alexa's side for very long, and even though Vanderbilt was accommodating him by allowing him to stay in her room, Jenny knew a recliner was no substitute for sleeping in a bed.

She shivered and sat up, turning on the light, blinding herself for a moment. When she could see again she noticed the curtains in front of the patio door move and it frightened her for a second until she remembered she had opened the door to let in fresh air when she'd first arrived. There was more than enough of that now, and she rushed over and closed the door.

Jenny hadn't eaten since the light meal she'd had on her flight and now she was beyond starved, but it was after midnight. Where would she get anything to eat this late? Room service? Some fast food joint? Neither really appealed to her. Besides, she was too upset to eat anything anyway.

She desperately wanted to see Marc. She wanted to let him know how much she loved him and how much she wanted to help him. If he was going to sacrifice the few remaining months of his college education, even for a while, then she would, too. Together they would help Alexa with her recovery and all she would have to go through with her physical and occupational rehab. It didn't matter how long it would take, she'd be there for both of them.

For now, though, she knew she needed to get some more sleep, but she also wanted to find out how Alexa was doing. She called the medical center and asked to be transferred to the Medical ICU nurse's station.

"Medical ICU. This is Sara."

"Hi, Sara, this is Jenny Kincaid. I was there yesterday afternoon with my boyfriend, Marc Janssen, visiting his sister Alexa and I was wondering if you could tell me how she's doing?"

"Hi, Jenny. Alexa is still resting at this time. Dr. Carr was able to start the procedure to bring her out of her coma – "

"What?! She's awake?"

"No, not yet. It typically takes quite a while for someone to awaken after being in a medically induced coma, so perhaps sometime tomorrow. Marc is with her now, would you like me to see if he's awake?"

"No! No, that won't be necessary. I'm hoping he's getting some sleep, so I'll just let you go and I'll come by in the morning."

"Okay, Jenny. Good night."

"Good night."

As Jenny set her phone down she rested her hand on it for a moment longer, pondering everything she'd seen and heard and felt since she heard Marc's voicemail what seemed like ages ago. She sighed heavily, and then got up and walked into the bathroom to get a glass of water and brush her teeth. Afterwards she pulled a nightgown out of her suitcase, slipped it on, and sat back down on the bed.

With her mind racing she knew she wouldn't be able to get back to sleep quickly, and in spite of how late it was she decided to call her mother.

They spent most of the next hour talking about Marc, with Adele attempting to calm her daughter's concerns about him. She tried to reassure Jenny that Marc's resistance to her help, even his attitude about her being there in Nashville with them, all stemmed from his exhaustion. She reminded her about how he felt about her, how kind he treated her, and how obviously in love with her he was before Alexa's accident and encouraged her to focus only on that.

'Just give him some time,' she heard her mother say more than once. 'Fine,' she thought to herself, 'I've got plenty of time', but her mother hadn't seen the look in Marc's eyes or, for that matter, the lack of it, when he'd talked to her the way he did, and there just wasn't any way Jenny could find to describe it. All she had to go on at this point was hope, and even that seemed to be fading fast.

After the phone call Jenny walked over to the patio door and quietly slid it open and stepped onto the patio. Looking up West End Avenue toward Broadway she gazed at the lights of downtown Nashville. She shivered from a cold breeze and stepped back into her room, slid the door closed, and locked it.

As she sat down on the edge of the bed she reached for the hotel phone and called the desk, asking for a 7:30 wake-up call. She turned off the light and slid off the bed and onto her knees and prayed ... for Alexa, for Marc ... and for the strength to live through whatever the next day would bring.

CHAPTER 37

Alexa

MARC HAD MANAGED TO get a few hours of restless sleep. Even though Dr. Carr had indicated that Alexa might not begin to wake up until mid-morning he had still been hopeful that she might beat the odds and awaken sooner. It was now after 6am and still no sign.

He closed his eyes once again, not to sleep, but to try to ease the pain from his persistent headache. He tried to clear his mind but the constant noise from the monitors prevented any relief. He thought ahead to what was coming next for Alexa. He remembered his own recovery and how long and painful it had been, and Alexa's injuries were much worse. She was going to need his complete attention and assistance throughout the coming ordeal. Her whole world, and his, had been turned upside down in an instant.

And Jenny. 'Why hadn't she stayed home?' he thought. 'It would have made everything so much easier. I love her so much but I can't deal with everything that's going on right now. And she deserves my attention, too. Why have I been so awful to her? And this stupid headache isn't helping. I need to – '

Voices outside the room interrupted his thoughts. Dr. Kendall entered.

"Good morning, Marc. Did you get any rest?"

"A little."

"Good. Well, let's see how your sister is doing this morning, shall we?" Dr. Kendall looked over the various monitors as well as Alexa's chart."

"I like what I'm seeing here, Marc. There's every indication that she should be waking up fairly soon."

Marc reached out for Alexa's hand. A few seconds later he thought he felt a slight twitch. He quickly looked up at Dr. Kendall, then looked back down at Alexa's hand, and then up to her face. His heart began to race in anticipation of Alexa finally waking up.

"Dr. Kendall, Alexa might be coming around," Marc said cautiously. "I thought I felt her fingers twitch a moment ago."

"That's good. Go ahead, Marc, talk to her."

"Alexa?" he whispered. "Alexa? Hey, sis." Several moments passed and nothing. Then another twitch sent his heart beating faster.

"Alexa?" he now asked louder, trying desperately to get her to wake up. "Alexa, it's Marc." This was followed immediately by Marc's hand being squeezed tightly as Dr. Kendall watched.

Marc leaned forward and kissed Alexa on the cheek. "I love you, Alexa," and they both watched intently as Alexa's lips began to move, trying to form words. Marc leaned closer to hear what she was saying, but then realized she wouldn't be able to talk because of the ventilator and leaned back up. "Don't try to talk, sis. It's okay. Just relax."

"Give her a few moments, Marc," Dr. Kendall said reassuringly. "This is typical of someone waking up after the kind of heavy sedation she's been under." Marc continued to stand next to his sister, still holding her hand, excited to feel a pulse increasing in strength as blood began rushing through her hands.

Alexa's lips began to move again, and her breathing began to come more quickly and deeper, flowed by a slight moan. As her eyelids began to flutter and she attempted to focus Dr. Kendall knew it was now his turn to talk to Alexa.

"Alexa? Alexa, if you can hear me I want you to relax and be comfortable. Try to breathe as normal as possible. That's it." Dr. Kendall's reassuring voice helped to calm her breathing just slightly.

Her eyes were trying to focus on her surroundings; trying to make some sense of where she was and what was happening.

Her eyes were still searching for understanding when Dr. Kendall asked Marc to say something to her. He leaned over and looked into her eyes.

"Hey, Alexa. It's Marc. I love you, sis." Alexa's eyes followed his voice and as their eyes met he saw so many questions in them. He knew his sister oh so well and he just knew she must be scared to death as she lay there on a strange bed, in a strange place, unable to talk."

"Just relax, sis, everything is going to be fine. You've been hurt and I'm here with you now to help you get better."

"Alexa?" Dr. Kendall asked, trying to get her attention from the other side of the bed. Unable to turn her head because of her injuries, she slowly turned her eyes toward the voice, until she saw where that soothing voice had come from. Once again she tried to speak, once again she was unable to, and fear began to grow in her eyes.

"Hi, Alexa, I'm Dr. Kendall. I know you're probably very confused right now about where you are and why, and I'll be able to answer your questions in just a moment. The tube you feel in your mouth and throat is helping you breathe and I'll be able to remove it soon. In the meantime, it's important that you lie as still as possible. Your brother, Marc, is right here with you, too."

Tears started welling up in Alexa's eyes as she looked over toward him, and Marc reached for some tissues nearby and gently wiped them away. He felt so horrible seeing the fear in her eyes and couldn't find the words to say to try to ease those fears. Dr. Kendall saw this, too.

"Alexa," Dr. Kendall continued in his soothing, reassuring voice, "you're in the medical center at Vanderbilt University. I'm one of your doctors and I'll be taking care of you. You were in an accident and suffered many injuries, but you're going to be fine. We have the finest staff here to take care of you, and all you need to do is stay calm and rest, okay?"

Alexa tried to speak and once again became agitated with the tube in her mouth and appeared confused.

"I'm sorry, Alexa, you're on a ventilator which has been helping you breathe, but we'll be removing it shortly. Try to lie as still as possible. In the meantime, to answer a question with a 'yes' just blink once, for 'no' blink twice, okay?"

Alexa blinked once. She closed her eyes and her pillow was moistened by a flow of tears.

"Dr. Kendall, how soon can you take her off the ventilator?"

"Right away, actually. I'll call for our respiratory specialist and Alexa will be able to talk in a little while."

"Okay. While you do that I'm going to step out for a few minutes."

"Sure, Marc. That's fine."

Marc looked at Alexa. "Sis, I'll be right back, okay?"

Alexa looked up at her brother and with tears still in her eyes she blinked once.

Marc left the ICU, found a water fountain, and then sat down in the waiting area. In spite of his exhaustion, his spirits were a bit lighter now that Alexa was awake. His headache was still there and he hoped the pain would begin to ease up soon.

So many thoughts were racing through his mind, all centered around Alexa.

§

When Marc returned to Alexa's room she was trying to talk with Dr. Kendall, but her voice was raspy. He rushed to the side of her bed and their eyes met.

"Marc, I'm scared!"

"I know, sis, but you're going to be fine."

"What happened to me?"

"You were in an accident but – "

"What?! I don't remember anything …" Alexa's voice trailed off.

"That's okay. That's not important now. What's important is that you just rest and everyone here will take care of you, including me."

Alexa tried to clear her throat and her face contorted in pain. Her eyes darted back and forth between Marc and Dr. Kendall.

"What's *wrong* with me?! Help me, *please!*" she pleaded with tears flowing down her cheeks. Her attending nurse, Rae Marie, increased the drip on her sedative as Marc and Dr. Kendall both did their best to calm her. Her eyes soon closed as she drifted off.

"She'll be okay, Marc," Dr. Kendall said. "This is perfectly normal for someone who's been through what Alexa is experiencing right now. The best thing you can do is just keep reassuring her, keep her calm, as we get through these next few days. It's going to take a while to work through this mentally and emotionally, as well as physically."

"Thanks, Dr. Kendall. I know you're right. I was in a bad accident a few years ago – "

"So, you know first-hand what's it like to be lying there helpless and scared."

"Sadly, yes."

"Well, then you'll be that much more of a help for her while she's here, and also while she's going through rehab."

"Yes, I'll be here with her the whole time."

"Alexa's a lucky young lady to have you, Marc."

Marc just nodded as he looked back to Alexa who was now resting comfortably.

§

An hour later Marc was resting in the recliner, allowing himself a chance to doze off for a few minutes. He couldn't help being deeply concerned for his sister. He had hoped that by his being here by her side it would have made enough of a difference that she would have taken the news better. But, then he realized that just the fact that he was here, she must have figured that her condition was very serious, if not worse.

There was a light tapping on the door. As he glanced over, expecting to see one of the nurses coming in, the door eased open and Jenny entered cautiously.

"Hi, Sweetheart," Jenny said softly with a warm smile.

"Hey," Marc replied calmly without getting up. Jenny walked toward him and sat on the chair next to him.

"Did you get any sleep?"

"A little."

"Oh, good!" she replied with a sigh of relief. "How's Alexa doing?"

"Okay, I guess. She woke up a couple of hours ago while Dr. Kendall was here. They were able to remove the ventilator so now she's breathing on her own."

"Oh, that's wonderful, Marc!"

"When she first woke up she was frightened and confused, and as the initial shock and reality of her situation set in she became very distraught. I did my best to calm her down, but nothing I said seemed to help. Dr. Kendall also tried to reassure her, but I remember how inconsolable I was for several days after my accident, mostly because of how scared I was. They increased the drip on her sedative and she eventually calmed down enough to go back to sleep. I just feel so helpless, Jenny."

Clearly remembering how Marc had responded to her touch the day before Jenny cautiously reached out her hand and rested it on his leg. He didn't pull away or even flinch. A good sign? Hopefully, she thought.

"Please don't feel that way, darling. Her doctors will take care of her, and what she needs most from you is what she already has – your love."

"I just can't help feeling like there has to be something more I can do. I hate seeing her suffer like this."

"I know, sweetheart, I know," Jenny said reassuringly.

"When she initially woke up she became so frightened about not being able to move or talk. She even looked at me strangely, almost as if she didn't recognize me. And because of the head trauma she suffered I'm just afraid – "

"You can't think like that, Marc."

"Why not?" Marc's reply was agitated. "It's possible, and I have to think of all of that really happened to her, and what's going to happen in the future."

"Marc, let the doctors figure that out, and then they can help you better understand everything, okay? Please … just give it some time."

Marc just sat looking at Alexa and didn't respond. Not wanting to cause any more possible agitation for him, Jenny moved her hand off his leg and sat back in her chair.

An uneasy silence pulsed through the room. After several minutes Alexa began to stir and both Jenny and Marc moved quickly and stood on either side of her bed, each holding one of her hands, waiting for her eyes to open. As they did, Marc saw the same expression begin to form in her eyes that he had seen earlier and he hit the nurse's alert button. Rae Marie arrived a moment later and asked if everything was okay.

"My sister just woke up again and I'm not sure if she needs anything."

"Well, let's see. Good morning, Alexa," Rae Marie said with a pleasant, cheery voice. Alexa's eyes shifted toward the new voice and searched for answers. She tried to move but the nurse calmed her down.

"Try to just relax, sweetie. We're taking good care of you, okay?"

"I'll try." Alexa responded, once again in a raspy voice. Her eyes searched from Rae Marie to Jenny to Marc, all the while seeking answers that wouldn't come.

"Is she going to be okay?" Marc asked, searching for his own sense of solace.

"Yes, it's just going to take some time," she replied loud enough for Alexa to hear, and at the same time trying to reassure Marc as best as she could.

Rae Marie continued to check Alexa's vital signs, along with the levels of her IVs, then made some notations on her chart. She shared a few more reassuring comments with Alexa, as well as with Marc and Jenny, and then left.

With Rae Marie gone Marc and Jenny took turns talking to Alexa. Tears filled Alexa's eyes and Marc reached for a tissue to wipe them away.

"I'm so sorry this has happened to you, sis. Because of my accident I know a little of what you must be going through right now, and I'm going to do everything I can to help you get better as quickly as possible."

"Thank you, Marc. I don't know what I'd do without you. May I have some water, please?"

Jenny reached for the cup of water on the table next to the bed and lifted it toward Alexa, placing the straw in her mouth. Relief came to her eyes as she felt the coolness flow down her throat.

"Thank you," she replied, whispering softly.

"Alexa, do you remember anything about this morning when Dr. Kendall was in here and explained about your injuries?" Marc asked.

"No," Alexa whispered.

"Do you remember being in an accident?" he continued. Alexa closed her eyes for several long moments before opening them again and whispered, "No. I'm sorry." Marc began to choke up, but fought back the tears so his sister wouldn't see him crying.

"Alexa," Jenny began, "you were in an accident a couple of days ago and were injured, but you're going to recover just fine, okay?" Tears filled Alexa's eyes once again and Marc wiped them away. Her fingers tightened their grip on their hands and loosened several times rapidly causing Marc and Jenny to look at each other and then back to Alexa, and Marc hit the call button again. They did what they could to calm Alexa down before Rae Marie came in a few seconds later.

"Everything okay in here?" Rae Marie asked. She looked at Alexa and recognized the typical signs of fear and disorientation and with a soft voice talked with Alexa for several minutes to calm her down. She adjusted the drip from the IV with the sedative, and then held Alexa's hand for a moment to help her calm down some more.

She turned toward Marc and Jenny and said, "Don't worry. This is a very typical reaction from patients who've been injured like this. There's so much they want to say and ask, and they're completely frustrated because they don't know where to begin. I've increased her sedation again and she'll be calming down right away, and she may even go back to sleep. If she does, she'll be fine, so just let her sleep."

"Thanks," Marc replied.

As she left, Marc's headache returned and he sat down in the recliner while Jenny walked around the bed to sit near him. Alexa's eyes were gently closing and her fingers were relaxing. They sat there quietly while Alexa once again drifted off to sleep.

Without warning Marc bolted up from his chair and walked out of the room. Jenny followed, and once outside she tried to get Marc's attention.

"Marc?" He ignored her and just kept walking. She jogged to catch up to him. "Marc, what's wrong."

"I just want to be alone," he replied sullenly.

"Sweetheart, I wish you'd talk to me," Jenny pleaded.

"Not now!" he replied firmly, trying his best to keep his voice down. They exited the ICU doors together and Jenny tried once more to talk to him.

"Marc, please … where are you going?"

"I don't know and I don't care."

"But—"

"But nothing, Jenny! I said I want to be alone!" and he took off for the elevator.

Knowing Alexa would be asleep Jenny decided to find a seat in the waiting area where she could watch for Marc to return.

§

"Hi, is this the Kensington residence?"

"Yes."

"Hi, this is Marc Janssen, is this Catherine?"

"Yes! Hi, Marc! How're you doing? How's Alexa?"

"I'm doing okay, and I think Alexa's going to be okay, but she's having a rough time right now trying to deal with everything that's happened. They removed the ventilator and she's breathing on her own but she's very distraught. The sedative they're giving her seems to be working to calm her down so she'll relax and go back to sleep."

"Oh, Marc, I'm so sorry. Is there anything we can do?"

"Actually, yes, and that's why I'm calling. Do you think you could ask Lacy if she could come by and see Alexa sometime? Maybe it'll help."

"Oh, sure. She's here right now, would you like to talk to her?"

"No, that's okay. Just tell her I'm going to leave her name at the Guest Services desk up on the ICU floor and the nurse's station so they'll know it's okay for her to visit. And I'll add your name and Robert's, too, for whenever you're able to come by whether Lacy happens to be with you or not."

"Oh, thank you, Marc. That's very thoughtful of you. Lacy's been so worried about Alexa. Well, actually, we all have, so I know she'll come right over."

"Thanks. I'll let you go, and I'll try to do better with keeping you updated."

"Oh, please, Marc, don't worry about it. We know you've been overwhelmed by everything so you just take care of Alexa, okay?"

"Will do. Thanks."

As Marc hung up the phone he paused before deciding what to do next. He didn't want to go back to the room. It made him depressed. He thought about his own accident and how afraid he felt after waking up in the ICU, and knew it was nothing compared to what Alexa must be experiencing right now. And there's *nothing* he could do about it!!

He also didn't want to go back upstairs yet because he didn't want to have to talk to Jenny. Not now. He was too upset about everything, and nothing he did or could think of seemed to ease the rising tension he felt building up between them. It wasn't her fault. Well, perhaps it was. He had told her not to come, but she did anyway. He felt guilty that she was missing her classes. He had a reason, she didn't. He'd told her that he'd call and keep her updated, but instead she'd ignored him and had come anyway.

Normally he would have been grateful for her thoughtfulness in wanting to do something like this for him and for Alexa. He knew Jenny and his sister had a special bond, but for some reason he found himself getting angrier by the minute about the whole situation. He decided to take a walk. Maybe when he returned he'd be calmer and have a clearer head. If not, he didn't know what he'd do, but he didn't want to think about that right now.

CHAPTER 38

Shattered

AFTER OVER AN HOUR of walking the streets around the medical center and the Vanderbilt campus Marc's headache and overall tension hadn't eased at all, but he felt a need to get back to Alexa. He hadn't come to any resolution about what he might say to Jenny, but perhaps something would come to him when they talked.

Part of his wanderings had taken him a few blocks east and he found himself in an area filled with scores of houses and buildings with signs out front that all had one thing in common … music.

'So this is Nashville's famous Music Row that I've heard so much about,' he thought to himself. He had dreamed many times that one day, after graduating from college and marrying Jenny, they'd move to Nashville and he'd pursue his dreams of being a songwriter.

But now that dream no longer mattered. All that really mattered was Alexa. He didn't know and didn't care how long it would take, but he loved his sister so much that he was willing to do whatever it took to help her recover, even if it meant sacrificing his own dreams.

He cleared his head and walked back to the medical center.

§

Jenny was still in the waiting area when she saw Marc approaching from the elevator. His head was down and he hadn't noticed Jenny off to his right. She got up from her chair to catch up to him.

"Marc?" she said timidly as she paused a few feet away from him.

He stopped and turned. "Yeah?" he replied calmly, but not warmly.

"Are you okay, sweetheart? You were gone a long time."

"Yeah," he replied in a noncommittal tone.

She stepped a little closer. "Marc, can we go somewhere to talk?"

"Yeah, maybe we should," and he turned around and started to walk toward the elevator with Jenny following close behind. They rode down without saying a word. When the doors opened Marc left the elevator first and headed down the hallway toward the inner courtyard they'd been in the previous day. Jenny could clearly see he wasn't in a good mood as she walked by his side. He'd never treated her this way. *Ever.*

They found two seats far away from the few other people who were already in the courtyard. Marc sat down heavily in his, and Jenny followed by sitting in the chair next to him but at a ninety degree angle so she could talk to him more easily.

She was afraid to speak, but the longer she waited for Marc to say something, the harder it was for her. The blank look on his face had returned, and the tone of his voice had been cutting. In spite of her fear, she spoke first.

"Honey, what's wrong? Please talk to me about what's on your mind."

Marc sighed heavily.

"Jenny, how many times do I have to go over this with you? I'm afraid for Alexa."

"I'm afraid, too, Marc, but I know there's something more that you're not telling me. I love you, Marc, and I want to help in any way I can. Please, talk to me."

Marc leaned forward, resting his elbows on his thighs, arms in front of him, and his hands almost touching Jenny's. Her heart prayed that he would take her hand, hold it gently, touching it lovingly, reassuringly, so that the aching in her heart would subside. Her wish went unfulfilled.

"What are you doing, Jenny? Why are you here?"

"I'm here for you, Marc, and I'm here for Alexa."

"I told you not to come—"

"No, you said it wasn't necessary for me to come."

"Same thing."

"No, it's not, Marc, and you know it."

"I just wish you hadn't come."

"You don't mean that, sweetheart."

"Yes, I do."

"Listen to me. You've been under a terrible stress, you haven't had a chance to really get any sleep, and you're exhausted."

"And your point is?"

"What kind of question is that?"

"You're telling me things I already know and I don't need to be reminded about them by you!" Frustrated, Marc leaned back and sighed heavily.

Neither of them spoke for several moments.

"I'm sorry, Marc," Jenny said softly.

Marc didn't respond. He wouldn't even look at Jenny.

"Sweetheart, I've got a room at a hotel a few blocks from here. I can give you my key and you can take a shower and sleep for as long as you want. I'll stay with Alexa—"

"No," Marc replied flatly.

"No? No, what?"

"No, I'm not going to your hotel. No, I'm not taking a shower, and no, you're not staying with Alexa."

"Why not, Marc? You're *so* exhausted. I know, don't tell you something you already know, but you're not doing anything about it and I'm giving you that chance. You need sleep, Marc, and you need it now before you crash altogether. In fact, let's do this. Let's go up to Alexa's room, if she's awake we'll visit with her for a few minutes until she falls asleep again, then I'll drive you over there myself because, quite frankly, you shouldn't drive in your condition."

"I'm not going anywhere, Jenny," Marc replied so softly Jenny couldn't hear what he'd said.

"I'm sorry, what did you say?" she asked softly.

"I said, I'm not going anywhere! Got it?!"

"But, Marc—"

"You know what? I'm tired of all of this. You're just making everything worse. Go home. Leave! You're not helping, and I don't want you around."

"Marc—" Jenny began to plead.

"NO! I don't want to hear any more, don't you understand?!"

Jenny burst into tears.

"Go home, Jenny. I don't want you here. I'll deal with Alexa by myself."

"But, Marc—"

"NOW!"

Jenny's sobbing was uncontrollable. Marc stood and walked several steps and stopped. With his back to Jenny he brought his hands together in front of him for a moment, then turned and walked back and stood in front of her. When she finally realized he was standing there, she tried to catch her breath as she looked up into Marc's vacant eyes. Without saying anything Marc held out his right hand, doubled up, palm down. Puzzled, Jenny timidly reached out hers to accept whatever it was he was about to give her. She watched as Marc's hand opened. Jenny had never experienced such pain in her whole life as she did at that very instant. Her heart shattered. As Marc walked away Jenny burst into tears once again and clutched her hand tightly around the last thing she ever expected Marc to give her ... the promise ring.

CHAPTER 39

One Month Later

WITHIN A FEW DAYS Alexa was able to grasp the full magnitude of her situation, and was coming to terms with how her life had changed so drastically in the blink of an eye. There had been some minor damage to the nerves running along her vocal chords but nothing that minor surgery a week after the accident, along with speech therapy, couldn't correct. She spent three weeks in the ICU before being transferred to a private room. She had just finished her dinner, and was resting as comfortably as could be expected, when Marc came in.

"Hey, sis, how are you?"

"Doing okay, considering."

"You're looking a little better this evening."

"Thanks. Mornings tend to be the worst for me because I'm so stiff when I wake up."

"Is there anything I can get you or do for you?"

"Yes! I want a pizza so bad right now!"

"Okay, I'll be right back."

"No, please don't leave. I don't want you to get in trouble for bringing me something I probably shouldn't have." Alexa looked at Marc in that way she had when she wanted to talk seriously and he sat down beside her on the bed. She reached out and held his hand.

"Marc, how's Jenny?"

He wasn't prepared for such a question. He'd previously managed to avoid telling Alexa anything about what happened by simply changing the subject, but not this time. Somehow he knew he had to say something, but definitely not all.

"I don't know. Fine, I guess."

"You guess? You don't know?"

"No, I don't."

"I … I don't get it. When was the last time you talked to her?"

"A while ago."

"Define 'a while ago'."

"Do we have to talk about Jenny?"

"Yes, we do. You've been in love with her for so long, and in case you've forgotten she's *my* friend, too."

"I know. It's just … ," Marc paused.

"It's just what, Marc?" Alexa asked softy.

"I guess … I guess in the end it just wasn't meant to be and she's better off without me."

"You can't believe that."

"Yeah … I can."

"But why? What happened to make you guys split up?"

"I'd rather not talk about it right now, okay?"

"No, it's *not* okay. I can see you're hurting, and I can see you're lost without her."

"No, I'm not."

"Yes, you are."

"Well, it doesn't matter anymore."

"Oh, yes, it does!"

"Not to me," Marc replied sullenly, lowering his head.

"Stop. Stop lying to yourself, Marc. And stop lying to me."

"Listen, some things were said, I hurt her, and it's over."

"Then fix them! Now! Before it's too late!"

"It already *is* too late."

Alexa tried her best to hide her frustration. She paused a few moments before continuing, looking deeply into her brother's eyes.

"Marc, you know I love you, right?"

"Of course!"

"And I'm SO grateful you've been able to be with me from the beginning of this ordeal."

"I wouldn't have it any other way."

"And now that I'm on the road to recovery I need you to do something for me."

"What's that?"

"Please, for me, would you please call Jenny and just talk to her. You *can* work this out, Marc. I *know* you can. Please?"

Marc's silence said everything.

"Wow," Alexa replied sarcastically. "I don't believe it. I never thought I'd see the day when my brother would be a quitter."

They didn't hear Dr. Carr begin to enter the room.

"I'm *not* a quitter, Alexa."

"Well, in my book you are. Whatever happened between you and Jenny needs to be fixed now."

"I'm not discussing this with you any longer, sis."

"Excuse me, am I interrupting?"

Marc and Alexa both startled.

"No, not at all, Dr. Carr," Marc replied, standing up from the bed.

"It's good to see you, Dr. Carr," Alexa added.

"It's good to see both of you, too. I'll just be a moment while I see how you're doing."

Dr. Carr examined Alexa and added some notes to her chart.

"I'm very pleased with how your recovery is going so far, Alexa. Your rehab seems to be going well. A few more weeks here and then we'll be able to transfer you next door where you'll receive more direct attention for exactly what you'll need to return home again in the not too distant future."

"Any idea when that will be?"

"Well, if all goes well, about seven months or so from now."

"Seven *months*?!" Alexa exclaimed.

"Sorry, I'm afraid so."

"Unfortunately, Alexa, she's right. My full recovery was seven months from the time of the accident until I could go home. You're injuries were a lot worse and so your total recovery time will be close to eight months."

Alexa was stunned. Another reality check.

There was a tap on the door and Alexa's roommate, Lacy, peeked in.

"Is it okay to come in?"

"Lacy!" Alexa cried.

Lacy walked quickly to Alexa's bedside and leaned forward to give her a cautious hug. Alexa, struggling through the pain, did her best to return it.

"It's *so* good to see you, Lacy!"

"You too, Alexa!"

"Well, I'll leave you all alone for now," Dr. Carr interjected. "You keep getting plenty of rest, Alexa."

"I promise I will, Dr. Carr."

Dr. Carr looked at Marc and whispered, "May I speak with you outside for a moment?"

Marc nodded and followed her to the hallway.

"Walk with me, Marc. I'd like to ask you something but I don't want to be near Alexa's room as we talk."

"Sure."

"Marc, as you know, as Alexa's attending physician I'm responsible for her total care while she's here with us."

"Yes, I remember."

"And my primary concern here is with her."

"And I'm grateful for that."

"Oh, you're welcome. But, what I want to ask is … how are *you* doing?"

"Me?" Marc asked uncomfortably.

"Yes. Over this past month I've observed your highs and lows and I've been concerned for how you're dealing with this."

"Oh, I'm fine, Dr. Carr. Really, I'm fine."

"Are you sure?"

"Yes, I'm sure."

"The reason I ask is … when Alexa was first admitted I saw your worry, concern, even fear for Alexa as just normal signs that loved ones always display when someone they love has been hospitalized, especially after a near fatal accident like Alexa's. But then, as she started to improve, even ever so gradually, there seemed to be something else distracting you, and your mood remained unusually reticent, as if you had some unspoken issue that you were dealing with aside from Alexa."

Marc didn't know what to say. He hadn't realized that all of his anguish over losing Jenny had been noticed by anyone else.

Dr. Carr continued. "I see by your reaction that I've probably nailed it, but I'm not going to pry into any details. Those are none of my business. But … I *am* going to ask you to deal with it, because I've noticed how it's also affecting Alexa, even going so far as to affect the progress she's making. If you're going to be here for her, then *be* here for her. If you're serious about wanting to help her, then shake off whatever else it is that's distracting you and pay attention to Alexa, or you'll become a liability to her and we may have to ask you to limit the amount of time you spend with her."

Marc nodded. "I'm sorry, Dr. Carr. You're right, there has been something. I'll get it resolved as soon as I can."

"Thank you, Marc. This is for Alexa's sake, *and* yours, because I care about you, too."

"Thank you."

Dr. Carr nodded her appreciation and walked off.

Marc decided to go downstairs to the cafeteria for something to drink and think about what Dr. Carr had just said, and also to give Alexa some time with Lacy. When he returned an hour later he found them chatting away with glowing smiles.

Marc smiled, too. 'Just what Alexa needed right now!' he thought to himself.

"Hi, bro!" Alexa exclaimed. "Welcome back to the crazy house."

"Hi, Marc!" Lacy added. "Yeah, we're just a couple of crazies!" The girls both laughed.

"Tell ya what," Marc began, "you guys just keep having a good time. I need some fresh air so I'm going to go for a walk."

"Okay, bro, be careful."

"I promise."

"It was good to see you again, Marc!"

"You too, Lacy. Thanks *so* much for coming. You really made Alexa's day."

"Oh, you're welcome. She made my day, too!"

Marc smiled and waved as he left the room.

His next stop? Parts unknown. All he knew was that he had a lot to think about.

"Lacy, I'm so worried about Marc," Alexa said, almost in a whisper.

"Why?" Lacy asked sadly.

Alexa sighed. "Something happened between him and his girl-friend, Jenny, right after my accident. Every time I mention her name he immediately changes the subject, and up until today he's refused to say anything about it. But this evening I was able to get a little bit out of him. Apparently, something was said, and he hurt her somehow, and now they're not together. I asked him what it was, but he wouldn't even give me a hint what it might be. I tried to tell him that whatever it was it's not too late to fix things, because I *know* Jenny and I *know* how crazy she is about him, but he refuses to listen to me. And ... I know you'll probably think this is crazy, but I blame myself for their breaking up."

"You're right, you *are* crazy. It's *not* your fault."

"Sorry, you can't convince me of that. If I hadn't been in that accident they'd still be together, happily in love, and about to grad-uate and get on with their lives together. Before the accident, Marc had been hinting during our phone calls that he was planning on asking Jenny to marry him some time after they graduated. Now look ... Marc quit college just before he graduates and he's deter-mined to stay with me throughout my whole time in rehab. Not only has my life been screwed up by this stupid accident, but I've destroyed Marc's life, too." Alexa began to cry.

Lacy moved closer to Alexa, reaching out for her hand as they cried together.

"Alexa, this really is absolutely not your fault."

"But what am I going to do? I can't stand to see him like this. He's tried his best to hide it from me, but the day I came out of my coma Jenny was there and we were talking, and then she was gone. I ... I just feel so terrible."

The door to Alexa's room hadn't quite closed behind Marc when he heard his sister say that she was worried about him. He had paused and, unbeknownst to Alexa or Lacy, had caught the door just before it closed completely. He had heard everything. As they cried he quietly eased the door closed and walked away broken hearted. Dr. Carr was right, he was hurting Alexa. But, what could he do? Any chance to apologize to Jenny had long since passed. Alexa was hurt, but would recover. He had to admit that Jenny was probably devastated, but he couldn't do anything about it. And as for him? He was ... lost. And so alone.

CHAPTER 40

Once

AFTER JENNY HAD RETURNED home from Nashville she found it nearly impossible to function. Her parents and friends had consoled her the best they could, but nothing seemed to help. She was living her life in slow motion, with every thought, every memory of what happened with Marc playing over and over in her mind.

It seemed like a waste of time to attend her classes; she couldn't concentrate, and at this point she thought 'what's the use?', but kept going just to have *something* to keep her mind off of Marc, if even for a little while.

As each day passed she slipped further and further into depression. She ached for Marc, to hear his voice, to look into his eyes, to have him hold her and make this nightmare go away, but every day brought no word from him – no call, no letter, no indication of any kind that he still cared.

If only she hadn't gone to Nashville! Her heart had said 'GO!', but Marc was too upset over Alexa to see how she could help them, too. All she had wanted was to be by his side, where she thought she'd always be for the rest of their lives, and now …

She and Lori had long talks. For as many years as Lori had known Marc, she had never seen this side of him before and she, too, was worried for him. At one point she told Jenny she was going to call him, just to see how he was, but Jenny begged her not to, saying he just needed time to figure things out for himself. Then, hopefully, he'd call, they would talk and work things out, and this nightmare would vanish. If only …

Weeks had now past without a single hint of his caring about her anymore. Tears still regularly soaked her pillow at night, and she was holding it together the best she could as she was preparing to graduate.

Once, she knew exactly what she wanted. Once, she knew what lay ahead in her future. Once, life was unfolding for her just as she had dreamed. Once, she had dreams of marrying Marc, and together raising their family in a home filled with love, and being so grateful to be the one he loved and cherished. Once, she had it all. Once.

CHAPTER 41

Seven Months Later

ALEXA'S RECOVERY HAD BEEN a grueling one for her to say the least, but she attacked it with her typical determination to not let it get the best of her. The surgery on her vocal chords and speech therapy had been successful, and after the early efforts at physical and occupational rehabilitation, she was moved across the street from the medical center to Vanderbilt's Stallworth Rehabilitation Hospital.

Taking Dr. Carr's counsel to heart, Marc had focused his attention on Alexa. He had proven to be invaluable to her during the early days of recovery, though it had taken an unknown toll on him emotionally. He did his best to hide this from Alexa, and his reticence to talk about Jenny sometimes made things difficult between them. They had always been so close as brother and sister, sharing even the deepest of confidences, but this was the one thing Marc refused to open up his heart to her about.

The time had finally arrived for Alexa to leave the rehab center and return to her apartment, and Lacy was so excited for her homecoming! Marc had kept up Alexa's share of the rent so Lacy wouldn't have to try to find another roommate. Besides, Lacy had spent most of her spare time visiting Alexa throughout these last eight months. The holidays were fast approaching and she'd decorated their apartment to make it as welcoming as she could for her best friend.

Alexa had regained most of her strength and nearly all of her mobility. It would still be a while before she would be able to run, but considering the critical extent of her injuries and the alternative of what might have been, she was just *so* grateful to be able to walk on her own once again. Lacy had even been brought in during the final phase of her in-house rehab so that she would be familiar with the exercises and could help Alexa with once she was back home on her own.

Alexa was surrounded with love as she prepared to leave. Marc was quickly gathering the last few items off the table near Alexa's bed and packing them safely away, and Lacy was there with her beaming smile, so proud of her roommate and the progress she had made. Lacy's parents, who had visited Alexa almost as much as Lacy, were also standing close by.

The worst was over, and now it was time for Alexa to return to living on her own again, and Lacy would be right there to help her make the necessary adjustments. As Alexa was escorted from her room in a wheelchair, the others followed close behind. She was overcome with emotion as the staff who had worked so hard to help her reach this day stood and applauded as she was wheeled by them. She asked the nurse pushing her wheelchair to stop for a moment.

"Thank you all so very much for everything you've done for me. I'm so grateful to each and every one of you, for your tireless efforts, for putting up with my frustrations, and yes, even my lowest days when I just felt like I couldn't do any more reps and you got the full brunt of those frustrations." The group of doctors, nurses, and assistants all laughed heartily, knowing exactly what she was referring to.

"I love you all so much, and I pray the next time we meet will be because of something happy and not ..." she let her comment simply hang in the air as she looked down at her wheelchair. Everyone certainly understood.

She turned and nodded to her nurse that she was ready to go, and then turned back and waved to everyone once again. The cheering and applause brought new tears to her eyes; happy tears that were washing away the horrible memories of how this journey had begun.

Alexa's homecoming was overwhelming to her. Not only did it feel good to walk into her apartment once again, but Lacy had fixed up their place beautifully with the decorations and scents of the holiday season, her most favorite time of the year!

"Welcome home!" Lacy exclaimed as Alexa took her first steps into their apartment. Lacy was right behind her, followed by Lacy's parents and then Marc.

"Oh, wow! This is so beautiful, Lacy! I can't believe how wonderful this looks. But, then again, I *can* believe it because of how immensely talented you are! Everything is just so, so ... beautiful!"

"Thanks, Alexa! My mom helped me because we wanted this moment to be *so* special for you. I've missed you so much, and our prayers have finally been answered that you're now back home where you belong!"

"Yes, and it feels so good!"

It took a while for Alexa to get settled back into her surroundings. Eight months had passed since she'd left her apartment that fateful day in March, never imagining the hell she was about to experience. As everyone else kept chatting Alexa wandered about the apartment, familiarizing herself once again with the place she called home.

Lacy and her mom had prepared a wonderful holiday spread, with plenty of things to eat and drink. As they transferred everything from the refrigerator to the dining room table, Lacy asked everyone to gather around and then asked Marc if he would mind offering a blessing. He gave thanks for Alexa's recovery and the wonderful blessings they were celebrating that day, as well as for Lacy and her parents, for their constant love and overwhelming support they had given both he and Alexa during her ordeal, and finished by offering a blessing on the food.

"So, Alexa" Catherine began, "now that you're free to get on with your life once again, what are your plans?"

"Well, I'm thrilled to say I'll be able to return to my studies at Belmont. Shortly after the accident Marc went over to the campus and met with the enrollment and scholarship staff and explained what had happened, and they were very gracious in not only holding my enrollment place open as a continuing student, but they also held all of my scholarships for me. I recently completed all of the necessary paperwork, and I'll be back in classes starting with the next term."

"Oh, that's wonderful," Catherine replied. "And I suppose you'll be getting back into your songwriting and performing again soon?"

"Yes! Very soon! I've missed that so much, and I can't wait to get back to all of it, the writing *and* the performing!"

"That's great," Robert added.

"And," Lacy added, "in anticipation of Alexa's homecoming I took her guitar in and had it all fixed up for her."

"Really?" Alexa asked with a puzzled look? "What do you mean 'fixed up'?"

"Well, your guitar was in need of a little work. You know, like new strings, a neck adjustment, those sorts of things. No big deal."

"Wow, thanks, Lacy! Hey, everyone I have the *best* roommate in the world!" Everyone agreed, and Lacy blushed and shared a brief wink with Marc that went unnoticed by the others.

"Maybe after we're finished here you'd like to play something for us?" Marc asked.

"No, bro, I don't think so, it's been too long since I held a guitar in my hands. I'd rather do that after I've been able to practice for a while."

"Yeah, that's fine. I just figured it wouldn't hurt to ask."

"Sure, that's cool," Alexa replied with a smile. Once again Marc and Lacy shared another wink.

When the meal was just about over Lacy asked if anyone had saved room for dessert, but she had no takers.

"I definitely want some," Catherine replied, "but in a while." To which there was a round of agreement from the others.

Everyone settled down in the living room to chat for a while, and after about fifteen minutes Alexa felt restless, in need of really re-acquainting herself with her old apartment, so she got up and began wandering around, while still remaining a part of the conversation. A few minutes later she walked down the hallway toward her bedroom. As the conversation continued without her, Alexa walked into the bedroom and sat down on her bed.

"Everything okay back there," Marc called.

"Yes," Alexa replied. "I'm just enjoying how comfortable my bed feels, and can't wait to sleep on a real bed!"

As the conversation continued in the living room Alexa let out a scream! Her motherly instincts instantly kicking in, Catherine bolted from the sofa and ran to Alexa's bedroom, Robert was immediately behind, while Marc and Lacy took their time getting up and walking down the hallway.

"What is it, Alexa?" Catherine asked frantically.

"Alexa, what happened," Robert pleaded. "Are you all right?"

Alexa couldn't speak through her sobbing. She pointed to her guitar case on the bed next to her, but everyone stood paralyzed, unable to figure out what she meant. Well ... almost everyone.

"Something in your guitar case?" Catherine asked, still fearful about what had happened. Holding her hands over her mouth and trying to catch her breath, Alexa nodded her head.

Catherine reached to open the case, and Robert started to stop her. "Wait, sweetheart–", but Alexa waved him off and nodded to Catherine that it was okay to open it. She carefully lifted the lid on the case and saw a brand new guitar, wrapped with a ribbon, and a bow resting on the top of the neck where it wouldn't get crushed.

"Oh ... my ... gosh, Alexa. It's beautiful!" She looked at Alexa and saw her nodding again while still holding her hands over her mouth, unable to control her sobbing.

"Where," Alexa tried to speak, "where .... did ... this come ... from?"

Catherine and Robert looked at each other, and then behind them at Lacy and Marc, each wearing the biggest grins.

"What's going on, Lacy?" her mom enquired.

Lacy walked past her parents and to the side of the bed, leaned forward to give her roommate a hug, and then leaned back.

"Welcome home, roomie!"

Still hardly able to breathe, Alexa jumped off the bed and gave Lacy a huge hug. As her crying began to subside, she sat back down on the bed and noticed everyone staring at her and the new guitar.

"Lacy, where did this come from? Where's my old guitar?" Catherine had found some tissues on the nightstand and handed them to Alexa to wipe away her tears.

"Well, first off, your old guitar is put away safely in your closet." Alexa sighed and smiled. "Secondly, I remember hearing you comment every once in a while about how you wished you could get a better guitar, believing that somehow it would make you sound better when you sing. Let me tell you, girl, you could play the washboard and your voice would still shine."

Alexa laughed and wiped away more happy tears.

"I wanted to do something very special for you, not only because of everything you've had to go through, but also for being so valiant in your determination to get your life back. There's nothing stopping you now, girl, and I can't wait to hear you sing while playing that hot, new baby lying on your bed."

Alexa reached over and cautiously removed the guitar from its case. "Oh, my gosh!!! I just realized I have a new case, too! Oh, wow!"

"You can't have a new guitar like that put in any old case, now, can you?" Marc asked with a smile.

"Were you in on this too, Marc?" Alexa asked, still trying to calm her breathing down as close to normal as possible. Catherine and Robert looked back at him and he just smiled and gave Alexa a wink.

"Oh, my gosh. Oh, my gosh. Oh, my GOSH!!! This is just ... so ... beautiful!" Alexa exclaimed.

"So-o-o-o ... let's hear it!" Lacy pleaded. Alexa rested the guitar in her lap and strummed a chord. She did everything in her power to fight back more tears.

"Oh, Lacy ... it's ... it's perfect. It really is perfect. I don't know what to say."

"Don't say anything," Lacy replied. "Just enjoy."

Alexa played a few more chords and then carefully returned the guitar to its case and jumped off the bed to give Lacy another big hug. "I love you, Lacy."

"I love you too, Alexa."

"Yeah, yeah, enough with all the mush, girls," Marc interjected. "I want to see some serious songwriting going on, ya hear?"

"You better believe it, bro! Now, while I get better acquainted with my new guitar why don't you guys go out and get dessert ready. I'll be out in, oh ... 20 or 30 ... years!" They all laughed heartily and then headed out to the living room, listening to Alexa strumming through a variety of chords and then finger picking her way through the intro to Marc and Jenny's favorite song, Restless Heart's "I'll Still Be Loving You". No one noticed Marc catch his breath as those notes began, and so many memories came flashing back.

Moments later he sat down next to Lacy on the sofa, looked at her and winked. "Yeah, she's going to be just fine," he said, even though he knew he wouldn't be.

CHAPTER 42

Marc

WITH ALEXA'S RELEASE FROM Vanderbilt and getting settled back into her life once again, it was now time for Marc to focus on the new career plan that he had come up with for himself during the long months of Alexa's rehabilitation and it gave him an exciting new lease on life. His dreams of success in the music industry would still be fulfilled, not for himself, but for and with others.

During the long hours he spent watching, and when allowed, assisting Alexa with her rehab, he had gradually formulated and designed a unique new career path for himself. Shortly after Alexa had been transferred to the rehab facility he started laying the groundwork to be able to launch his new enterprise as soon as possible after Alexa was on her own. In fact, it was Alexa's passionate spirit and incredible fight to survive and overcome her injuries so she could rise again and re-claim her dreams that deeply inspired Marc to develop this new direction in his own life.

All of the proper paperwork had been filed to prepare for the launch, and throughout the remainder of Alexa's rehab he waited anxiously for word to arrive that everything had been approved and he could finally make the long awaited announcement.

Lacy had invited Alexa and Marc to join their family for the Christmas holidays. Alexa was excited about being with Lacy and her family because of how completely they had welcomed her into their family. She missed her parents terribly, especially at this time of year, but the Kensington's treated her like a daughter and she felt cherished.

Marc had also grown close to them during Alexa's hospitalization. He had found a small, but comfortable apartment not far from the medical center where he had settled in not too long after Alexa was moved from ICU to a regular room, but he had also taken the Kensington's up on their offer for him to stay with them, which he occasionally did on weekends. Once Alexa recuperated enough that she wanted some quiet time for herself without her older brother around, and he didn't particularly want to hang around his apartment, he'd called the Kensington's and asked if he could come visit for a day or two. They always made him feel so welcome and loved. More than once Catherine and Robert had told him how much they admired him and how much they wish they'd had a son like him.

Occasionally when Marc visited, Robert would invite him to spend some time discussing a variety of topics. Before the chillier winter weather had set in, many of those discussions had taken place on a golf course. Even though Marc had worked at a golf course, he'd never had the opportunity to play. Cole had passed away before he was able to fulfill his promise to his son to teach him the game, but Robert was a capable and patient instructor, offering plenty of tips. Marc learned quickly.

Now, here they all were, gathered around a festive dining table decorated in the reds, greens, whites, and golds of Christmas with enough delicious smelling food to feed several families, and a warm fire blazing in the fireplace in the family room. A light snow was falling, adding a special touch to the season.

Robert rose to offer a toast. "It's so wonderful to be together this evening. On behalf of Catherine and Lacy we'd like to welcome our special guests and adopted family members, Alexa and Marc, and hope you'll enjoy this dinner with us. Alexa, we're so pleased that you've made such a wonderful recovery. It's been the answer to all of our prayers. So let's raise our glasses and offer a special toast to Alexa, and Merry Christmas everyone!"

"Merry Christmas!" came the response from around the table as they clinked their glasses.

While enjoying the wonderful dinner each of them took turns sharing special holiday memories and family stories.

As dessert was about to begin Marc cleared his throat and rose to say a few words.

"Well, Catherine … and Robert … and Lacy … on behalf of Alexa and me, I'd like to say thank you, and tell you how grateful we both are for accepting us into your lives, into your home and, most especially … into your hearts. We love you very, very much."

"And we love you!" Catherine replied.

"Here! Here!" Robert added.

Alexa and Lacy just looked at each other and smiled warmly.

"And … I have a special announcement to make."

If Marc didn't have their undivided attention before, he certainly had it now!

"As you all know from previous conversations, especially with Alexa, I had always dreamed of becoming a songwriter right here in Nashville. And, if I got the chance to sing some of my songs in some of the clubs in town along the way, then so much the better. But my true passion was in writing the songs that other artists, much more talented than I, would then record and make into big hits, making both of us very wealthy."

Laughter erupted around the table.

"But Alexa's accident changed things for me, and—"

"I'm so sorry, Marc," Alexa replied softly.

"No, no, sis! Please don't be sorry. Perhaps what I'm about to share with you is what I now believe my destiny was supposed to be all along."

The room drew quiet once more, with only the crackling fire in the fireplace breaking the stillness.

"Early in Alexa's recovery process I started jotting down some thoughts about what the future might hold for me once Alexa was able to return home and to school. As close as I was to graduating, I certainly gave some thought to returning home to California and finishing those remaining credits.

"However, something else came to mind as I was watching Alexa go through her recovery and rehab. I was so impressed, that in spite of the all of the pain and frustration she faced each day, her passionate determination to get well as quickly as possible was unbridled, and I knew I needed something in my own life that would make me feel that same passion and unbridled spirit.

"I wrote down my ideas and plans, talked to a few people about them, had some paper work that I needed to take care of, and, just a few days ago, I received word that everything was finally set and ready to go.

"So ... I'm excited to announce, that as of January 1st I will be launching an innovative foundation, dedicated to assisting worthy singers, songwriters, and musicians who are facing, or who have already faced, seemingly insurmountable obstacles in trying to fulfill their dreams. This foundation will provide the funding they need to make their musical dreams come true."

"That's wonderful, Marc!" Catherine replied.

"How exciting!" Lacy added.

"And the news gets even better," Marc added.

"How could it get any better than that?" Alexa asked.

"It's easy. I met with the foundation's Board of Directors this week and they approved my suggestion for our first recipient. Alexa."

"What?!" Alexa gasped as she began to shake from the excitement. "Wha ... what do you mean, recipient?"

"Well, in addition to the scholarships you have, I'm going to personally help you with your remaining educational and living expenses so you can concentrate on your classes and studying. The foundation has established a fund to cover the expenses for you to be able to concentrate on pursuing your singing and songwriting career, including studio time, promotions, etc."

"Oh, Marc," Alexa replied while jumping out of her chair to hug her big brother. "I don't know what to say."

"No need to say anything, sis," Marc replied softly as they held each other tightly with tears streaming down their faces. "I love you, and I'm honored to do this for you."

The Kensington's shared in the excitement with cheers of joy.

Finally, Alexa loosened her hug on her brother, and gave him a big kiss on the cheek before sitting down again.

"Now, two final announcements and I'll shut up and sit down so we can eat our dessert."

"It's about time!" Robert said jokingly, and everyone laughed.

"First ... I chose the name for the foundation based on watching my amazing sister over these last several months. She's so inspirational, and I know as the first recipient of funds from the foundation she will shine an amazing light on the work we'll be doing with her and others in the future. And so, in honor of Alexa's rise from the critical injuries she sustained in her accident to become the inspiration she is to all of us today, I've named it the Alexa Janssen Foundation!"

"Oh, Marc, that's wonderful!" Catherine exclaimed.

Lacy and Alexa looked at each other and bounced in their chairs like two giddy school girls. Robert looked on with genuine approval and nodded.

"And finally," Marc added, attempting to get everyone's undivided attention once again, and pausing for several intense moments for dramatic effect, "I'm thrilled to announce ... that I recently made an offer, and it was heartily and graciously accepted ... and one of the directors on our board is ... our very own ROBERT KENSINGTON!"

Robert raised his glass and nodded at Marc, and Marc raised his glass in return as the rest of the family erupted in cheers!

"Oh, my gosh," Catherine once again exclaimed, "this is all such wonderful news! I don't know if my heart can take any more!"

"Sure it can, sweetheart," Robert replied. "Now ... let's all celebrate over dessert!" to which everyone was in complete agreement.

§

Sitting in front of the fire later that evening, Marc and Alexa were sharing some special, quiet brother-sister moments. Finally, Alexa had to ask a few questions that had been on her mind ever since his announcements earlier in the evening.

"Marc, I'm really excited about your new venture."

"Thanks, sis, I'm excited, too."

"Have you decided where your office is going to be?"

"Yes, right here in Nashville. Why?"

"So … you won't be heading back out to California?"

"Sure I will, from time to time, but only for business."

"What about … our home?" Alexa asked hesitantly.

"We're keeping it for now. It's there for you whenever you head back home to visit friends or whatever, and after you graduate in a few years you might decide to move back to California and use that area as your base to build your career."

"What if I decide to stay here instead of moving back home?"

"When you're ready to make that decision we can sit down and discuss what we should do then, fair enough?"

"Sure." Alexa replied, still with some trepidation. She paused several long moments before continuing.

"What about … Marc, what about Jenny?"

Marc sat up and paused before replying, obviously upset by the question.

"Alexa … it's over," he replied softly, but firmly.

"It shouldn't be."

"Well, whether it should or shouldn't be doesn't matter. It's too late."

"No, it's not, Marc."

"Yes," Marc replied sadly, "I'm afraid it is. I lost her, and it's my own fault. And now I have to just live with that fact and move on with my own life."

"This is all my fault. If I hadn't—"

"Alexa, it's not your fault."

"Yes, it is. If I hadn't been in that stupid accident you and Jenny would have graduated, probably already be married by now and happily moving on with your lives."

"Alexa, none of this is your fault. Not the accident, not Jenny and I breaking up, nothing, okay?"

"No, it's not okay, Marc. You two were so much in love. You were perfect for each other. You had the kind of love and relationship that I dream of having some day. You *need* to call her!"

"Sis, please try to understand. What Jenny and I had once was beautiful and special, but it's over. I made a horrible mistake, and I just have to live with it. She deserves someone much better than me."

"That's where you're wrong, Marc. She deserves *you* and *only* you! I just wish you could see that."

"None of that matters any more, Alexa. It's too late. And can we please not talk about this anymore?"

"No. Not until I say this one last thing."

"What is it?" Marc asked with a long, exasperated sigh, definitely upset that Alexa insisted on hammering him about Jenny.

"This isn't your decision."

"What?!"

"You heard me, Marc. This isn't your decision."

"And just whose decision is it?"

"Jenny's."

"That's where you're wrong, sis. I broke it off, I sent her away, I'm the one who made the big mistake, and I'm the one and *only* one who needs to live with that decision. Period!"

"No! Not period! Whether you realize it, or will even find it in your thick skull to admit, Jenny's living with it, too, and she has been all along. And if you can't see that, then you're just plain stupid!" And with that Alexa got up and began to head to her room to go to bed.

"Wait, Alexa." She ignored her brother and kept walking.

"WAIT, please?" Marc insisted. Alexa stopped at the base of the stairs, her hand resting on the railing, but didn't turn around. He got up from the sofa and walked up behind her.

"Alexa ... I just can't. I can't call her, I can't write to her ... I just can't see her again at all. It's a lot more complicated than you think, and I can't even figure out how to explain it to you."

Alexa let his words hang in the air for several moments before saying anything.

"Is that all you can say?" she asked softly while looking down at the stairs in front of her.

"Yes," Marc replied in a whisper.

Alexa began walking up the stairs without saying another word.

"Good night, Alexa," he called out as his eyes followed her ascent up the stairs. She paused for only a moment as she reached the top, holding tightly to the stair rail post, and then walked down the hallway without a reply.

She softly closed the bedroom door behind her so she wouldn't disturb the Kensington's, praying they hadn't heard her 'discussion' with Marc just now. She laid down on the bed, clutching one of the king size pillows, and cried softly.

'If only there was something I could do to get you two back together again,' she thought to herself, 'but Marc ... I guess you're too determined to not let that happen. Why, Marc? Why? I just know Jenny still loves you.' She truly loved her brother, but sometimes he was just so blind to the truth that surrounded him.

CHAPTER 43

Present Day

THE LAUNCH OF THE Alexa Janssen Foundation had been a huge success. It didn't take long for the word to spread up and down Music Row, and then throughout the whole city. Nashville was a city where several thousand singers, songwriters, and musicians struggled daily for a break, *any* break that would lead to their dreams coming true and requests for funding deluged their office.

Funding the legitimate requests wasn't a problem … it was all of the filtering that had to be done to separate those that truly qualified for the funding from those who merely made up a bunch of lies to get their hands on what they thought was some quick, big money. Marc's staff, however, was up to the challenge.

Over the years, the foundation's reputation for integrity grew with every success they achieved, but Marc found himself being removed more and more from the day to day involvement with the talented singers, songwriters, and musicians they were developing, and having to be more involved with the executive requirements of his position. A change needed to be made and he knew just what it was and how he'd do it.

At the beginning of the next board meeting he stood up, shared some brief compliments with the members of the board, added his gratitude for all of the hard work they had put in, and then, without any warning, announced his resignation as Executive Director.

Stunned silence permeated the conference room. The board members looked at each other and then back at Marc with understandable disbelief. Suddenly, like a dam had burst, the questions overwhelmed Marc. He raised his hands in an attempt to bring some order to the meeting.

"Ladies and gentleman … you are all my very close friends, and I know this has come as quite a surprise to you. The main questions I'm hearing from you seem to be 'Why?' and 'What am I going to do now?' I assure you I have the answers to those questions, and if you'll allow me to explain, I believe I can alleviate any concerns you may have.

"First off, I'm quite sane, and—"

"I'm not so sure about that!" came a comment from Ron Campbell, a well known and highly respected Nashville producer sitting at the far end of the table. Laughter erupted, and Marc joined in the lighthearted exchange. He raised his hands to calm them down once again.

"I've been thinking about this for quite some time, so this is not some spur of the moment decision. Over the last twenty years our Foundation has become very successful in finding and developing worthy talent. I believe that as Executive Director I've come to the point where I've done all I can, and I'd like to see some fresh blood take over in my place.

"And the other question you have for me had to do with what I'm going to do now, and that's another fair question.

"When I launched the Foundation I found myself involved with every aspect of its operations, and the one thing I really loved the most, and the one thing I've missed the most as we've grown, is the one thing I'm going to return to now. I'm going to re-join the ranks of those who are out in the field every day looking for new talent that needs our assistance, as well as partner with our new Executive Director in making presentations to secure additional sources of funding to help us continue to expand our horizons."

The silence in the room was accompanied by nodding heads around the table as each of the members was keenly aware of how effective Marc had been at finding great talent, as well as his ability to consistently secure excellent funding, especially the yearly grants from the Pacific Far West Foundation.

"And now the answer to that question that wasn't asked earlier, but I know is on everyone's mind just the same ... who will take over as Executive Director?"

The room was still as every member of the board waited in anticipation for Marc's reply.

"Ladies and gentlemen of the board, it is my recommendation, and I hope you will go along with me in approving Robert Kensington to be the new Executive Director!"

Proper decorum was all but lost at that moment as applause and cheers filled the boardroom. When calm was finally restored Robert was heartily, officially, and unanimously approved as their new Executive Director and Marc immediately handed the balance of the meeting over to him. Marc moved to a chair at the far end of the room as Robert proceeded to thank everyone for their vote of confidence and then jumped right into the business at hand.

Before he could get very far, though, another member of the Board, Kent Phillips, joked, "Hey, Marc, I thought you said you wanted some *fresh* blood to take over, not *old* blood!" Everyone laughed, including Robert who seemed to be enjoying this the most.

"Well, it might be old, but, thanks to Marc's excellent counsel over the years, it's also wise blood," Robert countered, and after some other good natured bantering he guided everyone back to the work at hand.

§

With a bit more time on his hands Marc found his golf game gradually improving, while his golfing partner, Robert, jokingly complained about his game gradually declining. Regardless of whose game was improving or declining, their friendship grew stronger every day. Marc really missed his dad and the special father-son relationship they'd always enjoyed, but Robert had filled that emptiness in his life quite well. He trusted Robert and listened to his wise counsel intently and acted on it accordingly. That is, with one exception.

Robert had tried unsuccessfully to get Marc interested in taking more time off and less time in the office and on the road for business. He reminded Marc that a truly successful person was one whose life was in proper balance, not one who was so heavily involved in one pursuit that everything else seemed to take a faraway second place. He encouraged him to find a life away from business, and in order to really feel fulfilled in this life, he should think about settling down and getting married. Perhaps it wasn't too late to have a family.

Robert had had discussions like this with Marc many times over the years they'd been friends, but every time the subject came up Marc always changed the subject as quickly as possible. He didn't want to think about it, because he didn't want to have to deal with his past which he knew he'd need to resolve in his own heart before he'd ever have a chance to fall in love with someone else. He'd dated a few wonderful ladies over the years, but never seriously. After too many unsuccessful attempts Robert finally stopped bringing up the subject and that was fine with Marc.

Even though he was no longer Executive Director, the Foundation was still his baby and he was determined to do everything he could to make it as successful as possible, not so much in monetary terms, but in the number of amazingly talented people they would continue to find and develop. To Marc, the true measure of success for the Foundation was the number of dreams they could help fulfill.

Besides, Robert wasn't aware of the two times since this venture began that Marc had seen Jenny; the first time was ten years ago when he'd flown to San Francisco on short notice to make an updated presentation to the Pacific Far West Foundation, that resulted in the largest acquisition of new funding they'd received up to that point; a presentation he'd been grateful had gone well after being so overwhelmed from seeing Jenny in the airport earlier that morning. The second time was when he'd flown to California on that combined business trip and short vacation, and saw her in Carmel. Seeing Jenny that day, and with her husband, no less, had shaken him to his core. He had loved her so much, and knew he could never love anyone again as much as he'd loved Jenny.

And there was still the matter of the secret that he hadn't shared with anyone, not even Alexa; the one thing that had caused him the greatest pain and anguish in his life.

CHAPTER 44

Marc

MARC HAD BEEN WORKING virtually non-stop for years without taking any time off to really breathe. From the time of Alexa's accident and throughout her recovery he had focused his life on only one thing – Alexa. He'd sacrificed his studies … and Jenny. Nothing was more important to him at that time than making sure Alexa recovered, and then had the best chance possible to fulfill her dreams. He felt that if he couldn't have the career in music that he'd always dreamed of, then he would do everything in his power to make it possible for as many others to have that chance, beginning with Alexa. And for over twenty years he'd worked hard to make the Foundation a success and in the process the funding had allowed hundreds to fulfill their dreams.

Over those twenty years he'd occasionally thought about taking some time off to see if he could rekindle his musical drive and desire and make a few things happen for himself, but there was always just one more new applicant, one more new dream to fulfill, one more important presentation to make, one more new project to respond to. He was so used to putting others first that he had seemingly forgotten how to put himself first once in a while.

He was desperately in need of some good old fashioned R&R, and when he checked his schedule and noticed his 25th high school reunion was coming up in a few weeks, he found himself giving some thought to actually going. He had debated about whether or not to even add it to his calendar in the first place, but after several calls from some old friends he decided he'd at least put it on his calendar, and then if he had the time perhaps he'd go ahead and attend.

Then came the call that tipped the scale. It was Lori's party, early in their senior year, that had brought Marc and Jenny together and she had been a close friend to both ever since. She and Marc had kept up a casual correspondence over the years, touching base every so often. She had been the one who had alerted Marc to the reunion several months earlier since she was on the reunion planning committee. Perhaps they weren't so young anymore, but hearing from her had been like a wave of nostalgia overwhelming him with memories of high school, and he felt like he was 17 again.

Early on, and as painful as it was to hear about her, Lori had also occasionally kept Marc apprised with how Jenny was doing, that is ... when he asked. He knew he'd broken her heart and he knew he didn't deserve to have any part of her life anymore, but he still cared deeply about her. The memory of his high school and college sweetheart, even all these years after he'd broken up with her, still held a special place in his heart. Admittedly he still loved her. If only ... no, he just wouldn't go there. Why torture himself with something that could never be? Besides, he hadn't asked Lori about her in several years, especially not since ... no, he just couldn't allow his thoughts to go there either.

One favor Marc had asked Lori was that if Jenny ever asked about him (he doubted she would, but just in case) he asked Lori to please just tell Jenny he was doing fine, busy with his career, and if Jenny asked about his family Lori was just to tell her she didn't know because all he talked about was his career.

Marc was prone to bouts of melancholy as he thought about what might have been, and his only recourse had been to bury himself in his work. One of his hesitations about making the trip to California for the reunion in the first place was the possibility that he might run into Jenny. Sure, there was that brief moment at the airport ten years earlier, and then seeing her with her husband, Scott, in, of all places, Carmel two years ago. But this was different. The reunion was all about high school friends getting together to relive the good ol' days, to hear, and perhaps dance, to the music they loved back then, and to hopefully come away with new memories. If Jenny was there, fine. She had just as much right to be there as he had. And, no doubt, she'd be there with Scott. No big deal. If they got close enough to say "Hi" he'd simply be pleasant. He had plenty of other friends to visit with that night. He'd decided that he'd just deal with everything as it came and not worry about anything else in advance.

Marc's plans for his life had changed in an instant. One moment he was getting ready to graduate from college, marry his sweetheart, and pursue a career in music in Nashville, and the next moment he had left college to care for his sister, and lost his one true love to his anger. It had been hard to get over blaming himself for Alexa's accident, and he'd crashed into despondency with a deep and agonizing depression, but his unrelenting focus on Alexa and the Foundation had helped to pull him through.

To many casual observers he might have appeared indifferent about himself, but in his heart he was anything but. Not a day passed without him thinking about Jenny, wishing he could stop time and make it go back to before that fateful day of Alexa's accident. He wished he'd prevailed when Alexa had said she wanted to go out of state for college, but he knew he was only being unreasonable and selfish. She loved music, she was a wonderful songwriter, and had a voice that could literally melt anyone listening to her, and she was following her passion, just as he was at the time. She'd always looked up to him as her example, her mentor.

CHAPTER 45

Old Friends

MARC FLEW TO THE Bay Area on the Wednesday prior to the reunion. He planned to spend some time visiting a few old friends and neighbors before the actual reunion events planned for the coming weekend.

One bright spot on his calendar was coming up the next night. Lori had called him a month ago to see if he was actually going to make it to the reunion, and when he confirmed that he was, she'd asked if they could meet for dinner at a nice restaurant "for old time's sake" sometime during the week. They had decided to meet at The Spinnaker on Thursday evening.

He was looking forward to seeing Lori again, chatting about old times and finding out the latest on what was happening with her family and life since her divorce. There wasn't much to say about his own life since he never talked about it, always managing to switch to another subject like sports or the weather. His friends always got the hint. Lori knew, though, and that was enough, and he'd sworn her to secrecy from the beginning.

Arriving mid-afternoon on a flight from Nashville, Marc checked into the Claremont Hotel in the Berkeley hills, the site of the reunion later in the week, and settled into his room. Plans were already set for dinner that night as he'd talked with both Mike and Dave over the previous weekend and the three of them had decided to get together for pizza at one of their favorite hangouts from when they were in high school.

He kicked off his shoes, propped up the pillows on his bed, and laid back to relax and watch some TV before taking a shower and getting ready to meet the guys. He checked his cellphone for messages, then set an alarm just in case he got too comfortable.

While channel surfing he thought about how much he had missed the Bay Area. So much had changed from the time he and Alexa were kids and had grown up here.

He had watched many of the changes take place while he was young, but after moving to Nashville over 20 years ago, he had become disconnected, except for the rare occasions when he returned on a business trip. What new changes would he notice this time?

An hour later he was glad he'd set that alarm as he hadn't realized just how exhausted he was. He'd been on the road for most of the past few weeks and had been looking forward to these few days, knowing he'd have a chance to kick back and relax before his schedule went into hyper speed again after the reunion.

He picked out the shirt he wanted to wear with his Wrangler's, then took a hot and steamy shower to help loosen up his tense muscles. The long hours over the last month had been taking their toll on him both physically and mentally and he was grateful for this all-too-brief respite.

Just after he got out of the shower and dried off, his cellphone rang. Checking the caller ID he saw it was Lori.

"Hey, Lori!" Marc answered jovially.

"Hi, Marc! Are you finally in town?" Lori asked with excitement.

"Yes, I got in a little while ago. I just got out of the shower and I'm getting ready to head out for the evening."

"O-o-o-o, the man just gets into town and already he's got himself a hot date!"

"Ha! No, it's nothing like that. Just getting together with some of the guys to get something to eat."

"Oh, then I won't keep you. I just wanted to check to make sure we're still set for dinner tomorrow night?"

"Yes, absolutely! Eight o'clock at The Spinnaker, right?"

"That's the place!"

"I'm really looking forward to it, Lori. It's been way too long."

"It sure has. And the reunion this weekend is going to be great!"

"I hope so. Any idea how many of our class are going to be there?"

"The last I heard we had reservations for over 150, including spouses or dates."

"Hey, that's great!"

"So are you bringing a date, Marc?"

"Me? No. I'm just coming to see some friends and have a good time. I've missed all of the previous reunions so I've got some catching up to do."

"Well, I'm sure you'll have a great time."

"Yes, I'm sure I will. How could I not, with you on the planning committee?"

"Exactly!" Lori laughed. "Anyway, I know you have to get ready so I'll let you go. I'll see you tomorrow night!"

"Okay, Lori. Take care."

Marc clicked off his phone, set it on the bed, and proceeded to get dressed.

§

Getting together with the guys turned out to be just the right thing to help Marc forget about the present and relive the glory days of their past. They talked about football games with the usual embellishment of great catches, or how many yards they'd run on a particular play to win a game. Marc asked them about their families and careers, but when it came time to share the details of his own, he smoothly changed the subject back to sports. The Oakland A's were playing that night and they'd been half-watching the game on one of the large flat-screen TV's scattered through the place. By ten o'clock they were all talked out, at least for the night. No doubt they'd be ready for round two at the reunion.

As Marc drove back to his hotel he found his thoughts wandering once again as memories started rising and haunting him. As he approached his off ramp at Ashby Avenue, he decided to take the Powell Street off ramp instead and head west, out to the Point.

Reaching the end of the road he parked his car among the few others there at Marina Park, turned off his headlights and stayed in his car, listening to the night sounds. After several minutes he finally opened the door, climbed out, and leaned against the car, still just listening. A few moments later he walked between some nearby trees and out to Marina Park Pathway and sat down on the rocks, watching and listening as the waters of San Francisco Bay lapped up on them in a gentle rhythm. The view from the Point was amazing, with the lights of the Bay Bridge off to his left, the lights of the City straight ahead and the Golden Gate Bridge slightly off to the right.

Marc sighed heavily as he thought of moments like this with Jenny by his side. This was just one of the places around the Bay Area that they liked to go and talk ... and dream. It was quiet, they could be alone, and the view was ....

'STOP IT!' he thought. 'That was too long ago, and Jenny moved on ... without me. Maybe it's ... time ... for me to finally do the same.'

Before he could change his mind he quickly walked back to his car and headed back to the hotel.

§

The next morning Marc did something he rarely allowed himself to do ... he slept in. He didn't have much planned for the day so he thought 'why not?' After he finally got up and showered he went out for a light breakfast and then decided to take a drive.

He drove through his old home town, driving past his old high school, pulled into the student parking lot and looked out over the football field. It didn't take much for him to be able to hear the roar of the crowd, the quarterback calling plays, the crunching of pads, the cheers as another touchdown was scored, and the band playing the school fight song. Even the pretty cheer leaders in their short dresses leading the raucous crowd in one rousing cheer after another. It all came back.

He pulled out of the parking lot and drove past the houses where some of his best friends had lived and where he'd spent many happy days throwing baseballs or footballs, or just hanging out.

One of his last adventures was driving passed the home he'd grown up in just like he did nearly every time he came back to the Bay Area. After Alexa had graduated from Belmont and had chosen to stay in the Nashville area, they had decided to sell it. It hadn't changed much over the years, with each successive owner doing their best to keep up the attractive landscaping, as well as keeping the home itself in good repair, at least as far as he could tell from just driving by.

One last drive-by remained … the home where Jenny used to live.

He was fighting a losing battle with his emotions. In just a few days he'd be at the reunion. Would Jenny be there, too? He had to prepare himself for the possibility so he would handle it properly, like a gentleman, and not lose it altogether. He debated about calling Lori and asking, but decided not to. Besides, he'd be seeing Lori that night and he could ask her then.

He spent the balance of the day relaxing by just driving around the area, reacquainting himself with many of the fun places he and Jenny had gone to. He probably shouldn't have, but he just couldn't help himself. His thoughts always turned to her when he had too much time on his hands.

§

As Marc was driving through the City it dawned on him that he meant to ask Lori a question when she called the previous night. He switched on the Bluetooth feature and punched her number into his cellphone.

"Hello?"

"Hey, Lori!"

"Hi, Marc! How are you?"

"Doin' great!"

"What's up?"

"Well, I don't know where my head's been at, but how about if I come by and pick you up this evening and—"

"No, that's fine."

"Oh, okay, I just thought I'd offer. I was thinking that it didn't make sense for both of us to make the trip over there when I could just swing by and pick you up, and then drop you back home afterwards."

"Aw, that's sweet of you to think about it, Marc, but I'm visiting a good friend today and I'll be getting ready for this evening at her place."

"Okay. Well, have a good time."

"Till tonight!"

"Ciao for now!"

CHAPTER 46

Lori

EVEN THOUGH THE SPINNAKER didn't require their patrons to be dressed semi-formally or better, Marc still felt the need to wear the new navy blue pin-striped suit he'd bought and had tailored for the reunion. As far as he was concerned his special friendship with Lori dictated it. Of course, to add just a touch of casualness to the evening he still wore his trademark cowboy boots which he'd had the hotel staff polish that afternoon. And while he was doing some shopping in the City earlier that day he'd even managed to find a pair of cufflinks to match his brightly colored Jerry Garcia tie; the perfect combination of subdued class with a little splash of color.

Marc was ready to go but took a few extra moments to look at the view from his hotel window. The room he'd selected was perfect for its incredible view, especially of the evening lights he'd enjoyed so much. He'd moved back to the Bay Area for a while several years after Alexa's full recovery and had lived closer to the bay at the South Shore Beach and Tennis Club in Alameda. He had often walked across the street and up and down the beach at night, always alone, looking out across the bay toward the Bay Bridge and the City beyond. The shimmering lights always made him think of better times. But that was then, and this is now, and Marc shook his head to come back into the moment.

He gathered his thoughts, took one last look at the sweeping view, slipped on his coat, gathered his keys, turned off the lights, and closed the door behind him as he headed out for what he knew would be a special night.

Was it because he was going to see Lori whom he hadn't seen since shortly after they'd graduated from high school? Or was it the look of the lights of the bridge and the City? Or perhaps it was the silhouette of the Golden Gate Bridge with the brilliantly colored approaching sunset as a backdrop? Whatever it was Marc just felt that this evening was somehow going to be special.

Marc and Lori had been close friends from the time they met in Mr. McKay's freshman science class, and for the rest of their time in high school they'd shared several classes together. They'd never dated, but they were as close as if they'd been brother and sister, with Marc helping Lori with her homework from time to time as well as each of them sharing secrets about each other's latest crushes. They'd often studied together at Marc's house so Lori had also become close friends with Alexa. She'd even heard about Alexa's accident from Jenny after Jenny had flown home from Nashville after their terrible break-up.

Lori had done everything she could, along with Jenny's other girlfriend, Monica, to encourage Jenny to not give up on Marc, but Jenny had told them over and over about how adamant Marc had been about the breakup. Besides, in spite of his being so devastated over Alexa's accident, he'd broken her heart deeply when he returned her promise ring.

Knowing Marc was devastated by Alexa's accident Lori had tracked him down through some other mutual friends and had written him long letters of support and encouragement. He'd eventually responded to her letters, thanking her for her concern and encouragement, and explained that they had been one of the few things that had kept him going during the darkest hours of his life … losing Jenny and almost losing Alexa.

Now here they were, about to meet face to face after such a long time. Granted, she wouldn't be the young lady he'd last seen so many years ago, but he wasn't the same either. He'd managed to stay in great shape over the years. He'd worn his hair a bit long while they were in high school, touching about half way down his collar, the kind of singer-songwriter casual look, but for two decades now he'd assumed a more professional appearance befitting his role with his Foundation. He had trimmed his hair up a bit, and his once sandy brown hair had begun to show traces of a distinguished gray around the temples.

For a Thursday night the traffic through the City seemed to be lighter than Marc remembered from so long ago, and he made excellent time while heading to his rendezvous with Lori. For some reason crossing the Golden Gate Bridge always gave Marc a thrill. Maybe it was because he had so many memories associated with the bridge and good times, and dinner with Lori would certainly qualify as one of those!

Pulling into the lot near The Spinnaker he found a parking spot overlooking the Bay. He got out of his car, reached inside the driver's side rear door and eased his suit coat off the hanger. He took a moment to slip his coat on before closing the door, briefly catching his reflection in the car window. He straightened his tie, buttoned his coat, squared his shoulders and walked into the restaurant.

Marc glanced at his watch ... 7:40. He wasn't due to meet Lori until eight but was glad that he'd arrived early enough to be able to select a nice table in just the right spot to give them as much privacy as possible.

One of the fascinating things he'd always enjoyed about The Spinnaker was the incredible view of the lights of the City. Tonight he wanted a quiet, intimate setting because he and Lori had lots of catching up to do.

He approached the Maître d', identified himself, and said he was early for his eight o'clock reservation and would be joined soon by a friend.

"Oh, good evening, Mr. Janssen!" James replied warmly. "We've been expecting you! Your table is ready and I'll take you right to it."

"Thank you. May I ask a personal favor? Is the table in a nice quiet spot? I arrived early in hopes that I might be able to select just the right table that was available because this evening is rather special. I haven't seen the friend who's joining me in many years and we have a lot of catching up to do."

"Yes, Mr. Janssen, your table is in one of our best locations. I believe you'll be very happy. You might also like to know that your friend is already here and is waiting for you."

"Lori's already here?" Marc asked with a chuckle. He was totally surprised because Lori used to barely make it to class on time when they were in school.

"Yes, sir!" James replied with a smile. "I'll take you to her now."

"Thank you."

As James led Marc to his table he looked around and noticed that the restaurant was just as beautiful as he had remembered it, even though it had been a long time.

From several tables away Marc saw Lori and her radiant smile and he smiled back.

"Here you are, Mr. Janssen. And I hope you have a wonderful evening."

"Thank you, James. I'm sure we will."

"Gina will be your waitress, and she'll be with you in just a few moments."

"Thank you again, James."

Looking toward Lori, Marc smiled broadly. "Oh, Lori, it's *so* good to see you, and you look *amazing!*"

Lori had risen so they could share a warm embrace. "It's wonderful to see you too, Marc! You're too kind. Not to mention being VERY easy on the eyes," she added with a sly wink. Marc smiled in return, then helped her with her chair, and then sat down across from her.

"Well, they certainly put us at the perfect table," Marc said while glancing around the restaurant, noting that their table was rather private for that time of the evening, and the lighting was perfectly dimmed. Of course, the view of the City was appropriately breathtaking.

"Just the way I thought you might like it. I figured you'd prefer to be in a quiet area."

"Even after all this time you still know me well. Thanks, Lori. I appreciate it."

"Anytime!" Lori responded with a twinkle in her eye. "And I wanted to be sitting in just the right spot to see you the moment you arrived."

"I'm sorry, Lori. I don't mean to stare, but you really haven't changed since the last time I saw you, and we won't say how many years ago that was," he added with a wink.

"You sure know how to make a girl feel special, Marc. But look at you! My gosh! You're even more handsome than I remember you!"

"Well, either the years have been good to both of us, or we're the newest members of the Bay Area Chapter of the Liar's Club." They both enjoyed a hearty laugh.

"Oh, Lori, thank you so much for all of this. I have to tell you that ever since you called and we talked about getting together for dinner I've been so excited to see you and catch up with how you're doing."

"Actually, Marc, I'm just so glad you accepted! I wasn't even sure if you'd be able to make it to the reunion. I know how busy you've been for so long, and sometimes people just get into a routine that they find it hard to break for even a short time."

"Well, I have to admit that it took me a while to actually put the reunion on my calendar because I just wasn't sure if I could spare the time to come, but then I heard from Mike and Dave and we started talking about old times and the crazy stuff we did that we somehow managed to stay out of trouble over. It was great to hear from them and so I gave coming a second thought. I'll tell you, though, it was your phone call that sealed the deal. How could I pass up this opportunity to spend some one-on-one time with one of my best friends?"

"Oh, Marc, I'm honored you still consider me such a good friend."

"How could I not? After all we went through together in high school, and then everything you did for me after Alexa's accident? You were there when I needed it the most. You kept me sane when

I was ready to lose it so many times, and that kept me on the ball for Alexa. I owe you *big* time, Lori!"

"Actually, you don't because you were there for me when I was going through my divorce."

"I was so sorry when you told me about it. Actually, I was shocked because I really thought you and Gary were perfect for each other!"

"Well, we were ... at first. But he was doing a lot of traveling for his company and that started to really take a toll on our marriage. I was patient at first because he was only on the road a few days a month, but then over time it became more often and for longer periods. I tried to calmly talk to him about it but he said that it was just his job and he had to do it or lose it. The last time he used that line I firmly put it back in his face. I said, 'Okay, then look at it this way. This is your marriage and your family, and you're going to have to do more to be a part of it or you're going to lose it.'"

Marc's jaw dropped. "What did he say to that?"

"He just stared at me for a moment, said a disgusted 'Fine!', and walked off into the other room. We hardly talked at dinner that night. I tried everything I could think of to talk about something, anything, that he might be interested in, but he was just full of one word replies, if that. I was heartbroken, but I was also disgusted and decided to embrace that emotion instead because it was easier on my heart to handle. I'd rather be mad than upset *any* day. Mad I can get over rather quickly, sad I can't."

"I know what you mean, Lori. After Alexa's accident I was in a state of rage with the world and everybody in it. It took every ounce of patience I had when I was visiting with Alexa, and later while I was assisting her with her rehab. I just had so much rage built up inside with no way to get it out. One of Alexa's doctors noticed the symptoms and offered me a prescription, but I turned him down because I was afraid that if it really worked that I might become dependent on it and I didn't want to take that chance. Then he recommended that I see a psychologist or get into some kind of group counseling, sort of a support group for loved ones of accident victims. I thanked him for the advice, but decided to go it alone. It was hard, and looking back I can see the wisdom in his advice, but I was just too bull headed to really think straight and rationally at the time."

"Good evening! My name is Gina, and I'll be your server this evening. May I offer you a cocktail or something else to drink to start the evening off?"

The interruption was a welcome relief for both Marc and Lori as the mood had gradually become rather dark, and that's not what this evening was supposed to be about. They glanced quickly at each other after Gina's introduction before Marc replied, "Actually, Gina, we've been talking and haven't even looked at the menu yet. But in the meantime may we have two waters with lemon wedges?"

"Absolutely! I'll be right back."

Marc and Lori had barely begun their conversation again when Gina reappeared with their drinks. "I'll give you two a few more minutes to look over the menu and then I'll be back."

"That sounds good, Gina. How about at least five minutes, or so? We're not in a hurry this evening."

"Sure, Mr. Janssen. If you'd prefer you could just give me a nod when you're ready and I'll be right over."

"Thank you, Gina. That works for us."

Marc looked at Lori with a somewhat puzzled look on his face. "She knew my name? Hmm, that's interesting."

"Why shouldn't she know your name, Marc? You're famous!"

"Oh, sure. For what?"

"Oh, I told the Maître d' all about you so he had the whole staff on alert for you long before you arrived," Lori said with a mischievous smile.

"Yeah, right."

"No, I'm serious, Marc," Lori replied, though he found it difficult to believe her because of that look she had on her face.

"Why would you tell them I'm famous?"

"Why not?"

Marc knew Lori well enough to know he wasn't going to get anywhere with this line of questioning. No, she really hadn't changed a bit since high school. With a smile and a sigh of resignation he shrugged his shoulders and decided to just play along and changed the subject. "So, what would you like to drink?"

"Well, why don't I let you order for the two of us?"

"You trust me to do that?"

"Yes, I do, Marc."

Just then he caught Gina's eye and nodded that they were ready to give her their drink choices.

"So, have you decided?" Gina asked with a very sweet smile.

"Yes, we'll each have a Laguna Breeze."

"A very good choice, Mr. Janssen."

"Thank you."

"You're welcome, and I'll have them right to you. In the meantime would you care to order an appetizer?"

Marc looked at Lori who shook her head imperceptibly.

"Thank you anyway, Gina, but I think we'll pass."

"Very well, Mr. Janssen, I'll get your drinks right to you."

As Gina disappeared Marc looked at Lori and noticed that smile she'd been smiling earlier and couldn't stand it any longer.

"Okay, Lori, I need to ask a question. What's with this big smile you've had going since I arrived?"

"What big smile?" Lori asked coyly.

"You know very well what big smile I'm talking about. It's as if you have something up your sleeve and can't wait to surprise me with it. Come on, fess up."

Lori briefly looked away from Marc's gaze and in that moment she caught a glance and a nod from the Maître d' and without nodding back she took a quick glance at her watch. "Oh, look. I think it's time that I go powder my nose."

"Oh, look! I don't think so," Marc replied jokingly, but with a firmness that clued Lori in that he was willing to play along, but only so far.

"Marc, don't you remember how I used to tease you when we were in high school? We'd be doing something in class and you were usually the one that got caught by the teacher?"

"Yes, I remember that all too well. But what's that have to do with this evening?"

"Well, it appears that I haven't lost my touch, because I'm getting you all riled up like I used to, and it's fun to see you smile again. I always loved that smile."

Marc wasn't sure what to say, but the mood was temporarily broken as Gina delivered their drinks.

"Here you are. One Laguna Breeze for the lady, and one for the gentleman. Will there be anything else?"

"No. Thank you, Gina. It'll be a while before we're ready to order dinner so I'll just give you another nod, okay?"

"Certainly, Mr. Janssen."

"She's a good waitress," Marc replied as Gina walked away. "I love her enthusiasm."

"You know, Marc, you've always been one to notice good things in others. I've always found that so refreshing and admirable."

Once again Marc wasn't sure what to say. He just looked at Lori for a long moment.

"What?" Lori asked with a quizzical look on her face.

"Oh, I don't know." Marc paused again before continuing. "Did you ever wonder why we never dated?"

"Yeah, as a matter of fact, I did. From the moment I met you I had the biggest crush on you, but you just never seemed to notice. In fact, do you remember Debbie Taylor?"

"Yeah, weren't the two of you close friends for a couple of years?"

"That doesn't come *close* to describing us. We were best friends during our freshman and sophomore years, but during the summer before our junior year her family moved to Texas after her dad got a big promotion with his company. It broke our hearts to have to say good-bye. But we kept writing to each other for a few more years."

"So, what about her?"

"Well, I came so close to telling her about my crush on you, but before I could she told me *she* had a crush on you, and I just couldn't tell her then because I was afraid it might cause a problem between us. Even after she changed her mind a few months later and said she had a new crush on Roger Dean, I still didn't tell her because I was afraid she'd tell you."

"Would that have been so bad?"

"Yes. I've always believed that if someone I had a crush on didn't ask me out then it wasn't meant to be."

"Well, we were kinda young to be dating at that point."

"Yeah, I know, but it still would've been fun to have had you walk me home, carry my books, and so on."

"Hey, I did that! I carried your books every time we went to my house to study!"

"You know what I mean, Marc. That was different. I meant it would have been more … romantic—"

"Yeah, I knew what you meant, Lori. It was *my* turn to tease *you*," Marc replied with a wink.

"Touché, my friend," Lori replied, raising her drink in a mock toast. She took a sip and her eyes lit up! "Hey, this is good! What's in it?

"A couple of juices, sweet and sour mix, a syrup of some kind and club soda."

"Mmmm, it's good!" she replied after taking another sip.

"Marc?" Lori asked in a whisper.

"Yes?" Marc replied, curious about the change in Lori's mood and the look on her face. "May I ask you a personal question?"

"Sure." 'Okay,' Marc thought, 'here comes the heart-to-heart portion of the evening.'

Lori looked down at her drink, swirled it without taking a sip, then looked into Marc's eyes for a long moment before continuing.

"Have you talked to Jenny since the break-up?"

Marc was now totally speechless. Where to begin? He broke his gaze at Lori, downed more than half his drink in a single gulp, set the drink down on the table, took a deep breath and let it out heavily as he looked back into Lori's eyes. She saw sadness in his.

"Boy, you really know how to catch a guy off guard."

"I'm sorry, Marc. We can change the subject if you'd like."

"No, Lori. No … it's been too long since … since I was able to talk about this with anyone, and that was Alexa. She was a good listener. Initially, she let me get it all out without condemning me for being such an absolute jerk, but later she nailed me on it."

"Marc, you weren't a jerk. You were terribly distraught and—"

"That doesn't excuse me for saying and doing what I did." Gina was only a few tables away when Marc caught her attention and raised his glass to indicate he'd like another. She nodded and headed toward the bar.

Marc looked into Lori's eyes for a long moment. She remained silent allowing him to gather his thoughts.

"I have … a confession. Ever since that horrible day I've had a hole in my heart that nothing and no one has been able to fill. I've been empty. My heart, my soul, my spirit … my life. Everything. All empty. I've kept myself busy with the Foundation as a way of running from the truth." Marc paused again.

"There's more. And only Alexa knows about this. I've seen Jenny twice since that day."

"What?!" Lori's eyes searched Marc's deeply for understanding.

"The first time was about ten years ago. I had flown to San Francisco on a business trip. I was on my way out of the terminal and was just passing by one of the security check point areas when I saw her. She didn't see me, at least … I don't think she did. She looked in my direction and I thought our eyes met for a moment, but her expression didn't change and she didn't stop as she was gathering up her bag and purse so she had probably just looked in my general direction but didn't actually see me. Then she walked off toward her gate. My heart was pounding, it was hard for me to breathe … it was so painful. The hurt I know I caused her hit me deeply."

"Oh, my gosh, Marc!" If she wasn't before, then Lori was now glued to every word he spoke.

"Yes, that really hit me hard. I was already planning on spending some extra time in the City that weekend after my appointment that afternoon, but after seeing Jenny, even for that brief moment, it brought back so many memories. After my presentation I went back to my hotel, changed my clothes, and took off to retrace so many of the steps that Jenny and I had taken years earlier. By the time Sunday evening rolled around I was exhausted, but full; full of memories of the two of us … and full of such a deep regret.

"The weekend was a mixed blessing, because on the one hand I felt so lifted up, but on the other hand I felt so lonesome and empty. I had lost my sweetheart, my soul mate, someone I loved so much, and all because of my blind anger. I went to bed that night hating myself. If it wasn't for my need to take an early flight out the next morning I would have just stayed in bed and kept the covers pulled up over my head."

"Oh, Marc, I'm so sorry."

Marc shrugged, "I brought it on all by myself, Lori. Jenny had followed me to Nashville wanting to help out in any way she could, but I was too blinded by my rage over Alexa's accident. Plus, I was so exhausted from not sleeping that I couldn't even think straight. All I could think of was Alexa. I was all she had left in the world and I needed to be there for her every moment of every day. I realized too late that Jenny could actually have been a big help to me, *and* Alexa. They were good friends, too."

"Yes, Jenny told me."

"She did? When?"

"A long time ago. After she came back from Nashville. She said she just wanted to be there for you and to help out with Alexa in any way possible. She knew you wouldn't be going back to college that semester and she was prepared to miss the rest of the school year, too. She felt her place was by your side, and Alexa's."

"And I sent her away."

"Yes. And it broke her heart," Lori added, not in a mean spirited way, though it made Marc's eyes tear up.

Gina looked their way, but Marc shook his head slightly to let her know not to come yet. She nodded back that she understood. He made a mental note to leave her a generous tip when the evening was over.

"You mentioned you'd seen her twice since the break up?" Lori asked before taking a final sip from her drink. She lifted her glass slightly and caught Gina's attention who nodded that she'd bring her another in just a moment.

"Yes. A couple of years ago I flew out here on business and decided to take a couple of days and add some pleasure to my schedule. After concluding my business in the City I drove down to Carmel and checked into the Inn at Spanish Bay."

"Oh, I've heard that place is *wonderful!*"

"Yes, it is! I had stayed there once before when an associate of mine invited me out for a special benefit event at the Inn, and while I was there that week we played the golf course three times! It was amazing and so relaxing! I really needed that. It always seems like I cram too much work into my schedule and never have enough time for fun or just relaxing, and on that trip I got plenty of both!"

"Oh, Marc, that's wonderful."

"Anyway, this other time I was there I decided to take a drive through Carmel. Of course, once I got there I realized that I couldn't be satisfied with simply driving through that beautiful little town, I needed to stop and walk around a bit, see some of the places I loved to visit in the past, with Jenny.

"I found a place to park a few blocks from Ocean Avenue that wasn't metered so I could take as long as I wanted to just wander around and enjoy the sights. I began my slow and casual trek, in and out of little gift shops and art galleries, enjoying the scents in the air from many little cafés and restaurants, along with the gentle sea breeze from the nearby ocean.

"The weather was absolutely perfect that day, sunny without being too warm, and the breeze off the ocean actually made it quite pleasant, even when midday rolled around."

Marc took another swallow from his drink before continuing, realizing that he was once again about to share some very sensitive things. Gina arrived with Lori's drink and quietly placed it on the table, taking her other glass away without any comment as she realized they were in a very private and serious conversation. In spite of that, Lori whispered "Thank you" to Gina and Gina nodded before slipping quietly away.

"Anyway, I had just stepped out of a gallery and was headed back toward Ocean Avenue to find a place to get something to eat. Just then Jenny came around the corner up ahead holding hands with a gentleman, and she was talking about something quite animatedly while the gentleman politely listened. The moment I saw Jenny I froze in my steps. They didn't see me right away. As they came closer they looked toward me, and Jenny also stopped instantly while her friend took another half step before realizing Jenny had stopped. He looked back at her to see what the problem was and saw her looking at me with a look that's hard for me to describe. He looked at me with a puzzled look on his face, I'm sure wondering what was going on and why Jenny had stopped all of a sudden like that."

"Oh, my gosh, Marc! What happened? What did you guys say to each other?"

"Well, nothing for a moment or so. Finally I broke the silence and said, 'Jenny?' and she said, 'Marc?'

"I took a few steps toward her, while she just seemed frozen in place.

"'Oh, my gosh, Jenny, is that really you?' I asked, and she replied, 'Yes. Oh, Marc. I don't ... I don't know what to say.'"

"'I know' I replied, 'it's been ... so long.'"

"Just then I realized the gentleman standing next to her was looking a bit uncomfortable so I decided to make him feel a little more at ease. I said, 'Hi. My name's Marc. I'm ... a friend of Jenny's from several years ago. From college, actually.'

"'Hi, Marc. I'm Scott, Jenny's husband.' My heart stopped, Lori. Literally stopped."

"Oh, Marc. Oh, no!" Tears started to well up in Lori's eyes now.

"You know, it had crossed my mind several times over the years that by then Jenny was surely married and no doubt happily raising a family somewhere in suburbia, but when she was right there in front of me I felt paralyzed by both joy and despair!"

"Oh, my gosh, Marc, what did you do?"

"Well, after he said his name and told me who he was I looked right at Jenny. Hopefully I had a smile on my face at that moment, but to be honest with you I have no idea if I did or didn't. I do remember Jenny still had a stunned look on her face, and then I remember looking back at Scott and saying something like, 'Well, it's wonderful to meet you, Scott.'

"Then to kind of break the ice with Jenny again I asked, 'So, how've you been?' to which she had difficulty saying 'Fine. Just fine. And you?'

"'I'm doing pretty well myself. Keeping busy with work. I was in the City on some business and just decided to come down and visit some of our, uh, the old spots we, um, uh ... just wanted to see some fun sights again.'

"Then I looked back at Scott and said, 'Well, I'd better let you guys get on with your having a great day in this beautiful little town.' I looked back at Jenny who I could tell was valiantly fighting back tears and said, 'It was wonderful to see you again, Jenny.'

"'Yes ... it was, Marc. Take care.'

"'You too, Jenny. Nice meeting you, Scott!' and off I went. I was only a few steps away when I heard Scott say, 'Honey, are you alright?' and I heard Jenny say, "Yes ... I'll be fine.' After that I was too far away to hear anything further. Except ..." Marc paused for a long time.

"Except what, Marc?" Lori asked gently.

"I glanced back over my shoulder ... and Jenny was crying."

Lori remained quiet, gently dabbing away her own tears, and praying her makeup would survive.

"As I rounded the corner onto Ocean Avenue the sun hit me right in the face and I slipped my sunglasses on none too soon. My heart was racing, my breathing was erratic, and I felt the tears coming on strong. All I wanted to do at that point was just find a place to sit down and, hopefully, not in view of too many people. I found a park bench not too far away and spent the next half hour just trying to calm down and gather my thoughts. By the time I could stand up and walk again I realized I was really hungry, but at the same time I'd lost my appetite. 'Oh, great!' I thought, 'What do I do now?'"

"So, what did you do?"

"Well, I knew I had to have *something* to eat, but since I'd lost my appetite I figured I'd just find a small café somewhere and get a sandwich and something to drink."

"Oh, Marc," Lori replied, wiping away more tears. "I'm so sorry. That must have been so hard on you."

"Believe me, Lori, it was. It broke my heart to see her with another guy, especially someone who was her husband. That should have been *me*! But it wasn't, and it was all my fault. Why did I have to be such a fool?!"

"Oh, Marc. Try not to be so hard on yourself."

"How can I not be, Lori? I lost the only girl I ever really loved. How do I reconcile that in my life? There was nothing I could do about it that day in Carmel, and there's nothing I can do about it now. It's simply too late. The only thing I have to live for is my work with the Foundation. Alexa's doing great. She's married to a wonderful guy and they have four children, three boys and a girl, and she's still writing songs and sings occasionally at a variety of events. Seeing her come back from that accident, defying all the odds that she'd ever be able to sing and perform again, it was a miracle! And the work I do with the Foundation gives me a chance to see other miracles happen like that all over the country. We've even helped some people in a few other countries in the last couple of years. It's been amazing what we've been able to do."

"That's wonderful, Marc! I'm so proud of you!"

"I won't, I simply can't say that Alexa getting hurt was a blessing in disguise for me, because it wasn't. It derailed her career goals for at least a year, but she came back strong, and now has an amazing life. But my whole life was completely flipped on its head after her accident, and I had to move on from my dream. I don't mind, because I love Alexa so much. I've truly been blessed, though, to have been able to be by her side at the start of that grueling ordeal, and then blessed again to have been able to have the success I've had with the Foundation so her joy, and the joy of hundreds of others, could be fulfilled.

"I hope someday soon you get a chance to see her perform. She's simply amazing, Lori! Watching her you'd never know she'd ever been so badly hurt, nearly paralyzed, and told she'd be lucky if she ever walked again. And, on top of that, they thought she might never sing again, at least as well as she had before. I'm so grateful for all of the medical staff that worked with her, and I'm just so proud of her! She's worked so hard for what she's accomplished, she never gave up on her dream, and she deserves everything that comes her way."

"What can I say, Marc? I'm speechless. In the last half hour you've taken me from the highest mountain to the lowest valley and back up that mountain again. Now, if you don't mind, I'd like to visit that ladies room to freshen up a bit and re-do some of my makeup."

"Sure, Lori. Here, let me help you up." Marc rose quickly and slipped around to the other side of the table to help Lori with her chair.

"And while you're gone I'll let Gina know we'll be ordering dinner soon."

"What? Dinner? Oh, yes! Dinner! I almost forgot," Lori replied with a laugh to try to diffuse her momentary confusion. 'Way to go, lady.'

§

Sitting at the table alone, waiting for Lori to return, he closed his eyes for a long moment and pictured Jenny sitting across from him in a beautiful evening gown, sparkling necklace and earrings, and her meltingly unforgettable smile. He opened his eyes and sighed heavily as that recurring thought returned to haunt him once again. 'If only …' Ever since they'd met she had been the only girl he ever loved.

He'd been such a fool to make her go away, especially at such a critical time in his life. She could have helped him deal with Alexa's accident and injuries so much better. But the rage that had seemingly come out of nowhere had destroyed everything he had lived for. If only he could have controlled that rage, and shared his secret with her before it was too late.

Had she ever forgiven him? The day they'd met in Carmel was so unexpected, and neither of them was able to really talk to the other, especially with Jenny's husband right there. He hoped and prayed that she had. Chances are, though, he'd never know. Even if she showed up at the reunion, Scott was sure to be there with her, and that would prevent any chance for them to be able to spend even a moment together. No, it was best to try to simply put it all behind him … again.

§

When Lori returned from the ladies room Marc was once again ready to help her with her seat. After returning to his own seat he told Lori that he'd let Gina know they would be ready to order dinner shortly and they began to look over the many delicious sounding items on the menu, though Lori seemed a bit distracted.

"So … I have a question for you, Lori." After the emotional roller coaster he'd just been on Marc wasn't sure he really wanted to hear the answer to his question quite yet, but then decided he'd prefer to get it over with.

"Okay," Lori replied a bit apprehensively due to the subdued tone in Marc's voice.

"I figured that you'd probably know the answer because you've been on the reunion committee."

'Whew!' Lori thought to herself. 'This one I'm sure I can handle just fine.'

"So … I'm wondering … do you know if Jenny and Scott are coming to the reunion?"

'Oh, my gosh!' Lori tried not to gasp! She reached for her glass to take a sip before answering, all the while knowing that Marc could see her struggling with what to say. 'Okay, girl, relax. Perhaps it's finally time to bite the bullet. You've got to find a way to break the news to him.'

"Are Jenny and Scott coming to the reunion?" Lori re-asked his question in a stalling tactic.

"Yes, that's what I just asked. Is everything okay, Lori?"

"Yes! Sure! Why do you ask?"

"Well, I asked what I thought was a rather straightforward question and you seem to be having a difficult time trying to answer it. So, what's up?"

"Um, nothing's up, Marc." Lori replied quickly, realizing she wasn't handling this very well. She took another sip of her drink and then set it back down on the table.

"Lori, look at me," Marc asked calmly. He reached out and held her hands gently. "It's me … Marc. We're good friends, remember?"

Lori looked at Marc, though it was a bit difficult. She thought she'd been prepared for this, but somehow his question still caught her by surprise. "Yes, of course I remember."

"Okay, so why is it so hard to tell me if Jenny and her husband are coming to the reunion or not? If you're worried about how I might handle it if they show up, don't be, okay? I was fully aware when I made up my mind to come that I could possibly, even probably, see them there. And believe me, Lori, I'm okay with it. I can handle it. Crossing paths with her in Carmel that day simply caught me by surprise. But since then I've managed to make ... adjustments to my feelings, so I'll be okay if I see them there. Besides, I'll probably be hanging out with Mike and Dave most of the time that evening, just laughing about the good ol' days. And you'll be there too, of course, and I want you to promise to save me a few dances, okay?"

"Sure! I can do that! That sounds like fun!"

"So ... are they coming?" Marc asked again, maintaining his calm demeanor.

'Okay, Lori, this is it,' she thought to herself.

"Marc?" Lori asked almost in a whisper.

"Yes, Lori" Marc replied, matching her soft tone. "Oh, no!" he suddenly exclaimed.

"What?!" Lori was startled by Marc's sudden mood change.

"I think I just figured it out! You're having a hard time telling me if they're coming because ... something's happened to Jenny! That's it, isn't it?"

"What? No! Marc, nothing's happened to Jenny. She's fine."

"Really? Are you sure?" Marc's eyes were pleading for the truth.

"Yes, Marc, I'm very sure." Lori answered, trying her best to reassure him that Jenny was just fine.

Marc let out a big sigh of relief and took a large swallow of his drink. After setting it back down on the table he looked back at Lori once again.

"Okay, so we've established that Jenny is fine. So ... are they coming?"

Lori paused, looking deeply into Marc's pleading eyes, and reached out and took Marc's hands once again.

Nearly whispering Lori said, "Why don't you ask her yourself?" There! She'd finally let it out!

"Well, perhaps I would, or could, if I had a way to reach her, but I don't."

Still nearly whispering Lori replied, "Yes, Marc ... you do." She continued to look deeply into Marc's eyes to see how he'd react to her answers. The look in his eyes was kind and gentle, but still filled with bewilderment and pleading for an answer.

"I do? I'm sorry, Lori, but I ... I don't know what you mean. I lost track of her a long time ago. The way I broke it off with her was ... was reprehensible, and after I found out she was married I felt it wasn't right for me to try to reconnect with her again, especially after the way she reacted to seeing me in Carmel. So, when you tell me I do have a way to ask her ... what do you mean? How can I ask her?"

Lori kept her eyes right on Marc and squeezed his hands tightly. She took a deep breath and let it out softly. By now her heart was racing wildly, and all of a sudden she was finding it difficult to breathe. The moment ... this very moment ... was the moment she'd been waiting for for months.

Lori whispered something, unable to find her voice, with tears welling up in her eyes.

"Pardon me?" Marc asked.

"Turn ... around, Marc." Lori saw the bewildered look in his eyes grow as he searched her eyes for understanding. "Look behind you."

Lori watched as the look on Marc's face went from bewilderment to anticipation and felt the increasing pulse of his heartbeat all the way down in his fingers.

Still not fully understanding what Lori had asked him to do he released his hold on her hands, sat up straight and turned around.

"Hi, Marc," Jenny said softly.

CHAPTER 47

The Reunion

MARC FROZE FOR A long moment, unable to find the words to say. Everything in his world suddenly disappeared. Every sound, everyone that would have been within his vision ... everything gone. He could only see Jenny. The only scent that he was suddenly aware of was a classic perfume that Jenny wore on special occasions, Oh! de London. He wondered why he hadn't noticed it before. Finally, after Jenny gave him a warm smile, along with a wink that had always been a special signal to him of her love, he realized that his heart was pounding heavily in his chest. His breathing had all of a sudden begun again, and he flashed back to when he'd had that same feeling when he'd seen her at the airport all those years ago.

"Jenny?" Marc replied, almost in a whisper.

"Hi, Marc," Jenny softly replied again, maintaining her sweet smile.

He slowly rose from his chair, his knees weak, his mind spinning, unable to fully comprehend what was happening, and still oblivious to virtually everything and everyone else around him.

"Jenny? It's ... it's really you? You're here?"

"Yes, Marc. It's really me, and I'm really here." Jenny rose from her chair as she saw Marc get up and take a step toward her. By the look on his face she knew a hug was inevitable, and she didn't mind one bit.

"Oh, my gosh, Jenny! Oh, my gosh!"

Jenny laughed, and just then Marc heard Lori's tearful laughter behind him. He turned around to look at Lori, then back at Jenny, and finally back at Lori. "Okay, what's going on?"

"Surprised?" Lori asked with a big, bright smile while dabbing away her tears. So much for her fresh makeup!

"Surprised isn't the word for it." Then something very unsettling hit Marc and he looked back at Jenny.

"Wait a minute. Oh, no ... wait a minute. I'm really in trouble here, aren't I?"

"What do you mean, Marc?" Jenny asked.

"Where's ... where's ....—"

"Scott?"

"Yeah, where's Scott? Is he about to walk in here and join us? Did I overstep my bounds by hugging you? Oh, Jenny, I'm sorry if I—"

"No, Marc. You're fine. Scott's not here. And don't worry, he won't be joining us Saturday evening at the reunion either."

"He won't?"

"No."

Just then Lori spoke up, "Listen, Jenny, it's time. Come over and join us."

"Yes, please join us," Marc replied, holding out the chair that was between his and Lori's.

"Ahhh, always the gentleman," Jenny replied as she gently kissed Marc on the cheek before sitting down. "Thank you, kind sir," she added with a smile.

Marc found it hard to take his eyes off Jenny but he finally looked at Lori and asked, "So, is this what that smile was all about earlier?

Lori blushed. "Yes."

"And just how long have you been planning this?" his eyes darting back and forth from Lori to Jenny and back.

The ladies smiled at each other, then Lori replied, "Hmmm ... a while. And when you said you were coming to the reunion after all, well ... that's why I asked to meet you for dinner a few days before."

Lori took a sip of her drink and continued. "I just had this feeling about the two of you, that you just needed to see each other again and have some time together, away from the reunion. And now, since I have you both here together, my job is finished and it's time for me to leave."

Marc and Jenny both looked at Lori at the same moment and exclaimed together, "What?!"

Lori smiled, and as she took a final sip of her drink and gathered her clutch she explained, "You two need some time together, alone. I've already made arrangements with the Maître d' to bill my card, so this evening is on me. Please enjoy it, OK?"

Marc rose from his seat to help Lori with hers, gave her a big hug, then held her a moment longer as their eyes met. "What can I say?"

"You don't need to say anything, Marc. Except, perhaps, 'Thank you.'"

"Thanks, Lori. For *everything!*"

"Yes, Lori," Jenny added as she also got up to give Lori a hug. "Thank you *so* much!"

Marc and Jenny just stood there, stunned, while Lori excused herself from the table and started to head for the door. They both said, "Thanks, Lori!", and Lori looked over her shoulder, winked, and said, "You're welcome!" Then Marc turned toward Jenny and asked, "Shall we?" as he held her chair. As she turned to sit down Jenny smiled a nervous but happy smile and softly said, "Yes, I'd like that."

They sat next to each other for several moments just looking ... without saying a word; their smiles were hard to contain.

"I know you must be wondering," Jenny began, "so let me clear something up for you."

"Okay," Marc replied, wondering exactly what Jenny was referring to.

"Scott and I are divorced. It happened six months after we saw you in Carmel. It wasn't brought on by what happened that day, but it probably hastened its eventuality. We'd been having problems for several years. I won't go into the details other than to say he was abusive to me ... and my children."

Marc's eyes lit up. "Wait! You have children? Oh, of course you'd have children! You'd always been looking forward to being a mother. But how old are they? They weren't with you two—"

"You're right. They weren't with us that day you saw us. My parents were watching them for a few days while Scott and I were in Carmel ... trying to work things out."

Just then Gina appeared and Marc noticed that she wasn't surprised to see Jenny instead of Lori.

"Another round, or are you ready to order dinner?"

"I'm not sure about you, Marc, but I'd like another before we order if that's okay with you?"

"Sounds good to me," Marc replied and then, looking at Gina he said, "It looks like we'll have another round."

"I'll be right back!" and once again Gina was off.

"Jenny, did you see how she didn't seem to notice it wasn't Lori sitting with me?"

"Hm-mm. Sure did."

"Don't you find that kind of odd? I mean, she's been so observant all evening, always attending to our drinks and just knowing what we'd like when we'd like it."

"What's so odd about that? She's seems like a very good waitress, if you ask me."

"But, not noticing you weren't Lori?"

Jenny smiled her warm, loving smile that had always melted Marc in the past.

"What?" Marc asked, trying to figure out what Jenny was thinking.

"She knew."

"She knew what?"

"She ... knew ..., Marc."

"I'm sorry. I don't get it." Marc seemed genuinely confused.

Gina returned with their drinks and quietly set them down, retrieved their empty glasses before giving Marc a wink, and slipped away without disturbing their conversation.

"Oh, Marc, I guess I'm going to have to take back my nickname for you, Mr. Dean's List, because for someone who was always so keen, alert, and smart I can't believe this one has gone over your head."

Marc remained silent, letting Jenny do all of the explaining.

"Marc … she knew, just like our Maître d' knew. Lori set this whole evening up ahead of time and clued in everyone on what she was doing and why. You were the only one that was kept out of the loop … for obvious reasons."

"Obvious reasons?"

"Just in case the earlier part of your conversation with Lori didn't go as we all hoped it would."

"Okay, speaking of my earlier conversation with Lori … at what point did you arrive? How much did you hear of our conversation?"

"From the point where you were ordering your drinks."

"So … you heard it all?"

"Every word. To begin with, I was sitting right behind you, so I could hear everything perfectly. This has to be the most perfect spot in the whole restaurant because I could even hear when the two of you were whispering. Then, because everything had gone so well before Lori left for the ladies room, I knew I was going to stay. When she returned she gave me a slight nod, which was my cue to wait 30 seconds, then I slipped around the table and got in position without you noticing."

"Well, the two of you were pretty sly, you know it?"

"Yes, we were. But Lori more so because this was all her idea."

"So … she planned out this whole evening?"

"Well, everything up through the point where she left. The rest is now up to us." That's when Marc noticed Jenny wink at him.

"Now … as I remember, there's something I'm supposed to do anytime you wink at me like that."

"You're right. So … what are you waiting for?" That was all the invitation Marc needed, and he leaned over to give Jenny a tender kiss.

"If you'd like, there's more where that came from."

"I'd like, Marc," Jenny replied with a loving smile, "but let's save them for later, shall we?"

"Sure."

Clearing his throat Marc suggested that they should probably take a look at the menu so they could finally order their dinner. A few minutes later Marc nodded at Gina and she came and took their order.

As they waited for their dinner Marc and Jenny talked about a variety of light subjects, both trying to avoid getting too serious. This was, after all, the first time they'd been together, really together, since that horrible day in Nashville, what seemed like a lifetime ago. A lot had happened in both their lives since then, and they knew it was going to take time to sort through everything and see if there just might be a chance for the two of them again. That old saying 'The third time's the charm', just might apply to them, but they needed time, and neither of them wanted to ruin their chances this time around.

After their dinner finally arrived Marc was the first to approach a possibly sensitive subject.

"Jenny, would you mind telling me about your children?"

"Oh, Marc, I'd love to! I have three and they're all *so* wonderful. Let's see, Joanna is my oldest. She's 16 and takes after me a lot. She loves sports and music and she's an excellent student.

"Then there's Kate, and she's 14, and loves being in high school with her older sister. They love to hang out together, and if it weren't for them having birthdays nearly two years apart you'd think they were twins."

"You know? Your eyes just dance when you talk about your children."

"Do they? Well, I'm not surprised. I'm so blessed because they're such good children."

"Sorry to interrupt, but I just couldn't help telling you that. You said you have three children?"

"Yes, and finally there's my 8-year-old … Marc."

"Marc?! Really?" Marc asked as his jaw began to drop.

"Yes. The whole time I was pregnant with him it just felt different from the way I felt with my girls so I had a feeling it would be a boy, and the first name I thought of was yours. The moment the doctor confirmed that I was, in fact, carrying a baby boy I knew beyond a shadow of any doubt that I would name him Marc."

"Even after …?" Marc couldn't finish his question.

"Yes. Marc, you've always been everything to me. *Everything.*" Jenny replied softly.

"What did Scott have to say about that?"

"He didn't know anything about you until after we saw you in Carmel. After he saw my reaction to seeing you he demanded to know why I seemed so upset. I told him the truth."

"All of it?"

"Yes, all of it. From how we met and became high school sweethearts, through the huge fiasco of my stupid Dear John letter and our getting back together the next year, through Alexa's accident and … our break up."

"Jenny … about that—"

"Don't, Marc. Please, let's not talk about that right now, okay? I know we will eventually, and that's soon enough for me, but for now, for this evening, let's set that one aside, shall we? Please?"

Marc looked deeply into Jenny's eyes. If he couldn't say it he hoped that he could at least convey to her how terribly sorry he was for breaking her heart. He had a feeling, though, that she knew. After all … she was here, sitting right next to him, wasn't she?

"Okay, as long as you promise that we'll talk about it soon, alright?"

"Fair enough." Jenny let out a long, soft sigh, and then reached over to hold Marc's hands. "Oh, Marc … I wish I could tell you how I feel right now. About what Lori did for us this evening. About everything. But I'm just having a problem finding the words."

"I know, Jenny. I know. Boy, do I ever know, because I'm having that same problem." With a shared wink and a smile they squeezed each other's hands tenderly and then resumed eating.

A few minutes passed, and finally Jenny had to ask Marc about his family. She had tried to get the details from Lori, but Lori had said he had never talked about his personal life to anyone. She wasn't sure about anything from the last twenty plus years of his life, and she wanted to know. Had he ever been married? Did he have a family somewhere? She doubted it. Not the way he'd been so busy with his Foundation. He's too good of a man, and he would have been a great dad to his children and wouldn't have spent so much time at work. But she just needed to know for sure.

"Marc?" Jenny asked softly.

"Yes, Jenny?" Marc replied in kind.

"I've had a wonderful time this evening."

"Oh, me too. I still can't believe how you and Lori were able to pull everything off the way you did."

"You need to give all of the credit to Lori. It was all her idea from the very start. In fact, she told me she'd been planning this for a long time ... long before any of the serious planning for the reunion started."

"How far back?"

"A year ago."

"A year? Really?" Marc sat in silence for several moments. The silence was finally broken by Jenny's next question."

"Marc, why haven't you told anyone about ... about your personal life?"

"Pardon me?" Jenny's question caught Marc off guard.

"Anyone I've talked to knows nothing about your personal life after you left college. All we know is that you left to take care of Alexa, and then your involvement with your Foundation, but no one, not even your best friends Mike or Dave, know anything about your personal life."

Marc took a deep breath before responding. He paused and looked over Jenny's shoulder, out the window and across the bay toward the City. Thinking. Just thinking.

"There's nothing to know, Jenny," Marc finally answered reluctantly.

"Nothing?"

"Nothing."

Jenny touched his arm to bring his attention back to her. She looked into his eyes, trying to express as much love and compassion for him at that moment as she could. She hoped and prayed her next question wouldn't bring this evening, this beautiful evening, to an abrupt end.

"Marc … would you … would you tell me? Please?"

Marc looked away without answering, closed his eyes for several moments, trying to keep his emotions in check and keep tears from forming. He opened them, took another deep breath, let out a long sigh and looked back at Jenny.

"Jenny," he began calmly, "there's really nothing to say about it, because I've had no personal life. Just my work with the Foundation."

"None at all? You … never got married?" This caused Marc to look away again to gather his thoughts, but it also caused Jenny to worry if she'd pressed him too far.

"No … I never got married. I guess you could say I was just married to my work."

"Marc, I'm sorry if this is causing you any … pain or—"

"No, Jenny, no. It's … it's just awkward, I guess, because I've never talked to anyone about it. I've always maneuvered the conversation to something else, because thinking about … thinking about marriage was just too painful."

"Painful? Why, darling?"

"Because … how could I … how could I marry someone … when I never stopped loving you?"

Marc saw the look on Jenny's face reflect a full range of emotions.

"Oh, Marc. I'm so sorry."

"Wait a minute, Jenny. What do *you* have to be sorry about? You didn't do anything wrong. It was *me*. I'm the only one to blame for our break up."

Jenny leaned in closer to Marc.

"I know, but I heard from Lori about Alexa's recovery and rehab and how successful they were, and she also told me that Alexa was not only able to return to college, but also her performing. What miracles both of those things were for her, and you, for that matter, because you were so deeply involved in all of it. Marc, what I'm trying to say to you is … after I knew you were able to continue on with your life after Alexa was fine … I desperately wanted to see you, to call you, to somehow reach out to you to see if there was anything I … anything I could do for you after you'd given so much of yourself to Alexa."

"Oh, Jenny." Marc took a deep breath to fight back the tears. "You know, in a way I wish you had, but on the other hand even though Alexa was better ... I wasn't. I was deeply overwhelmed with guilt over how cruel I'd been to you. I loved you so much and in my rage I sent you away. I said terrible things that I hope you know I didn't mean."

"I know, darling, I know. I understand. And I understood then, too. All I wanted to do was help, to be there for you and Alexa. Whatever you needed I wanted to help."

"Oh, how I know that now, Jenny ... but it was too late. Once I realized what had happened I was delirious with guilt, shame, and despair over it all, and the only thing that pulled me through it was my love and commitment to Alexa, doing all I could to help her survive and recover, and then help her get back to normal again.

"One evening about a month after Alexa had been released from rehab we were having a heart to heart talk. I had just announced the creation of my Foundation and she was very happy and excited for me, but there was something else on her mind. She said that was all well and good with regard to my career, but she wanted to know what I was now going to do with my *life*. You know what the first thing was that she told me to do?

"No, what?"

"She told me to call you."

"So ... why didn't you, huh?" Jenny poked him in the arm to keep the mood as light as possible so she wouldn't start crying.

"Because ... as much as I loved you, as much as I wanted, *needed* you back, I knew I no longer deserved you, and I told Alexa that. Then she said that wasn't my decision to make, it was yours."

"She was right, Marc."

"What?"

"Marc, she was right. She knew. You should have given her credit for being an intelligent woman. Women just know these things. Even though we hadn't talked since her accident, she still knew what I must have been feeling. She *knew*, Marc."

Marc just sat there in silence. His entire well-thought-out defense for his thoughts and actions had just been completely destroyed.

"Darling, I waited for you." As valiantly as Jenny tried she couldn't hold back the tears any longer. "I waited for you for three years after Alexa's accident, hoping and praying that somehow we'd get back together. When you said you never wanted to see me ever again, as much as it broke my heart to do so, I did my best to honor and obey that request because of how much I loved you. I kept waiting for you to call or write or something, *anything* … but nothing. Not even a message through Lori. Then, once I'd heard from her that you had apparently moved on with your life, and it was obviously without me, I tried to move on with mine. The only good things that came out of it were my children."

"I'm so sorry, Jenny. But I know to say that just isn't enough. I've lived and relived our breakup over and over and it just tears me up inside every time. I see your face in my mind, how hurt you were, and I can only imagine what my rage must have looked and felt like to you. Jenny, I need to tell you something I've never told anyone."

Jenny looked intently and lovingly into Marc's eyes and saw his deep concern, perhaps even a touch of fear that whatever it was, the fact that he was about to reveal something so private was scaring him. She tried to find the right words to say to ease his fear, but couldn't.

"Jenny, remember all those years ago I said that I needed you and I added the words "now more than ever?""

"Yes, I do. I remember them very well. And, if I remember correctly, you also had a strange concern in your voice when you said those words, but you never told me why."

"Well," Marc cleared his throat, "here's the 'why'."

Jenny remained silent and kept looking into Marc's eyes, trying to convey her love and trust. She held his hands, gently stroking the back of them with her thumbs.

"One of the things I didn't tell anyone about my accident was regarding the severity of my concussion. Normally, concussions can clear up within a few days or weeks. Some that are a bit more severe may last a few months, but sweetheart, my symptoms didn't go away for years."

"Oh, Marc, are you okay now?" Jenny asked with her own deep concern.

"Yes, but it took a long time. When the symptoms didn't go away after about four months the doctors ran more tests and found out that my concussion was more severe than they had originally thought, based on the details of the accident. And here's the hardest thing I had to deal with all that time ... one of the side effects was that I could go into a sudden inexplicable rage, no warning or reason whatsoever. After several visits with a team of specialists they determined that those sudden outbursts were brought on by extreme stress."

"Really?"

"Yes, and that was another one of the reasons I returned to California to go to college, more specifically to be near you."

"I don't understand," Jenny replied quizzically.

"Because, sweetheart, you always had such a calming effect on me, so I not only wanted, I needed to be near you as much as possible not only because I loved you, but also because I believed you could help save my life."

"Oh, honey, I ... then that day—"

"About the day I broke up with you?"

"Yes."

"That fit of rage I burst into was brought on from the extreme stress I'd been under after Alexa's accident, compounded by my exhaustion. I had no control of it, only warnings from my doctors to avoid stressful situations. I wasn't thinking about how stressful everything was surrounding Alexa's accident. At first, I was surprised to see you, and I was so glad you were there, but somewhere inside me I was in such turmoil because of Alexa and her injuries. I was furious over her accident and how and why she got hurt. On top of all of that I was extremely exhausted from not having slept for so long.

"At first I was so upset with myself for not being more insistent that Alexa not go away to college, but I later realized that was irrational. With our mom and dad gone, I was the only one left to watch over and protect her, and with her so far away I was constantly worrying about her, but I never expected anything like that accident to happen to her."

"Oh, Marc, how could you?" Jenny responded sympathetically. "No one could have known that."

"Yes, I know, but it took me a long time to understand that. In fact, it took one of Alexa's doctors pulling me aside one day to challenge me to get a hold of myself and my emotions. I wasn't aware of it, but apparently I was a total basket case when I was around her in those early days and the doctor told me I was no use to her and her recovery that way, and if I didn't snap out of it she'd prevent me from seeing her until I could.

"That really shook me up and we had a long talk about everything, including my telling her about my own accident, my concussion, and what my doctors had warned me about. Alexa's doctor gave me some great counseling and things began to improve after that.

"But that's when everything that happened between us hit me head on, and I ran back to Alexa's doctor again for more counseling. She was the one who initially told me to call you right away and explain everything, but I was too ashamed."

"Oh, how I wish you had, Marc," Jenny replied, wiping away tears.

"Yes, me too, now. But even after Alexa was well enough, and told me to call you, I still couldn't. I believed you deserved someone else, someone so much better than me, someone who wouldn't bring this kind of problem into a relationship. Someone—"

Jenny placed her fingers gently on Marc's lips to stop him.

"Marc, may I share something with you?"

"Sure."

"Marc, it's okay for us to look back, because there are still so many wonderful memories and experiences for us to remember and keep sacred in our hearts, but let's only claim those embers of love and not the ashes of sadness and pain. We both have to let go of the pain before we can truly move forward … together."

They sat there in silence for several moments. Jenny cried silently and Marc reached into his pocket and retrieved his handkerchief and handed it to her. He leaned forward, resting his arms on the table, thinking about what to say next. Finally, he leaned up and looked toward Jenny. She was looking down at his soaked handkerchief as he spoke.

"Jenny?" he said softly.

"Yes, Marc?" she whispered. He reached over and gently touched her cheek with the back of his fingers. Jenny leaned into his touch and sighed. She held his hand against her cheek for a moment, kissed it, and then looked into Marc's eyes. She saw deep sadness and regret, but his touch told her something more.

"I love you."

"Oh, Marc!" Jenny leaned into his arms and sobbed. "You have no idea how long I've waited to hear you say those words to me."

"Actually ... I think I do, sweetheart."

"I love you so much, Marc."

The rest of the evening was a blur as they ate and laughed and talked about everything they could think of. When it was time to leave, Marc reached for his wallet and pulled out two fresh hundred dollar bills, folding both into fourths, and slipped one into his coat pocket and put his wallet away.

Marc caught Gina's attention one last time and when she reached their table she said, "If you're waiting for your check, Mr. Janssen, remember that you're friend, Lori, already took care of it."

"Oh, I didn't forget, Gina. We just wanted to thank you and make sure you got this."

"What's this?" she asked without looking down.

"Just a little something for you."

"Oh, thank you so much, Mr. Janssen! I really appreciate it!" And without looking at the tip she slipped it into her pocket.

"No, Gina. Thank *you*! You really helped to make this evening so very special for me, Lori and Jenny, and because of that we'll remember you for a very long time."

Gina blushed through her smile as they noticed tears come to her eyes. The three of them hugged and Gina watched as Marc and Jenny left.

"Bye! Be happy!" Gina called out to them.

"Bye, Gina. We will," Jenny called back.

As they approached the Maître d', Marc reached into his coat pocket and retrieved the other hundred dollar bill.

"Thank you so much, James," Marc said as he extended his hand to shake James' hand and pass him the tip. "It's been wonderful."

"Well, thank you, Mr. Janssen. We've enjoyed having all of you here with us this evening, and we hope you'll come back and see us again very soon."

"We look forward to it, James. Good night."

Suddenly Gina came running up to Marc, crying.

"Mr. Janssen! Thank you SO much!!! I've never received a tip like that!"

Marc looked at Gina with a big smile.

"That's a shame, Gina, because you certainly deserve it, and I'm sure we're not the first patrons to have ever been so professionally served like you served us."

Gina just couldn't hold back and she threw her arms around Marc to give him a big hug. "Bless you, and thank you," She said through her tears.

"No, thank you, Gina."

"I'm sorry," Gina said as she stepped back. "I guess that wasn't very proper or appropriate, but I—"

"No, that's perfectly fine, Gina," Marc replied with a wink. "Have a good evening."

"You too! Bye."

"Good night, sir. Good night, ma'am," James added, nodding to Jenny. She returned his nod and gave him a wink and a very sweet smile.

As they stepped out of the restaurant into the balmy evening air Marc offered to walk Jenny to her car.

"Actually … it's not here," Jenny replied. When Marc looked puzzled she continued. "I rode here this evening with Lori. We were hoping that things would turn out exactly as they did, and so … I guess I'm going to need a ride back to the hotel."

"And what if things hadn't turned out this way?" Marc asked with a teasing smile.

"Well, the two of you would have had a nice dinner, and I would, too, of course. Then I would have finished and left ahead of you so there wouldn't have been a chance of your seeing me. Lori and I had it planned out so that if it did come to that, she would just drive down Bridgeway until she found me, picked me up, and taken me back to the Claremont herself. But … I'm really glad the way things *did* turn out."

"I am too, Jenny. So … may I offer you a ride back to our hotel?" Marc asked with a sly smile.

"That would be wonderful, kind sir," Jenny replied with a wink. They embraced and shared a brief kiss, looked at each other for another moment and then fell into each other again, kissing much longer this time, both of them remembering how wonderful it felt and not wanting it to end. Their kiss seemed to go on forever.

"May I?" Jenny asked softly as she indicated she'd like to slip her arm through Marc's as they began to walk toward his car.

"Sure, I don't mind at all," Marc replied with an inviting smile. They walked the rest of the way to his car in silence, simply enjoying each other's company. He helped her into his car, walked casually around the front, and noticed that Jenny was watching every move he made. He climbed in and put the key into the ignition, pausing to glance at the beautiful lady sitting next to him. They looked at each other without saying a word, but their hearts said 'I've *missed* you!'

"Marc … would you wait just a moment before you start the engine?" she softly asked.

"Sure. Why?"

Jenny didn't respond, she simply opened her clutch and removed something from a deep corner. She reached for Marc's hand and gently placed hers on his open palm, allowing her long, slender fingers to open ever so slowly. Marc's eyes went from curious to almost tearful as he felt something cool and round touch his palm … and he knew.

ABOUT THE AUTHOR

JACE CARLTON HAS HAD A diverse career as a freelance writer & photographer, award-winning poet, author, a former Adult Contemporary radio DJ in the San Francisco Bay Area, and twelve years as a popular and award-winning play-by-play football announcer. He now enjoys a career as a romance novelist, as well as a songwriter, predominantly in the Country genre, but also enjoys occasionally writing for A/C, Pop, R&B, and Smooth Jazz. As a freelance writer he has contributed reviews on new music and singer/songwriters to online publications, and regularly contributed book and concert reviews, along with personal commentary on the music industry, to Nashville's *Songwriter's Connection* e-Zine.

Jace is also the creator behind ChangeYourStars.com and its companion motivational / inspirational e-mail messages that have been read by tens of thousands of people all over the world. He is currently writing a new series of books based on the *Change Your Stars!* theme.

Originally from the San Francisco Bay Area, Jace and his wife, Kathi, spent many years in Nashville and now call the Eagle Mountain, Utah area home.

The Reunion is Jace's first novel.

Coming Soon

Novels
Second Chance
A Stranger Passing Through
The Last Letter
All of Her Heart

Poetry
Breaking the Stillness

Motivational / Inspirational
A series of 8 books based on
his website ChangeYourStars.com

www.ingramcontent.com/pod-product-compliance
Lightning Source LLC
Chambersburg PA
CBHW030700120726
47905CB00001B/296